Praise for Carla Neggers and her novels

"Neggers captures readers' attention
with her usual flair and brilliance and gives us
a romance, a mystery and a lesson in history."
—*RT Book Reviews*, Top Pick,
on *Secrets of the Lost Summer*

"Only a writer as gifted as Carla Neggers
could use so few words to convey so much action
and emotional depth."
—Sandra Brown

"With a great plot and excellent character
development, Neggers' thriller *Saint's Gate*,
the first in a new series, is a fast-paced, action-packed
tale of romantic suspense that will appeal to fans of
Lisa Jackson and Lisa Gardner."
—*Library Journal*

"*Saint's Gate* is the best book yet
from a writer at the absolute top of her craft."
—*Providence Journal*

"*Cold Pursuit* is the perfect name
for this riveting read. Neggers' passages are
so descriptive that one almost finds one's
teeth chattering from fear and anticipation."
—*Bookreporter.com*

"[Neggers] forces her characters to confront issues of
humanity, integrity and the multifaceted aspects of
love without slowing the ever-quickening pace."
—*Publishers Weekly*

CARLA NEGGERS

CIDER BROOK

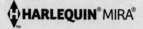

Recycling programs
for this product may
not exist in your area.

ISBN-13: 978-0-7783-1588-9

CIDER BROOK

For questions and comments about the quality of this book, please contact us at CustomerService@Harlequin.com.

Printed in U.S.A.

www.Harlequin.com

To my friend Fran Garfunkel

CIDER BROOK

One

Samantha Bennett slipped her grandfather's antique silver flask into an outer pocket of her khaki safari jacket. He'd claimed the flask was from an old pirate chest, but she'd discovered in the three years since his death at ninety-six that not everything he'd told her had been factual. Harry Bennett had been a grand spinner of the strategic tall tale. He'd probably been drinking rum from the flask when he'd spun the pirate-chest story.

No rum for me, Samantha thought, glancing around her grandfather's cluttered office on the second floor of the Bennett house in Boston's Back Bay. She'd filled the flask with the smoky Scotch he had left in one of his crystal decanters. If she was going to hunt pirate's treasure, she figured she ought to have whiskey with her.

Although what could go wrong in little Knights Bridge, Massachusetts?

Her grandfather smiled at her from a framed black-and-white photograph hanging on the wood-paneled wall behind his massive oak desk. At the time of the photo he'd been forty-seven, roguishly handsome, wearing a jacket much like hers. He'd just arrived back in Boston after the Antarctic trip that had sealed his reputation as a world-class explorer and adventurer. It had almost killed him, too. Her couple of nights' camping in an out-of-the-way New England town hardly compared to an expedition to Antarctica.

She buttoned the flap of her jacket pocket. There were endless pockets inside and out. She was already forgetting where she'd put things—her phone, compass, matches, map, the earth-tone lipstick she'd grabbed at the last second, in case she went out to dinner one night during her stay in Knights Bridge.

Out to dinner? Where, with whom—and why?

If nothing else, a few days away from her grandfather's clutter would do her good. He had been born on a struggling New England farm and had died a wealthy man, if also a hopeless pack rat. Samantha hadn't realized just how much he'd collected in his long, active life until she'd been hired by his estate—meaning her father and her uncle—to go through his house and his London apartment. She swore she'd found gum wrappers from 1952. The man had saved *everything*.

The morning sun streamed through translucent panels that hung over bowfront windows framed by heavy charcoal velvet drapes. Her grandmother, who had died twenty-five years ago, when Samantha was four, had decorated the entire house herself, decreeing that gray and white were the perfect colors for this room, for when her husband was there, being contemplative and studious—which wasn't often, even in his later years. He'd spent little time in his office, mostly just long enough to stack up his latest finds.

Samantha appreciated the effect of the filtered sunlight on the original oil painting that she'd unearthed from the office closet a few weeks ago. The painting was unsigned and clearly an amateur work, but it had captivated her from the moment she'd taken it out into the light. It depicted an idyllic red-painted New England cider mill, with apples in wooden crates, barrels of cider and a water wheel capturing the runoff from a small stone-and-earth dam on a woodland stream. She'd assumed it was untitled but two days ago had discovered neat, faded handwriting on the lower edge of the simple wood frame.

The Mill at Cider Brook.

Her surprise had been so complete that she'd dipped into the Scotch decanter.

She didn't know if the mill depicted in the painting was real, but there was a Cider Brook in Knights Bridge, barely two hours west of Boston.

Of all places.

A quick internet search had produced a year-old notice that the town of Knights Bridge was selling an old cider mill in its possession. Had someone bought it? Was it still for sale?

Samantha had checked the closet for anything else her grandfather might have stuffed in there related to Cider Brook. Instead, she discovered a legal-size envelope containing about fifty yellowed, handwritten pages—the rough draft of a story called *The Adventures of Captain Farraday and Lady Elizabeth.*

She suspected but had no way to prove that the story was by the same hand as the painting, but it didn't matter. It had sealed the deal, and now she had Harry Bennett's antique silver flask tucked in her jacket and her plans made for her return to Knights Bridge—a town she had expected, and hoped, she would never have to visit again.

Plans more or less made, anyway. Samantha had no illusions about herself and knew she wasn't much on detailed planning.

Her first visit to the little town had been two and a half years ago, on a snowy March day a few months after her grandfather's death. She had expected to slip in and out of town without anyone's knowledge, but it hadn't worked out that way.

"A carpenter told me he saw a woman out here. You, Samantha?"

Yes. Her.

The carpenter had been her undoing. She didn't know who he was, but it didn't matter. She would be more careful on this trip, even if careful wasn't a Bennett trait.

This was her chance to put things right.

Samantha returned the painting to the closet, pulled the drapes, locked the doors and met her uncle and cousin out front. They had collected her grandfather's forty-year-old Mercedes from its parking space behind the house. It was a staid gray and had Massachusetts plates, but it was destined to stand out in Knights Bridge. In some ways, Harry Bennett's frugal upbringing had never left him. While he'd bought an expensive car, he'd decided to keep it until he ran it into the ground. It would have helped if he'd driven it once in a while, but he'd never liked to drive.

His younger son, however, loved to drive. Caleb Bennett was a rakishly handsome maritime historian in his early fifties. He and his wife, a rare-books specialist, lived outside London and were the parents of four, the eldest of whom, Isaac, a high-school senior, was strapped into the seat behind Samantha. Isaac and his father were heading to Amherst, the first stop on a tour of New England colleges. Samantha, who didn't own a car, was hitching a ride with them.

"This will be great," Caleb said as she got in next to him. "I can't remember the last time I drove into the New England countryside."

"Are you sure you don't want me to drive?"

"Nah. Sit back and enjoy yourself."

The three youngest Bennetts would be arriving in Boston with their mother that evening for a weeklong visit. At some point, Samantha's parents were due to arrive from the Scottish coast for an even shorter visit. A sort of family reunion. Her uncle and Isaac would pick her up in Knights Bridge on their way back to Boston.

Caleb pulled out onto busy Beacon Street. It was late September, a great time to be in Boston—or anywhere in New England. He glanced at Samantha. "You look as if you're about to walk the plank."

"Do I? I don't feel that way. I'm excited."

"That bastard Duncan McCaffrey fired you, Sam. Going back to Knights Bridge just picks the scab off a wound that should be healed by now."

Isaac leaned forward. "Duncan McCaffrey? The treasure hunter?"

Samantha's throat tightened, but she tried not to let them see her tension. She and Isaac shared the Bennett golden-brown hair and dark eyes, but he was lanky, angular and a gifted tennis player. She was active but had no patience for tennis, and, at five-five, she had obviously not inherited the Bennett height. Even her mother, Francesca, a marine archaeologist, was taller. Samantha considered herself lucky to have inherited her beautiful mother's high cheekbones and full mouth.

"That's right," she said finally. "I worked for Duncan for a short time. He's gone now. He died two years ago this past June."

"He fired your cousin three weeks before he died," Caleb put in.

Seventeen days, to be precise. Samantha let it go. "I didn't tell him things he believed he was entitled to know," she said.

Isaac's eyes widened. "You lied to Duncan McCaffrey?"

"Not exactly."

Her cousin sat back in the soft leather seat. "Wow. That's got to haunt you. Talk about bad timing. What does Knights Bridge have to do with him?"

"I've heard stories in treasure-hunting circles, but I don't have all the details. Apparently Duncan was searching for information on his birth parents and ended up buying property in Knights Bridge. His son inherited it. Dylan. He's now engaged to a woman from town."

"Wait," Isaac said. "You're going there for revenge because Duncan fired you?"

"No. I'm not going for revenge." Samantha took a breath, not knowing what to say to her cousin, especially with her uncle right next to her. She'd already told Caleb more than she'd meant to. She exhaled, her tone matter-of-fact as she continued, "I'm going to test a theory."

Caleb grimaced next to her. "You're stirring things up for no good reason."

"Dylan McCaffrey doesn't even have to know I'm there."

"Sam…" There was a note of dread in Isaac's voice. "Sam, please tell me this trip isn't about pirates."

She swiveled around to look at him. "What, you don't like pirates, Isaac?"

"I got over pirates when I was twelve. Are you searching for the lost treasure of Captain Hook?"

"Show some respect, Isaac," his father said. "Samantha's an expert on East Coast privateers and pirates. Captain Hook is fictional. She's only interested in real pirates and such. Right, Sam?"

Samantha ignored the skeptical note in his voice. "I'm researching Captain Benjamin Farraday, a Boston privateer-turned-pirate who disappeared before he could be hanged for his crimes."

Isaac yawned as the Mercedes sped west on Storrow Drive, along the Charles River, which was dotted with small sailboats and Harvard rowers. "You think this Captain Farraday buried treasure in Knights Bridge?"

"It's possible."

Her cousin groaned. "Sam, nobody believes in buried treasure anymore."

His father glanced sideways at her. "You see? His mother's influence. He's got both feet planted firmly on the ground."

"He wants to go to Amherst College. That's Grandpa's alma mater." Samantha winked at her cousin in the backseat. "There's some Bennett in you."

Isaac rolled his eyes. "Don't remind me."

* * *

Dozing—and pretending to doze—on the drive west at least allowed Samantha to stop trying to convince her uncle that she hadn't lost her mind. He'd interrogated her on the contents of her backpack—he was pleased she had a first-aid kit and an emergency whistle—and her reasons for venturing to Knights Bridge on her own. *"You and this damn pirate, Samantha. You're obsessed with this Captain Benjamin Farraday of yours."*

No argument from her.

She hadn't mentioned the cider mill painting and the story she'd discovered in his father's Boston office. She had enough to overcome with her uncle without telling him she was off to Knights Bridge because of an anonymous painting and the fanciful writings of an unknown author—a woman, Samantha would guess given the feminine handwriting. She had no doubt her uncle would have dismissed *The Adventures of Captain Farraday and Lady Elizabeth* as worthless to a proper historian and tossed the pages into the fire.

Samantha had copied them and brought them with her, possible clues to her pirate mystery, as well as a reminder of the reasons she was undertaking this mission and returning to Knights Bridge. It was a fun story. One particular passage had stuck in her mind.

Lady Elizabeth Fullerton refused to choke on the terrible rum the black-haired, black-eyed pirate had thrust at her. "What's your name?" she asked, returning the flask to him.

"Farraday. Benjamin Farraday. And yours?"

"Bess." She'd already considered what name

to give him. Something simple and not too far from the truth, so that she wouldn't forget. "Bess Fuller."

He grinned and leaned in close to her. He obviously didn't believe her. "Well, Bess Fuller, drink up. We've a long way to go before you'll see England again. You can thank me later for saving you."

"I'd rather have drowned than to be rescued by a pirate rogue."

It was a rousing tale of a spirited high-born British woman who'd been captured for ransom by a dastardly enemy of her remote but wealthy father and then "rescued" by a dashing pirate. Although entertaining, the story bore only marginal resemblance to the life of the real Farraday—at least his known life. There was much not yet known about the Boston-born pirate and his exploits.

Samantha had her grandfather to thank for sparking her interest in Captain Farraday. A few months before his death, he had plunked a copy of an eighteenth-century broadside in front of her. It detailed the crimes credited against Farraday, then a wanted man. *"You like pirates, Sam. Check out this guy."*

She had dived in. As her grandfather's health quickly had begun to fail, he loved for her to sit at his bedside and tell him every new development in her research. She had theorized that Farraday might have hidden treasure in the wilderness west of Boston, first as his personal insurance policy against his capture, arrest and ultimate execution, then to finance a new sloop to continue his raids on other ships.

She had little to go on—no proof beyond snippets here and there and her leaps to connect the dots of her research. She didn't know why her grandfather hadn't told her about the painting and the manuscript pages in his closet—he could have simply forgotten they were there. Now she suspected at least the story had brought Captain Farraday to his attention in the first place.

"Samantha—Samantha, we're here."

She sat up straight at her uncle's voice. "Right. So we are."

He slowed the old Mercedes as they came to the Knights Bridge town common, an oval-shaped green encircled by a narrow main street with classic homes, a town hall, a library, a general store and a few other businesses.

Caleb shuddered. "This place is straight out of 1910."

"It just looks that way on the surface." She pointed vaguely. "You can drop me off anywhere here."

He stopped in front of the Swift River Country Store. "What about mosquitoes? Ticks? I hope you packed DEET."

"DEET and Scotch," Samantha said lightly. "The necessities when hunting pirate treasure."

Caleb looked at his son. "You're going to be an engineer."

Isaac managed to stir enough to wish her luck. As she grabbed her pack out of the backseat, she caught him smirking and muttering something about hoping she found herself a sexy pirate of her own.

"This isn't about sexy pirates," she told him.

He gave her a knowing grin. "Right. It's about scholarship."

She ignored him. "Enjoy your college tour." She smiled at her uncle. "Thanks for the ride. I'll see you in a few days."

"Have fun. Steer clear of carpenters."

Samantha wished she hadn't told her uncle how Duncan McCaffrey had come to fire her. Being spotted in the snow by a small-town carpenter paled in comparison to some of the ways her father and his baby brother had gotten themselves into trouble over the years.

Caleb and Isaac didn't linger. Samantha waited for the Mercedes to disappear back out the winding road to the highway before she set off. There was nothing she needed to pick up at the general store. She didn't have to ask for directions—she had a paper map and a map on her phone, but she'd committed her route to memory.

Ninety minutes later, Samantha slipped off her backpack and set it at her feet as she paused on a simple wooden bridge. It spanned a rock-strewn stream that had to be Cider Brook. She was on a back road that meandered among green fields, old stone walls and woods that were changing color with the arrival of autumn.

She could see a sliver of the Quabbin Reservoir in the distance, its quiet waters shining blue in the afternoon sun. Before Quabbin, three branches of the Swift River had run through a valley of peaceful New England villages. The valley's abundance of freshwater streams, rivers, ponds and lakes had proved too tempting for growing, thirsty metropolitan Boston to resist. In the 1930s, the villages had been forcibly cleared out, razed and the valley flooded to create a pristine source of drinking water for their neighbors to the east.

The "accidental wilderness," as it was called, was a stunningly beautiful sight on an early-autumn afternoon.

Samantha wished the weather was cooler. The day had turned warmer and more humid than she'd expected. She unbuttoned her jacket and was tempted to take it off altogether. She doubted she would have use for the merino wool throw she'd packed, in anticipation of a chilly night looking up at the stars. With little ambient light out this way, the night sky would be spectacular.

Across the bridge, the narrow road curved uphill to a rambling white clapboard farmhouse with black shutters and a red barn set on a hill that overlooked the valley. Huge maple trees, their leaves just starting to turn color, shaded the front lawn. A dark brown dog slept in the driveway, and a white duck—a pet, Samantha assumed—paraded across the grass as if it owned the place. She could hear an unseen rooster crowing in the summerlike stillness.

If she remembered her map correctly, the farmhouse was at a hairpin turn in the road, which then wound back toward the village. That meant the stream under the bridge definitely was Cider Brook.

She lifted her backpack again and slung it over one shoulder. She would strap it on properly once she was on her way again. She crossed the bridge and left the road, pushing through knee-high ferns down a steep incline to the edge of the brook. The brook was narrow here—far too narrow to support even a small cider mill—but would widen farther downstream. The coppery, clear water was shallow, winding downhill over and around rocks and boulders that created natural pools and mini waterfalls.

She brushed away a mosquito buzzing by her head. A hundred years ago, this area had been largely farmland. Now much of it had been reclaimed by a mixed hardwood forest.

An old cider mill could easily be tucked in the woods, and she could walk right past it.

At the rate she was going, she would be finished with Knights Bridge well before her uncle and cousin headed back this way. She hadn't calculated the exact distance from the bridge to the reservoir, but it would be a pretty hike—an adventure, even if she didn't come across a nineteenth-century cider mill.

More mosquitoes found her, and she stopped alongside the brook to refresh her bug spray. Thunder rumbled off to the west. She looked up at the sky, hazy and blue directly above her but with ominous dark clouds behind her. Tucked in the trees as she was, she couldn't see far enough to get a sense whether the storm was coming her way or moving off in another direction. This late in the season, she hadn't considered she might run into a thunderstorm. Of course, once she thought about it she realized a storm wasn't out of the question.

She noticed a trail on the other side of the brook. She had a feeling she was close to the spot where Cider Brook curved toward a dirt road that jutted off the paved one she had followed to the bridge. If she got in trouble with the weather, she could always work her way out to the road and find a house or a shed or flag down a car. Something. Right now, she wanted to get across the brook and on the trail.

Adjusting her backpack, Samantha tested a jagged, half-submerged rock. When it didn't move, she stepped onto it, then jumped to a flat-topped hunk of granite, the cold brook water swirling and gurgling, soothing her sudden sense of dread as more thunder growled. She leaped to the opposite bank, sinking slightly into the soft ground, and thrashed through ferns and skunk cabbage onto the trail.

Lightning flashed, and the darkening clouds created eerie shadows. She picked up her pace. She didn't need a detailed weather forecast to know a nasty storm was bearing down on her. The trail continued to follow Cider Brook into the woods. As she'd anticipated, the brook widened as smaller streams joined it on its gentle descent toward Quabbin.

As the trail curved past a huge, old red-leafed tree, she could see sunlight ahead—a clearing of some kind. A simultaneous bolt of lightning and ferocious clap of thunder propelled her into an outright run. Trees swayed in strong wind gusts, and she could hear the hiss of rain in the woods behind her. Fat raindrops splattered on the dirt trail.

Breathing hard, debating whether she should seek shelter in a protected spot in the woods, she emerged into a clearing. She came to an abrupt halt in front of an old rough-wood building, maybe thirty feet by twenty feet, tucked next to a small stone-and-earth dam and quiet millpond.

Damned if she hadn't found her cider mill.

Or *a* cider mill, anyway.

It resembled the one depicted in the painting in her

grandfather's office, but it was run-down, obviously abandoned and definitely not new or painted a rich, vibrant red.

Hail pelted her, an unpleasant reminder of her immediate situation. It was dime-size and quickly covered the ground.

"Ah, damn."

Of *course* there was hail.

She bounded up to the mill's solid wood door, but it was padlocked. Why, she couldn't imagine. Three small windows were encased in thick, dirty plastic. A garage-style door, where wagons had once unloaded apples and loaded cider, was boarded shut.

She knew how to pick a padlock. Her uncle had seen to teaching her that particular skill himself. *"It's only to be used in self-defense, Sam. No breaking into a vault or anything like that."*

She noticed faded Do Not Enter and Danger signs to the left of the door.

Lightning lit up the sky, and thunder echoed in the woods.

She needed to get inside.

Now.

Two

The storm was fierce, intense and downright unnerving, but Samantha rode it out inside the dusty, empty cider mill. With the rain stopped and the thunder clearly off to the east, she had her grandfather's flask out of her jacket pocket and was debating whether to imbibe now or wait until after dark.

Then she smelled smoke.

Smoke? She groaned in disbelief. Wouldn't *that* just top off her day?

She tucked the flask back in her pocket and breathed in deeply, hoping the smell of smoke had been a trick of her imagination. The mill consisted of a single room with rough-wood walls, wide-board flooring and a pitched ceiling with open rafters. It would go up in flames in no time if it caught fire.

The smell didn't dissipate, and it wasn't her imagination. It was definitely smoke.

Could the wind have carried smoke from a chimney in a nearby farmhouse?

What nearby farmhouse?

She could taste smoke now, feel it burn in her eyes.

She reached into the open compartment of the backpack at her feet, grabbed her four-by-nine-inch documents pouch and slipped it into an outer jacket pocket, opposite the one with the flask.

A strange hissing noise seemed to come from beneath the floor by a half-dozen old wooden cider barrels pushed up against the wall. In another moment, smoke, visible now, curled through cracks in the floorboards and floated up to the rafters as if it were a living thing. Samantha stared at it, transfixed. She couldn't delude herself. She was in a fire.

She didn't have a minute to waste. She clicked into action.

She knew she had to leave everything—tent, sleeping bag, food, water, toiletries, bug spray, first-aid kit, flannel pajamas and her merino wool wrap, a gift from her mother. So much for watching the stars come out, envisioning life here in the early eighteenth century.

More smoke poured through the floorboards.

Samantha dropped low, remembering that was what someone was supposed to do in a fire, with rising smoke. She pulled her jacket collar over her mouth and nose and launched herself toward the door.

She swore she could hear flames under her in the mill's cellar.

Her eyes were blurry and watery with smoke, but she could see an orange, fiery glow by the north wall. She felt the heat of the fire now. Sudden, intense.

How long did she have before the old, dry wood exploded into flames?

Stifling a surge of panic, she crouched even lower, coughing as smoke filled the enclosed space. She kept moving. She had to get out of here before she collapsed due to smoke inhalation.

Flames burst through the floorboards by the barrels and crawled up the wall, bright and terrifying in the gray light. Fire and smoke seemed to join, forming a monster ready to consume everything in its path.

She got onto her knees, gasping for air. Her hand fell from her jacket, exposing her to more smoke. She covered her mouth and nose with the crook of her arm and decided she would crawl on her belly if she had to…but she couldn't move, couldn't breathe. There was no pirate rogue to save her. She had to save herself. She had to stay conscious, get moving, steer clear of the flames.

The front door banged open, startling her.

"Is anyone in here?"

A man's voice. Soothing, firm, maybe a little annoyed. Or was it her imagination, or a passage from the pages she'd discovered in her grandfather's office?

Samantha tried to stagger to her feet. "Captain Farraday?"

"Easy. Are you hurt?"

She shook her head and blinked, but she couldn't focus—couldn't see the man through the smoke and her own burning tears.

Strong arms reached around her. "Stay low," her rescuer said. "We need to move fast."

He had her up off her feet before she realized he had lifted her. In a few long strides, he had her out the door and down the stone-slab step, then flung onto the bank of the small millpond. She landed in cold, wet grass, rolled onto her stomach, coughing, spitting, sucking in the clear air.

"Do you have medical issues?"

The man again. Samantha sat up, her eyes and throat burning, aching. She tasted smoke and grime and felt her heart thumping in her chest. She blinked rapidly, peering up at the man standing between her and the mill. He was tall, looming over her. She made out dark short-cropped hair, deep blue eyes, a firm mouth, a square jaw, broad shoulders. He wore a black canvas shirt over a black T-shirt, jeans, scuffed leather boots.

Hauling her out of the mill had obviously not taxed him to any degree, but he didn't seem happy about it. She had no idea who he was. A hiker? A local man? Did he own the cider mill? She hadn't considered she might have to contend with an owner, or that it might be a tough, humorless man not much older than she was.

"I'm sorry," she said, clearing her throat. "What did you ask me?"

He sucked in a quick breath. "Do you have asthma, allergies, a heart condition, anything—"

"No. Nothing. No medical issues." Her voice was raspy, tense. "I'm fine. Thank you."

He showed no sign of lowering his guard. "Fire department's on the way. I have to get to work. You sit tight."

"What can I do to help?"

"Stay out of the way."

He hadn't hesitated even half a beat before firing off his answer. He didn't wait for a response and set off toward the mill. Thick smoke billowed from the open door into the cool, clear air. Flames glowed orange behind the dirty plastic and cracked glass in the windows.

Samantha watched as her rescuer stopped at a dusty-gray pickup truck, parked with its hood facing out the pitted dirt driveway. In seconds, he had donned fire gear—hat, mask, jacket.

A firefighter?

He grabbed an ax and headed for the mill.

The fire seemed to have sucked the door shut. He kicked it open and went inside.

Whoever he was, her rescuer was strong and utterly fearless.

She shivered in the cooler air. She hadn't called him Captain Farraday, had she? Not out loud. It just wasn't possible.

She heard sirens and realized a road was closer than she'd thought. In another thirty seconds, fire trucks and a lone police car descended. Samantha moved to a small boulder by the brook. With the downpour from the storm, the water was high, rushing over rocks, moss and mud.

As she watched firefighters set to work, she could feel the padlock in her jacket pocket.

If no one asked about it, she saw no reason to mention it.

Three

Her rescuer's name was Justin Sloan.

Or so he told Samantha right before he demanded she produce his padlock.

He put out a callused hand. "Where is it?"

The fire was out, the mill intact if damaged. The firefighters had loaded up their gear and left, and the two uniformed police officers had followed them along the rutted driveway to the road. One of the officers had interviewed her. She'd told him the truth about how she'd ended up in the cider mill—that she'd ducked inside to get out of the thunderstorm. He'd asked if she'd noticed the Do Not Enter and Danger signs. She'd said she had. He'd scowled and hadn't requested further details.

He was a Sloan, too. Eric Sloan.

One of the firefighters was also a Sloan. Christopher.

Small towns, she thought.

Justin, she now realized, was a volunteer firefighter. After helping put out the fire, he'd returned his gear to his truck and then joined her by her boulder. Samantha had dipped a hand into the cold brook water and done what she could to wipe the soot off her face, but she doubted she'd gotten it all. The acrid fire smells wouldn't be easy to eliminate from her skin or her clothes. She had travel wipes and fresh clothes in her backpack, assuming it had survived the fire and wasn't too contaminated by smoke.

Telling Justin Sloan that his missing padlock was in her jacket pocket didn't seem like a particularly wise course of action at the moment. Although he gave no indication, he had to be in high-adrenaline mode after coming upon the old mill in flames, discovering a woman was more or less trapped inside, carrying her to safety and then helping to put out the fire.

Samantha realized she was in high-adrenaline mode herself. She stood, the seat of her pants wet, and flicked an ant off her knee. Casual. As if she hadn't picked the padlock to get into the mill and didn't have it in her jacket.

The banter she'd overheard between the firefighters had confirmed her suspicion that her rescuer owned the old cider mill.

"Hell, Justin, this place is even more of a dump than I thought."

"I can't believe you spent real money on it."

"Firetrap, Justin. Told you."

That last had come from Christopher Sloan. Apparently he was one of two full-time firefighters in Knights Bridge. Everyone else was a volunteer.

"They're your brothers?" Samantha asked. "Eric and Christopher?"

"My brothers. Yes." Justin snapped two fingers of his outstretched hand. "My padlock."

Not a man easily distracted. She tried to look as if she didn't quite understand him. "Padlock?"

"The one you picked or broke to get into the mill."

He lowered his hand to his side, but she could tell from his set jaw that he wasn't giving up. She didn't feel guilty at what she'd done, but she didn't want to explain herself to a man who'd just carted her out of a burning building and had helped put out the fire. He didn't look as if he'd be a willing listener on a good day. Since one of his brothers was a police officer and another was a professional firefighter—and he himself was a volunteer firefighter—she wasn't *afraid* of him. He wasn't a thug. He was just not in a great mood.

"It was a dangerous storm. Downright scary, and I've been in some scary storms." She decided to change the subject. "My name's Samantha, by the way."

His deep blue eyes narrowed on her. "What's your last name, Samantha?"

"Bennett," she said, sounding more tight-lipped and reluctant than she would have liked. She hadn't volunteered her last name on purpose. She'd told Eric Sloan, the police-officer brother, but he'd asked, leaving her no choice. She doubted the Bennett name meant anything to him, Justin or the other firefighters who'd rushed to the old cider mill, but she'd intended to get in and out of Knights Bridge without the knowledge of any of its residents.

"Are you a Sam or a Samantha?"

"Either works."

"Mostly Sam?"

"Mostly Samantha, actually."

"Well, Samantha, you're damn lucky you got out of there in time."

"No argument from me. I noticed the smoke about fifteen minutes after the storm ended. Lightning caused the fire?"

He gave a curt nod. "Looks as if it struck the roof and traveled down the side wall to the cellar. The fire started there and worked its way up the wall. We've had a string of severe storms this past month." He looked at her as if she might have caused the recent bad luck with the weather. "A microburst hit the center of town a few weeks ago. It uprooted a bunch of trees and damaged some homes and businesses. No serious injuries."

"That's good. About the injuries, I mean."

Samantha glanced up at the sky, graying now with dusk. It would be the kind of cool, beautiful night she'd anticipated. She'd checked the forecast on her phone on the drive from Boston, but she'd missed any reference to the force and speed with which the cold front would move into this part of New England.

Of course, it was just like a Bennett to be struck by lightning.

"What were you doing out here?" Justin asked her.

"Hiking."

"Most people hike in Quabbin or one of the state forests. Why'd you pick here?"

"I wanted to follow Cider Brook to where it empties into Quabbin."

"Any particular reason?"

"It seemed like a good idea this morning." She smiled, feeling less jittery now that the fire was out. "That could be my family's motto. 'It seemed like a good idea at the time.'"

Justin didn't appear amused.

She added, truthfully, "I like the name Cider Brook. Pretty, isn't it?"

"Never thought about it. Where's your car?"

"I don't have one."

"Someone picking you up?"

"Not today." She gestured vaguely toward the mill and surrounding woods. "I planned to camp out here."

He shook his head. "Not happening. Most of your gear's wrecked, and I can't let you inside the mill until I'm satisfied it's safe."

Well, that was inconvenient. Samantha considered her options. Amherst, where her uncle and cousin were spending the night, wasn't that far—but she would have to figure out how to get herself there. If they had to make a detour to pick her up early, she would never hear the end of it. Uncle Caleb would carry on about why she hadn't known about the storm before it hit, the odds against a lightning strike setting the mill on fire and what she was going to do now that she'd come to the attention of the locals. She could just hear him: *You never should have gone to Knights Bridge in the first place.*

But she had, and now she needed to figure out what to do. Send Justin Sloan on his way and then…what? Buy a new tent and sleeping bag? Where? What about dinner? Water? Clothes? If her things were trampled, soaked, burned up in the fire or just out of reach, she would have to start from scratch. She didn't even have a toothbrush.

"There's an inn down the road," Justin said, interrupting her thoughts. "You can stay there tonight. I'll drop you off."

The Farm at Carriage Hill. Had to be.

It was owned by the woman who was engaged to Dylan McCaffrey, Duncan McCaffrey's son.

Samantha carefully arranged her features so she wouldn't look as if her rescuer had just invited her into the lion's den. She could be hard to read herself. It just wasn't her natural state. Her natural state was to be open, honest and straightforward, but she had to be circumspect now that a fire had put an end to her low-profile presence in Knights Bridge.

"Thank you, Justin." She even managed a smile. "I appreciate all you've done."

"Not a problem."

"I'm glad the damage to your mill wasn't any worse. It's a good thing you got here when you did, isn't it?"

"Yep." He took a half step closer to her and pointed at her jacket. "My padlock is in the inside pocket on the right. I felt it when I rescued you."

"I didn't need you to 'rescue' me."

"Yeah. You did." He tapped the lower left pocket where she'd tucked her grandfather's flask. "Booze?"

"Scotch. Lagavulin. I was going to sip it under the stars."

He gave just a hint of a smile. "I'll bet you were."

He went back up to the cider mill and disappeared inside.

Samantha exhaled but didn't relax. She'd had a close call with the fierce storm and then the fire—closer than she wanted to acknowledge. It wasn't easy to admit that if Justin Sloan hadn't come along when he had and swept her out of the burning mill, she could have been overcome by smoke and gone up in flames.

She would return his padlock to him. Just not right

now. Better to wait until they'd both had a chance to deal with the adrenaline dump of the fire.

Justin emerged from the mill with her backpack. He opened the passenger door to his truck and tossed the pack inside. "Hop in," he said. He left the door open as he circled around to the driver's side. "Carriage Hill is a ten-minute drive."

"Are you sure you don't mind?"

He got into his truck, shut the door and started the engine, clearly in no mood to wait. Samantha suspected his terse manner was the way he was, although the events of the day might have exacerbated his natural tendency. She reminded herself she wasn't in Knights Bridge to make friends, or even because of Captain Farraday, as intriguing and as entangled with her true reasons as her colorful eighteenth-century pirate and his illicit treasure were.

She looked up at the old mill, bits of barn-red paint visible in its worn exterior. The fire smells were strong in the cool late-afternoon air. She wanted to know about the painting she'd found in her grandfather's closet. She wanted to know how the author of *The Adventures of Captain Farraday and Lady Elizabeth* had ended up writing a fictional story about a real pirate, and why Harry Bennett had put her—his eldest grandchild—onto the trail of the mysterious New England pirate.

All of that was interesting, but Samantha knew it was only a small part of the reason for coming to Knights Bridge. The main reason—the real reason—was to make peace with Duncan McCaffrey, a man who'd hired her and mentored her.

Who'd *trusted* her.

"Damn, Samantha. It never occurred to me not to trust you."

She tightened her jacket and headed for Justin Sloan's dusty-gray truck.

The combination of adrenaline, an enclosed space and an intense man behind the wheel turned the ten-minute drive to The Farm at Carriage Hill into something that felt a notch short of an eternity. Samantha was accustomed to being around rugged men, but this was different. Even if she could have gotten out of the mill on her own—and she remained convinced she could have—Justin Sloan had, in fact, rushed into a burning building and carried her out. A courageous deed by any standard. As the beneficiary, she felt a mix of gratitude and guilt but also a physical aware-ness that had taken her completely by surprise.

Justin had rolled up the sleeves of his canvas shirt to just below his elbows, revealing taut, well-developed forearms. Samantha guessed that his volunteer fire-fighting plus whatever he did for a living kept him in shape. She wasn't going to ask for details. Personal questions on her part risked personal questions on his part.

He pulled in front of a cream-colored center-chimney house, the last home on a narrow road that once had been a main route from Knights Bridge into the Swift River valley towns—long before major highways and interstates. Now it dead-ended at a Quabbin gate. Not only had she studied her map and the history of the area but she'd been out here before, if only that one time on a snowy March day.

She shook off that thought. Couldn't go there. Later, maybe. Not now.

Justin turned off the engine. He'd parked next to a sign for The Farm at Carriage Hill painted with its signature blossoming chives. Although Samantha hadn't done nearly enough planning for her trip to Knights Bridge, she knew that Olivia Frost, the owner, was a graphic designer, as well as Dylan McCaffrey's fiancée.

Samantha unlatched her seat belt and pushed back a surge of regret that she hadn't stayed in Boston and walked the Freedom Trail with her aunt and young cousins. No point second-guessing herself now. Dylan had only ventured to Knights Bridge earlier that year, meeting Olivia in the process. After his career in the National Hockey League had ended, he'd teamed up with his childhood friend, Noah Kendrick, an MIT genius. Together they had transformed Noah's fledgling NAK, Inc. into a profitable high-tech entertainment company that had gone public last fall. Samantha had never met Dylan during her weeks working with his father, and she wasn't in Knights Bridge to intrude on his and Olivia's lives.

But here you are, on their doorstep.

Justin pushed open his door. "Carriage Hill's just opened. It's not a regular inn." He glanced sideways at her. "Your hands are trembling. A little wobbly? It's normal after a fire."

"I'm okay. Hungry. What about you? Are you wobbly?"

"Me?" He grinned. "No. Not wobbly."

"You've had experience with fires, but this one was on your land."

"Doesn't change anything."

A dark-haired woman was arranging pots of yellow-and-white mums on the steps to a one-story ell off the main part of the house. Olivia Frost, presumably. Samantha turned to Justin. "Am I expected?"

"I didn't have a chance to call ahead. It'll be fine."

She didn't move as he headed to the stone walk. He'd left the door open. She could hear Olivia as she approached Justin, dusting off her palms on her baggy cargo pants. "Dad just called about the fire. He says it was a lightning strike. Yikes, Justin. You're all right?"

"Yep. Fine."

"The storm must have gone right over the mill. It wasn't that bad here. Dad says a woman was camping there—"

"Samantha Bennett," Justin said. "She needs a place to stay tonight."

"Of course. We have loads of room."

He motioned to the truck. "Hop out, Sam. Come meet Olivia."

Samantha could think of a hundred other places she would rather be. She wished she'd at least found refuge somewhere else besides Justin Sloan's cider mill. The chicken coop at the farmhouse upstream would have done nicely.

She stepped out of the truck, misjudged the distance and felt her knees buckle under her. Even as she steadied herself, Justin was there, one hand on her elbow. "I guess you're wobbly after all. No shame in it."

"I'm not that used to trucks is all."

He lowered his hand. "I'm not surprised."

Olivia stepped forward with a smile and introduced

herself. "My father was at the fire. He's a volunteer firefighter. I'm so glad you weren't hurt."

"Thanks," Samantha said. "It's been quite an afternoon."

"You must be beat. We'd love to have you stay with us."

"If you're sure it's not too short notice—"

"I'm positive," Olivia said graciously. "Did Justin explain that Carriage Hill isn't a regular inn? We're just getting started with destination events. Showers, weddings, meetings—that sort of thing, mostly on weekends. My friend Maggie and I are having a blast so far."

Samantha stood back. "You mean you don't take in overnight guests? I can find a place to pitch my tent. Really. I don't mind."

"Your tent didn't make it out of the fire," Justin said.

She frowned at him. "It burned?"

"I told you most of your gear was wrecked."

Olivia shot him a disapproving look, apparently not appreciating his bluntness.

He shrugged. "Your tent and sleeping bag were trampled and soaked. They're easily replaced."

"Is there some place in town I could buy new ones?" Samantha asked.

"The Swift River Country Store on the town common," Olivia said. "We call it Hazelton's—they were the original owners. It's got everything. They must have tents."

"Then I could pop over there," Samantha said.

Justin shook his head. "They're closed." When Olivia glared at him again, he softened his expression and added, "You'll like Carriage Hill. Maggie and Olivia are even making their own goat's milk soap these days." He glanced at Olivia as if to say *"Better?"*

She ignored him and shifted back to Samantha with an encouraging smile. "We do take in overnight guests, of course, and we'd be happy to have you stay with us. Welcome."

"I love goat's milk soap," Samantha said. "I appreciate this very much. Thank you, Olivia. I'm still a bit rattled, but a quiet night will help."

With a slightly muddy hand, Olivia pointed at the door to the ell. "The kitchen's through there. I'll be right in. Help yourself to whatever strikes your fancy. Maggie and I made applesauce this afternoon. No sugar added. The apples are perfect on their own."

"Sounds wonderful," Samantha said, feeling less tense. "Thank you again."

Justin headed to his truck, grabbed her backpack and brought it to her. "I can bring it up to your room if you'd like."

"Got it, thanks." She took the pack from him and slung it over one shoulder. Picturing him in her guest room at Carriage Hill wasn't helping her heart rate at all. She could feel heat rushing to her cheeks. *Ah, hell.* She wasn't the blushing type. She forced a quick smile. "Thank you for all your help today. I hope the fire won't set back your plans for the mill."

"It won't." He glanced at Olivia as if expecting her to scowl at him for being so abrupt, then shifted back to Samantha and added, less bluntly, "I have more dreams than actual plans. I'll adjust. Glad you weren't hurt today."

"Same here. That you weren't hurt, I mean."

He grinned. "I appreciate that."

She couldn't get inside fast enough but turned to Olivia. "I look forward to that applesauce," she said, then headed up the steps past the mums and through a blue-painted door into a cozy kitchen.

A white mixing bowl of applesauce was in the middle of a butcher-block island. She set her backpack on the floor by the door and went over to the island, felt the sides of the bowl and realized the applesauce was still warm. As she found a small bowl and spoon, a big dog wandered out from the adjoining mudroom and yawned at her. He was mostly German shepherd, she guessed.

She heaped applesauce into her bowl and sat with it at a white-painted table. The dog flopped down at her feet. She patted him, wondering at how her day had started in the cluttered office of Harry Bennett and now was ending in a warm, inviting kitchen on the edge of the Quabbin Reservoir, in a little town that time seemed to have forgotten.

She still smelled like the fire at the cider mill, though.

Maybe a bath with the goat's milk soap would help.

Four

Justin knew he was in trouble with Olivia, but it wasn't unexpected. She'd been giving him a hard time ever since she and her little friend Maggie O'Dunn had caught him and a couple of his brothers raising hell out by Frost Millworks when they were teenagers. Now Maggie was married to his younger brother Brandon, and Olivia was engaged to a California multimillionaire.

And he'd just dumped a problem on her doorstep.

Samantha Bennett. Treasure hunter, expert on pirates and a woman who had an uneasy relationship with the truth. What was it Duncan McCaffrey had told him?

"Samantha Bennett isn't your problem, Justin. She's my problem."

Justin watched as Olivia picked up a yellow mum in a clay pot and glared at him. "I know you've had a rough day with the fire at the mill, but could you be any more brusque?"

He winked at her. "Yeah, probably."

She tucked the pot under one arm. "Samantha needs

a little time to get her feet back under her. You did the right thing bringing her here."

He suspected Samantha already had her feet back under her, but he made no comment.

"What was she doing out at the mill?" Olivia asked.

"She says she'd been following Cider Brook and ducked into the mill when the storm hit. We didn't get into details."

Olivia tilted her head back, frowning at him. "Justin, are you sure you're okay?"

"Yep."

"Sounds as if you arrived at the mill just in time."

"I stopped by after the storm. I knew it'd gone right through there, and I wanted to check for damage. Figured at most I'd run into a fallen tree."

"Instead the place was on fire." Olivia let out a breath. "Really scary, Justin. Was Samantha trapped inside?"

"Overcome with smoke. She was right by the door. Rescue was a piece of cake."

"That's what you always say."

Probably so, he thought. He'd learned a long time ago that if he dwelled on the dangers and the might-have-beens of his life, he'd never do anything. He trusted his training, preparation and experience. Beyond that—not much he could do. Which wasn't to say that discovering a semiconscious woman overcome by deadly smoke in his old cider mill hadn't taken a toll.

He appreciated the cool breeze in the wake of the storm. It helped clear his head. He wanted to talk to Dylan about Samantha Bennett.

He realized Olivia was eyeing him with concern.

He preferred her scowls to outright worry, but she said, amiably, "You're welcome to stay for dinner, Justin."

"I'm good. Dylan's up the road?"

She nodded. "He rode out the storm in his car. As I said, it wasn't that bad here."

"Olivia," Justin said, "if you're not sure it's okay for Samantha to stay here—"

"I'm sure. I imagine she's still in shock. She might not be able to grasp how close she came to real harm." Olivia took in an audible breath. She'd had close calls of her own and was palpably tense, as if she were picturing Samantha collapsing in the burning mill. She seemed to give herself a mental shake. "I'll keep that in mind tonight."

"Dylan will be here, right? He's not going out of town?"

"He'll be here." Olivia smiled and leaned toward him. "You're free to go, Justin. Your good deed for the day is done."

She'd always thought it about killed him to be nice. He pointed at the mum in her arm. "I like the yellow." He grinned. "Autumnal."

"You'd say that no matter what color it was."

He laughed. "Probably. See you around, Liv. Call if you need me."

He returned to his truck, aware she was still frowning at him. As he got in and started the engine, she set the yellow mum off to one side at the base of the kitchen steps. He doubted arranging flowers was foremost on her mind. She had good instincts. She'd sense he hadn't told her everything he knew about her guest.

Justin's grip tightened on the wheel. Was Samantha helping herself to applesauce in Olivia's kitchen?

Thinking about taking a crowbar to the walls in search of pirate treasure?

Looking for a place to hide his padlock?

In the immediate aftermath of the fire, bringing her to Carriage Hill had made sense. Now he wondered if he should have left her to her own devices. But that hadn't been a viable option. One, because of who she was. Two, because she'd had a scare and shouldn't be on her own out in the woods.

But mostly because of who she was.

She was younger and more attractive than he would have guessed from the one glimpse he'd had of her two and a half years ago. He hadn't recognized her when he grabbed her out of the mill and plunked her down by the brook, her face smudged with grime and just pale enough that he had no doubt the fire had affected her. She had golden-brown curls that framed angular features, dark, almond-shaped eyes and a full mouth. She'd struck him as a curious mix of unflappable and vulnerable.

Then again, who wouldn't look a touch vulnerable after escaping a fire?

But that was before he'd learned her name.

He'd been tempted to rifle through her backpack when he'd retrieved it from the mill, but he had a feeling most of the interesting stuff was in her jacket. She was the type to grab any incriminating evidence at the first smell of smoke.

Maybe he should have driven her to Amherst or Boston—away from Knights Bridge.

Or just loaned her a damn tent.

It was almost dark when he pulled into the gravel driveway just up the road from The Farm at Carriage

Hill and parked behind Dylan McCaffrey's Audi sedan. A new house and barn were going up on the site where Grace Webster, a retired teacher now in her nineties, had lived for more than seventy years. Dylan's father had bought the property from Grace but hadn't told his only son. Dylan had found out this past spring, when Olivia had contacted him about the mess in his yard. Before that, he'd never even heard of Knights Bridge.

Justin knew Grace, but she'd been long retired when he was in school. She'd moved to Knights Bridge as a teenager with her father and grandmother. After they'd died, she stayed on in their simple house and taught high-school Latin and English. She never married and had just moved into an assisted living facility in town when Duncan, a respected treasure hunter, had shown up and bought her crumbling old house.

Duncan had died a few months later while on an expedition in Portugal, without revealing the reasons for his interest in Knights Bridge. Dylan had figured out the truth on his own. His father hadn't come to the little Massachusetts town for treasure but to investigate a long-dead British jewel thief and the young woman he'd met while on the run more than seventy years ago. Grace Webster and Philip Rankin were star-crossed lovers and Duncan's birth parents.

Philip, a Royal Air Force flyer, had been killed early in World War II and never returned to Grace. She'd secretly delivered their baby boy—Duncan— who'd been adopted by a Boston couple. Grace had never held her son and had never seen him again, until he'd ventured to Knights Bridge seventy years later.

It was a hell of a story that had taken Justin and everyone else in Knights Bridge by surprise, but it had changed Dylan's life. He had fallen for Olivia Frost and was making a home in Knights Bridge, launching the adventure travel business his father had dreamed they would start together one day.

Not one to let the grass grow under him, Dylan had hired a local architect, drawn up plans for a house and barn that could be used for the business and enlisted Sloan & Sons to do the construction. Justin—one of the sons—was in charge of the project. The foundations were in, and he anticipated finishing basic exterior work before cold weather set in. The original house hadn't been worth saving. Grace had often said she had considered tearing it down and wasn't at all sad to see it go, although she'd been pleased when Dylan had put aside bits and pieces to incorporate into the new house.

Olivia was involved in every decision about the construction, particularly those having to do with color. Dylan, she maintained, would default to "cappuccino" if she didn't step in. Justin had never pictured her with a Southern California businessman and former hockey player worth upward of a hundred million, but no question she and Dylan were right together—a good thing since they were planning a Christmas wedding at Carriage Hill.

As Justin got out of his truck, he noticed the air had cooled even more in the time it had taken for the short drive. The unseasonable humidity had gone with the line of thunderstorms that had moved through. He walked up the driveway to a stack of two-by-fours that had been delivered just before the storm. Dylan was adjusting a blue tarp over the lumber. He wore a sweater, jeans and boots, looking like any other guy in Knights Bridge—except he wasn't like any other guy in Knights Bridge.

Dylan stood straight. "I just talked to Olivia. She told me about the fire. She said you dropped off the woman you rescued. Damn, Justin. Hell of a day's work."

"It wasn't that big a deal."

"I imagine this woman thinks otherwise."

Justin wasn't too sure about that. "Her name's Samantha Bennett."

Dylan's eyes narrowed. "Someone I should know?"

He obviously didn't recognize her name. Justin wasn't surprised, although he would have less explaining to do if Dylan was familiar with her. "She's not from town."

"So I gathered." Dylan, known for his keen instincts about people, stood back. "What's going on, Justin?"

"I don't know. Maybe nothing. Your father had me out here when he was in town. I mentioned I'd seen a woman checking out the place a couple of weeks before that. I thought she was his daughter or an assistant or something, but he got quiet, asked me to describe her. He recognized her right away. He told me her name was Samantha Bennett, and she worked for him as an expert on pirates."

"Pirates."

"That's right. He said she was his problem." Justin left it there. "I never thought much about our conversation after that."

Dylan nodded thoughtfully. "My father never liked the term *treasure hunter*. He loved the work, and he was serious about it. I don't recall him mentioning pirates or a pirate expert—or this woman. Not that he would have. I wasn't involved in his treasure hunting. Most of his unfinished projects have been taken over by colleagues. I've only just started sorting out the orphaned ones."

"Maybe Samantha is in town to get in on one of them." Justin rubbed the back of his neck, feeling the effects of fighting the fire. Hauling Samantha Bennett out of the mill hadn't been a strain at all. She couldn't weigh more than a few sticks of lumber. "I don't know what she's up to, Dylan, but maybe it wasn't such a great idea to have her stay at Carriage Hill."

"No, it's fine. I'll be there."

Justin pulled at the tarp, letting loose a small pool of water from the earlier downpour. It streamed onto the ground. "When I described her to your father, it was clear she hadn't told him she'd been out here."

Dylan winced. "He wouldn't like that. Trust was important to him. He worked hard to establish and maintain his reputation. He didn't take well to anything that might threaten it."

"Understandable."

"That doesn't mean he was thorough. He thought he was good at reading people. He hated taking the time to check people out, even people he hired. He relied on his gut. Usually it worked out, but maybe not in this case." Dylan looked out at the rolling fields behind his house, dark now with the increasingly shorter days of autumn. "I didn't know my father had come to Knights Bridge, and I'm his son. How did Samantha Bennett find out?"

"I don't know." Justin placed a rock on top of the

tarp to hold it in place. "We only had that one conversation about her."

"Did you recognize her today?"

"Just her name. I don't know why I remembered it, but I did."

"And it's the same Samantha Bennett?"

"Doubt there are two, don't you?"

Dylan nodded, sighing. "My father never mentioned her to me, but he wouldn't have. Treasure hunting was his passion." Dylan's voice was laced with pain and loss, but he maintained his composure. "Hell, I miss him. I guess I always will."

"I see that as a good thing," Justin said simply.

"Yeah, me, too. Anyway, having Samantha stay at Carriage Hill gives us a chance to find out who she is and what she's up to."

"I doubt she knows I'm the one who told Duncan about her."

"Just as well, maybe."

Justin shrugged. "I'm not worried."

"You're not the worrying type," Dylan said with a grin that quickly faded. "I'll call Loretta and see if she knows anything about her."

Justin had met Loretta Wrentham, Dylan's longtime San Diego attorney and friend, when she'd blown in and out of Knights Bridge a few weeks ago. He'd spent less than ten minutes with her but could easily believe she would be someone Dylan would turn to about a mysterious woman from his father's past.

"Let me know if I can do anything," Justin said.

"Will do. Thanks for stopping by. My father and I got along, but we didn't spend much time together his last few years. I guess we thought there would be more time than there was. He didn't tell me everything, as you know."

"I can go back and get Samantha if you change your mind."

"There's plenty of room at Carriage Hill. She must be exhausted after today." Dylan eyed him with obvious concern. "You, too, Justin."

"I'm good. Just need a beer and a good night's sleep." He started back to his truck. "Give a yell if I can do anything."

"You saved a woman's life today. I think that's enough." Dylan paused, then added, "Besides, my father was right. Samantha Bennett isn't your problem."

Justin got into his truck and pulled the door shut. *The fire, the padlock. Pirates.*

Somehow he doubted he'd heard the last of the dark-eyed woman whose butt he'd just saved.

Five

Instead of calling it a night, Justin headed back to the cider mill. He parked his truck, got out his flashlight and navigated the pitted patch of dirt that passed for a driveway. Cider Brook was quieter now that the immediate rush from the downpour had eased. He ducked under the yellow caution tape his fellow firefighters had strung up, the bitter, unmistakable smell of smoke and burnt wood still heavy in the sharply cooler air.

He pointed the beam of his flashlight at the mill door. It didn't show any obvious damage from where he'd kicked it in earlier that afternoon.

A moth fluttered in the light and disappeared.

He'd bought the property a year ago when the town, which had seized it due to unpaid back taxes, had put it up for sale. His brothers, sister, father, mother, uncle, grandmother and everyone else who had voiced their opinions—all of them unsolicited—said he should convert the mill into a residence or, better yet, tear it down and build a new house. Then sell the property at a profit. He didn't disagree that would be the practical thing to do. It made a hell of a lot more sense than thinking he would find pirate treasure out here.

He turned and shone his flashlight at the small millpond and spillway and across the brook to a stone wall that had once marked off farmland and now snaked into the woods. How could he sell this place?

Not that he knew what he *would* do with it.

He heard an owl hooting in the dark trees and turned back to the mill.

"I like the name Cider Brook. Pretty, isn't it?"

Yeah, but it wasn't what had drawn attractive Samantha Bennett to Knights Bridge.

Justin gritted his teeth and went into the mill. The smoke and burnt-wood smells were stronger. He shone his flashlight on the blackened wall and floor where the fire had done its damage. He hadn't planned to stop at the mill today. He only had because of the storm's path. He'd ridden it out in his truck. He hadn't been in a hurry to get out here, and it was by chance he'd arrived in time to call in the fire before it devoured the mill.

And by chance he'd arrived in time to save Samantha.

She struck him as the sort who relied on miracles.

He'd just known that whoever had broken into his mill was in danger. He'd acted quickly, certain the situation was worsening and time wasn't on his side.

It'd been a cinch to lift Samantha and carry her out to the brook. She was small but obviously fit—strong legs, flat abdomen, and she'd recovered immediately when he'd dumped her in the wet grass.

All the junk she'd stuffed in her safari jacket hadn't seemed to get in her way.

He shifted the stream of light to the things she'd left behind. He hadn't lied to her about her tent and sleeping bag. They were in a trampled, sodden heap. He pictured her stretched out in her sleeping bag. He had no doubt she hadn't thought twice about being alone out here in the dark.

Why had she decided to come to Knights Bridge now?

Why alone?

He sucked in a breath. Picturing her in a sleeping bag wasn't helping him. He squatted by her destroyed camping gear and maneuvered his flashlight beam to the edge of the tent and then past it to something that caught his eye. He held the light steady on a red-covered journal or notebook. It looked intact, as if it had been dropped or had fallen there after the fire. Had it fallen out of Samantha's backpack when he'd grabbed it for her? He'd been in a rush. Preoccupied. He could easily not have noticed.

He picked up the notebook. The cover was a little wet, but the inside pages looked to be dry, with no sign of fire damage.

Definitely a journal of some kind.

He tucked his flashlight under one arm and opened to a title page.

Notes on Captain Benjamin Farraday, Pirate and Privateer.

Please return to Samantha Bennett.

Neatly printed on the lines provided were her email address, telephone number and a Boston post office box.

Justin stood back. "Well, well."

He took the journal with him and headed back outside. He could drive to Carriage Hill and return Samantha's journal to her.

Or he could hold on to it, at least for now.

Either way, she would discover it was missing at some point, and she would want it back.

He had no desire to read her personal notes. He wasn't the sneaky type. At the same time...

"Pirates."

Damn.

He heard vehicles out on the road, through the woods. In another minute, a truck and a Jeep drove into the small clearing. All four of his brothers got out of the vehicles—Eric, the eldest, and their three younger brothers, Brandon, Adam and Christopher.

They had a six-pack and wood for a fire.

"Just like the old days," Brandon said. "Except then it used to be a keg."

"Sloan solidarity," Eric said. He'd changed into jeans like his younger brothers.

Adam, who also worked with Sloan & Sons, dumped an armload of cordwood into a fire circle on the edge of the driveway. "Christopher says you pulled this woman out of the fire in the nick of time."

Brandon grinned. "Our brother, the hero."

"I just was here at the right time to help," Justin said with a shrug.

"How'd she get into the mill?" Christopher asked. "Don't you keep it locked?"

"She either broke the lock or picked it," Eric said. "Or it wasn't intact—"

"It was intact." Justin heard the abruptness in his own voice. Olivia would have scowled at him, but his brothers barely noticed. "Good that she got herself out of the storm," he said, less irritably.

"Better the mill caught fire than she was struck by lightning," Christopher said.

Justin nodded. "Agreed."

They left it at that and got the fire going and the six-pack opened. In a little while, more of the crew who fought the fire turned up, all of them volunteers like Justin.

Time to decompress.

An hour later, the impromptu gathering broke up. Eric insisted on driving Justin's truck back to the converted antique sawmill where Justin had an apartment a few miles away, on another stream. The mid-nineteenth-century sawmill was owned by Randy and Louise Frost, Olivia's parents. They ran a custom millwork business up the hill, on the same property. Their younger daughter, Jessica, had vacated the sawmill apartment a few weeks ago, ahead of her wedding that Saturday. Justin was renovating the place in exchange for rent.

He and Eric got out of the truck. Stars glittered in the night sky, and a quarter moon had appeared above the dark silhouette of trees.

"A missing padlock isn't much to go on," Eric said, "but let me know if you have any concerns about this woman."

"I will. Thanks."

"You know more about her than you're saying, don't you?"

Justin debated a half beat, then said, "Some. Not much."

"I see. Well, I don't see, but I'll leave you to it."

Christopher pulled up in his Jeep. Eric hesitated, then climbed in without another word. He was engaged to a great woman, a paramedic. Christopher was seeing someone in Amherst. Justin doubted it would go anywhere.

He wasn't seeing anyone. Hadn't in a while. Which wasn't like him at all.

He climbed the narrow stairs to the small apartment. He'd added a few things of his own, but most of the furniture belonged to the Frosts. He'd always lived in Knights Bridge and always would, but he didn't need a permanent address at this stage in his life.

His head was clear. He'd only had one beer. Eric had insisted on driving him because of the close call today, for him and for the woman he'd found in his burning mill.

He tossed Samantha's journal onto the coffee table and sat on the couch.

Notes on Captain Benjamin Farraday, Pirate and Privateer.

"Uh-huh. Pirates. No surprise, Samantha. No surprise."

Justin picked up a small wooden box he kept on a side table and placed it in his lap. He removed the lid and set it on the couch next to him, then lifted out a small padded envelope. He opened the envelope and slid out a gold coin about three inches in diameter, with faded etching. He'd found it at the cider mill as a teenager and figured it wasn't worth much. He'd never had it appraised, but he'd thought it was worth keeping, a memento of the mill's past.

He wasn't one to hang on to things—he could move in one trip with his truck—but the coin was one of the few possessions he had never thrown out, given away or sold.

Now he wondered if the old coin had something to do with Samantha Bennett and her Captain Farraday.

He returned the coin to its envelope and closed up the box again.

He would take a shower and get something to eat, but he doubted he would get much sleep.

Six

Samantha opened a small bar of pure goat's milk soap handmade at The Farm at Carriage Hill and breathed in its light lavender scent. The packaging was as charming and sophisticated as the inn itself. Olivia Frost did have an artistic eye.

"I'm lucky I know how to match a pair of socks," Samantha said aloud, turning on the water in the shower as hot as she could stand. A bath was tempting but out of the question. As tired as she was, she would go straight down the drain.

The private bathroom, off her pretty room at the top of the stairs, was small and perfect, with a sparkling white tub, pedestal sink and fluffy towels. Framed prints of herbs decorated the walls, and an oval mirror reflected her soot-smudged face back at her. All she could think was that she looked like hell. In Justin's place, she would have suggested a night at Carriage Hill, too. Still, she couldn't help but think she should have curled up with a blanket in the woods.

She peeled off her smoky clothes and noticed her right knee was slightly bruised. She figured she must have hit the deck in the midst of the fire with more force than she realized at the time. Her muscles ached all over, undoubtedly from tension. Justin hadn't hurt her when he'd carried her out of the mill. He'd known what he was doing and had been efficient but also very gentle, even if it had been his property on fire.

She stepped into the tub, welcoming the hot water and steam. The goat's milk soap was mild but worked well on her accumulation of dirt, mud, soot and sweat. A pleasant-smelling shampoo cut through the grime in her hair, and a dab of conditioner got rid of any remaining tangles in her short curls. She'd never been any good at fussing with her hair.

Clean and calmer, she wrapped up in a soft white towel and went back into the bedroom. She gathered up her smoky clothes and stuffed them into a garbage bag that she kept in her backpack for various purposes. It could even be used as an emergency shelter, but not a comfortable one, certainly not compared to The Farm at Carriage Hill. Her room was decorated in an attractive, soothing combination of vintage and contemporary furnishings and eclectic odds and ends. The queen-size bed was covered in soft white linens, throw pillows embroidered with herbs and wildflowers and a down comforter. A dresser, mirror and side chair were painted in shades of green that she wouldn't have thought went together but somehow did.

She resisted the temptation to collapse onto the bed. She'd told Olivia she'd meet her downstairs for a light dinner. She had no idea if Dylan would be back from the house he and Olivia were building up the road. Olivia had explained that he was staying late, making a few calls and doing a bit of work at the construction trailer.

Samantha stood at one of the two windows that looked out toward Quabbin, no lights visible in the seemingly endless dark woods. She would have loved to have followed Cider Brook into the reservoir, but she suspected she would have ended up camping at the cider mill, even without the storm.

A hike, a wild thunderstorm, a fire.

Rescued by a taciturn, good-looking firefighter.

Secrets.

No wonder she was struggling to get her bearings.

Her phone vibrated with a text message. She sat on the edge of the bed and saw the text was from Caleb. Cider mill fire? Was that you?

Of *course* he'd found out. Samantha texted him back. Yes. Lightning.

You okay?

Yep. How'd you know?

Internet. Need me to fetch you?

All she needed now was to have Caleb Bennett burst into town. He wouldn't be discreet. He never was—it wasn't in his nature. He was larger-than-life, impossible to ignore and not the least bit subtle. He would do anything for her, but he wasn't in New England because of her. He was here to visit colleges with his son.

Besides, she still had work to do.

No, thanks, she texted.

Where are you staying?

She debated, then decided on a vague answer. Knights Bridge.

Don't get arrested.

Samantha didn't respond. She dug through her backpack and pulled out a change of clothes that didn't smell too much of smoke.

A fresh sweater, fresh jeans—she felt more like herself again.

She hung her safari jacket on the back of a painted wooden chair and felt the weight of its contents. She withdrew the documents pouch and set it on the bedside table, thinking of plucky Lady Elizabeth as she adjusted to life aboard her pirate ship.

Lady Elizabeth dreamed of castle gardens and the sweet scents of lavender and roses, but she woke to the smells of whiskey, rum and men. It wasn't a nightmare. She was trapped in a claustrophobic berth on a pirate ship. Home was far, far away.

For poor Lady Elizabeth, it had been out of the frying pan of being kidnapped by her father's enemy and into the fire of being rescued by a notorious pirate. After today, Samantha supposed she could identify with the eighteenth-century British aristocrat and her plight more than she had the first time she'd gone through the rousing handwritten pages.

Of course, she hadn't been kidnapped and rescued on the high seas. If things didn't work out for her at Carriage Hill, she could just call a cab or a car service and be back in Boston in a couple of hours.

Steep, narrow stairs landed Samantha in an entry hall with the same wide pine-board floor that extended into the adjoining living room and dining room, each with painted wainscoting and fireplaces off the same center chimney. The living room was quiet and inviting with its casual sofa and chairs and end tables stacked with books on decorating, herbs and soap making. In her room at her grandfather's house in Boston, she had dozens of books on pirates, privateers, eighteenth-century sailing ships and Colonial New England. She didn't own a single book on anything remotely crafty or design-oriented, but she appreciated Olivia's obvious talents.

She continued into the cozy kitchen. A big pot of soup was simmering on the gas stove. She'd enjoyed her helping of applesauce earlier and hadn't thought she would want anything else tonight, except maybe a sip of Scotch, but now she realized she was starving.

The big dog burst through the back door into the mudroom, Olivia right behind him with his leash in hand. She'd introduced him as Buster when she'd shown Samantha to her room. He ran to her, wagging his tail. "He's obviously taken to you," Olivia said, hanging the leash on a hook. "We've been working on his socialization skills. He showed up here this past spring, about the same time I did. He was rambunctious at first."

Samantha patted him. "He seems very friendly."

"He does have his moments. We took a good walk down the road, but he would have stayed out longer if I'd let him." Olivia shivered as she entered the kitchen. "It's chilly out there. I wonder if today was the last gasp of summer. Buster's going to love fall, I think. He likes to chase every leaf he sees."

"That could get to be a challenge when the leaves really start falling." Samantha stood back as Buster abandoned her and flopped down by the mudroom door. "I've never owned a dog. Too many moves."

Olivia peered into the bubbling soup pot. "Where do you live now?"

Nowhere. "I'm on the road a lot. I've been in Boston lately." Samantha stifled an unexpected yawn. "I'm more worn-out than I thought I'd be. Adrenaline as much as anything."

"I imagine so." Olivia grabbed a long-handled spoon from a pottery crock. "Most women in Knights Bridge would tell you that one consolation of being caught in a fire would be getting rescued by a Sloan."

"It happened so fast, I'm not sure it would have made any difference who hauled me out of there."

"Trust me. Better a Sloan than my father. He's been a volunteer firefighter for thirty years. He'd have managed, but it wouldn't have been the same as having Justin rescue you."

Samantha eased onto a chair at the white-painted table in front of a double window, its curtains shut against the dark night. She could feel Justin's arms around her. He hadn't hesitated. "All the firefighters seemed to know what to do."

"They're a good crew."

"It was my first fire."

"And I hope your last," Olivia said as she gave the soup a quick stir.

Samantha noticed a small basket of some kind of whole-grain bread already on the table, but her mind was on the events of the afternoon. She almost jumped at the memory of the fierce bolt of lightning and simultaneous clap of thunder.

"You okay, Samantha?"

"Yes, thanks. Sorry. I was thinking about the storm. I think the lightning struck before I got into the mill and the fire smoldered for a few minutes before it took hold. I wish I'd noticed sooner. By the time I did notice…" She sat up straight, focusing on her surroundings. "There was nothing I could do. Even if I'd managed to get out of the mill safely on my own—and I'm sure I would have—I never would have been able to call in the fire in time to save the mill."

Olivia set her spoon crosswise over the bubbling pot. "It's a great old place, but no one would have blamed you if it had burned up."

"Does Justin work in town? Is that how he can serve as a volunteer firefighter?"

"He's a carpenter. One of the Sloans of Sloan & Sons. They're based up on Cider Brook above the mill. They're doing the construction on the house and barn Dylan and I are building up the road."

Samantha almost jumped out of her chair. Justin Sloan was a *carpenter?* She forced herself to contain her reaction. He wasn't the only carpenter in town, obviously, and he hadn't shown any sign he recognized her. A different carpenter—even a different Sloan— could have spotted her two years ago, described her to Duncan and ended up ruining everything for her.

Olivia watched her with obvious concern. Samantha pulled herself together. "How many Sloan sons are there?" she asked.

"Five."

"I met three of them this afternoon. Justin, Eric and Christopher."

"Eric is the eldest, then Justin, Brandon, Adam and Christopher. There's also a sister, Heather, the youngest. She was born after the company was already named."

"Five older brothers?"

"Yes, but don't pity her. She can hold her own with anyone, including her brothers. Justin, Brandon, Adam and Heather all work full-time for Sloan & Sons. Brandon is also getting involved in adventure travel with Dylan. He's married to my friend Maggie. They just moved back here from Boston."

"Long story?"

Olivia laughed. "There are no short stories in Knights Bridge, I swear. The Sloans are a big family. Knights Bridge wouldn't be Knights Bridge without them. What about you?"

"I'm an only child." Samantha decided not to try to explain her family further.

Olivia got two pottery bowls out of a cupboard and set them on the butcher-block island. "It's potato-leek soup. All right with you?"

"Perfect. Thank you, but please don't go to any trouble."

"It's no trouble at all. We have one restaurant in town and a couple more out by the highway, but you're tired. If soup's all right—"

"Soup is perfect. It smells wonderful."

"It's my own recipe. We also have apple cake." She pointed at an iced cake under glass on a pedestal on the counter. "I've already had a taste. It's outrageously fantastic. Maggie dropped it off before the storm. She and her sons picked the apples themselves. She's a caterer, but it's her grandmother's recipe."

Samantha felt herself relaxing in Olivia's easy company. "How could I resist an invitation like that?"

Olivia smiled. "You're not meant to."

"What can I do to help?"

"Not a thing. Just relax. Maggie slipped a few handfuls of herbs in the soup. Parsley, thyme and chives, I think. We're still harvesting herbs from the gardens out back. I'm lucky the house came with such well-established landscaping. Anyway, we've been drying herbs, freezing herbs, trying out new recipes with herbs. It's fun." Olivia brought the two bowls to the table. "We're even trying our hand at our own herbal essential oils."

"I'm lucky if I can tell parsley from basil," Samantha said as she breathed in the fragrant steam rising from the soup.

Olivia went to the counter and opened a drawer, producing silverware and bright yellow cloth napkins. "I know what you mean. I've gotten better at it. Just to add to the fun, there's more than one kind of parsley and basil." She placed the silverware and napkins on the table and sat across from Samantha. "I've no doubt Dylan's life would go on quite happily if he never heard me say 'herb' again."

Buster wandered over from the mudroom and squeezed under the table. Samantha placed her napkin on her lap and lifted her spoon, and tried to concentrate on the smell of the soup instead of the memory of the fire.

"You're done in, aren't you?" Olivia set her own spoon down. "You don't have to sit here, Samantha. Why don't you finish your supper in your room?"

"I'm more tired than I expected."

"I can make some chamomile tea and bring it up— with a piece of cake, of course. If I'd just survived a fire and could only eat one thing, it'd be Maggie's apple cake."

Samantha ate some of her soup. She had to rein in her emotions. Second-guessing her every move and every decision wouldn't get her anywhere. "I can't thank you enough, Olivia. I know I'm here on very short notice."

"No notice, but that's Justin for you. Everyone in Knights Bridge knows the easiest way to get along with him is just to do what he wants. It's like that with all the Sloans. Even Heather." Olivia smiled. "But we love them all."

Samantha hoped her own dealings with the Sloans had ended that afternoon. She wanted to know more about the cider mill, but she would figure out a way to get information without involving its present owner.

"Knights Bridge seems like a great town," she said.

"I love it," Olivia said without hesitation. "I lived in Boston for a while, but I always wanted to come back home to Knights Bridge. Dylan still has a house in San Diego. Coronado, actually. We were just out there. It's gorgeous."

"Will you two divide your time between here and San Diego?"

"We'll see. I'm trying not to launch myself too far into the future."

Samantha stood up from the table, her legs steadier under her than she would have guessed they would be. The soup and conversation had helped. She hadn't touched the bread. As good as it looked, her mind was now on cake and snuggling under the comforter in her pretty room upstairs.

Waiting until morning to meet Dylan McCaffrey seemed like a smart idea, too.

"You definitely look beat," Olivia said, easing to her feet. "I'll get you your cake."

She went to the counter, lifting the glass lid off the round, double-layer cake, just the tiniest sliver already cut out of it. She grabbed a knife from a rack and cut a generous slice of the cake, setting it on a small plate.

Samantha stifled a yawn. "I guess I am falling over."

"Please, go on up to your room and relax."

"Tea, cake and a warm bed do sound great right now."

"I'll make tea and bring it up with the cake." Olivia raised a hand, stifling any protest from Samantha. "I'm happy to do it. You've had a tough day. Relax and make yourself at home."

Samantha was tempted to tell Olivia about her connection to Dylan's father. She hadn't lied, but she hadn't been forthcoming, either. She was too rattled to trust herself to be able to explain properly. She didn't want to end up causing more problems than she solved.

Best to head up to her room, keep to herself and call it a night.

After her cake and tea, Samantha changed into her flannel pajamas—which didn't smell that smoky—and sat cross-legged on her bed under the comforter, her back against an array of fluffy pillows.

She breathed deeply, listening to an owl outside her window.

It was such a tranquil spot.

She knew how to settle in to new places. A ship sailing the Caribbean Sea, a friend's apartment in Paris, her aunt and uncle's house in the Cotswolds, her grandfather's house in Boston and apartment in London. She had no home base of her own, but she'd always liked being able to pick up and leave a place without a lot of fuss. Her grandfather had enough possessions to keep her mind off anything she might want to buy for herself. She couldn't figure out what he'd wanted even with a tenth of what she'd sorted through so far.

The owl went quiet. She couldn't hear anything now, not a passing car, not even a breeze. She couldn't see Duncan ever making his home in Knights Bridge. He'd seemed more suited to Los Angeles, where she'd first met him—*after* she'd heard about his interest in Knights Bridge and she'd ventured out here.

She lifted her documents pouch off the bedside table and opened it, pulling out the copy of the trifolded, yellowed handwritten pages she'd found in her grandfather's office closet. The original was still safe at his Boston house. As painstaking and tedious as it could be at times, Samantha had to admit that going through his cluttered house and apartment had brought her closer to him. She knew him better in some ways now than she ever had in his long life.

She smiled at the feminine cursive handwriting.

The Adventures of Captain Farraday and Lady Elizabeth

She had no idea how the captivating tale had ended up in her grandfather's possession, or what it could possibly have to do with the real Benjamin Farraday or a painting of a nineteenth-century New England cider mill.

She put the pages aside and pulled out a 1903 map

of the Swift River Valley, then an idyllic setting of picturesque towns and villages. She carefully unfolded the worn, yellowed sheet onto the comforter. The towns of Prescott, Enfield, Dana and Greenwich lay before her. By most accounts, they had been blissful places, but as early as the late-nineteenth century, engineers and politicians had eyed the valley as a potential site for a massive reservoir, given its abundance of streams, rivers and lakes. Less than a hundred miles from Boston, the valley's upland location meant a reservoir there could deliver water through an elaborate aqueduct by gravity alone, eliminating the need for artificial filtration. The planners had been right. Damming Beaver Brook and the three branches of the Swift River that wound through the valley had solved Boston's water problem for the foreseeable future. It had also dislocated thousands of people.

Samantha ran her fingertips over lakes, roads and landmarks that were long gone from the landscape. So few were left who remembered life in the lost towns. She touched hills where children once sledded that were now uninhabited islands surrounded by the beautiful waters of the reservoir. She traced the twists and turns of the middle branch of the Swift River, long before it had been allowed to overflow its banks and flood the surrounding valley.

She located the faded line that was Cider Brook.

What if she'd simply told Duncan McCaffrey the truth?

But she hadn't, and not without reason.

Seven

Loretta Wrentham paced in her La Jolla living room. She didn't want to fly back East to Knights Bridge. She'd been there recently, and it was a pleasant town and the people were nice—but she didn't want to go again this soon. She would be flying out there for Dylan and Olivia's Christmas wedding, and she had things to do at home.

Such as figure out what to do about this Hollywood private investigator.

Damn him.

His name was Julius Hartley, and he was a smart, sardonic, all-too-good-looking, all-too-knowing divorced father of two grown daughters. He was sitting on her butter-colored leather couch with one arm across the back and one leg thrown over the other as he watched her pace. He had on golf clothes and looked as if he'd just stepped out of an expensive country club. Loretta hated golf.

He was also a private investigator for a law firm in Los Angeles. She swore he knew where every skeleton in Southern California was buried, locked or cremated.

One of those skeletons had brought him to her attention in August and then led to her traveling with him to Knights Bridge.

It was all crazy, confusing, complicated and more fun than either of them had had in a long time.

Without pausing, Loretta threaded her fingers through her short gray hair. She'd stopped dyeing it when she'd turned fifty. Instead of thinking she was older because of the gray, people thought she was younger. Hell if she could figure out that one, but she was good with it.

Julius uncrossed his legs and put both feet flat on her floor. "What do you know about Samantha Bennett?"

Loretta stopped dead in her tracks. "Samantha Bennett? Why do you ask?"

He shrugged, all innocence. "I overheard you on the phone with Dylan."

Of course. That made sense. Julius might not even have been eavesdropping, although she wouldn't put it past him. But she'd shrieked. Samantha Bennett was the *last* name she'd expected to hear Dylan utter. She hadn't uttered it herself in the two years since his father's death.

"You have to fire her, Duncan. You have no choice."
"I know, I know."

Loretta composed herself. She hadn't told Dylan all or even a lot of what she knew about Samantha. She needed time to get her bearings. She'd promised to call him later tonight or in the morning. He'd been intrigued but patient, obviously sensing that he'd stepped into another emotional minefield that involved his late father.

Samantha Bennett.

Of all the people from Duncan's past to turn up, why her?

"You can tell me what's going on," Julius said. "I won't tell Dylan."

"I'm not keeping secrets. I'm just…" She reined in her irritation. She wasn't one to be at a loss for words. "I need to think."

"She's a treasure hunter? This Samantha Bennett?"

Loretta gave a reluctant nod. "She specializes in pirates and privateers who roamed the East Coast and Caribbean in the seventeenth and eighteenth centuries."

"Jack Sparrow."

"*Real* pirates, Julius. Blackbeard, William Kidd, 'Black Sam' Bellamy. That ilk."

"Cool."

"It's not cool. Samantha lied to Duncan about herself, and he fired her."

"She lied? About what? And what does this have to do with you?"

Although Loretta hadn't known Julius that long and had told him little about her past with the McCaffreys, he was adept at picking up on clues. "I wasn't Duncan's attorney if that's what you're asking. I work for Dylan. I never worked for Duncan."

"I get that. Did you tell Duncan this Samantha lied and suggest he fire her?"

"I didn't give him legal advice of any kind."

"Not what I'm asking, Loretta."

She knew it wasn't. "Duncan discovered Samantha had sneaked into Knights Bridge between his visits. She didn't tell him. Then she showed up in his office in Los Angeles. He hired her on the spot to work on his Portugal project. Once he found out she'd neglected to tell him some important details about herself, he couldn't take the chance that she was spying on him."

"Spying on him? To what end?"

"To get information she could use for herself."

"Do an end run around him you mean? Get to some lost treasure before he did?"

"Possibly. Or just ruin his reputation."

"Why would she want to do that?"

"I'm not saying she did." Loretta stood by the open patio door and let the breeze hit her. She was hot. It was all this emotion. She turned back to Julius. "I'm saying Duncan couldn't take that risk once he knew she hadn't told him the truth about herself."

Julius stretched out his legs and leaned back against the comfortable couch. He didn't look emotional at all. "People lie all the time. Doesn't always mean they're up to anything underhanded."

"Knights Bridge was too important to Duncan. I didn't understand why at the time, but it wasn't a part of his work as a treasure hunter. That Samantha inserted herself there and then lied about it was too much for him to ignore."

Julius nodded. "I get that, too."

"Then what don't you get?"

"Why you're pacing. Dylan's a big boy. He can handle this woman if she's up to something in Sleepy Hollow."

Loretta plopped onto a chair across from him. She worked at her house—she had an office in a front room, with views of the street. She liked to see who was pulling into her driveway, and it allowed her to keep her living area separate. This room was home, where she relaxed and enjoyed looking out at her pool and the Pacific. Both were glistening now, with roses and bougainvillea along the pool fence adding splashes of bright red. She'd moved here before she'd known anything about ice hockey—before she'd met a driven young hockey player named Dylan McCaffrey. She'd worked with him throughout his years with the National Hockey League and then when he'd joined forces with Noah Kendrick and his high-tech entertainment company, NAK, Inc.

Dylan hadn't heeded all her advice, but he'd done fine for himself. He was like a son to her. Noah was, too.

And now both of them had fallen in love with women from little Knights Bridge.

Loretta leaned forward, elbows on her knees, hands clasped. She had to calm down. "There's more. Samantha painted herself as a quiet researcher. Duncan hired her and took her under his wing."

"I gather she isn't a quiet researcher," Julius said.

"She's Harry Bennett's granddaughter."

Julius was silent a moment. "Ah. She's not just any Bennett."

"Her father is underwater explorer and salvage expert Malcolm Bennett. Her mother is Francesca Bennett, a prominent marine archaeologist, and her uncle is Caleb Bennett, a maritime historian and adventurer."

"Didn't Harry die in Antarctica?"

Loretta shook her head. "He survived a tough expedition fifty years ago and died three years ago at home in his bed at the ripe old age of ninety-six."

"Duncan didn't make the connection between his Bennett and *the* Bennetts?"

"He did not."

"You'd think having a Bennett on his team would be an asset."

"Maybe it would have been, but Samantha didn't tell him—and he didn't ask."

"He didn't check her out before he hired her? Why not?"

"He said he was distracted by his reasons for being in Knights Bridge—his search for his birth parents—but I think it had more to do with his nature. He didn't like getting bogged down in details. He preferred to trust his instincts."

"Did he have good instincts about people?" Julius asked.

"Sometimes. I don't know." Loretta sprang to her feet. "It's a mess."

Julius eyed her from the couch. "If Samantha slipped into Knights Bridge before she met Duncan, how did she know he was there?"

"She's part of the treasure-hunting community." Loretta realized she had resumed pacing in front of the patio doors. "Apparently word got out that he'd been to Knights Bridge. Everyone assumed it was for personal reasons, which it was."

"So this Samantha heard he was there and tried to see him, missed him, and came out to L.A. What's the big deal?"

"The big deal is that she didn't tell him. Duncan didn't fire her because she's a Bennett or because she sneaked into Knights Bridge. He fired her because she didn't tell him the truth about herself. Trust is vital in the treasure-hunting world, given the stakes, the controversies."

"It's vital in any relationship," Julius said.

Loretta frowned at him. "Yes. Right. I'm just pointing out its value in Duncan's world."

"He was worried this Bennett woman was a spy for her father or grandfather—"

"Her grandfather was already dead when she and Duncan met. He died the previous fall."

"My point stands. Was she good at what she did for him?"

"Very good, apparently. She was in Portugal with him and his team right before he died. She was involved in planning that trip."

"Not his fall, I hope."

Loretta gave him a cool look. "Duncan had a heart attack. The heart attack caused his fall."

Julius shrugged. "Don't tell me it didn't occur to you there was a connection."

"You and I obviously live in different worlds, Julius, because you're wrong, it didn't occur to me. I knew this wouldn't move your needle given the scandals and skulduggery you've unearthed up in Hollywood."

"But this Samantha is sneaking around your Dylan, and that concerns you and therefore it definitely moves my needle." He walked over to the patio doors and looked out at the pool, a classic kidney shape, its water sparkling under the blue sky. "How did Duncan find out what was up with Samantha? Did you investigate her for him?"

"*Investigate* isn't the word I would use," Loretta said, easing next to him. "I looked into her background once Duncan became aware she'd been to Knights

Bridge. That by itself set off alarms. It wasn't hard once I got started. She hadn't lied so much as omitted things."

"Why do you think she's in Knights Bridge now?"

"Because Dylan's there. Other than that, I don't know."

"Is she looking for treasure?"

"In Knights Bridge?"

Julius grimaced. "Right. What was I thinking? Goats, herbs, country roads, antique houses and hardheaded people. Although Duncan was after stolen British jewels. Think Samantha got wind of them?"

"I told you, I don't know what she was up to then or now. I just know that she didn't tell the truth, and Duncan fired her."

"Did he give her a chance to explain?"

"Explain what? No. There was no point. He said he wanted her to go on her way."

Julius looked at her. "Did you two discuss his work?"

His scrutiny made her feel self-conscious. It wasn't like her. She shook off her discomfort and said, matter-of-fact, "I didn't know Duncan that well. I've known Dylan for years, but I didn't meet his father until a few months before his death."

"Ah," Julius said, knowing. "Regrets?"

"I don't have a lot of serious regrets, but I'm in my fifties, Julius. You are, too." She avoided his eye and watched the pool water ripple in a breeze. "If we don't have regrets at our age, we haven't been living."

He slung an arm over her shoulders. "Does Dylan know about you and his father?"

She swallowed. "Yes, but we don't discuss it."

"Does that mean you're not discussing it with me?"

"Tenfold."

"Dylan had never heard the name Samantha Bennett until she showed up in Knights Bridge this afternoon?"

"That's right. His father never told him about her. Neither did I. Why would I?"

Loretta didn't wait for an answer. Instead she quickly relayed what Dylan had told her about the fire at an old cider mill up the road from Carriage Hill.

Julius grinned. "A cider mill? You're kidding, right?"

"People could have been killed, Julius."

"Yeah, but…" He shook his head. "All right, all right. I'm glad no one was hurt."

"I haven't told Dylan what I know about Samantha, but I will. Whatever she's doing in Knights Bridge, he can handle her without my help."

"You want to believe that, but you don't." Julius drew her close and kissed her on the top of her head. She was almost as tall as he was. "Let's grab something to eat. You're a desk lawyer, Loretta. You know contracts and money. You don't have a sixth sense about people."

She gave him a skeptical look. "And you do?"

"Damn straight. Come on. We can walk. It'll be good for us."

She grabbed a lightweight jacket, and they headed out. It was cool, but it would be cooler in Knights Bridge. She'd found she liked to check the weather there. She supposed it helped her feel as if she was still a part of Dylan's life. The emotions of this new chapter in his life had hit her hard—harder than they would have, no doubt, if she hadn't slept with his father during his last days. Duncan had died before their relationship had had a chance to move beyond a mad night of sex to wherever it could have gone.

Now, two years later, here she was holding hands with Julius Hartley. Was he a new chapter in *her* life, or was he a passing fling? A distraction?

"How can you walk in those shoes?" he asked her, interrupting her thoughts.

She glanced down at her strappy sandals. "They're fine. What's wrong with them?"

"The heels. Don't they kill you?"

"I'm used to them. I like them. I think they make my legs look sexier, don't you?"

"Sexier than what?"

She sighed. "Than without heels."

"That's one of those 'do these jeans make me look fat' questions women should never ask men, and men should never answer if they do."

"Oh, for Pete's sake, Julius—"

"Your legs always look sexy." He winked at her. "How's that?"

"You sound like a prepared witness."

"But you're laughing."

She tugged him closer to her. "Yes, I'm laughing."

They walked a few blocks to her favorite seafood restaurant. It was early for dinner, but she'd worked through lunch, after a late rising thanks to Julius turning up last night. He said he'd had business in San Diego. She hoped she wasn't out of her mind getting involved with him. She wasn't worried about getting hurt. If he decided she was nuts and moved on, she would manage. She just didn't want to hurt him.

They sat at a cozy round table overlooking the water below them. She gazed down at the waves. She loved this place. She'd grown up here and had moved back after she'd graduated from law school. She had no desire to live anywhere else. Zip, zero. As far as she was concerned, the hillside, seaside community of La Jolla, California, was paradise, never mind the high cost of living.

But she found herself picturing Dylan on the sunlit stone terrace at The Farm at Carriage Hill, with the flower and herb gardens, the shade trees, the open fields and the old stone walls.

The leaves were turning in New England, he'd told her. She should come back out there and see them.

She pushed back the image and focused on the handsome man across the small table from her. "Why do you think Samantha Bennett is in Knights Bridge?"

Julius didn't hesitate. "To redeem herself."

Julius left after they got back from dinner. He headed back up to his house in Beverly Hills or Hollywood Hills or wherever it was. Loretta hadn't been there yet. It was his world. His daughters were there. His ex-wife. His clients and the law firm he worked for. She envisioned him with a Sam Spade sort of office but supposed that was nonsense.

She hated to see him go but at the same time was relieved.

She'd never married—she'd never *wanted* to marry—and she'd had damn few long-term relationships in her life. It hadn't been a plan, it had just worked out that way. She wasn't promiscuous. She'd had long dry spells between men.

"Like a decade," she muttered as she went out to her pool. It was heated. She hated cold water.

She kicked off her sandals and dipped a toe into the water. She'd gone skinny-dipping with Duncan their one night together. Talk about madness. She in her fifties, he in his early seventies. They'd had a blast, laughing, enjoying life. She didn't know why she'd fallen for him, but she had no regrets, not about that. She'd been his last love. They hadn't fought, or really had a chance to get to know each other.

She hadn't told his son because—well, because her relationship with his father was none of Dylan's business. That was just a fact. It wasn't good or bad. What she and Duncan had shared was about them. It wasn't about Dylan.

With no indication that Duncan was in anything but excellent health, it had been a terrible shock when she'd gotten word of his death.

What a two years it had been since that dark day.

Loretta didn't dare trust what she had with Julius. It wasn't just lust, and that scared the hell out of her. Did she want to get serious with a man at this point in her life?

What if Julius freaking dropped dead, too?

She blinked back tears. How had her tidy life become so complicated?

"Damned if I know what I want."

She splashed the water with her foot and almost fell into the stupid pool. Wouldn't that serve her right? An independent, successful professional falling ass-over-teakettle into the pool over a *man*.

She was more raw than she'd realized after Duncan's death and now Dylan's engagement to a woman in this little New England town. She hated not knowing what to do about Julius. About her feelings for him. That wasn't like her. She *always* knew what to do.

Duncan had known he had no choice, but he'd still disliked firing Samantha Bennett, then wondered if he'd done the right thing. *"In my work, Loretta, I can't take chances on someone who deliberately lied to me—whatever her reasons. But I'm not a heartless SOB, either."*

"She'll be fine, but it'll help that she only worked for you a short time," Loretta had told him. She remembered how much she'd enjoyed their long calls and occasional video chats. They'd shared an intense intimacy that she'd never expected would last—but she hadn't expected he'd die, either. *"Did you ask her why she looked you up in Knights Bridge?"*

"Not specifically, no. Maybe she would tell me, but it doesn't matter. She needs to get on with her life, and I have work to do."

Loretta sank onto a lounge chair, letting her feet dry in the fading sun. She had a damn good life here. She couldn't relate to Dylan's life in Knights Bridge. Maybe if she had some reason to be there—like he did.

She'd felt all crazily warm and fuzzy and maternal when he'd called to ask her what she knew about Samantha Bennett.

She groaned. "I've gone off the edge."

Her phone vibrated on the table next to her lounge chair. She grabbed it and saw Julius had texted her. You're angsting, aren't you?

The man did have a sixth sense about people. She typed her answer. Obsessing. There's a difference. Where are you?

Almost home. Stopped for gas.

She debated asking him to turn around and come back to La Jolla, but there was nothing to keep her at home except work that could wait. He'd been asking her to come up there. If he understood she wasn't ready to meet his family...

She texted him back. Do you have wine?

I collect wine. Noah would approve.

Noah Kendrick, Dylan's best friend and the billionaire founder of NAK, Inc., owned a winery on the central coast of California. He was there now with Phoebe O'Dunn, the Knights Bridge librarian. They would be returning to Massachusetts soon.

Loretta felt abandoned, alone—she didn't know what the hell was wrong with her.

She responded to Julius. I'm on my way.

His answer came within seconds. I'll be waiting with the Chardonnay.

Eight

Samantha awoke to sun streaming through her windows. She hadn't pulled the curtains, but she'd overslept, anyway. She bolted upright, knowing it was after eight before she checked the time on the bedside clock.

Eight thirty-four.

She had planned to be on her way by now. On her way *where* she didn't exactly know, but out of The Farm at Carriage Hill, away from the herbs and the big slobbery dog and the happy engaged couple.

Late last night, exhausted but unable to sleep, she'd decided she would get an early start. She didn't need to meet Dylan over coffee and eggs. She could stick to her plan and accomplish what she'd come to Knights Bridge to do without a face-to-face with her ex-boss's son.

With a groan, she sank against the padded headboard. She'd ended up deep under the comforter, finally and totally dead to the world after days of digging through her grandfather's office and then her uncle and cousin's arrival in Boston and then yesterday. The drive west, her hike, the thunderstorm, the fire, the rescue, the irritable volunteer firefighter. Then the gracious hostess, the warm applesauce, the soup, the cake. The big dog. The goat's milk soap.

No *wonder* she'd had a hard time winding down and hadn't fallen asleep until well after midnight. Hearing what she took to be Dylan McCaffrey's voice out in the hall hadn't helped.

Justin Sloan had to have known she would be more like a *house* guest at The Farm at Carriage Hill than an *inn* guest. She supposed he and Olivia both had tried to warn her, and she'd just been too shaken and rattled for it to sink in that her hosts *lived* here.

She stood up, the braided rug warm under her bare feet. Without warning, her mind flashed to the hiss and near-roar of the fire in the dark, claustrophobic cider mill.

She could feel Justin lifting her as she'd gasped for air. She could smell his shirt, his skin. . . .

"Gad," she said under her breath.

She'd dreamed about him, and now that she was awake she was going to keep thinking about him?

She shook her head. "I need coffee."

Despite traipsing through the woods, her tense escape from the fire and her dreams, the stiffness and achiness she'd felt last night had eased and she wasn't particularly sore this morning. She ducked into the pretty bathroom, her reflection in the mirror not as deadly as yesterday when she'd arrived.

She took another shower, getting any residual smoke smell off her, and quickly got dressed. She unloaded her backpack on the floor and went through every item for smoke damage. She would figure out what she needed to replace and stop at the country store in town. She wanted to go back to the cider mill this morning. It and the village were both within relatively easy walking distance of Carriage Hill.

She stared at the contents of her backpack on the floor with a feeling of dread.

She got down on her knees and went through every item again.

No journal.

She hadn't thought about it until now. It was always with her. It must have been displaced in the mad dash from the fire.

She stood straight, her heartbeat quickening as she considered the possibilities. Had it burned up in the fire? Had it fallen out of her pack after Justin had rescued her?

Had one of the other firefighters found it? His cop brother?

Was it still in the mill? Would someone stop there this morning and find it?

She had no memory of the small cloth-bound journal beyond slipping it into her backpack yesterday morning before she left Boston. She was *positive* she'd had it with her when she'd shoved her pack into the backseat with Isaac.

Maybe she'd dropped it in her grandfather's Mercedes.

She texted her uncle and asked.

He responded immediately. No journal.

Check under the seats. Please.

She paced, waiting for his next text. Not in the car. Burned?

I don't know.

Uh-oh.

Yeah, no kidding. How's Amherst?

The ghost of Harry Bennett haunts the ivy-covered buildings.

Only her uncle would take the time to type such a text. Samantha typed a quick response. No doubt. Good luck.

You, too, Sam.

Marginally calmer, she headed downstairs, arriving to an empty kitchen. A cool draft drew her into the mudroom and out to the stone terrace, where Olivia sat at a round wood table having coffee and toast. She smiled cheerfully. "Well, good morning. Did you sleep well?"

"Great, thanks." Samantha pushed aside her panic over her missing journal and pulled out a chair in the sun, taking a seat. "It's a lovely day."

"It is, isn't it? I'm not letting a single reasonably warm, sunny morning go to waste. It'll be snowing before we know it. Dylan played ice hockey for years, but he's never done a real New England winter. Should be interesting." Olivia rose, grabbing her breakfast plate but leaving her coffee mug. She wore jeans and an oversize, paint-spattered white shirt, her dark hair pulled back loosely, her casual attire a reminder that Carriage Hill was also her home. "We're having our wedding here on Christmas Eve."

"Do you hope it snows?"

"I hope there's snow on the ground. I wouldn't want a blizzard to keep people from traveling. What can I get you for breakfast? We have almost anything you can think of, including wild blueberries for pancakes."

"I'd be happy to make my own breakfast—"

Olivia held up a hand, silencing her. "I wouldn't

dream of it. We're still getting up to speed, but the larder is full, so to speak. So, what do you think? Cereal, muffins, toast, yogurt, fresh fruit, eggs—"

"Yogurt with fruit and toast would be fabulous. Thank you."

"Done. I'll bring it out to you." Olivia grinned, heading to the mudroom door. "This is so much fun."

When Olivia disappeared into the kitchen, Samantha breathed in the crisp air, hoping it would help settle her down. She wanted to enjoy her surroundings. If her journal was in the cider mill, she would find it before anyone else did. If it had burned up…well, then, it had burned up. If Justin or any of the other firefighters had found it, surely they would return it unread. They were professionals.

Who was she kidding? They would read at least enough to realize she was in their little town because of a long-dead pirate.

Buster rolled onto his back in front of a bench at the edge of the terrace. The yard was a mix of lawn and raised beds of herbs and flowers, with mulched paths that led to a garden shed and a stone wall and shade trees along the edge of a rolling field. A small hill rose across the field. Carriage Hill, presumably.

Samantha imagined a Christmas Eve wedding with freshly fallen snow, lights, a soft winter-blue sky. It would be beautiful. Then again, this place would be beautiful anytime of year—including now, with the autumn-tinged leaves, colorful mums and New England asters. She thought she could smell mint on the light breeze.

"My friend Maggie will be here soon," Olivia said as she returned to the terrace with a breakfast tray.

"We're getting ready for my sister's wedding here this weekend."

Samantha sat up straight. "This weekend? Today is *Thursday*. You look so calm."

"It's not a huge wedding, and Maggie's doing most of the heavy lifting, since the bride is my sister and I'll be participating in the ceremony. Maggie's unflappable. I'm more like the old saying about the duck—calm on the surface, paddling like crazy underneath." Olivia laughed as she set the tray on the table. "But I'm calmer than I used to be, and it'll all work out. Jess—that's my sister—and Mark, her fiancé, are both from town, and the weather looks good for Saturday."

"A New England fall wedding. It'll be wonderful."

Olivia unloaded a plate of whole-grain toast and small bowls of plain yogurt, fresh-cut fruit—apples, plums, peaches—and butter and jams. A coffee press, mug and cream pitcher came next, then the silverware and napkin.

"This is perfect," Samantha said with a smile. "Thank you so much."

"If you think of anything else you need, just let me know."

"You'll join me for coffee?"

"Happily." Olivia sank into a chair, looking relaxed. "Maggie and I have a full day ahead of us."

"I imagine so." Samantha poured coffee, breathing in its strong smell. "Is your sister nervous about the wedding?"

"She says she's too busy to worry. She works at my family's mill in town. Mark is a local architect. Mark Flanagan. He did the plans for the house and barn Dylan's building up the road." She paused, then added with a smile, "The house and barn Dylan and *I* are building. Sometimes I still have to remind myself."

"You two will live there when the house is finished?"

"Yes. We have so many plans." Olivia took a quick breath, as if to keep a rush of anxiety at bay. "It's been quite a year. A good one, but it's come with a lot of changes."

Buster stirred, and Samantha heard men's voices in the kitchen. She resisted the temptation to jump up and run and instead buttered toast and spooned out yogurt and fruit. Then the back door opened, and Justin Sloan and another man walked out onto the terrace. Olivia got up and introduced Dylan, her fiancé. Not that it was necessary, given his resemblance to his father.

"Good to meet you, Samantha," he said. "Sorry your first day in Knights Bridge wasn't the best."

She chose her words carefully. "It's a beautiful day today. I can't thank you and Olivia enough."

"Not a problem. Glad to have you."

Justin pulled out a chair and sat next to her. "You don't look any worse for wear this morning." There was just the slightest edge of suspicion in his voice. "What are your plans for the day?"

Samantha ate some of her fruit and yogurt and got her bearings before she responded. "I thought I'd resume my hike. I'm not positive yet."

Buster rubbed against Dylan's knee. He patted the big dog. "Take your time. There's no rush on our account."

"You've got a wedding to put on."

"It's under control," Olivia said. "You're welcome to stay."

Samantha thanked them as she got to her feet, feeling like a total liar. When he'd fired her, Duncan hadn't been mad so much as disappointed—harder to take in many ways than outright anger. *"I can't have you work for me, Samantha, but I wish you the best as you get on with your life."*

Dylan slipped an arm around his fiancée. It was easy to see why he'd fallen for Olivia. She was kind, generous and creative. She'd obviously had her struggles. Without knowing any details, Samantha sensed that Olivia's return to her hometown had come with obstacles and a story, if one with a happy ending— The Farm at Carriage Hill and a Christmas wedding to Dylan McCaffrey.

Samantha stared down at her breakfast on the table. Her throat tightened with emotion. She didn't belong at Carriage Hill, inserting herself into these people's lives. "Thank you all so much for helping me out. The fire affected me more than I realized." She was aware of Justin watching her, head tilted back, deep blue eyes narrowed with a certain skepticism. She couldn't let him get to her. Couldn't be distracted by wanting to convince him that she wasn't up to no good. "I'll grab my things and be on my way."

Before anyone could respond, she bolted into the mudroom and through the kitchen, not stopping until she was back in her room. She shut the door behind her, leaned against it and caught her breath. Her head was spinning. She couldn't blame smoke inhalation. She wasn't experiencing any aftereffects from her close call with the fire. Physically, she was fine.

She shut her eyes, breathed deeply, trying to quiet her heart rate.

Meeting Dylan had thrust her back to the difficult days when his father had taken her under his wing and then died believing she was a liar and a spy.

Then there was Justin. Her taciturn rescuer.

She gave an inward groan. She wasn't practically gasping for air because she'd been in the company of a McCaffrey, or even because of her missing journal. It was Justin and his suspicious deep blue eyes, his hard jaw and abrupt manner. She wished Olivia's father *had* been the one to rescue her. At least then she'd have been able to keep a clear head.

She exhaled, standing up straight. "Damn."

Of all times *not* to let herself be swayed by a good-looking man, regardless of what he thought of her. She glanced around the sunlit room. If only she could stay here all day. Read. Take a hot bath. Look out at the view of the forest with its changing fall colors.

Hide. Avoid.

That wouldn't help her situation any more than running away would.

Dylan and Olivia seemed like decent people. Olivia's sister was getting married here on Saturday.

They didn't need someone stirring up the past.

Samantha stuffed her things into her backpack, made up the bed and scoured the bedroom and bathroom for anything she might have dropped—especially anything that could give away her history with Duncan McCaffrey. With a deep breath, she slung her backpack over one shoulder and headed downstairs.

She would find her journal. Then she would figure out what was next. Once she was on her own, at least she'd be able to think.

* * *

Samantha expected to find Olivia in the kitchen and perhaps her friend Maggie, and hoped to say thank you, make her goodbyes and be on her way. Instead she found Justin there, alone, leaning against the sink, his powerful arms crossed on his chest as he watched her grind to a halt on the other side of the butcher-block island.

"In a hurry, Sam?" he asked.

"Not really, no, but I am getting a later start than I wanted." She glanced into the mudroom but saw no sign of Olivia or Dylan, or even Buster. She tightened her hold on the strap of her backpack. "It got quiet all of a sudden."

As far as she could see, Justin didn't move a muscle. "Dylan and Olivia went up the road to meet with their architect."

"Mark Flanagan. The almost-brother-in-law."

His eyes leveled on her. "You're getting to know the players."

She felt a rush of awareness that she couldn't explain. *Had* to be the aftereffects of yesterday. She tried to keep any hint of her physical reaction to him from showing in her voice or manner. "Olivia and I chatted over breakfast. It's a beautiful morning. I'm looking forward to a good walk."

"Are you planning to finish following Cider Brook into Quabbin?"

"I'd like to try. I thought I'd start where I left off at the cider mill. I can collect my stuff at the same time."

"No point. It's ruined. I'll toss it when I clean up."

"I don't mind—"

"The mill's taped off until I go through it and decide it's safe."

The man did have a cut-to-the-chase way about him. Samantha debated what to say next. Normally she was one to plunge in and think and talk at the same time, but Justin's directness combined with her missing journal had her rattled.

"I still want to go back there," she said, firm but not argumentative.

He stood straight, lowering his arms to his side. "Why?"

"I had nightmares last night." True, as far as it went. "It would help to see the mill on such a nice, sunny morning. I don't have to go inside." Assuming she found her missing journal out by the brook. If not, she *would* have to go inside the mill. She wanted that journal back—she needed to know what had happened to it, even if it meant asking Justin for his help. But she wasn't there yet. "I won't stay long."

"I have some stops I need to make. I'll give you a ride over there."

Not what she had in mind. "Really, I don't mind walking—"

"That's good." He pointed at her backpack. "Want me to carry that for you?"

"I'll manage. I hiked with more yesterday."

He shrugged. "Suit yourself."

"Are you always this abrupt?"

His sexy look caught her off guard. "Not always."

He went out the front door, obviously expecting her to follow him. Samantha could feel his padlock in her jacket pocket, but she'd slipped the documents pouch and her grandfather's flask into her backpack. She'd meant to return the lock, but Justin's manner had her second-guessing herself. Now she wasn't sure what she'd do. Keep acting as if she didn't have it, maybe.

She supposed she should appreciate his offer of a ride, but it felt off, too. It wasn't just a grudging offer, and it wasn't impromptu—because he was heading out on errands, anyway. He had waited for her in the kitchen. Keeping an eye on her? Suspicious of her?

If she didn't accept his offer of a ride out to the mill and kept arguing and finding excuses, she would look as if she had something to hide.

Which, of course, she did.

She would also come across as ungrateful and rude, although she wasn't sure Justin would even notice.

There was also nothing to stop him from driving out to the cider mill and waiting for her while she walked away.

Hoisting her backpack onto one shoulder, she headed outside. Justin had left the passenger door to his truck open and was behind the wheel. Presumptuous, but Samantha realized she had little choice at this point and continued out the stone walk. A few red leaves had fallen from a nearby tree and lay scattered on the lush grass. Chickadees swooped from pine branches. She wished she could relax and enjoy the gorgeous day, but meeting Dylan and now the prospect of driving to the cider mill with Justin had her feeling unusually self-conscious. She didn't like skirting the truth and wasn't one to waffle, but she needed to find her journal and regroup.

She had good reasons for being in Knights Bridge.

She slid her backpack onto the floor in front of the passenger seat and climbed in, grimacing when the first thing she noticed was Justin's right thigh. Not good. "This is a beautiful place," she said, pulling her door shut. "It was a good idea for me to stay here last night. Thanks for your help with that."

He started the engine. "Sure thing."

"Olivia couldn't have been nicer. She wouldn't take any payment from me."

"That's Olivia for you." He pulled out onto the narrow road.

"You two grew up together?"

"More or less. I'm a few years older."

"You've always lived in Knights Bridge?"

"Yep."

The stiff movements, the abrupt manner. He definitely didn't trust her. Samantha decided she would be smart to keep her mouth shut and head out on her own again as soon as possible. She had a lot on her mind, and one wrong word—one slipup—and Justin would be all over her. It wasn't just his mood, she realized now. He was like that. Alert, observant and not one to suffer fools gladly.

Or liars.

Except she hadn't lied. Not to him, anyway. Not really.

And not really to Duncan, either, even if he hadn't seen it that way.

A Sloan & Sons van and several trucks were in the driveway at the McCaffrey construction site up the road. A trio of men stood at one of the trucks with to-go cups—coffee, undoubtedly—and were going over what appeared to be a set of blueprints spread out on the hood.

"Would you be with those guys now if you weren't carting me around?" Samantha asked.

"Probably."

"You'd have waited to do your errands. You're just doing them now because of me." She decided to match his bluntness. "Were you elected to keep an eye on me?"

He glanced at her. "Self-appointed."

His response took her by surprise. He was as much as admitting he was suspicious of her. "So, you didn't offer to drive me to the mill just to be nice. Okay, I get it, but there's no need for me to inconvenience you. I can walk from here. I like to walk."

"I mind you walking." He didn't ease off the gas pedal. "At the rate you're going, you'll end up tripping and falling into the millpond."

"So what if I do? It's not deep."

"I was trying to be funny. You're not laughing?" He drove with one hand loosely on the wheel. "If we're going to spend the next couple of hours together, we might as well laugh, right?"

Samantha shook her head. "We're not spending the next couple of hours together. We're spending the next ten minutes together." Her heart was pounding now. "You're dropping me off at the cider mill and then going about your business."

He slowed for a curve on the narrow road. "I'm not leaving you alone out there."

"Why not?"

"I told you. It's not safe."

That wasn't the reason. She knew it wasn't. "The mill already caught fire. That's not going to happen again, and you said yourself the damage is minimal."

She sat back in her seat but didn't relax. "The odds are with me. I'll be fine."

"Is that how you live your life? Calculating the odds?"

"Actually, I don't often take the time to calculate the odds at all. I usually just plunge in headfirst and hope for the best."

"Is that what you did yesterday?"

"I planned my hike, maybe not down to every possible scenario, but I had everything I needed—"

"Including Scotch."

"Exactly." She kept her tone light despite her self-consciousness. He had her rattled. She suspected he knew it, too. "I admit the thunderstorm caught me by surprise, but I managed. I took quick, decisive action."

"Quick, decisive action, huh? Was that before or after you broke into the mill?"

She ignored his sardonic tone. "Both. Not that I broke in. Technically."

"Right." He didn't bother to hide his skepticism. "Breaking into the mill kept you from getting struck by lightning. What was your 'quick, decisive action' once you were inside?"

"Dropping low and making for the door when I smelled smoke. If I'd stayed by the wall where the fire came up from the cellar, we could both be dead now."

Justin glanced at her, his deep blue gaze going right through her. "You want me to thank you for saving my life?"

"I wouldn't go *that* far."

He grinned. "I wouldn't, either. I'm not reckless. I knew what I was doing when I rescued you."

"That word again. Rescue."

"Tough for you to admit when you're in a mess, isn't it, Sam?" He didn't wait for her to answer. "Did you know the mill was there?"

"How would I have?"

"Lots of ways, I imagine, and that doesn't answer the question."

She knew it didn't, but she had no intention of getting into what she did or didn't know about his cider mill. "I wasn't surprised to run into an old mill on a winding New England brook."

"Uh-huh."

Justin turned onto the dirt road out to the mill. He had a sure manner and not a hint of self-doubt—a plus in the fire but disconcerting now. Samantha sighed. "You can be uncompromising, can't you? Hard on other people—hard on yourself."

"Calling me a bastard, Sam?"

She smiled. "I don't know you well enough to call you a bastard."

"Ha."

"Maybe having five siblings taught you not to beat around the bush."

He slowed as the truck bounced over a series of deep ruts. "You're just not used to having someone see through you. You've parsed nearly every word you've said about yesterday. You don't want to tell me what you're up to out here, but you don't want to outright lie, either." He glanced sideways at her, his expression unreadable. "Am I right?"

Samantha pretended he had no effect on her. "You're the second eldest, right? So that's three younger brothers and one younger sister. They must have gotten into your stuff a lot. You had to figure out who did what. Protect your space."

"We're not talking about my siblings."

"Ah. So it's not a two-way street. You get to analyze me, but I don't get to analyze you." She kept any note of irritation out of her tone. "Got it."

"I'm not analyzing you. I'm telling you what's what."

"You and Dylan seem to get along. He strikes me as intuitive about people but not as blunt as you are."

Justin's hands tightened visibly on the steering wheel, but he said nothing.

Duncan, Samantha remembered, had been smart, imaginative, daring and scrupulous. After he'd fired her, she'd buried herself digging out her grandfather's London office, still feeling terrible about how her first and only non-Bennett job had ended. She would sort through a box or a drawer and plot how to fix things with Duncan. Then had come word of his sudden death.

She became aware that Justin was eyeing her as he came to a stop at the cider mill. She could feel the heat in her cheeks and realized she must have turned red, thinking about the past—about those awful weeks two years ago. She unfastened her seat belt, anxious to get out of the truck and away from her driver's scrutiny.

He turned off the engine. "You haven't said if I'm right about you."

"Of course I haven't told you everything about me. We don't know each other." She pushed open the door and looked over at him. "I didn't think I'd see you again once you left yesterday."

He winked at her. "Maybe that explains your nightmares."

"I had nightmares about the fire. I didn't have nightmares about never seeing you again. You know, you've accused me of breaking into your mill and basically of lying to you. Why would I want to see you again?" She held up a hand. "Don't answer."

"Don't need to, anyway. You already know the answer."

Cocky as well as taciturn. She changed the subject. "What would you have done if I'd insisted on walking out here?"

"Made my stops and met you here."

"Lucky me."

"Yeah, Sam." He smiled, real amusement in his deep blue eyes. "Lucky you."

Nine

The brook had returned to its normal level after yesterday's rain, but Samantha could still smell the fire in the cool morning air. She stood on the bank, arms crossed on her chest as she watched a red-orange leaf float in the small millpond, dragged inexorably to the dam by the strong current. Finally the leaf plummeted over the spillway, then spun downstream. It would likely get hung up on a rock, a fern, driftwood or a patch of mud or moss long before it got near Quabbin—and it wouldn't care, because it was a leaf and it had no plans, no goals, no one to disappoint or cheer it on. Footloose and fancy-free or pathetic?

Samantha lowered her arms to her sides and glanced at the boulder where she'd sat yesterday, recovering from her relatively minor bout of smoke inhalation and waiting for the firefighters.

No journal.

She would have easily spotted its bright red cover among the tall grass, ferns and rocks. If it had slipped into the brook, the water was clear and shallow enough that she would have seen it.

That meant she hadn't dropped it out here, or someone else had found it.

Justin? Had he come back here last night or early this morning? Wouldn't he have said something if he had found it?

Not necessarily, she thought. In his place, she might not have, either. Wait, say nothing, let the outsider with his padlock in her pocket show her hand.

Samantha didn't want to show her hand.

She needed to get into the mill and look for her journal there.

Justin had asked her to wait outside while he checked out the mill. He was inside now. He didn't appear to be in any hurry to get on with his workday. If not for his obvious suspicion, she might not have minded his direct manner. She was used to straightforward people.

She stepped over the drooping yellow caution tape. If the fire was out, how unsafe could the place be? She mounted the stone step and peered inside, almost choking on the strong, acrid smell of charred wood and wet ashes. Her heartbeat quickened, and her breathing was rapid and shallow, as if she were just now smelling smoke for the first time and realizing the place was on fire.

A minor flashback, she told herself. She would be all right in a second. She placed a hand on the door-jamb and blinked deliberately a few times, letting her eyes adjust to the dim light, giving herself a chance to accept being back here. She could see Justin, standing between her and the spot where she'd dumped her things yesterday. She remembered how happy she'd been to be out of the worst of the storm, unaware the mill had been struck by lightning and a fire was brewing under her.

She could see her destroyed tent and sleeping bag and the remains of her wool throw. She felt her mouth go dry, her hands tremble as her gaze leveled on the spot where Justin had found her yesterday. She hadn't gone as far as she'd thought before the smoke had overcome her.

Without warning, her stomach lurched. For an awful moment, she thought she would vomit.

Justin was there, his hand on her arm, steadying her. "Easy, Sam." His voice was soothing, firm, deep— as if he knew just what she needed to hear to get her bearings. "You're having a flashback."

It wasn't a question, but she nodded. "I'm okay. I just…" She shut her eyes, letting the nausea pass, his hand still on her. When she opened her eyes again, she attempted a smile. "I'm not going to faint or be sick."

"Good to know." His tone was casual, reassuring, sincere. "A bit of a panic attack isn't uncommon after a scare like yesterday. One can grab you from behind when you least expect it."

"Has one grabbed you?"

"Yesterday wasn't a scare for me."

"More of an annoyance," she said.

"At first, maybe." He let go of her arm but stayed close. "Sure you're okay? You looked like Casper thirty seconds ago."

She nodded. She hated feeling vulnerable, but she noticed the change in his tone. The abruptness, the sarcasm—the suspicion—were gone, if only for the moment. "How long have you been a volunteer firefighter?"

"Since I graduated high school. There are about forty of us. It was a natural thing for me to do." He spoke pragmatically, without any detectable bravado. "I can jump off the job easily enough to respond to a call."

She raised her gaze and met his eyes. But the flashback wasn't over yet. Again she remembered the feeling of his arms coming around her, remembered clutching his canvas shirt—remembered the hard muscles underneath.

Those strikingly blue suspicious eyes of his narrowed. "Sam?"

"Sorry. Mind wandering." She cleared her throat and stepped over the threshold into the mill. "It doesn't look unsafe in here."

"There's damage, but the roof and walls won't cave in on you, and you won't crash into the cellar."

"That's good."

The bright morning sun shining through the open door and filtering through the dirty plastic-covered windows helped the interior of the mill seem less claustrophobic—less threatening—than it had been not even twenty-four hours before.

"Imagine making cider here a hundred years ago," Samantha said.

"This area was very different then."

"I imagine so." She took a few steps deeper inside. "When was this place built?"

"Mid-1870s. 1874, I think." Justin remained by the door. "It operated as a cider mill until a few years after World War II. My grandmother says it was the best cider she's ever had."

"What a nice memory to have."

He shrugged. "She's got a bad case of nostalgia, but I'm sure it was good cider."

The floorboards creaked as Samantha edged toward him. Her grandfather's house in Boston had been built around the same time but was completely different from this place.

"Do you have any of the original workings of the mill?" she asked.

"The original water wheel was here. It attached just below the pond and powered the grinding mill and press. They were auctioned off a long time ago, probably before either of us was born."

"It's hard to think of the pool of water outside as a 'pond,' but obviously the dam is big enough to create enough energy to run a cider mill. I assume the apples came from local orchards."

He nodded. "Some of the orchards are still around."

"Picking apples in the fall. Turning them into cider. It sounds idyllic."

"The whole apple was used. Seeds, peels, core and all. Helps the flavor. Cider was a staple drink of early New England families." Justin leaned against the doorjamb, watching her, looking at ease despite the fire damage, the smell of smoke. "Do you like cider, Samantha Bennett?"

"I love cider."

"We have a press up at the house. We make our own cider every fall."

His words reminded her that Knights Bridge was his home, and she was the outsider with an agenda— and he knew it. "I'm really glad the fire wasn't any worse, Justin," she said quietly.

"Yeah. Me, too."

A dead Bennett with his padlock in her pocket would have complicated his quiet life, perhaps up-ended his plans for the mill. All she needed was her missing journal. Then she could go on her way, and he could patch up the fire damage and carry on as if she'd never been here.

"Is your family home nearby?" she asked.

"Everything's nearby around here. My folks are a few miles up the road."

"Rambling white farmhouse with black shutters, a red barn and a duck wandering in the yard?"

"That's the place. The company offices are there, too."

"I was on Sloan land the whole time yesterday, wasn't I?"

"Yes, you were." His eyes settled on her as he stood straight. "The duck's name is Fred, by the way. My mother got him for my brother Brandon's boys. Fred took over. He thinks he runs the place."

Samantha smiled. "Does Fred the Duck like cider?"

"Only the hard stuff."

"Lame, Justin," she said with a laugh.

He grinned. "Wait until you meet Fred."

She had no intention of meeting Fred or any of the other Sloan animals—or any of the other Sloans, for that matter. Justin, his cop brother, Eric, and his fire-fighter brother, Christopher, were plenty.

Justin by himself was plenty.

"Any pets of your own, Sam?" he asked her.

"My lifestyle doesn't allow for pets right now. I wanted a pet alligator when I was a kid. My father said no. I think my mother might have been game." She wondered if her answer had opened up too many doors. She didn't want to say anything that would invite more questions, more scrutiny. "What about you?"

"Do I have a pet alligator, you mean?"

"A pet. Do you have a pet?"

He stepped closer to her. "We're going to have to work on your sense of humor." He paused, his eyes lost in the shadows. "No pets other than the ones at my folks' place. Our chocolate Lab likes to come to work with me whenever he gets the chance."

"Quite a life you have." She nodded toward the burned area and her sodden gear. "I'd like to take a look."

He shrugged. "Watch your step."

She was aware of him behind her as she squatted by her destroyed things. She had no desire to pick through them and wouldn't have ventured this deep into the mill if not for her journal. She'd started jotting notes in it well before she'd met Duncan—from the time she and her grandfather had first discussed her pirate, Benjamin Farraday.

She didn't see her bright red journal in the mess on the floor. She supposed it could have burned to ashes, but more likely she'd dropped it on her hike yesterday, perhaps when she'd broken into a run on her mad dash to get out of the storm.

Or someone had found it.

She walked back to Justin, still watching her from the doorway. "I had a small journal with me yesterday. I can't find it and might have dropped it. By any chance did you or one of the other firefighters find it?"

"Like a diary or something?"

"Or something."

"Could it make for interesting reading?"

"Not like what you're thinking. I was hoping I'd find it out here. I didn't want to make a big deal of it. I'd like it back if one of your friends has it."

"Noted."

"I could have dropped it on my hike. It has a red cover."

She caught a lungful of the acrid air. Her stomach lurched, and she bolted past him, plunging down the stone step and racing to the brook. She bent over, hands on her knees, but the clean air and the steady, rhythmic sounds of the water pouring off the dam and swirling among rocks soothed her immediately. She wouldn't vomit.

"Okay?" Justin asked behind her.

She nodded and sank onto her boulder from yesterday. She breathed out, smiled up at him. "I'd hate to puke in front of you."

"Better than on me."

"It's the smells. They turn my stomach."

He stood next to her rock. "It is pretty rancid in there."

"Are you used to the smells? Because you're a firefighter?"

"I guess. I haven't thought about it."

"You must have to take precautions—to make sure you don't get contaminated."

"Always."

He wasn't abrupt now so much as steady, matter-of-fact. It was reassuring in its own way. Samantha peered up the trail, shaded by an arch of white pines, but she didn't see her journal. Its title page alone would confirm she wasn't in Knights Bridge just for an early-autumn hike. Her grandfather had often cautioned her on the need for what he liked to call "operational security" in her work. Pirate treasure was a temptation, no matter how remote the possibility it existed, never mind whether it could be found after hundreds of years.

She noted the dappled shade of an oak tree on the quiet millpond. Three hundred years ago, European settlers to the east had considered this area the wilderness frontier. Today Knights Bridge was an easy drive from Boston. A day trip. Shop, visit museums, go to a ball game. Be home at a reasonable hour. She'd had options besides camping here. She could have postponed her trip until her uncle and cousin had finished their college tour and then taken her chances with the old Mercedes. She'd wanted to stay a few days and explore the area—leave no stone unturned, as it were.

She wondered if Justin ever ventured to Boston.

"You don't trust me," she said without looking at him.

"I wonder why that is." He picked up a fallen leaf, twirled it by the stem, then tossed it into the water coming off the spillway. "For someone caught in a storm, you weren't exactly drenched yesterday."

"My jacket is water resistant, and I got here just before the heaviest rain."

"Convenient."

"I had to run, if that makes you feel any better."

His eyes were half-closed as he turned to her. "It's not about how I feel."

Samantha jumped up from her boulder. She took a breath and, without thinking, pulled the sturdy padlock out of her jacket pocket and handed it to him. "Here you go. I guess I needed the adrenaline from yesterday to wear off before I gave it back. A mistake, maybe, but it doesn't change the facts."

Justin slipped the lock into his canvas shirt pocket. "Sure doesn't."

"I mean the fact that I ducked into the mill because of a nasty storm."

"How do you know how to pick a lock?"

"I didn't say I picked it."

He grinned at her unexpectedly. "You have a stubborn streak, don't you, Samantha?"

"Maybe it's just a healthy mix of self-preservation and determination."

"Or maybe it's a bullheaded stubborn streak."

She avoided his eyes and looked down at a clump of browned, sodden leaves stuck in a small, stagnant pool of water on the edge of the brook. Being in such close proximity to the man who had rescued her yesterday wasn't helping her regain her emotional equilibrium. The shock of finding a cider mill like the one in the painting she had discovered in her grandfather's office closet would have been enough for one day. Add a fire, smoke inhalation and a tall, rugged firefighter—dreaming about him—and no wonder she wasn't her usual self.

Did Justin Sloan have to be so damn sexy? The spark in his deep blue eyes when he grinned by itself could buckle a woman's knees.

"You can relax," he said calmly. "You don't have to confess to picking the lock. I've got it back, and you didn't burn up and the mill didn't burn up. We're good."

"You make it sound so simple."

He shrugged his broad shoulders. "It is simple."

That was part of his appeal, she realized. He was a man who zeroed in on what he needed to do and didn't overburden himself with details. "I sometimes complicate things that don't need complicating, but pretending things are simple when they're not can be a problem, too."

"So it can."

She ignored his knowing tone and ran her fingers on the rough, cool granite of a waist-high boulder. "Do you know much about the history of the mill? Are there any interesting stories, rumors or tall tales associated with it?"

"Like what?"

"I don't know. I'm the one who decided to follow Cider Brook, remember? I'm curious. The history of this area is fascinating."

"I haven't heard stories associated with the mill, but I'm not the type to pay attention to that sort of thing."

"What sort of thing *do* you pay attention to?"

It was the wrong question. She saw her mistake right away, but it was too late to take back her words. He laughed and gave her a sexy wink. "Bet you can guess."

"Bet I'm not going to."

He pointed across the brook at a stone wall that went up the hill into the woods. "That stone wall marks the edge of what used to be farmland when the mill was built. Quabbin changed transportation routes in this area. Many of the roads that used to lead into the Swift River Valley towns are now dead ends, or they've been bypassed by newer highways. You have to remember that the reservoir is a large body of water that didn't exist a hundred years ago."

"Have you ever considered living somewhere besides Knights Bridge?"

"Where?"

"I don't know. Boston, Florida, Seattle. Idaho. Paris. Someplace else."

He shook his head. "No. I haven't considered living anywhere else."

Samantha tried to put aside how they'd met and all she was hiding and get a better sense of him. Most of the men she knew were adventurers, divers or crew on her parents' research ship, and liked to be on the move. They didn't have the roots Justin did. They would probably get hives thinking about living in the same small New England town their entire lives, being a volunteer firefighter, having five siblings and a family duck named Fred or owning a nineteenth-century cider mill off a winding dirt road.

"What about you, Sam?" Justin asked, his tone unexpectedly quiet. "Olivia said you live in Boston."

"For the moment. I've been staying at my grandfather's house. He died three years ago." She stopped herself before she could go too far, say too much and put him on alert again. She looked back at the mill with its solid construction and deceptively simple lines—not unlike its owner. "It's a nice spot, Justin," she said, sincere. "What are your plans for the mill?"

"Right now the land is more valuable than the mill. I'd hate to demolish it, but I might have no choice."

"That would be sad, wouldn't it? It would be like razing a piece of New England history."

"I'd salvage what I could. Saving bits and pieces of the mill beats watching it all rot."

"Or burn down," she said.

He said nothing. Samantha regretted reminding him of yesterday's close call. She glanced again up the trail, wishing she would see her journal tucked under a fern or something. A cool breeze rustled in the woods. The sun was higher in the clear sky. Before long, the entire landscape would be alive with vibrant color, her favorite time to be in New England.

"Do you know who built the mill?" she asked.

"The Hazelton family. They also built the general store on the common."

"Do any of them still live in Knights Bridge?"

"Not in a long time. I don't know much about them. I took a chance and bought this place when the town put it up for sale. I've always wanted to own land." He nodded to the remains of a fire circle on the edge of the driveway. "My brothers and buddies and I used to sit by a campfire and drink beer out here. We did again last night after the fire, but it'd been a while."

"What do you do for fun nowadays?"

He grinned at her. "Do you ever think before you speak?"

She groaned. "Apparently not today." She stood straight. "The mill has possibilities. Of course, now I have a mad urge for apple cider and another piece of apple cake. Will you be at the wedding on Saturday?"

"I'm the best man."

Samantha pictured him in a tuxedo. Not that hard to do, surprisingly. She smiled at him. "I'll spare you more questions. I've kept you from your work long enough."

"I have a feeling you could keep asking questions all day."

She squinted up at the blue sky. "The weather's

great. Fortunately I'm in no hurry. I imagine you'll get a lot done at the McCaffrey site today."

He shook his head. "Forget it. I'm not leaving you out here on your own."

He wasn't being argumentative, she realized, so much as stating a fact, and it was up to her to decide what to do about it. No doubt that would be easier if she hadn't found herself noticing everything about him. Reacting to him, tingling in a way she hoped he didn't notice. It had to be the fire, the danger she'd been in, the half truths, being back out here. Her attraction to him was primal somehow. Adrenaline-fueled. Completely mad, of course, but she wondered if he felt it, too, then reminded herself yesterday wasn't his first fire.

"It was helpful to come back here," she said, deciding to state her own facts. "I'll walk up the trail and see if I can find my journal. Then I'll walk into town. It's not that far. It's a gorgeous day. I won't run into another storm."

"You are one stubborn and relentless woman, Sam Bennett." Justin studied her a moment. "All right. We'll do this your way. I have to get to work. You have a phone, right?"

"I do, yes."

"Call me if you run into trouble."

As he gave her his number and she added it to her phone, Samantha felt as if he could see inside her—see through her careful answers and battery of questions to her vulnerabilities, hopes, fears. It felt as if she was meant to be right here, right now, with intriguing, suspicious Justin Sloan and his old cider mill.

All the more reason, she told herself firmly, to make sure he went on his way.

She slipped her phone into her jacket pocket and smiled at him. Polite, not giving away the raging mess she was on the inside. "Thank you for everything, Justin."

He hesitated for a fraction of a second, just long enough for her to know he was still reluctant to leave her to her own devices. "Do you have a job you have to get back to?"

"I'm self-employed," she said. "I make my own hours."

"Self-employed at what?"

"Research, cataloging, curating. Lately, anyway. Nothing too exciting." It was close enough to the truth, she decided. "Doesn't that sound fascinating?"

"Depends on what you research, catalog and curate, I guess." He walked back to his truck and glanced at her as he opened the door. "I imagine you wouldn't get into anything boring."

"People have different ideas of what constitutes boring."

"They do indeed."

Heat rushed to her face, but she managed, for once, to resist opening her mouth and didn't respond.

Justin smiled, as if he knew the effect he was having on her. "Be good." He climbed into his truck. "I have a feeling you aren't done with Knights Bridge."

Samantha waited for him to pull the door shut, then watched the truck head back out to the road. When it disappeared through the trees, she still didn't move. She couldn't remember when she'd felt so alone, but she looked up at a tall white pine outlined against the blue sky and listened to birds singing behind her, on the other side of the brook. She realized she couldn't smell the fire.

Maybe the wind had shifted. Maybe it was a positive sign that the worst of her adventure in Knights Bridge was behind her.

Then why did she feel so alone?

She pushed that question aside, leaving it unanswered as she retraced her steps back up the trail. She went all the way to the bridge just below the Sloan farmhouse and then climbed up to the road, but she didn't find her journal. Frustrated, she paused in a patch of sunlight on the wooden bridge. She must have left her journal in Boston after all, or her uncle had missed it when he checked the car.

She noticed a dusty-gray truck parked up by the Sloan barn—which apparently served as the offices of Sloan & Sons. The chocolate Lab was rolling in the grass. No sign of the duck.

Justin hadn't exactly left her to her own devices. He would be able to see her from the barn. Could he tell she hadn't found her missing journal?

What if he'd found it? What if that was why he'd insisted on driving her to the mill and had let her ask so many questions?

Why not tell her?

He would have his reasons, she thought. He was the sort of man who always had his reasons, and pirate treasure was a damn good reason.

She debated marching up to Sloan & Sons and asking him outright if he had her journal, but if he didn't, she would only look paranoid, and if he did—well, then what?

She hoped she *was* being paranoid, because she cringed at the idea that Justin Sloan had her personal notes and musings about Benjamin Farraday.

Gritting her teeth, Samantha adjusted her backpack and started back down the narrow road toward Knights Bridge. Maybe she would get lucky and find her journal in a ditch before she reached the spot on the town common where Caleb had dropped her off. But she didn't think she would. She kept glancing back at the Sloan farmhouse, and by the time it was out of sight, she was pretty damn sure that Justin had her journal.

Ten

Samantha was out of sight by the time Justin headed back to the building site on Grace Webster's old property. It was the place where he'd spotted Samantha that snowy March afternoon—no idea who she was, no idea he would ever see her again. How fast everything could change, he thought as he made his way to the construction trailer. He hadn't liked leaving her to trek into town on her own, but except for getting tired of the weight of her backpack, she would be fine.

She wouldn't find her journal, of course, but she would eventually figure out he had it. He was confident of that. And when she did, she'd come find him and no doubt want to throttle him.

That could be interesting. Smart, feisty Samantha Bennett trying to throttle him.

He did feel mildly guilty about not returning her journal to her. He'd planned to tell her he had it, but while he was poking around inside the mill, he'd received a text from Dylan letting him know that Loretta Wrentham had called. She had more information on their treasure hunter. Dylan had ended the message succinctly: We need to talk.

A cold wind blew fallen leaves across the driveway and whipped the tarp still covering the lumber. The crew was making good progress on the framework for the house. Justin stepped into the small trailer, used mostly for storage of tools and supplies and occasional shelter from the weather.

Dylan was standing inside looking at the plans for his house and barn that were taped to the wall, marked up here and there in pencil and ink. "When I was playing hockey for a living," he said, "I never thought I'd own a house. I lived in rentals. Loretta talked me into buying in Coronado."

"Olivia says it's nice out there," Justin said. "All that Southern California sunshine would get on my nerves after a while."

Dylan grinned at him. "Loretta feels that way about New England's changeable weather. She likes her Southern California sunshine. One ice storm, and she'd be on a plane west."

Justin knew Dylan's first trip to Knights Bridge early that spring had involved ice—and a testy encounter with Buster, the stray who had adopted Olivia. Justin hadn't met Dylan until a later visit.

He unfolded a brown metal chair and set it next to a box of nails but didn't sit. "What did Loretta have to say about Sam Bennett?"

"She worked for my father briefly. He fired her after you told him about her coming here. Samantha is the granddaughter of Harry Bennett. I'm not that familiar with him. He was an explorer and adventurer—"

"Antarctica," Justin said. "Harry Bennett led a near-fatal expedition there about fifty years ago. I watched a documentary on Antarctica while I was painting woodwork one night."

Dylan sighed heavily. "Then you know more about him than I do. Loretta says he died a few months before my father died. His wife died way back. They had two sons." Dylan glanced out a small window. "Samantha's father is the older brother, Malcolm, an underwater explorer and salvage expert. His wife's a marine archaeologist. Samantha's their only child. She spent her early years on their research vessel."

"Not quite Knights Bridge."

"Not quite."

Justin could hear the guys working outside. In his mind, he'd shirked his duty that morning by charging off to the mill with Samantha, but they wouldn't see it that way. Normally he was the first on the job in the morning and the last off in the afternoon, and the circumstances were unusual—the fire, the woman camping out on his property without his knowledge or permission.

Daredevil Harry Bennett's granddaughter.

No wonder she refused to believe she'd been in serious danger yesterday.

"Is Samantha an expert in pirates or did she make that up?" Justin asked.

"She didn't make it up," Dylan said. "Loretta said she told my father that old Harry got her interested in pirates and undiscovered sunken pirate ships."

"Especially ones that sank with treasure on board, I bet." Justin plopped onto the chair, stretched out his legs, pictured Samantha's ashen, soot-smeared face. Her big eyes. She'd been genuinely shaken, but she'd also bounced back quickly from her ordeal. A fast thinker. Good in a crisis. A Bennett, he thought, gritting his teeth. "Does Loretta know what Samantha's been doing since your father let her go?"

"Loretta checked out what she was up to right after my father fired her but hasn't since. She was in Scotland helping her parents explore for sunken World War II ships and submarines in the North Atlantic. They have a long-term grant, but it doesn't look as if Samantha continued working for them."

"I asked her what she does," Justin said. "She gave me some vague answer about researching, curating and archiving."

Dylan went over to the open doorway, as if he needed air. "It could be true."

Justin got to his feet. "Did your father know the Bennetts?"

"Not personally. Loretta says he knew their work. He got into treasure hunting in his fifties. It was a second career for him. A passion. It's not like Samantha comes from a family of bartenders. He would have wanted to know about them. He would have wanted her to tell him."

"But she didn't, and he found out the hard way."

"Loretta told him."

"That would be the hard way," Justin said.

It was a halfhearted attempt at levity—maybe not even that much—but Dylan seemed to appreciate it. "She says she didn't pull any punches with him. She told my father that Samantha had to go. No choice. Not telling him she was a Bennett on top of sneaking out here was too much."

"How did Samantha explain herself when your father confronted her?"

"I don't know that she did. He might not have given her much of a chance."

Justin shrugged. "I'm not sure I would have, either. What would you have done in his position?"

"I'd like to think I wouldn't have been caught off guard in the first place, but you've met her. You see what she's like. She doesn't come across as someone with a lot of secrets." Dylan zipped up his jacket as the wind picked up again, blowing more leaves, flapping the tarp on the lumber. "Maybe she's figured out it's easier not to get into her background. Being a Bennett comes with a certain amount of baggage. Maybe she just wanted to carve her own path."

Justin pictured Samantha fishing his padlock out of her jacket pocket and handing it to him. She didn't strike him as a woman who had any issues carving her own path.

Dylan glanced back, his gaze narrowed on Justin. "Does Samantha know you're the one who told my father she'd been out this way?"

"Not that I'm aware of, but I think she'd have said something if she knew."

"She's alone here, and outnumbered by the rest of us."

"Doesn't seem to bother her."

"We're not that threatening," Dylan said with a grin.

"Neither is she."

"Loretta says my father liked Samantha and looked forward to working on pirate-related projects with her, but he couldn't take the chance that the Bennetts were up to something that would blow back on to him."

Dylan stepped out of the trailer and looked back inside at Justin. "Do you have any idea why she's in Knights Bridge?"

"Pirates."

"She wants to make a pitch to me to help her find a pirate shipwreck?"

Justin joined him outside. "I don't know about that," he said, then told Dylan about her journal, adding, "I haven't given it back to her yet."

"But you didn't read it?"

"Not the type."

"I've never heard of Benjamin Farraday," Dylan said. "Have you?"

"No, but I'm not up on my pirates. I was going to tell her I have her journal, but I held off once I got your text that you'd heard from Loretta."

"You weren't sure if Loretta had given me good reason to check out this journal. No, I'm not the type, either, to read someone's private research notes and musings." Dylan grinned suddenly. "Damn, though, it's tempting."

"No argument from me," Justin said.

"Where is it?"

"At my place. I'll return it to her, then. No rush. I have plenty to do around here this afternoon. Samantha isn't going anywhere until she gets her journal back. What about you?"

"Olivia called right before you got here. Jess is at the house."

The sister with the wedding on Saturday. Also Olivia's only sister. "Any problems?" Justin asked, not sure he really wanted to know.

"Olivia didn't sound too concerned," Dylan said.

"She says Jess is having her requisite nervous breakdown about the wedding. Maggie's there, too."

Justin gave a mock shudder. "Stay here, then. I learned in sixth grade never to get in the middle of any combination of the O'Dunn sisters and the Frost sisters. It's a rule I live by."

Dylan laughed. "I have a feeling you're not exaggerating. I probably should grab a hammer and get you to put me to work. It's what you'd do in my shoes."

Knowing Dylan, Justin figured he was perfectly capable and would do fine helping out. "What's Jess freaking out about? Anything in particular?"

"I gather that her anxieties boil down to whether the plumbing at Carriage Hill can support the number of guests. If it doesn't, Jess says she'll hear it from her grandmother. Why, I don't know. I didn't ask about that part."

"Audrey Frost hates old houses," Justin said, matter-of-fact. "She remembers Carriage Hill when it still had an outhouse."

"That was a while ago, I assume."

"Not in Audrey's mind. The plumbing's fine, by the way. The previous owners planned to turn the place into a bed-and-breakfast themselves and renovated accordingly. I can reassure Jess if it would help."

Dylan shook his head. "It wouldn't help. Her anxiety doesn't really have anything to do with the plumbing. That's just what she's hanging it on."

Justin agreed but said nothing. Dylan had to know by now that the two Frost sisters were prone to anxiety, although Jess less so than Olivia and neither one of them as much as their mother. Over the years, Louise Frost had gone from an occasional case of nerves to suffering from full-blown panic attacks. Over time, she'd gotten to the point where she was hardly able to leave town by herself. She wanted to take trips with her husband of thirty years but couldn't manage to go shoe-shopping in Northampton. She finally entered therapy, and a couple of months ago, she and Randy had headed out to California, one of Louise's dream trips.

Dylan was frowning, looking preoccupied. An anxious future sister-in-law and a disgruntled former Duncan McCaffrey employee would do it. Then Olivia walked up the driveway, waving at him, and Dylan smiled.

"Jess just left," Olivia said, joining Justin and her fiancé on the patch of grass between the trailer and the stack of lumber. "Maggie distracted her by talking about adventure travel. Jess thinks it's right up your alley, Dylan, after your years playing hockey and swimming with the corporate sharks." She hooked her arm into his. "You've had a hockey stick to the teeth a time or two. Whisking adventurers off to Newfoundland should be simple by comparison."

He pulled her close to him, his mood obviously lightening with Olivia here. "I got out of the NHL with all my teeth intact, thank you."

"Good," Justin said, "because my nephews are looking forward to playing hockey with you this winter. We'll be filling the ice rink on the common before we know it."

"A New England winter," Dylan said. "Can't wait."

"You'll love it," Olivia said, grinning.

Justin winked at them. "You two could always go on a long honeymoon."

"It's a good thought," Dylan said, "but Buster would miss us."

"I don't know." Olivia leaned into his arm, obviously at ease with him. "Buster might like Southern California. Can you see him getting loose at your house and charging through the Hotel del Coronado?"

"I can, yes. He'd have a blast and cost us a fortune—or get us thrown in jail."

"He did just fine when we were in San Diego. Maggie doesn't mind looking after him. He liked Loretta when she was out here. Maybe she can come dog-sit."

Dylan's eyebrows went up. "Loretta? Dog-sit?"

Olivia kissed him on the cheek. "Kidding."

Soul mates, Justin thought. The pair of them. "All set for the wedding?" he asked.

Olivia nodded. "Maggie's meeting me here soon. We need to run into Hazelton's for a few things. Is Samantha still in town?"

"As far as I know," Justin said, keeping his tone neutral.

"You'd know. There are Sloan spies everywhere."

Justin grinned at her. "It's true."

Olivia looked at him with amusement. "You all wish you struck fear into the hearts of everyone in Knights Bridge, but you don't. You never did."

"I'm crushed."

Dylan lowered his arm from Olivia's waist and nodded to the trailer. "I need to talk to you before Maggie gets here."

"Is something wrong?" Olivia asked, frowning.

"Loretta called."

"Oh. I see. And not about dog-sitting, I take it." Olivia sighed, serious now. "I'm guessing she called with more information about Samantha. That must explain the dour looks I noticed when I came up the driveway."

"Dour, Liv?" Justin made a face, wanting to lighten her mood. Samantha wasn't her problem, either. "What the hell's a dour look?"

"Troubled? Irritated? Preoccupied?"

"More like all of the above," he said with a grin. "So, Liv, if you lost your personal journal, and I found it and told you I hadn't read it, would you believe me?"

"You? Yes, not because you wouldn't like to read it but because you're not particularly introspective yourself. You wouldn't be that curious about someone else's personal ramblings." Olivia paused a moment, then added, "Your brother Eric, though. He'd have read it in a heartbeat."

"Probably true. If it wasn't a diary but research notes—"

"Research notes? On what? Justin, are we talking about Samantha?"

He wished he hadn't brought up the journal. Wasn't even sure why he had. "Never mind. I'll let you and Dylan talk. I need to get back to work, anyway."

Olivia hesitated but said nothing as she followed Dylan into the trailer.

Justin was relieved when the door shut behind them. Dylan's presence in Knights Bridge had already changed the town. His friend Noah Kendrick's would, too, when he and Phoebe returned from California. There was no question in Justin's mind that Phoebe wouldn't be moving full-time to San Diego or that Noah wouldn't be coming back East with her.

Samantha hadn't met Dylan or Noah when she'd

worked for Duncan—Dylan would have remembered—but she must have heard about them. What if her reasons for slipping into Knights Bridge two years ago and again now had nothing to do with pirates and instead had to do with two wealthy, single men?

Seriously, Justin thought—what were the odds the gold coin he'd found at the cider mill had anything to do with an eighteenth-century pirate?

Fifteen minutes later, Justin had sorted out a routine problem with the framework and taken a call from the electrician and was back by his truck when Christopher texted him that Samantha had made it into town. Spies everywhere, indeed, Justin thought, but his humor was short-lived when Maggie O'Dunn Sloan, his sister-in-law, pulled up in her van, jumped out, slammed the door and pointed at him.

"You, Justin," Maggie said, her red hair pinned up, a flour-covered apron tied over dark jeans and a sweater. "Over here."

He ambled over to her. "What's up, Maggie?"

"You have to be careful about what you say to Mark right now. He repeats it to Jess, and then she gets into a state."

"Mark and I didn't talk about anything that should worry Jess. Dylan said she was concerned about the plumbing at Carriage Hill. Mark and I didn't discuss the plumbing, Maggie. Trust me."

Maggie didn't back down. "You two discussed septic tanks."

Justin settled back on his heels, trying to remember. "Oh, yeah. We did. So?"

"Jess had visions of the septic tank overflowing in the middle of her wedding."

"Even if it did, the leach field isn't anywhere near where people are going to be standing—"

"Justin."

He sighed. "The septic tank isn't going to overflow, Maggie. Mark and I were talking about options for up here. We were taking into consideration zoning and the different ideas for using the barn as well as the house. Then we thought about the septic system at Carriage Hill as things get busier there. No big deal."

"Maybe not to you two." Maggie pulled a pin out of her hair, then shoved it back in again, tightening things up some. "I know it was something for Jess to focus on because she was having a case of the jitters, and she's fine now—but you can't be talking about septic tank capacity and such right before our very first wedding at Carriage Hill."

"You sure Jess is the one with the jitters?"

Maggie flashed her turquoise eyes at him. "I'm cool as a cucumber. Calm as ice. Always. I don't get the jitters in my work."

He grinned at her. "Right, Maggie."

"I don't, but you can think what you want to think."

"You and Olivia are partners now. The success of this wedding is important to—"

"To Jess and Mark," Maggie finished for him. "Period."

"I agree. They're the bride and groom. You're doing a great job on their behalf."

She scowled at him. "You just manipulated me, didn't you, Justin? You managed to get yourself off the hook."

"Hell, I hope so. You going to take off that apron before you go into town?"

She told him to shut up, but she removed the apron. She looked less agitated as she turned her attention toward her husband, Justin's younger brother Brandon, in hard hat and work boots, hammer in hand down by the barn-in-progress. "He's working long hours. It's like he's trying to make up for the months we were separated. You won't let him overdo it, will you? You're the boss."

"Shh. Don't tell him and the rest of the guys. And my sister. Damn. Don't tell her."

"I'm serious, Justin."

A year ago, Maggie and her two young sons had moved back to Knights Bridge from Boston—without Brandon. She'd launched her own catering business and bought a house just off the common—an old Gothic Revival "gingerbread" house that needed work—and their separation had started to look permanent. Then Brandon, who'd never wanted to return to Knights Bridge, decided to come home and be a part of Sloan & Sons again. Bit by bit, he'd won Maggie back.

Justin wasn't doing anything to get between Maggie and his brother. Another of his rules. "I agree that rest is important," he said, his tone neutral, professional.

His answer seemed to satisfy her. "It's good having him back here. He's looking forward to getting into adventure travel with Dylan—on the side, of course. He's committed to his work with Sloan & Sons."

"For now, anyway. It's not a prison sentence. He can do what he wants."

"If you're insinuating I'm pushing him—" Maggie stopped herself. "Never mind. You're right. I'm feeling the pressure of the wedding. It's our first big event at Carriage Hill, and Olivia and I want it to be perfect, probably more than Jess does. She'll just be happy at this point if the septic tank doesn't overflow."

"The wedding will be great, Maggie."

She smiled. "Thanks. You can be very reassuring when you put your mind to it, you know?"

"I'm just trying to get rid of you," he said with a grin. "I need to get back to work. We're knocking off early tomorrow for the wedding rehearsal and I'm running behind."

"You're behind because of this Bennett woman," Maggie said, tossing her apron into the van. "You wouldn't have lost ten seconds of work today if you'd rescued Olivia or Jess or me instead of Samantha Bennett. What is it with her? I haven't met her, but from what Olivia says—it's what you see is what you get with her, isn't it?"

"I doubt it."

Maggie's eyes narrowed on him. "Justin…" She tucked a few fresh stray hairs behind her ear. "Maybe you should watch yourself with her. I mean, rescuing someone—anyone—from a fire has to have a certain effect on both parties. You know. Adrenaline and all that. There must be some kind of chemical bonding thing that goes on."

"There's no 'chemical bonding thing.' Talk to Olivia on your way to town. She can fill you in."

Maggie didn't seem to hear him. "You have to admit you aren't always the best judge of women. Remember that architect you dated last year? Where is she now? Atlanta, right?"

"Goodbye, Maggie."

"All right, all right. I just don't want this woman taking advantage of you."

Justin grinned at his sister-in-law. "Well, isn't that sweet?"

She groaned. "Right. What was I thinking? Big-city girl takes advantage of small-town volunteer firefighter and carpenter. It could happen, but not to you."

Olivia came out of the trailer, but Dylan stayed inside—a wise move, Justin thought, if only a coincidence. "I have to go," he told Maggie, then didn't wait for her to respond before he headed back to the guys. This was his world. Construction. Building and rebuilding homes, barns, businesses. Not wedding jitters and treasure hunting, or the granddaughter of a famed explorer.

His older brother, Eric, texted him. SB just bought a sandwich at Hazelton's.

Justin texted Eric back: What kind of sandwich?

It was just a way to take the edge off his own mood. He didn't expect his brother to respond, but he did. Sloan. She'll eat us for lunch.

Funny.

Who's being funny?

Justin left it at that. He knew he should return Samantha's journal to her, but she'd had multiple opportunities to tell him the truth about herself and her reasons for being in Knights Bridge.

If she stewed a little longer, it served her right.

Besides, he really did have work to do.

Eleven

꧁꧂

Samantha took the sandwich she'd bought at the Swift River Country Store—also known as Hazelton's—across the street to the town common and sat on a bench next to a statue of a Civil War soldier, in the shade of an old oak tree that seemed to be a favorite with the local gray squirrel population. The chattering squirrels paid no attention to her, and she did likewise with them.

Several miles of hiking and thinking had her no closer to figuring out how to get her journal back from Justin. She'd kept looking for it while she retraced her steps, but she wasn't surprised when it hadn't turned up.

The bastard had it. She knew he did.

Maybe lunch would help her figure out what to do. Her sandwich was made with local cheese, cucumbers and lettuce on store-made multigrain bread. She hadn't eaten much for breakfast, and her walk from the cider mill had left her hungry. She'd also bought a few energy bars and refilled her water bottle at the country store. She felt better knowing she had at least minimal provisions, never mind that she had a phone and could call her uncle or a car service and go back to Boston whenever it suited her.

It didn't suit her yet.

She would put the matter of her missing journal out of her mind for the moment and surreptitiously peruse a few pages of *The Adventures of Captain Farraday and Lady Elizabeth* while enjoying her lunch. Let the perils of Lady Elizabeth serve as inspiration as well as a cautionary tale about her own troubles.

She set the copied pages on her lap and placed her sandwich on top of them, keeping them out of the view of prying eyes—such as those of Eric Sloan, the police officer Sloan brother, who was walking toward her from the country store side of the common, where, she'd noticed, the town offices, police station and fire station were all located.

"Good afternoon, Ms. Bennett," he said amiably as he approached her bench. "I thought I recognized you. Cool for a picnic, isn't it?"

"It's refreshing." Samantha tried to keep any annoyance with his brother out of her voice. Eric had the same deep blue eyes as Justin, although his manner didn't seem as blunt—if only because it hadn't been his mill that burned and his padlock that she'd picked. If Justin read even one line of her journal, he would know she hadn't told him everything about her reasons for being in Knights Bridge. Then again, he'd already suspected as much. She realized his older brother was frowning at her. "It's a perfect day, isn't it?" she said, maintaining her pleasant tone.

"Better than yesterday. How're you doing after your close call?"

"Great, thanks."

"I heard you stayed at The Farm at Carriage Hill last night."

Of course he had. "I did. It's a beautiful place. I can imagine what it must have been like out there before Quabbin was built. Justin drove me back to the cider mill this morning and I walked into town from there. I love walking along New England back roads, especially this time of year." She patted her backpack, upright next to her on the bench. "I'll probably chuck this when I get the chance. It smells like smoke."

"We're all just glad you're okay. Let us know if there's anything we can do to help."

"I will, thanks."

"Will you be staying in town again tonight?"

"I'm not sure yet."

"All right, then. Enjoy your sandwich. Hazelton's makes a good one."

Samantha didn't ask him how he knew her sandwich was from the country store. It wasn't as if there were many options, but at the same time, she wouldn't put it past Justin to have his army of siblings keep an eye on her.

She thanked the eldest Sloan and watched him start back across the common the way he'd come. Based on her twenty-four hours in Knights Bridge, she suspected it was a fair guess that the Sloans were all cut-to-the-chase types.

With Officer Sloan safely on his way, she returned to her sandwich and *The Adventures of Captain Farraday and Lady Elizabeth.* Two squirrels chased each other along a low-hanging oak branch, then hopped onto the grass and scampered to another tree. She couldn't help but feel a little alone. Maybe a little vulnerable, too.

She peered down at the feminine handwriting of the long-ago, unknown author.

Despite the rough seas, Lady Elizabeth hadn't experienced so much as a moment of seasickness, either while held captive by her father's enemy or now aboard Captain Farraday's sloop. Her strong stomach was a point of pride with her, one she pressed upon the pirate over breakfast. "I'll keep down every bite," she told him.

"Good. You'll need your strength."

"For what?"

He grinned at her. "Your father's dear friend who lately kidnapped you has a ship loaded with Spanish gold."

"My father?"

The pirate's black eyes held hers. "Lord Edgar Fullerton." He shook his head at her. "Bess Fuller. You should have chosen a more obscure name for yourself."

"Would it have mattered?"

"No. I've known who you were from the moment I rescued you."

"A rescue implies going from an unsafe situation to a safe one, and that hasn't happened, has it, Captain Farraday?"

"Admit it, Lady Elizabeth," he said, moving closer to her. "You're safer with me than with your father's enemies."

"This ship loaded with gold. You want it?"

He didn't hesitate. "I'll have it by nightfall."

Samantha smiled as she returned the pages to the pouch. Lady Elizabeth's pluck was matched only by her loneliness after weeks away from her beloved castle and not-quite-so-beloved family back home in England. Then there was her forbidden attraction to Farraday—and his to her. All good fun, Samantha thought as she retrieved her phone from her jacket, saw it had a good signal and dialed her father's cell phone.

He picked up almost immediately. "Where are you?" he asked her.

"Knights Bridge. I just had a picnic lunch on the town common with the squirrels." She didn't mention Officer Sloan or her missing journal. "What about you?"

"Your mother and I just got into town. I'm hiding in your grandfather's library." The library was just down the hall from his second-floor office. "You won't catch your cousins in here."

Caleb's three youngest children—Keith, fifteen, Ann, twelve, and Eloisa, nine—had arrived with their mother last night. Samantha pictured them careening through their grandfather's Back Bay house. Of course, he used to tell her stories of her father and uncle doing the same as boys. "It'll be good to see everyone," she said, leaving it at that.

"Your aunt is organizing tours for the kids. Freedom Trail, Emerson House, Walden Pond, Kennedy Library. They just want to go to the mall and a Red Sox game."

"Autumn is a beautiful time to be in New England no matter what you like to do."

Her father grunted, obviously unimpressed. "You pay for New England autumn foliage with a New England winter. Caleb just called, by the way. He's worried about you in that little town by yourself."

Her father and his younger brother got along well but often said they wouldn't if they "lived in each other's pockets." Samantha had learned to navigate the sometimes treacherous waters between them. "I appreciate his concern," she said, keeping her tone neutral.

"He thinks you'll be lucky to get out of there without being tarred and feathered. This fire—the locals don't blame you, do they?"

"It was clearly caused by lightning, which no one can possibly blame on me."

"You still aren't ready to let go of the idea of pirate treasure out there?"

"I just want to know more." Samantha tried not to sound defensive. "The trail leads where it leads. You're sure Grandpa didn't mention Benjamin Farraday to either you or Mom?"

"I'm almost positive he didn't. Your mother's absolutely positive. We'll see you soon, right?"

"Yes. I was hoping..." Samantha sighed and looked up at the oak tree, its leaves still a deep green against the blue sky. They would turn burgundy or rust later in the season. She would be long gone from Knights Bridge by then. She put that thought aside. "I don't know what I was hoping. Maybe surviving a lightning strike and a fire's enough adventure for this trip."

"Caleb and Isaac won't be back your way for a few more days." There was a note of genuine concern in her father's voice. "They've got Pop's old Mercedes, but I can always rent a car and come fetch you. Anytime. Hear me?"

Just what she needed was Malcolm Bennett blowing

into town. She smiled into her phone. "Do you even remember how to drive?"

"Of course. If it's got gears, I can make it run. Caleb's the academic in the family. I'm a mechanic at heart."

Samantha pictured her father up to his elbows in grease, working on a boat engine. Her mother had been drawn to his practical skills. Uncle Caleb, while an academic, also could manage just fine in the field. Samantha wasn't always sure where she fit in with her family. "Don't worry about me," she said. "I'll figure something out."

"You always do. I believe in you, Samantha, and I'm sorry this thing with Duncan McCaffrey is still bugging you. He was a hell of a treasure hunter, but he lost out when he fired you. I wish I'd known at the time. I'd have punched him out."

"That would have helped," Samantha said dryly.

She could feel her father's grin. "From what I hear, Duncan was a pretty good brawler himself. He'd have held his own. His son was a professional hockey player for a while. Didn't happen by accident."

"Dylan seems like a decent sort."

"Met him, have you?"

"This morning. Briefly." She decided not to get into details. "He and Olivia Frost, his fiancée, were decent to me."

"You like everyone you meet," her father said, not for the first time in her life. "It's not a flaw, but it's something you need to be aware of. Not everyone wishes you well. It has nothing to do with you. It has to do with them."

"I didn't tell Olivia or Dylan that I'd worked for Duncan."

"Smart, if you ask me. Why make things harder than you need to? For you or for them." He sucked in a quick breath. "I hear your cousins. I think they're on to me. Stay in touch, okay, Samantha?"

"I will. Say hi to Mom and Aunt Martha and the kids for me."

"Your mother's whipping up something in the kitchen. She's always loved the kitchen here. Beats me why. Wish us luck with your cousins. You would think jet lag would slow them down, but if anything, it's the opposite. Hell…the little devils are pounding on the door."

Samantha was smiling when she disconnected, part of her father's mission, she suspected, when he'd answered her call. She could see him in his father's library. He'd be wearing shorts, even if it was chilly. He was tanned and leathery, with fierce dark eyes, unevenly graying golden-brown hair and a boisterous laugh—a man of great intellect and passion. That he and her quiet, gifted mother had stayed together for thirty years and counting was a mystery to many, but not to Samantha. Her parents were soul mates. It wasn't just that they were meant to be together. They had decided that was the case, and they had lived accordingly—with love, laugher and great optimism. They liked to say they looked themselves and their lives straight in the eye. They didn't want—or need— rose-colored glasses.

Finding a true soul mate was rare, if not impossible, Samantha thought, crumpling up her sandwich wrapping. About as rare as getting struck by lightning—

which pretty much had happened to her yesterday. Did that mean the odds were now against her finding a soul mate of her own?

"The odds were *always* against you," she said under her breath as she returned her documents pouch to her backpack, really noticing the hint of smoke now. She wasn't sure a casual passerby would notice, but the smell—unpleasant and unmistakable—was a tangible reminder of her ordeal yesterday.

A bolt of lightning, a fire and Justin Sloan in less than thirty minutes.

A lot for one person to handle.

Mentally adding a new backpack to her shopping list, Samantha walked back across the common and Main Street. She wondered if any Sloans were watching her, or if other townspeople had heard about the fire yesterday and were speculating whether she was the woman Justin had rescued.

Worrying about small-town gossip would get her nowhere. She put it out of her mind as she reentered the country store. She'd been focused only on lunch earlier. It was a traditional general store that offered everything from rubber boots to a decent selection of wine. There was nothing deliberately quaint or touristy about it—it was a store for local people who didn't want to drive to one of the larger nearby towns.

Samantha made her way to a jam-packed section in the back that offered a range of sturdy basic gear for hiking, camping, hunting, fishing, canoeing and biking. She zeroed in on the camping gear and picked out a new tent and sleeping bag. Considering the amount they cost, she decided to wait to buy a new backpack.

Maybe she would try dunking hers in Cider Brook to see if that got rid of the smell.

A large, detailed map of the area was tacked to a bulletin board. She noticed several campgrounds where she could pitch her new tent, assuming she wanted to avoid Sloan land—assuming she wanted to stay in Knights Bridge at all. She could find Justin, get him to return her journal and clear out of town. Give up on figuring out how and why her grandfather had introduced her to Benjamin Farraday and how the painting of the cider mill and the story featuring Farraday had ended up in his closet.

Give up on redeeming herself with Duncan Mc-Caffrey.

Leaving would feel like a defeat, but she could regroup and come back another day—without drawing attention to herself. Two and a half years ago she'd thought she'd managed to slip into and out of Knights Bridge on her one-day trip without drawing attention to herself, but a carpenter had spotted her and reported her to Duncan.

Justin? *Had* it been him?

As she turned from the map, Samantha noticed three framed five-by-seven-inch black-and-white photographs hung in a vertical row next to the bulletin board. She took a closer look and saw they were copies of originals, old photographs depicting an earlier incarnation of Justin Sloan's cider mill. All three photographs looked as if they had been taken on the same day, probably about a hundred years ago. The land was cleared and the mill was tidy, painted in a dark color with white trim. The top photograph showed the waterwheel and part of the dam and millpond. In the bottom photograph, a wagon full of apples stood in front of the carriage-door entrance, ready to be unloaded.

The middle photograph in particular caught Samantha's eye. In it, a young man and woman stood by the wagon. The woman had light hair pinned up and wore a simple, high-collared ankle-length dress. The man was dark-haired, wearing a dapper suit. At the bottom of the frame, in nearly illegible handwriting, the couple was identified as *Zeke and Henrietta, 1915*.

Who were Zeke and Henrietta?

Although curious, Samantha couldn't imagine what the Zeke and Henrietta of 1915 could possibly have to do with her eighteenth-century pirate. If Benjamin Farraday had, in fact, ventured into the Swift River Valley, it would have been two hundred years before the three grainy photographs of the cider mill were taken.

The painting and the manuscript weren't proof that Farraday had walked this ground. He could have ended up in one of the now-drowned Swift River Valley towns, or he might never have come this way at all.

Samantha still wanted to know who Zeke and Henrietta were.

When she headed to the front with her tent and sleeping bag, Olivia Frost entered the store with a redheaded woman. "Samantha!" Olivia said cheerfully. "I didn't expect to see you here. This is my friend Maggie. I mentioned her this morning. She's catering my sister's wedding on Saturday and works with me at Carriage Hill." She turned to Maggie. "This is Samantha Bennett, Maggie."

"The woman my brother-in-law pulled out of the

fire yesterday," Maggie said with a smile. "Good to meet you."

"You, too," Samantha said. "You're married to—"

"Brandon Sloan. Third of six, as he likes to say. He's a carpenter."

Another carpenter, Samantha thought. Olivia was frowning at the sleeping bag and tent on the counter by the register. "You're not planning to camp out tonight, are you, Samantha? Please. Come back with us to Carriage Hill. You can stay in the same room as last night."

"We insist," Maggie said. "Save your tent for another time."

Samantha didn't know what to say. "But the wedding—"

Maggie waved a hand in dismissal. "Not a problem. The wedding isn't until Saturday. No one's staying over tonight."

"Dylan and I would love to have you stay with us," Olivia added.

There was no turning them down. Samantha paid for her tent and sleeping bag while they grabbed milk, bread, cheese, local apples and cider. Ten minutes later, she found herself in the backseat of Maggie's van, among grocery bags and kids' books and toys, on the way back to The Farm at Carriage Hill.

Twelve

As Samantha stood at a window in her room at Carriage Hill—the same room as last night—she could see bright red-and-orange leaves, touches of yellow, and the deep green of pines and spruces in the endless woods that led to the shores of the vast Quabbin Reservoir. The temperature had dropped. It would be a chillier night tonight—one for wrapping up in her soft wool throw and watching the stars, if her throw hadn't been wrecked in the fire.

She turned away from the window. If Benjamin Farraday had buried his treasure in the drowned valley, it had either been found long ago or was now lost forever. No one would find it under the reservoir waters or in their protected watershed. Not without a treasure map, anyway. In all her studies of pirates, she had never come across a real treasure map.

Or real buried treasure, for that matter, she thought, heading downstairs to the kitchen.

Maggie's two young sons had arrived with their father, Brandon Sloan. Given his resemblance to the three brothers she'd already met, Samantha didn't need anyone to tell her he was a Sloan. Dylan was there, too, getting a casserole out of the freezer and setting it on the butcher-block island. Brandon introduced the boys—Tyler, seven, and Aidan, five—who said a quick hello and then charged out through the mudroom, their father right behind them.

Dylan nodded to Samantha. "Come on out with us. Brandon and I are just talking about adventure travel. You strike me as the sort who likes to travel. Am I right?"

"I've done some traveling," she said. "I can't say I've liked all of it."

"What's your favorite place?"

"So far? I don't know that I have a favorite."

Dylan smiled. "That probably means you've been to lots of places." He grabbed a pitcher of iced tea and placed it on a tray with several glasses. "Make yourself at home."

Samantha thanked him but hesitated as he went out. She could hear Maggie and Olivia in the dining room, where they were putting together wedding favors. They had handmade, hand-wrapped chocolates, cookies and goat's milk soap heaped on the table. Maggie was lecturing her friend. "Promise me you're not going to worry about a single thing on Saturday. Jess is your sister, and you're her maid of honor. That's all you need to think about. I'll do the rest. I have an excellent team—except for Brandon." Maggie gave a long-suffering sigh. "He likes to help. I indulge him."

Olivia laughed. "Brandon's a huge help and you know it."

"We'll see. After Saturday, you might change your

mind and decide to move your own wedding to San Diego."

Samantha smiled and left them to their work. She headed out to the terrace. The air was decidedly cooler, but she would be warm enough in her sweater, especially if she followed Buster's lead and stayed in the sun. She sat on a bench, Buster sprawled at her feet. The Sloan boys were racing on the mulched paths among the herbs and flowers. Brandon and Dylan, neither of whom looked cold, were seated at the table across the terrace.

Dylan offered her iced tea, but she shook her head. "I'm happy to sit here and enjoy the day," she said.

They were, in fact, discussing adventure travel. Samantha remembered Duncan mentioning adventure travel as one of his interests. He'd wanted to spin off some of his treasure-hunting projects and plan trips—get his son involved.

That son was Dylan, she thought. A real, flesh-and-blood man not five yards from her.

She regretted succumbing to Olivia and Maggie and was ready to bolt with her new tent and sleeping bag when Justin appeared on the other side of the old stone wall along the field at the back of the house. He climbed over the wall, jumped over a wild-looking herb and hopped up onto the terrace. He wasn't wearing a jacket, either, his canvas shirt open over a T-shirt. As he approached her, Samantha noted his strong build and flat abdomen and again considered slipping off into the woods with her tent.

After she confronted him about her journal.

She dreaded the idea, and she had no intention of bringing it up in front of Dylan.

Justin nodded to her, not a hint of awkwardness about him. "Afternoon, Samantha."

"Knocking off early today?"

"Waiting for a plywood delivery. I'll head back up in a few minutes. I see you've met Brandon and my nephews."

"I have, yes. I didn't expect to be back here, but I ran into Maggie and Olivia in town."

"So I heard."

Of course he'd heard. Samantha realized that her pulse had quickened, but she hoped it didn't show. As much as she was accustomed to being around men— hardheaded men—it was always on her own turf, or at least Bennett turf. Here, she thought, she was a stranger. An outsider. She tried to think of something to say besides, *"I want my journal back."* She'd never been good at small talk. Her mother was the expert. Justin showed no sign of letting her off the hook and going over to chat with his brother and Dylan. Time to channel Francesca Bennett.

Samantha took a breath. "It looks as if you're making good progress on the house and barn you're building up the road."

"We are, but we have a lot to do before cold weather sets in." Justin flicked a large spider off a white mum in a stone pot beside her bench. The spider landed in the grass and scurried out of sight. "There was a house on the site that had to be demolished first."

Before Samantha could respond, Dylan got to his feet and walked over with his iced tea. "It was owned by a woman who turned out to be my father's birth mother. In a way she's the reason I ended up in Knights Bridge. It's quite a story."

"Her name's Grace Webster," Justin added.

Samantha felt her mouth go dry. "She's still alive, then?"

Dylan nodded. "She moved into an assisted living facility here in town. My father ended up buying her old house. For various reasons, he never told me. He died two years ago this past June. I didn't know I'd inherited the property until earlier this year."

Samantha leaned over and rubbed Buster on his stomach. He gave a contented sigh, and she looked up at the three men, all of them, including Brandon, watching her, as if gauging her reaction to the story about Grace Webster. Given Dylan's background, a certain level of scrutiny of people wandering into town made sense. It didn't mean they'd figured out who she was.

It didn't mean they hadn't, either.

She didn't want to lie and she didn't want to explain. So she got up, stepped over Buster, mumbled something neutral and innocuous and stepped off the terrace into the gardens. The Sloan boys were enthralled with another spider—or maybe the same spider—on a rock. Samantha continued down a mulched path and paused in front of the stone wall, looking out across the field toward Carriage Hill.

"There are trails up Carriage Hill," Justin said, easing in next to her.

"The views must be spectacular this time of year. Any time of year, I imagine."

"You can snowshoe and cross-country ski in winter."

She wished she didn't feel so self-conscious. "Sounds like fun, although not on a frigid day."

"What's frigid to you?" he asked.

"Under ten degrees. The temperature has to be in double digits for me to strap on skis."

Justin placed one foot on a boulder, probably collected by farmers clearing the fields around the time the house was built in 1803. She noticed nicks and scars on his boot, bits of mud at the frayed hem of his jeans, the hard curve of his thigh—of his jaw, his mouth. His eyes narrowed and then met hers with no detectable change in his expression, but she suspected he knew she was taking in all the sexy details about him. Then again, maybe he was just picturing her snowshoeing up Carriage Hill.

"I didn't find my journal," she said, deciding to give him the chance to come clean. "I retraced my steps from yesterday but no sign of it."

He glanced away from her. "Would it be much of a loss if you don't find it?"

"It contains research notes."

"I see." His gaze narrowed on her, but he didn't take the bait. "My delivery should be there by now. See you around, Sam."

"Right. Sure. Maybe, anyway."

She didn't know if he heard her. He hopped over the stone wall, landing in tall grass and late-blooming wildflowers, and started up along the edge of the field back toward his construction site and plywood delivery.

His nephews called to their father to come look at a "gigantic" spiderweb they'd found. Brandon responded and followed Buster off the terrace. Dylan went back inside, the screen door shutting behind him. Samantha thought she heard a crow off in the distance, toward Carriage Hill.

There was a chill in the breeze, but it did little to cool the heat building inside her.

"Would it be much of a loss if you don't find it?"

A carefully worded question, wasn't it?

She wasn't paranoid. She was *right*.

Justin Sloan had her journal.

"Damn."

With a burst of energy, she bounded over the stone wall and followed a well-worn trail through the grass and wildflowers, ignoring all the cautionary voices in her head that warned her to think first. She was alone in this little town, among strangers—she didn't even have a car. It wasn't the time to be impulsive.

But she *knew* Justin had her journal.

She caught up with him and grabbed his arm. It was like grabbing a tree trunk. He stopped only because he decided to stop. She was breathing hard, more from emotion than from exertion. "You found my journal, didn't you?"

He shrugged. "Last night after the fire."

"Why didn't you tell me?"

"Thought I'd see what was what with you first."

She lowered her hand from his arm. "Did you read it?"

"The title page. That's it." He didn't sound at all guilty. "I'm not the kind of guy who reads women's journals."

"You let me twist in the wind."

"That wasn't the purpose of my not saying anything." He didn't explain further. "You're here about a pirate?"

"I thought you said—"

"I read the title page. *Notes on Benjamin Farraday, Pirate and Privateer.*"

"Farraday is a little-known privateer who turned to piracy and appears to have escaped capture by fleeing west."

"To Knights Bridge?"

"It wasn't Knights Bridge then. It's possible he ended up in this general area."

"With pirate's treasure?"

Samantha ignored the sarcastic note in his voice. "Why would you think that?"

"Why else would anyone be interested enough in a little-known pirate to hike out here by herself? Is that why you chose to follow Cider Brook—something to do with your Captain Farraday?"

"I didn't say I was here because of him."

"Right," he said, skeptical.

She took in a breath. "I just want my journal back. Unread."

"I'll drop it off in the morning—"

"Now. Tonight. I'll come get it myself. Just tell me where it is."

"It's at my place."

His words were challenging and sexually charged, and he knew it—knew exactly what he was doing. He was deliberate, calculating and enjoying himself, and she couldn't pretend otherwise.

Which didn't mean she had to play his game.

"After work will be fine," she said. "Since I don't have a car, I'd appreciate it if you dropped it off."

Just the slightest smile. "Sure thing."

"You don't feel guilty, do you?"

"Nope." He pointed up the field. "I have to get back to work."

"Of course. Don't let me keep you." She stood straight. "I just want to say…" She paused, forced herself to think first. "Anyone conducting research into pirates learns to be circumspect. It's not meant to be secretive, disingenuous or rude."

"*Disingenuous.* Good word." He leaned in close to her and winked. "I'll be back here with your journal in an hour."

Dinner was vegetable lasagna, garlic bread and salad. Maggie, Brandon and their sons stayed, but Samantha fled to her room with a tray. She didn't know if Justin had told Dylan, Olivia, Maggie, Brandon, his cop brother, his firefighter brother—everyone in Knights Bridge—about her journal and Benjamin Farraday. She wished she'd asked Justin who else knew but couldn't bring herself to tell her hosts. She was too raw, and too caught up in her reaction to him. She needed to get her bearings. *Think* for a change.

She was so convinced that either Justin wouldn't return with her journal at all or would leave it in the kitchen for her that when she heard a heavy footfall outside her door, it didn't occur to her it was him.

But it was. He knocked. "Here's your journal."

She opened the door, aware she was barefoot, holding a glass of red wine and wearing the plush, too-big white bathrobe she'd found in the closet. He was exactly as she'd left him. Canvas shirt, black T-shirt, worn jeans, scuffed boots, deep blue eyes, short-cropped dark hair and far too sexy for a man with her private journal in his hand.

"Thank you," she said, trying not to snatch it from him.

He placed it in her outstretched palm. "Wore yourself out today?"

"A lot of walking between yesterday and today, but it's been great. I'm just relaxing this evening." She motioned with her wine. "Dinner was perfect."

"Good to know. Olivia offered me leftovers. I see you decided on wine instead of dipping into your Scotch. Or is Scotch just for when you're hunting for pirate treasure?"

"Actually, my uncle thinks I should take rum— which isn't to say I'm confirming your suspicion that I'm here hunting pirate treasure. Most historians agree that stories of buried pirate treasure are apocryphal."

"Meaning they're bullshit."

Samantha sighed. "Thank you for not reading my journal. It's mostly just ramblings."

"You're welcome."

"You're being sincere, aren't you? You really didn't read it."

"Life's easier if you don't lie. Less to remember." With one hand, he adjusted the collar of her robe, then pointed to the belt. "This thing's about to come undone."

"It's a little big for me."

"I noticed."

Of course he noticed. Of course he'd *tell her* he noticed. With a wineglass in one hand, her journal in another and the tie to her robe about to come loose, she didn't dare move. "You might want to get back downstairs while the lasagna's still warm."

"Yeah." He gave her a knowing grin. "I might."

"Would you—um—mind shutting the door? My hands are full."

"Not a problem."

He kept his gaze on her as he pulled the door closed.

Nothing more deadly, Samantha thought, than a man who knew he was sexy.

Once she heard the door latch, she spun around, set her wine on a small table and tossed her journal onto the bed—and tripped on the hem of her robe. She pulled it off and slipped into her flannel pajamas. Probably should have stuck with them and skipped the robe altogether. There was nothing provocative, sexy or alluring about navy flannel pajamas.

She sat on the edge of the bed and picked up her wine, sipping it as she replayed her two days in Knights Bridge in her mind.

"They know."

With a shaking hand, she set her wineglass back on the table, next to a vase of fresh-cut yellow mums.

"They know who I am."

Her voice was a hoarse whisper, her throat tight as she stood, stiff and hardly breathing.

"Justin is the carpenter who told Duncan about me, and they all *know.*"

She paced in her flannel pajamas. It was dark out now. Cold.

"Hell's bells. *Now* what?"

She was in the middle of *nowhere.* On a dead-end road, with people who had every reason to think she'd deliberately misled them and was up to no good in their little town.

The thunderstorm and fire explained some of her predicament, but not all. It was also the haunting painting of the cider mill, the handwritten, fanciful pages about Captain Farraday and Lady Elizabeth and the memory of Harry Bennett and Duncan McCaffrey, two men she'd loved and admired and who'd died within months of each other.

Her own family didn't understand her reasons for being here. How could she expect Dylan, Olivia, Justin and all of the other Sloans to understand?

Sometimes she wasn't sure she understood herself. Duncan was dead. How could she redeem herself with him? What difference did it make if she proved her theory about a three-hundred-year-old pirate?

Why had an amateur painting and story buried in her grandfather's office closet intrigued her to the point she'd had to be rescued in a fire?

"Things can get out of control fast," her grandfather had said when he'd told her about some of the close calls he'd had over his long, adventurous life. *"You can't anticipate everything. Sometimes you just have to play the cards you're dealt and do your best."*

Samantha finally sat back on her bed and picked up her wine.

Harry Bennett had survived the harsh conditions of Antarctica, the coldest, iciest continent on earth.

She could damn well survive Knights Bridge, Massachusetts.

But if she could find a way to do it without being noticed, she would go out the window on her bedsheets.

Thirteen

Treasure-hunter Samantha Bennett in a bathrobe two sizes too big for her did nothing for Justin's sense of calm as he downed a helping of lasagna, then drove back to the Frost sawmill. He couldn't stop thinking about her almond-shaped eyes, the touches of gold in her dark curls, the creamy curve of exposed breast as her robe drifted dangerously close to falling open.

She was a resourceful, plucky sort. She'd have figured out something before she found herself standing stark naked in front of him.

It was a hell of an image for a cold autumn night.

He noticed the office light was on at Frost Millworks and headed up there. He found Randy Frost standing at his wife's desk, shaking his head at pictures she'd taped up on the wall. "Holland," he said, pointing at the images of Dutch streets and sights. "That's where Louise wants to go next. Delft, Rembrandt, canals, cheese and windmills."

"Sounds good to me."

Randy was a big, salt-of-the-earth man who would do anything for his wife of thirty years and their two daughters. Justin had served with him as a volunteer firefighter for over a decade and couldn't imagine anyone more reliable or trustworthy.

"Six months ago, Louise wouldn't go to Northampton by herself. Now she's got us applying for passports." Randy pointed at a picture of thousands of tulips in waves of bright colors. "She wants us to go during tulip season so we can visit Keukenhof."

"Gardens?"

"Yep. Gardens." Randy seemed to pull himself out of his thoughts. "Two weddings in three months and then the Netherlands."

"You can drink Dutch beer."

Randy grinned at him. "I like how you think. There's a lot going on, but it's all good."

"All set for Jess's wedding?"

"I just do as I'm told. Louise and I both like Mark. He's already like a member of the family. Took him and Jess a while to figure out what we've all known for years."

"They're a good pair," Justin said.

"Yeah, they are. We like Dylan, too, but he's different from what we're used to."

"He's rich, you mean."

Randy sighed. "There's rich and then there's Dylan and Noah."

Justin couldn't argue with that. "They keep things interesting around here."

"No complaints." Randy switched off the desk lamp and walked past Justin out into the showroom. A single overhead light was on above the front door. "How's the cider mill?"

"Minor damage. Nothing I can't fix over a couple of weekends."

"A wonder that place didn't burn down years ago. There was a time I thought you and your brothers would set it on fire horsing around out there."

Justin grinned. "Brandon, Adam and me, maybe. Eric and Christopher? Never."

"I don't know how you made it past thirty without being arrested."

Randy switched off the light, and they headed outside, Justin continuing on to the old sawmill while the older man went home to his wife. With the rehearsal for Jess and Mark's wedding tomorrow and the service on Saturday, Randy Frost had good reason to be pensive, to need a little time to himself.

When Justin reached the sawmill apartment, he took off his work boots and sat on the couch. Growing up together, he and Mark had often joked about which one of them would get married first. Which one would marry a girl from Knights Bridge. Mark hadn't lived in town his whole life. But he'd come back. It was where he wanted to be. What he and Jess had together was the real thing. It wasn't perfect—it had taken work to get to this late-September wedding of theirs—but it was right.

Unlike Justin and the Worcester architect Mark had introduced him to last year.

They'd worked out for a while. Then she'd gotten a job in Atlanta and assumed he would follow her. She couldn't understand why he wasn't interested. She didn't get it that his life was in Knights Bridge. *He* was in Knights Bridge.

She'd never have slipped into town in search of pirate treasure. She'd never have picked a padlock, or even come close to getting caught out in the woods in a fierce thunderstorm. She'd thought Justin's service as a firefighter "quaint." They weren't a good fit. But although Samantha was much more his type, pursuing his attraction to Harry Bennett's granddaughter was another mistake. A different kind of mistake.

Justin checked Netflix and found the special on Antarctica that mentioned Harry Bennett and his expedition there fifty years ago, well before Samantha was even born.

"The South Pole. Hell."

Harry came onto the screen, with the same energy and dark eyes as his granddaughter up in her room at Carriage Hill. Justin watched for a few minutes before he switched off the television. He got out his gold coin. Was it part of Captain Farraday's treasure? Was there more gold buried out at the cider mill?

It didn't matter, Justin told himself. He returned the coin to its box. He saw no point in telling Samantha about it.

Let Harry Bennett's granddaughter give up on Knights Bridge and go on her way.

Justin got an early start in the morning. Fog had settled in the dips and low areas but would burn off with the rising sun and warmer temperatures. He had a long list of things he had to do before quitting work at noon to get ready for the wedding rehearsal and rehearsal dinner that evening.

When he reached the construction site, he received a text from Mark. Nervous as hell.

Justin called him, and they chatted for a few minutes. He knew part of a best man's job was reassuring the groom, even one as solid as Mark Flanagan, that a case of nerves before his wedding was normal.

Mark asked about Samantha. "I hear she's feisty and pretty, Justin."

The man was looking for distractions. Justin obliged—to a degree—and told his friend about the fire but didn't get into the rest of it. Pirates. Being a Bennett. Getting on the wrong side of Duncan McCaffrey. That all was for Dylan to sort out.

Mark seemed satisfied. "How long will she be sticking around town?"

"No idea, but it won't be forever."

Justin hung up and got things organized for the day. Within an hour, the crew started to arrive with coffees and breakfast sandwiches. Maggie sent apple-walnut muffins with Brandon. Justin tried one. It was still warm from the oven. Only Maggie. Brandon swore she baked in her sleep.

"Isn't that Samantha?" Brandon asked, pointing down the driveway.

Indeed it was. She had on her safari jacket with her backpack on her shoulders, her new tent and sleeping bag strapped to the top and bottom.

Brandon gave a low whistle. "She's hoofing it. Must be in good shape."

And in a hurry. Justin took his muffin with him and walked down to her. Sunlight was sparkling through the fog now, and it was already warming up. "Hey, there," he said.

She gave a curt wave. "Good morning."

"Where you off to?"

She didn't slacken her pace. "Not sure yet."

"You're moving awfully fast for someone who isn't sure where she's going." He eased in next to her. "Need a ride?"

"No, thanks."

"Still mad about your journal?"

She gave a tight shake of her head. "No. It's fine."

"Samantha." Justin resisted the urge to touch her arm. "You okay?"

She slowed slightly and seemed to make an effort to smile. "I had an epiphany this morning. I should have rented a car. It's not as if I can hop on a subway out here."

"Just now figuring that out?"

She adjusted her pack. "I think it took walking from Carriage Hill with this new tent and sleeping bag to convince me. I've logged a fair number of miles since I arrived in Knights Bridge. Anyway. I'm in good shape. All's well."

"Is someone with a car meeting you?"

"Eventually. I'm…" She sucked in a breath, looking away from him, across the road to the woods. "I appreciate all that you, Dylan and Olivia have done for me. Thank you."

"No problem."

"I'm not a liar," she said, almost to herself.

Justin settled back on his heels. "Not a good one, anyway."

She frowned at him in obvious surprise. "What's that supposed to mean?"

"It means that a good liar would just lie and wouldn't bother parsing her words the way you do."

"When did I parse my words?"

"When you talked about my padlock, for starters."

"I didn't—" She stopped, as if she were trying to keep herself from saying anything else. If so, it didn't work. "It was an awkward situation. I hadn't expected to end up in a fire. Then staying with Dylan and Olivia. My missing journal."

"Awkward," Justin said, not sure why he was so amused.

Samantha nodded. "That's right."

His brother Adam slowed as he passed them in his truck, frowning at Justin, who waved him on. Of all his brothers, Adam least appreciated his people skills. At least once a day, he would say, "You know you can be a bastard, right, Justin?" With a big Adam Sloan grin, naturally.

"Another brother?" Samantha asked.

"Adam. He's a mason, one of the best in southern New England."

"Adam. Got it. He's between Brandon and Christopher. I think I've seen all your brothers now. What about the two older men?" She motioned up the driveway. "Your father and—what, an uncle?"

"Uncle Pete. He's a pain in the ass but he can do anything. He's retiring soon."

"Is your sister here?"

"Back at the office."

"And you all get along?"

"Most days. I irritate Adam a lot, but neither of us holds a grudge. My father pays no attention. My mother is just happy she never had to make bail for any of us." He was watching Samantha, saw that she wasn't as stiff and abrupt—but she wasn't calm, either. More like she was trying to fake it. "Do you want to get whatever's bothering you off your chest, Sam? Trust me. Whatever it is, I can take it."

She bit down on her lower lip, not, he thought, because she was tentative but because she was pushing back a range of emotions, none of which she liked. Finally she looked at him, her dark eyes squinting against the bright morning sun behind him. "How much do you know—or think you know—about me?"

So that was it. He grinned and leaned closer to her. "Not nearly enough."

She snapped up straight. "I'm serious."

"So am I."

"I worked for Duncan McCaffrey for a little while two years ago. Which I know you know but I want to tell you myself. You're the carpenter who told him about me?"

"I told him I saw a pretty brown-haired woman out here in the snow. No hat, no gloves, driving a car that appeared to be rented."

"I learned the hard way that driving my grandfather's old Mercedes draws attention. Duncan recognized me from your description?"

"Instantly. He said your name was Samantha Bennett and you were his problem."

Pain flickered across her face. She breathed in through her nose, then said, "He was a good man. The best. I'm sorry I disappointed him, but that's—" She faltered, tears in her eyes as she cleared her throat and continued, "It's something I have to live with. He was right. I'm not your problem."

"Sam—"

"I should go." She flicked a tear out of the corner of her eye with a fingertip, obviously attempting to rally. "You have work to do, and you have a wedding tomorrow."

Not the time to push her, Justin decided. "All right."

"I'll be stopping at the library. You can tell your spies so they won't get all excited thinking I'm up to something."

"What's at the library?"

"Books." She flashed him a smile. "Sorry. I have some research I want to do."

"About the couple in the photos at Hazelton's?"

She looked surprised. "How do you know—"

"Those spies of mine," he said. "Maggie and Olivia told me last night."

Her smile was gone now. "I'm sorry I wasn't straight with you from the start. That's why you didn't return my journal right away, isn't it?"

"That's part of it."

She didn't seem to hear him. "You recognized my name. Duncan told you, and you remembered." Without waiting for an answer, she sucked in a breath. "Serves me right."

She spun around and headed down the road at a fast, determined clip.

Justin let her go. He wondered if her research into the old photographs would lead her to his gold coin, but he didn't know how that was possible.

Maybe I should just tell her.

He shook off the thought. What was wrong with him? Let Samantha Bennett run out of steam and go back to Boston or London or wherever.

But she was a lot like her grandfather, and old Harry Bennett hadn't been one to give up. Frostbite, hypothermia and the prospect of dying at the ends of the earth hadn't stopped him. His granddaughter might be upset and mortified, but she wouldn't leave Knights Bridge until she'd finished what she'd come to accomplish.

Justin was relieved when she rounded a bend and was out of sight. Damned if she didn't have him hot, uncomfortable and distracted.

He got back to work. Dylan was at the trailer. "I came up through the field," he said. "I didn't want to run into Samantha and make things worse for her."

"She's on her way to the library."

"You talked to her?"

"Yeah. It didn't go well."

Dylan didn't look surprised. "She left Olivia and me a note apologizing for omitting details about who she is and why she's here."

"That's what she did with your father," Justin said. "Omitted details."

"She wrote in her note that she thought it was a good idea at the time and never meant to cause any problems for anyone."

"What do you think?"

Dylan shrugged. "I think she doesn't give up easily. You?"

"I think she doesn't give up at all."

"No wonder my father liked her."

Justin opened the trailer door but didn't go inside. "Did your father ever mention this pirate of hers? Captain Farraday?"

Dylan shook his head. "He was getting into shipwrecks but never mentioned pirates in particular. The idea that one could have buried treasure in Knights Bridge or even in this region is far-fetched, isn't it?" He looked at the skeleton of the house he was building on land once owned by his grandmother, a woman who'd fallen in love with a British jewel thief as her town was being swept out of existence. "Then again, given my family history, maybe I shouldn't be surprised."

Fourteen

Loretta sat with a pot of coffee on a small garden terrace off the den of Julius's home in the hills above Santa Monica Boulevard. It had multiple patios and terraces, a natural given that it was built into a hillside with expensive houses above and below and stunning treetop views. In fact, she sort of felt as if she was in a tree house. The interior had high beamed ceilings, a fireplace, skylights, hardwood floors and white cabinets. She loved white cabinets. Julius had told her he hadn't picked them out. They'd come when he'd bought the house after his divorce five years ago. His ex-wife and daughters lived nearby.

No ex-husband for her. No daughters, either.

Loretta knew more about Hollywood and Beverly Hills from watching movies and television than she did from living in Southern California.

"This Samantha Bennett is sophisticated and smart," Julius said.

"*Irresistible* is the word Duncan used. He meant it in a fatherly way."

"Want me to look into the Bennetts?"

Loretta thought a moment. "Not yet."

"Anything I should know about the Sloans?"

"There are a lot of them, and they're doing the construction on Dylan's house and barn." A barn, she thought. Dylan was building a damn barn. She grabbed her coffee cup. "You met a bunch of Sloans when we were out there with Daphne."

Daphne Stewart, aka Debbie Henderson. Maybe it was the other way around, since she'd been born Debbie Henderson. She was a costume designer in Hollywood who'd fled Knights Bridge as a teenager.

"I remember Brandon Sloan," Julius said. "He's married to one of the O'Dunn sisters."

"Maggie."

"Right. The caterer. Phoebe's the eldest. The twins are the youngest. Ruby and Ava. The theater majors." Julius reached out and plucked a dried leaf off one of the plants in the lush greenery along the edge of the terrace. "Their mother raises goats. What do you think Noah's going to do about the goats?"

"Nothing. They're not his goats."

"That's what I'd do. Nothing. Not a damn thing."

Loretta had no idea why they were talking about the O'Dunns and goats. That was Julius. His mind pinged from one thing to another, and he could talk about anything. "It's good to see Noah happy and in love. For years, all he's thought about is this high-tech stuff. Math equations or whatever. Women have thrown themselves at him because of his money, but Phoebe…"

"Phoebe's a special woman," Julius said.

Loretta nodded, picturing Phoebe O'Dunn with her long strawberry curls, turquoise eyes and sweet smile.

At first she'd struck Loretta as shy and a little wishy-washy, but she was smart, kind and strong, secure in who she was—she didn't need Noah and his bazillions to create an identity for her.

Julius was frowning from across the table. "You tearing up, Loretta?"

She scowled at him. "No. I am not tearing up, Julius."

He grinned. "I wouldn't have taken you for a romantic, but you are."

"Nothing wrong with being a romantic." She jumped to her feet, restless, out of sorts. "This is the first time in two years that I've wanted a cigarette. Last time was when Duncan died. I quit smoking a million years ago, but that doesn't mean I don't want a cigarette every now and then."

"I bet Dylan and Noah are usually involved when you do."

"True." She sighed, rubbing her fingertips on a glossy, pointed leaf of something. She'd never been good at remembering the names of plants. "Dylan listened to all my advice, but he only heeded about a tenth of it."

Julius shrugged, standing next to her. "If he'd heeded more, he wouldn't have been sleeping in his car when Noah knocked on his window and asked him to come work at NAK with him. Think of the millions they've both earned because Dylan didn't take all your advice."

"That's twisted logic, Julius."

"Maybe." He hooked an arm around her and drew her close. "You have to make peace with whatever

Duncan McCaffrey was to you, Loretta. It'll eat you alive if you don't."

"Samantha Bennett's a schemer."

"That's a leap, don't you think? And Dylan can handle her."

"I know, but I hope he doesn't hold it against me because I didn't tell him about her sooner. It didn't occur to me since she'd gone on her way. I haven't kept tabs on her. No reason."

"Go, Loretta. Meet Samantha Bennett and see for yourself that all is well." Julius kissed her on the forehead and whispered, "Make your peace with Duncan's ghost."

"Julius—"

"No. Not now. Go to Knights Bridge and then come back and we'll have wine."

Loretta nodded and left without another word, her throat tight as she went back inside, packed, dragged her overnight bag out to her car and started the drive south to La Jolla. Julius was right. She couldn't share the same space with him right now. She needed to get her head together and decide what came next in her life.

Julius was still out on his terrace, contemplating Loretta and how crazy he was about her, when he heard someone on the spiral stairs up from the street. Then came the familiar voice of Daphne Stewart. "Knock, knock." She waved a hand at him as she stepped onto the terrace. "Don't get up."

"Good morning, Daphne." He pushed out a chair across the table from him with one foot. "Have a seat. What brings you out here?"

"GPS. I'd have gotten lost without it. The streets over here are a maze."

She plopped down as if she'd walked a hundred miles instead of driven a few. She lived in a bungalow decorated with the artistic flair she'd demonstrated during her brief stay in Knights Bridge as a teenager, dreaming of the life she'd come to live as a Hollywood costume designer. She was a petite woman in her sixties, copper-haired and elegant. Over the summer, Julius had helped her figure out that Dylan McCaffrey and Noah Kendrick's interest in Knights Bridge had nothing to do with her. In the process, she'd decided to reconnect with her past and had returned to the little town a few weeks ago for what she'd insisted would be a one-time visit. Julius hadn't been so sure.

"I want to go back to Knights Bridge," she announced.

There it was. He shrugged. "Nothing stopping you."

"There isn't, is there? All my secrets are out. No one ever cared except me. I had to change my name, wipe the dust of my past off my feet and start fresh." She sank back in her chair. "Oh, Julius. What a life I've lived."

"And are still living, Daphne."

"Yes. Right. Of course. I don't have a dread disease or anything. I'm healthy as can be." She leaned forward, forearms on the table. She had on bracelets and rings, all eye-catching but all in good taste. "I've stayed in touch with the O'Dunn twins. Ava and Ruby."

"The theater majors."

"That's right. We're talking about doing something theater related in Knights Bridge."

"You mean like Shakespeare?"

"Could be. More likely a master class on costume design to start. Maybe something with children. We've got lots of ideas."

"Why?"

"They're great young women, Ava and Ruby, and it would be fun. I'd forgotten how lovely Knights Bridge is, and it's not far from Amherst and Northampton, or from Boston. Who knows where this could lead."

Julius picked up his coffee, remembered it was cold and set it back down again. Daphne was great, but she wasn't exactly low maintenance. "Are you thinking of relocating?" he asked her.

She didn't hesitate. "Oh, no. No, no. I couldn't take a New England winter again."

"You like being a local celebrity," Julius said, grinning at her.

"You're a horrible man, Julius Hartley. I don't care anything about celebrity, and you, of all people, should know it." She fingered one of her big rings. "I'd like to help Ava and Ruby if I can. I had no help when I started."

"Things worked out. Maybe it's better that way."

"Well, whatever, I think it'd be fun, and I want to do it if I can."

Julius really wished he had hot coffee. "Why tell me? Just buy a plane ticket and go."

"I was wondering about Noah Kendrick and Phoebe O'Dunn...." Daphne looked awkward, a rare state for her. "And about Dylan McCaffrey and Olivia Frost. I don't want them to think I'm doing this to curry favor with them, or that I want to ask them for money. Anything like that."

"Ah. They're rich. They probably get hit up for money all the time."

"That's what I was thinking."

Julius could see how uncomfortable Daphne felt. "You can't control what other people assume. You know that, Daphne. You can only control what you do."

"And sometimes barely that," she said half under her breath. "What about you and Knights Bridge?"

He shuddered. "There is no me and Knights Bridge."

Daphne eyed him knowingly. "Loretta is like a second mother to Noah and Dylan."

"In her head, maybe. I'm neutral about Knights Bridge." It was close enough to the truth, Julius thought, flicking a small leaf off the table onto the deck. "I don't care if I see it again or if I don't see it again, or if Noah and Dylan or one or the other make a home there. Irrelevant to my life."

"Do you ever think about retiring?"

"I am right now with you going on and on."

She waved a hand at him. "Be serious."

"I can't afford to retire yet."

"Can Loretta?"

"I don't know. Ask her if you want."

"Do you think she'll move East?"

"And what, help you open a children's theater in Sleepy Hollow?" Julius grinned at the thought. "Loretta is a hard-nosed lawyer, Daphne. She knows more about ice hockey than she does about theater."

Daphne pointed a bejeweled finger at him. "Ha. I'm right. You and Loretta are an item. I knew I saw something between you two on our trip East. Have you told your daughters?"

"Told them what? I'm seeing a lawyer from San Diego? So what?"

"You're serious about her. I can see it in your eyes." Daphne swept to her feet. "Just don't be a fool, Julius, okay? You're good at finding out things about people, but that doesn't mean you're good at knowing someone's heart, including your own."

He stared up at her from his seat. "I have no idea what you're talking about." He held up a hand. "Don't explain. Did the O'Dunn twins mention anything about treasure hunters?"

"Treasure hunters? You mean like Dylan's father?"

"For starters."

"I can find out—"

"Don't find out. Don't do anything." Julius tried to keep any sharpness out of his tone, but he'd learned to be direct with Daphne. "What about a local guy named Justin Sloan? Ava and Ruby mention him?"

"Only their brother-in-law, Brandon Sloan." She frowned at him, obviously curious. "Why? Do you want me to ask?"

"Don't ask. Forget I mentioned him. When were you thinking about going back to Knights Bridge?"

"I might go this fall for a quick trip, but we wouldn't be able to do anything until spring at the earliest. Ava and Ruby will be graduating. Well. We'll see." Daphne smiled, kissed him on the cheek. "Always a pleasure, Julius. See you soon."

She glided down the stairs. Julius watched her, realizing Loretta didn't glide. She consumed ground when she walked. She was an exhausting woman. Maybe that was what Daphne, who hardly knew Loretta, had picked up on.

If so, no argument from him.

Fifteen

Samantha was almost to the library when she decided she'd had her fill of walking Knights Bridge's back roads, at least for a while. She was ready to toss her backpack into the nearest trash bin and call a cab.

Not much farther, she told herself. She could see the library just ahead, on the corner of South Main Street and a narrow side street. She would hide out in a quiet spot, catch her breath, see what she could find out about Zeke and Henrietta of 1915 Knights Bridge and decide what to do next about her own life. She had outlined options in her head while trying *not* to think about Justin and the mess she was in, simply because she had ventured to his town in the snow a little over two years ago and hadn't told anyone.

Of course, it wasn't quite that simple.

She should have known better, given that her decision to keep quiet had involved Harry Bennett and a long-dead pirate, both of whom had lived complicated lives.

Complicated lives that had now complicated *her* life.

Except she had no one to blame for her decisions except herself.

She slowed as she came to a patch of shade under an old maple tree and recognized Maggie Sloan loading a crate into the back of her van, parked in front of a small "gingerbread" house.

"Well, good morning, Samantha," Maggie said, red hair flying as she stood straight.

Samantha eased her backpack off her sore shoulders. "Morning."

Maggie's smile turned to a wince. "Uh-oh. You've got the look that says you've just had a run-in with a Sloan."

"Do I?"

"I had that same look for months when Brandon and I were on the skids. Now it's only from time to time. The Sloans are good at building things and putting out fires and such. You want one of them around when it's your house being built or you're in an emergency, but subtlety isn't in their nature. Every last one of them should have 'blunt as hell' as their middle name." She shut the van doors. "You don't look daunted, though."

"It's my own fault. I wasn't as forthcoming as I should have been—"

"You worked for Duncan McCaffrey. I heard. My mother met him on one of his visits to town. I never did."

"I thought it would be easier for everyone if I didn't mention our history." Samantha rubbed her stiff right shoulder. "I was a bit rattled after the fire, but it's no excuse."

"Are you kidding? It's a damn good excuse." Maggie tightened her long, flowing sweater around her.

"You don't seem like trouble, Samantha. You seem more like someone on a mission. A personal mission. Maybe you're telling yourself it's professional, but it's not, is it?"

"In my world, the lines between professional and personal can get blurry before you know it." She picked up her backpack. "You've got a wedding to put on. I won't keep you."

"Will you be staying in town a while longer?" Maggie asked.

"Not if your Sloan brother-in-law can help it."

The words were out before Samantha could take them back. Maggie gave her a knowing look, but Samantha said goodbye and continued on her way. She'd been too impulsive in coming to Knights Bridge. She should have had contingency plans. A damn *car*.

But how could she have planned for a fire—or for Justin Sloan?

The Knights Bridge public library was located in a solid Victorian stone-and-brick building with its own grand piano, a small stage, a fireplace, an imposing oil portrait of its founder and all sorts of nooks and crannies. Samantha settled into a quiet corner in a small reading room on the main floor and immersed herself in finding out more about the Hazelton family, early settlers of Knights Bridge and the original owners of the country store and Justin's cider mill. She quickly discovered that the library was a treasure trove of information on the history of the town and the Swift River Valley. There was also a local historical society, headquartered in one of the oldest houses in the village.

She felt more at ease. Musty books, archives, old

photographs—this was a world she knew well and could navigate with confidence, without second-guessing herself.

Unlike navigating the loyalties and suspicions of the people in a small town.

She got to work, losing herself in the history of one family. In a little over an hour, she discovered that the Hazeltons had settled in Knights Bridge in the 1740s, three decades before the American Revolution. They became farmers along Cider Brook and a small spring-fed pond—the same parcel of land where, in 1874, their descendants built a prosperous cider mill. In 1915 the family opened the general store that became a town institution.

Now, another century later, not a single Hazelton resided in Knights Bridge.

Samantha didn't discover so much as a hint of any Hazelton family association with Benjamin Farraday as a semirespectable privateer or, later, a wanted pirate. At least not in Knights Bridge. She supposed the two parties could have met prior to the Hazeltons' arrival in town. She didn't know where they had originated.

That was a question for another day. She could dig up more information—births, deaths, marriages—but she didn't know what that would accomplish, and in the meantime, she needed a break. She collected her backpack and headed outside. It was sunny, brisk and beautiful, but she opted against a sandwich on the common. She decided to try Smith's, the only restaurant in the Knights Bridge village.

As she crossed the street to the common, she glanced around, in case a Sloan was watching her, but she didn't see anyone. She was on her own, and that was just fine with her.

Smith's was already filling up with locals when Samantha arrived at the converted 1920s house just off the town common. Its wide front porch was decorated with magenta-colored mums and hanging baskets of deep pink geraniums, still vibrant in late September. She sat in a small booth at the far end of the main dining room, where she could see everyone but wouldn't be easily spotted herself.

Her waitress, a stout, cheerful middle-aged woman who didn't appear to be a Sloan, recommended the turkey club. Samantha went with it and coffee, figuring she needed sustenance after her encounter with Justin, her hike into town and her research at the library. She also had no idea what she would be doing the rest of the day, or where she would be sleeping tonight. Not, she thought, at Carriage Hill.

Her coffee arrived first. She sipped it as she dug out her documents pouch. She'd jotted down notes on the Hazeltons in her newly returned journal but would look at them later. Her eye was drawn to a passage in the anonymous story of the kidnapped aristocratic Lady Elizabeth and her worldly pirate captor.

Lady Elizabeth appreciated the simple pleasures of a good cup of tea. Captain Farraday seemed to have no idea what that meant to her. She didn't tell him that it reminded her of home, of soft scents and sweet memories. She wouldn't tell him.

Better, she thought, that the man with her fate in his hands not know everything about her.

Samantha understood that sentiment. She folded the pages and tucked them back into the pouch, sliding it into her pack on the bench next to her. When she looked up, she saw that Justin had arrived. What were the odds? He was laughing with two men she recognized from the fire. Her throat tightened with an uncomfortable mix of guilt, attraction and lingering jitters. She hadn't counted on meeting local people—meeting Duncan's son.

Liking them.

The two men eased away, and Justin walked straight to her booth and sat across from her without waiting to be invited. "I heard you were still wandering around town," he said.

"Your brother Eric told you?"

"He keeps an eye on the goings-on in town."

The cop brother. And she was a "goings-on." *Great.* She picked up her sturdy coffee mug, tried to look casual. "Are you surprised to find me having coffee and a sandwich after I was run out of town?"

"You weren't run out of town. Obviously, since you're still here."

She pointed at his menu. "I ordered the turkey club. What else is good here?"

"Not the chef's salad. It's the worst. Everything else is fine." He leaned back, clearly amused. "Feeling claustrophobic?"

"It's a lovely place. I feel…" She sipped her coffee, set the mug back on the table and smiled at him. "Watched."

"I wonder why we'd watch you, don't you, Sam Bennett?"

"I just spent over an hour in the library doing dull, tedious research."

"Into what?"

She decided to tell him. "The Hazeltons."

His eyes held hers just for a split-second longer than was comfortable. "Why?"

"Curiosity. I doubt they have anything to do with Captain Farraday, but a lot of what I do is dry and uninteresting, even if it involves pirates and missing treasure."

"Why pirates?"

The waitress returned and took Justin's order. He went with iced tea and grilled chicken on a green salad, which made Samantha feel marginally guilty about her club sandwich and fries—but he hadn't walked to town with a loaded backpack.

He rested his arm across the back of the bench, looking casual, at home. Of course, he *was* at home. She was the stranger. He tapped the table with his free hand. "Pirates, Sam. Why pirates?"

"I became enthralled with them when I was a kid on my parents' research-and-salvage ship. I was often alone. Pirates were good company."

"During the summer?"

She shook her head. "I was privately tutored until I started high school."

"What did you do for friends?"

"I hung out with members of the crew and their families. My parents' friends and colleagues at various stops. It was a different upbringing but not as isolated as it sounds."

"And high school?"

"Boston. My grandfather lived there. I spent a lot of time with him. But he wasn't always there. He was active into his nineties."

"Was he interested in pirates, too?"

"He was interested in everything."

Justin lowered his arm and sat up straight. "You have an interesting life. Why hire on with Duncan McCaffrey and become a treasure hunter?"

"It just happened. My grandfather and I…" She picked up her coffee again, covering for an unexpected wave of emotion. "He died a few months before I came out here and you saw me. I often kept him company. He's the one who introduced me to Benjamin Farraday. Grandpa was such a presence—so resilient, so full of life. Sometimes it's still hard to believe he's gone."

"I'm sorry for your loss," Justin said.

His simple words and obvious sincerity caught her by surprise. "Thank you. He had a good, long life. I've spent most of the past two years—since Duncan fired me—going through Grandpa's things."

"Your curating, archiving and research."

She smiled. "Exactly."

The waitress returned with the turkey club and a heap of fries. Samantha noticed Justin's eyebrows go up. She picked up a fry and motioned at her plate with it. "Help yourself. I could eat every one of these fries, but I'm not going to."

"It's real bacon on the club," he said.

"So I see."

He snatched a fry. "What was the fate of your Captain Farraday?"

"We don't know for sure. I'd like to find out what

happened to him. I have my own ideas. He wasn't captured and executed, but there's no question he was guilty of piracy."

Justin popped the fry into his mouth. "Did he look like Johnny Depp?"

Samantha sighed. "There are no likenesses of Captain Farraday that I'm aware of. Popular culture through the centuries has painted a different portrait of what pirates were like than what current scholarship would suggest was actually the case."

"Ah."

"You don't care, do you?"

"I'm interested but, no, I don't care."

His salad arrived. It looked good, but not as tempting as her meal. Their waitress also brought his iced tea and questioned him about the upcoming wedding, the rehearsal that evening, whether Mark and Jess were really, finally, ready to tie the knot. Justin responded without any of the curtness or suspicion that Samantha had been getting from him.

"Is she a cousin?" she asked when the woman withdrew.

"Millie? No. She's not a cousin, but her son worked for us through college." He picked up his fork and looked across the table at her. "Did you think if you could prove Farraday was in this area, it would somehow absolve you for what happened between you and Duncan at the end of his life?"

Samantha squirted ketchup onto the edge of her plate, avoiding his gaze. "Maybe. I don't know. I guess I wanted to prove to myself that I wasn't out of line in wondering if Duncan had come here because of Captain Farraday."

"That matters to you."

"Yes."

"But Duncan didn't come here because of a pirate."

"No," Samantha said. "He came to find out who he was."

Justin started on his salad. "That made you feel like an even bigger heel, didn't it? Then he dies. You go into hiding, sorting out your grandfather's closets and drawers. Find anything interesting? The skeleton of a mastodon or an old pirate hat or something?"

She smiled. "Nothing like that."

"Think you're going to find buried treasure out here?"

"That would be fun, wouldn't it?"

"Not an answer. I'm not fooled, Sam. You're sophisticated—"

"And you're just a simple country boy?"

He grinned. "Yeah. Just a simple country boy."

It didn't bother him at all.

She didn't want to lie, but she saw no point in telling him the rest now—about the painting of the cider mill or the fictionalized account of Farraday's adventures.

He watched her a moment, then drank some of his iced tea. "It's been two years. Why come to Knights Bridge now? Is it because you realized Dylan was in town?"

"Partly. I'm not sure there is a logical reason for my coming here now."

"It's emotional?"

"Emotional and intuitive."

He leaned over the table. "That means you don't want to tell me the real reason." When she started to protest, he held up a hand. "I'm just telling you what I believe. I'm not trying to put you on the defensive."

"Thank you. Just because I don't answer a question doesn't necessarily mean I have anything to hide."

"Doesn't mean you don't, either. Anyway, Maggie and Olivia instructed me to be nice. They also want me to invite you to the wedding tomorrow."

"The wedding—Justin—"

"They think that I as the best man should have a guest. Doesn't matter that my entire family will be there. They say it's not the same."

"It isn't," Samantha said.

He gave her an easy grin. "Good. That means you'll be there."

"That's not what it means. I…" She picked up a triangle of her sandwich, then set it down again. "Who says I'm even going to be in Knights Bridge tomorrow?"

"That's what I told Maggie and Olivia. They said you'll be here. Woman's instinct or something."

"If there's a woman's instinct, I don't have it."

"But you're not going anywhere, are you?"

She tried to ignore his knowing tone. "I can't stay at Carriage Hill with a wedding there tomorrow. And why would I go as your guest? You've accused me of being a liar and a thief."

"I never said you were a thief. You did break into my mill, though. Now that I know you're Harry Bennett's granddaughter, I'm not surprised you can pick a lock."

"My uncle taught me. And you still haven't answered the question."

His deep blue eyes sparked with amusement.

"You'll go to the wedding with me because I'm ir-resistible."

She shook her head. "I'll consider it because it's decent of Maggie and Olivia to think of me, and it's more than I deserve after misleading them about my reasons for being here."

"That, too. We bonded when I rescued you, Sam. Just one of those things."

He took a sip of his drink, set the glass down on the table. She noticed a scar on his right hand, cal-luses on his fingers, and wished she hadn't—but he seemed oblivious to her discomfort, her intense aware-ness of him.

"Do you own a dress?" he asked.

"A closetful." Samantha smiled. "That might be an exaggeration, and I don't have one with me."

"I don't know why Duncan ever believed you. You're a terrible liar. Come on. I've got the afternoon off to get ready for the rehearsal tonight. We'll find you a dress."

Her eyebrows rose.

He grinned and winked at her. "I'm a man of many resources."

Sixteen

Samantha drove with Justin out to Frost Millworks, a private company that produced quality custom millwork for homes and businesses. He led her into a sunlit meeting room with tall windows overlooking another brook, stone-and-earth dam and millpond. The old sawmill had been converted into an apartment and storage space. It was bigger than Justin's cider mill but not by much.

He motioned to a long table piled with old clothes sorted into stacks—dresses, pants, jackets, shirts, sweaters, accessories. "Help yourself."

Samantha stared at him. "Seriously?"

"There's bound to be something here. Louise Frost collected clothes leftover from a vintage fashion show at the library a few weeks ago. She's figuring out what to do with them. She says some of them are in great shape."

"A vintage fashion show." Samantha smiled, although she still wasn't convinced she would find anything that would both fit and be suitable for a wedding. "What a great idea for a fund-raiser. Did you attend?"

"I don't remember. If I did, I've blocked it."

"Ah. I see. A tough Sloan can't be going to fashion shows."

He winked at her. "You're catching on. Brandon went, but he's married to Maggie. She was modeling a gown. He had no choice."

"What about your other brothers and your sister?"

"They probably don't remember if they were there, either."

"Which means you all went."

He nodded to the overflowing table. "You'll find something."

"I'll give it a shot," she said.

She fingered an old brown tweed woman's jacket, the fabric soft and worn. Had it come from someone from town? She wasn't at all certain she wasn't out of her mind for being here—or why, exactly, she'd been invited to the wedding. Had Dylan had a hand in it? Were they all just trying to keep tabs on her, find out what was up with her and her interest in Benjamin Farraday? She wouldn't blame them if they were.

She reminded herself that her predicament was entirely self-inflicted, and she had options—including getting out of town.

"I don't have suitable shoes for a wedding," she said.

"Olivia and Maggie have already thought of that," Justin said. "They told me that between them and their sisters, they would find a pair that fits and will go with whatever dress you choose."

"This is very decent of you all, but—"

He shook his head. "No 'buts.'" His expression softened, maybe for the first time since they'd met two days ago. "Just enjoy yourself, Sam. You've had a rough week."

"My own fault—except for the lightning. I didn't cause that."

He tucked a few stray hairs behind her ear. "No one's trying to pull a fast one on you. If we didn't want you there tomorrow, we wouldn't have invited you." He smiled, stepping back. "We sure as hell wouldn't turn you loose in our vintage clothes department."

She laughed, but only for a moment as she stood straight, basically at a loss. "Thank you, Justin."

"You can try on stuff in here. No one will bother you, but there's a restroom down the hall if you prefer. I'll be down at the sawmill."

"That's where you live?"

"There's an apartment upstairs. I'm renovating it in exchange for rent." He headed to the door, glanced back at her. "Have fun."

After he left, shutting the door behind him, Samantha dug through a stack of old skirts. She remembered playing "dress up" with her mother's clothes on a stormy day at sea, pretending she was a princess. It was easy to do with her mother's flowing, elegant clothes. Even aboard a research-and-salvage ship, Francesca Bennett had made sure she had a proper wardrobe.

The Knights Bridge vintage clothes ranged from fun and different to stolid and traditional. Any truly ratty pieces must have been culled already, as well as any real "finds." Samantha ran across everything from hippie bell-bottoms to ladylike hats and dumpy pleated skirts. Her favorite was a Pat Nixon wool coat, but unless the temperature dropped even more, it wasn't suitable for tomorrow's wedding.

A pile of cool-weather dresses yielded a timeless, caramel-colored lightweight wool shift. If it fit and didn't have too many moth holes, it would be perfect. She pulled the blinds on the windows and tried it on. Except for one tiny moth hole in the hem, it was in great shape, and the fit was fine—just a little tight around the hips.

All she needed now was a pair of shoes.

She raised the blinds and headed out with the dress hooked over one arm.

"You must be Samantha." A middle-aged woman with auburn-dyed hair poked her head out of a small office. "I'm Louise, Olivia and Jess's mom. Come. I have shoes for you."

Samantha entered the office. "Thank you."

"Our pleasure. We're all having fun outfitting you." Louise, in a navy fleece vest over a turtleneck, jeans and rubber boots, pointed at a half-dozen shoe boxes stacked on her cluttered rolltop oak desk. "I think the top pair will work. I hope they're the right size."

Samantha lifted the box off the stack. Louise—or someone—had taped pictures of Holland to every available space on the desk and wall. "Planning a trip to the Netherlands?"

"Randy and I are going this spring. He's my husband. He was at the fire the other day. Have you ever been to Holland?"

"Not in several years, but, yes, I have. I love Dutch bread and cheese." Samantha smiled as she pulled a neutral-colored pump out of the box. "And the museums, of course."

"I want to see Rembrandt's *Night Watch* at the Rijksmuseum and take a canal tour of Amsterdam. We'll get out into the Dutch countryside, too. We're going during tulip season." She paused, her breathing shallow, her cheeks flushed. "I've never flown overseas."

"It'll be an adventure," Samantha said.

Louise touched her fingertips to a picture of a Dutch canal. "That's right, it will be. Both my girls' weddings will be behind us. Spring will be a good time for Randy and me to get away." She seemed calmer as she turned to Samantha. "We were out in California a couple of months ago. We did the Pacific Coast Highway from Los Angeles up to San Francisco."

"That sounds very romantic," Samantha said, slipping off one of her trail shoes.

"It was like a second honeymoon. Such beautiful country. Dylan is from Southern California."

Samantha nodded. "I knew his father."

"Oh, right. Liv told me."

Louise sounded matter-of-fact, as if nothing she'd learned from her daughter troubled her. Samantha didn't pursue the subject. She peeled off her wool sock and tried on the pump. It was a bit loose in the heel, a common problem for her with shoes, but otherwise fit perfectly.

"What do you think?" Louise asked her.

"They'll work great. Thank you so much. I'll return the shoes tomorrow after the wedding."

"You can just leave them at Liv's place. I'll get them back to Heather—Heather Sloan. Justin's sister."

"I haven't met her yet," Samantha said. "Are you sure I won't be the skunk at the wedding?"

Louise didn't hesitate. "The more the merrier, and we're all delighted that Justin won't be on his own."

"We're not—this isn't—" Samantha stopped herself with an inward groan. She placed the shoe back with its mate, popped on the cover and tucked the shoe box under one arm. "Thank you again."

But Louise Frost wasn't finished. "It's not that Justin needs help getting a date. I don't mean that. He's just…" She waved a hand, obviously feeling awkward despite having been the one who brought up Justin Sloan's love life. "He'll settle down one of these days."

Samantha wasn't going there. "It should be a beautiful weekend for a wedding." She thanked Louise again and nodded at the Holland pictures. "I hope you have a great trip."

"Half the fun is planning the trip. I'll be heading out soon to get ready for the rehearsal. Let me know if there's anything else I can do."

Samantha went back outside with her vintage dress and borrowed shoes. She wondered what came next. Cold feet and a return to her senses, probably. It was absolute madness even to consider attending the wedding tomorrow.

Especially with Justin Sloan.

She'd let herself get caught up in events. Guilt, maybe, after misleading everyone. At least Louise Frost seemed to appreciate the distraction of helping her find a dress and shoes.

It was cool outside, a refreshing breeze stirring in the trees across the brook. Samantha didn't expect to see Justin there, but he was tossing a stone in the millpond, bright red leaves reflected in its clear water. She walked down to him, struck by just how incred-

ibly sexy and good-looking he was—rugged, fit, in
sync with his surroundings in a way she wasn't. She
couldn't help herself, but she'd have to be a rock not
to notice the shape of his strong shoulders and thighs,
how his black canvas shirt hung over his hips. His
square jaw and his eyes as he turned to her, as clear
and penetrating a blue as the September sky.

He pointed to her dress and shoe box. "Looks as
if you're all set."

She nodded. "I got lucky. I tried on one dress and
it fit, and one pair of shoes and they fit." She smiled,
trying not to look as if she had any interest at all in the
shape of his shoulders. "I should shop at Frost Millworks more often."

"Anything you'd wear in Boston or London?"

"Absolutely."

He stood close to her. She noticed the collar on his
canvas shirt had a frayed edge. He wouldn't be a man
who replaced things that still did the job, even if a bit
worn. He looked comfortable out here, at ease with
the rocky brook flowing behind him, the faint smell
of sawdust in the air, the sound of leaves rustling in
the breeze.

"What are you thinking about, Sam?"

No *way* was he getting a complete answer. "Just
taking in the day," she said.

"Do you like weddings?"

"Sure." She hadn't expected his question. "I haven't
been to that many, but I've always enjoyed them."

"Any at a country inn on a dead-end road?"

"Not one. This will be my first."

"Olivia's new to event planning, but Maggie's a pro.

It'll be good." He gave her an easy grin. "Just have to keep Buster out of the punch bowl."

Samantha laughed, relaxing somewhat. "Definitely." She felt the soft wool of the dress on her arm. "You can change your mind about having me there, you know."

"You'll do fine."

"I should warn you that I'm not that great at small talk. My grandfather wasn't, either. His sons took after him, but my mother has managed to teach my father the basics in the art of social chitchat. She's a natural."

"Francesca," Justin said. "Marine archaeologist."

"That's right. She has a knack for making people feel comfortable. I remember as a teenager going to a cocktail party in London. I didn't know a soul. Grandpa and Uncle Caleb were in a corner having an intense conversation with a geologist about Antarctic ice formations. My mother and father were laughing with a half-dozen people, talking about their favorite restaurants."

"Where did you fit in?"

"I eavesdropped on both conversations."

"Unnoticed?"

"Maybe. I don't know. I didn't care one way or the other. I was the only kid there. My cousins are much younger." She smiled, not sure why she'd told Justin so much about herself—wondered if he'd even wanted to know. "I had an unusual upbringing, maybe, but it was great. No complaints. It's not like you and Mark Flanagan and the Frosts and the O'Dunns. You all have known each other forever."

Justin picked up a small flat stone. "'Forever' is a long time. We grew up together."

He skimmed the stone across the millpond. He wasn't as curt and irritated as he had been after the fire—but at that point he'd just recognized her name, knew she was the woman who had misled Duncan McCaffrey. She'd put him on high alert right from the start. A man to have on your side in a fight, she thought. He was straightforward if not uncomplicated, and she appreciated this easier, less intimidating side of him.

"It must be great to know someone since nursery school," she said. "And you have a big family, too."

He winked at her. "Always something going on and someone with an opinion."

"My uncle and aunt have four kids, but they live in England. I don't know if it'll be forever, but I don't see them as much as I'd like. I saw them more, of course, when I was in London sorting through my grandfather's apartment there. Still more to be done but I moved on to Boston."

Justin toed another stone loose in the mud and grass on the edge of the stone walk. "What about friends?"

Samantha pushed back a sudden surge of self-consciousness. Friends. Why were they talking about her friends? What was it about him that kept making her feel so self-conscious? She adjusted her shoe box and dress in her arms. "I have friends all over the place," she said, almost dismissive.

"You live in a big world." He picked up the loosened stone and tossed it into the water, ripples going out from where it landed. He leaned in close to her. "It wasn't a good skipping stone."

"I wouldn't know a good one from a bad one."

"Easy to learn. Who did you grow up with, Sam Bennett?"

"Pirates," she said with a smile.

"I don't doubt it."

His tone struck her as sexy—deliberately sexy. She took a quick breath. "I should go."

"I need to get ready for the rehearsal," he said casually, then nodded to the sawmill entrance. "Come on up. You can check out an old sawmill while I get ready and decide what you want to do with yourself tonight. I can drop you off somewhere on my way to the rehearsal."

"I can manage on my own. You've done enough—"

"Sam, you don't have a car." He smiled. "You're at my mercy."

"It's been that way since the fire, hasn't it?"

He laughed, taking her shoe box and dress from her. "Now you're catching on."

Justin's apartment was cozy and sparsely furnished, with windows—obviously added when the mill was converted—that looked directly down at the millpond and dam. It was so *not* like her grandfather's Back Bay house or London apartment that Samantha wasn't sure what to make of it—or the man who lived here. On the way up the steep stairs, Justin had explained he hadn't started renovating the apartment yet. He was gathering ideas and might reconfigure the space altogether, even incorporate the lower level, now used for storage for Frost Millworks.

The place reminded Samantha of life aboard her parents' research ship when she was growing up, but maybe only because it was small and had a temporary feel to it. The living room was furnished with a simple couch, sturdy coffee and end tables and an inexpensive lamp. A flat-screen television sat on a turned-over apple crate. The adjoining galley kitchen had a mug and coffee press on the counter, a few dishes on open shelves and two empty beer bottles on the windowsill above the sink.

"Still planning to camp out tonight?" Justin asked, laying her dress over the back of a chair and placing her shoes on the seat.

Samantha shrugged. "I'm not getting in the way at Carriage Hill with a wedding tomorrow. I have a new tent, remember. Maybe the Frosts will let me camp out here."

"I'd look like a heel if I let you camp out in the cold when I have a warm place right here." He spoke casually, as if he were talking to one of his firefighting buddies. "You can spread out your sleeping bag on my couch."

"On your couch?"

"It's comfortable. I've fallen asleep there lots of times watching movies."

"Right." She pointed vaguely outside. "I left my backpack in your truck."

"I won't go off with it."

"That's not what I mean. I just…" She just was imagining herself sleeping on his damn couch. That, on top of going with him to the wedding tomorrow, and her head was spinning. "Never mind. I don't see many personal items in here. When did you move in?"

"A few weeks ago," he said, snatching up a couch pillow and brushing it off. "Dog hair. Our chocolate Lab sneaks onto the couch when I'm not looking. He likes to hang out with me, but he's going to get himself disinvited if he keeps this up."

"Where did you live before here?"

"Another house in town I renovated. That was for almost a year." He set the pillow back on the couch. "Before that, I lived in a cabin we own on a pond across the field from my folks' place."

"Did you fix it up, too?"

"Some."

Samantha sat on the edge of the couch, restless, certain she'd pop up again at the least provocation. "And all the while you've also been a volunteer firefighter. How often are you on call?"

"Depends on the week." He grabbed another pillow, gave it a shake, set it back down. "Ever live in a town that has a volunteer fire department, Sam?"

She shook her head. She didn't know what she was doing, what she was saying—why she wanted to know any details about his life. It was a long walk back to town, and even if she waited for Justin to drive her, she had no idea what she would do once she got there.

"You had my journal up here with you?" She got up again. "And you didn't read it? Really, Justin?"

"As much as I was tempted to read about pirates and brigands on a chilly autumn night, you can relax, Sam. As I said, I only glanced at the title page." He stood between her and the door, his gaze on her, no sign that he was offended by her skepticism. "I had a beer instead and hit the sack early."

She walked over to the window. "I was going to tell you everything this morning, but you already knew."

"We like a good mystery around here."

"I didn't lie. I didn't want to get you involved—"

"Save it, Sam. It's okay."

He ducked into what appeared to be the sole bedroom. Samantha stared out the window, watching the shadows on the brook as the sun sank lower in the sky. She hadn't realized so much time had passed since lunch. She looked out at the dense woods. She couldn't imagine pitching her tent there. She'd have to find a clearing of some sort.

She heard Justin emerge from the bedroom. She turned from the window and had to force herself not to gasp. He was nothing short of breathtaking in a dark gray suit, deep maroon tie and cordovan wing-tip shoes.

He grinned at her. "Mark gave me the name of a men's store in Boston. He doesn't want me showing up for his wedding in camouflage. Architects. The rehearsal dinner is at a country club just outside town."

Samantha recovered her composure. It wasn't good, this effect he had on her. "It's a nice suit. Will you be wearing a tux tomorrow?"

"Yep. Prepare yourself."

She wanted to tell him just how *not* funny that was. "Well, then." She cleared her throat. She couldn't stay here. Just couldn't. "I'll be on my way—"

"On your way where?" He moved toward her, the suit falling perfectly, sexily. "To pitch your tent on the dam?"

"I'll figure something out."

"There's that stubborn streak again." He was between her and the door now. "You don't give up, do you? Even when it's in your best interest."

"Grandpa liked to tell me I was plucky."

"Plucky." Justin smiled. "It's an old-fashioned word."

"Probably sexist, too. I've never needed rescuing before, but I did on Wednesday. I was in real trouble. I know it. I'm glad you were there." She swallowed past the tightness in her throat. "Enjoy your evening. Don't worry about me."

"Does anyone ever worry about you?"

His intensity combined with his quiet self-control made her stomach clench. She wanted this man on her side. Anyone would. And yet she found herself brushing off his concern with a quick smile and a flippant comment. "My family doesn't include many worriers."

"Why am I not surprised?"

"But we care about each other," she added, suddenly wanting to connect with him—to not let him think they had nothing in common, that the Bennetts were a bunch of thrill-seeking, self-absorbed lunatics. Because it wasn't true. She and Justin did have a few things in common. Their can-do natures, their outspokenness, their pragmatism. And the Bennetts were tight-knit in their own way, even if they didn't all live in the same small town the way the Sloans did.

Justin was watching her as if he could see her inner turmoil, as if he could read her jumble of thoughts and emotions. He was standing close enough to her that he could reach out and push loose curls behind her ear. He let his fingertips trail along the curve of her jaw, then, with one fingertip, raised her chin so that his eyes were leveled on hers.

She thought he said her name as he lowered his mouth to hers, easing his hand along her collarbone, around to the nape of her neck. His lips grazed hers not so much tentatively as with a promise—a hint of what he wanted to do, would do. His control just inflamed her more, her pulse racing, her blood heating. She grabbed his hand, intertwined her fingers with his.

"Justin…damn…"

Their kiss connected, deepened. His hand eased down her back to her waist, drawing her closer. All the toughness and hardness of Wednesday when he'd rescued her was there, but so was a warmth—a longing and urgency that had built over the past two days. It was as if their kiss was meant to be, unfinished business after the fire.

He stood back with an almost imperceptible smile. "I've been wanting to do that since I felt my padlock in your jacket." He winked at her and started for the door. "Be good, Sam."

Samantha tried to look as if she weren't about to melt into a puddle on the floor. "Was that payback for rescuing me?"

He paused, his hand on the door latch, and glanced back at her, his gaze unflinching. "Something like that."

"Or was it part of keeping an eye on me while I'm in Knights Bridge?"

"Something like that, too, but my couch does beat pitching a tent in the cold."

Once the door shut behind him, she raked both hands through her short curls and groaned. She'd let things get out of hand between her and Justin. She'd *helped* them get out of hand. Now the sexual electricity between them—however adrenaline-induced—had erupted into a kiss that had been anything but simple.

She went back to the window. The sun was lower in

the sky, a golden glow on the millpond. She wondered what it had been like here when the dam and sawmill had been built more than a century ago.

Whoever had painted *The Mill at Cider Brook,* whoever had written *The Adventures of Captain Farraday and Lady Elizabeth*—however they'd ended up in Harry Bennett's Boston house—had nothing to do with the contemporary Knights Bridge of Justin Sloan and his family and friends.

Samantha watched a large bird swoop down low over the millpond, then arc into the trees on the other side of the brook and disappear. She had no idea what kind of bird it was. Some kind of hawk? A raven?

Probably just a crow, she thought, turning away from the window.

All she had to do was stuff her dress and her shoes into her backpack and go find some quiet field where she could camp for the night. Who would know? Who would care? She could decide about the wedding in the morning. With no shower facilities, surely she would come to her senses and realize she couldn't attend the first-ever wedding at The Farm at Carriage Hill.

What would Duncan think of Olivia Frost? Had he run into any of the Frosts on his few trips to Knights Bridge before his untimely death?

Had he ever imagined his only son would find his way to the small New England town that Grace Webster had called home for more than seventy years—ever imagined that Dylan would discover the truth about Grace and her British flyer and their secret affair? Grace had already been expecting Duncan her first autumn in Knights Bridge as a teenager.

Pregnant, unmarried, displaced by the construction

of Quabbin from the only home she'd ever known, living in a new town with her father and grandmother and hopelessly in love with a man who was off to war, never to return to little Knights Bridge.

By comparison, Samantha thought, her biggest challenge at the moment was whether to clear out of Justin's apartment now or to stick around until he returned.

She could still taste his kiss, feel his mouth on hers. "Gad."

She was almost ecstatic when her phone rang and she saw it was her uncle.

He was shocked when she mentioned she might be attending Jessica Frost's wedding tomorrow. "Sam… are you out of your mind? Sneaking into Knights Bridge was one thing, but sneaking into a wedding?"

"I'm not sneaking," she said, sitting on the couch despite her restlessness. "The best man was going alone and—"

"So this is a *date?*" Uncle Caleb moaned as if he had a migraine. "That's even worse."

"It's not a date-date. It's a date of convenience." Samantha picked up one of the throw pillows and fought back an image of Justin's hands as he'd tossed it back on the couch. "The best man didn't invite me. Olivia Frost did. She's the bride's sister and Dylan McCaffrey's fiancée."

"Dylan McCaffrey," her uncle said. He might have said *the devil*.

"I know, I know. I'm playing in the lion's den, but it's not what you think. They know Duncan fired me. They know who I am. Anyway, Olivia and her friend Maggie, a caterer who helps run Carriage Hill, like the idea of the best man not being at the wedding on his own. Maybe they just want someone to keep him occupied. I don't know."

"There's a Maggie?"

"Yes, why?"

"My head's spinning."

"Maggie is also the best man's sister-in-law, by the way. She's married to one of his younger brothers. He has three. And an older brother. And a younger sister."

"That's six kids total."

"Correct."

Her uncle sighed into the phone. "I actually think I'm getting the players sorted out. It's scary. Who's the best man? He must have a name."

"Justin Sloan." She tried to keep her voice as matter-of-fact as possible. "He's the volunteer firefighter who grabbed me out of the cider mill after it caught fire."

"Hell, Sam," Caleb said without so much as a split-second's hesitation. "Isaac and I are in New Hampshire. Or maybe it's Vermont. Wait a sec—no, Isaac says we're in Maine. Bowdoin College. It'd take a while, but we can come fetch you."

The confusion over his location was all show. A distraction to get her mind off the wedding, Justin, Knights Bridge. Refocus her. Isaac's college tour. The upcoming Bennett family reunion. Her *life*.

It didn't work. "Thanks, but I'll manage." Samantha sank against the back of the couch and glanced over at her vintage dress hanging neatly over the chair. She didn't notice a big stain or tear or *something* that would help bring her around and provide her an excuse to demur from attending the wedding. "I know I'm not good at figuring out people's ulterior motives.

Do you think the wedding invitation is tactical—so they can keep an eye on me?"

"Yes. There's also a chance they're just being polite and they expect you to say no. I get invited to a lot of weddings that it's understood I'm supposed to send my regrets."

"I don't get why people do that."

"I know you don't, Sam."

She stood, not as tired or as stiff as she would have expected. The kiss, maybe. It had energized her. She bit her lip, wishing she hadn't even thought about it in case her uncle was in one of his mind-reading veins. "You think I shouldn't go," she said

"Didn't I just say that? And how can you go? You didn't pack a dress, did you?"

"I found a dress in castoffs from a vintage fashion show."

Caleb was silent. She almost could picture him pacing, scratching the back of his neck, debating whether to skip Bowdoin and head down to Knights Bridge. Finally he said, "You've spent too much time alone in your grandfather's house and apartment. Where are you sleeping tonight?" He added quickly, "No, don't answer. Damn. If you need me, you have my number."

"Thanks, Uncle Caleb. How's Isaac?"

"He's still sold on Amherst."

"Because of Grandpa," she said.

"Harry Bennett's shadow is long and impossible to ignore. I'm afraid it's having unforeseen and unexpected consequences for you and for Isaac." He added knowingly, "You should keep that in mind, Samantha."

She promised she would, and after she disconnected, took a deep cleansing breath. She noticed the sun had gone down. The millpond was gray and still, and vibrant red leaves stood out against the dusk sky. Her uncle was no doubt right, and attending tomorrow's wedding *was* utter madness, but she did have a great vintage dress to wear and shoes that almost fit.

Why not put aside the mysteries of Benjamin Farraday for a day?

It would, after all, be rude to let Olivia, Maggie and Olivia's mother go to such trouble and then back out for no good reason.

In the meantime, dinner and where to sleep remained problems to be solved.

Samantha went into the outdated galley kitchen and examined the contents of the refrigerator.

Beer. Local cheddar cheese. Three apples. Milk.

"Works for me," she said.

She got out the cheese and an apple and placed them on a plate, then found a knife and tore off a couple of sheets of paper towel to use as a napkin. She headed back to the living room and stood by the chair with her dress and shoes. She thought about her backpack, her new tent, and then she looked at the couch. She did have those navy flannel pajamas that covered her from chin to anklebone.

And there was a quilt folded on the back of the couch.

She could curl up under the blanket, and Justin wouldn't even know she was there. It wasn't a bad option. She liked camping and wanted to try her new tent, but where would she hang her vintage dress? What if spiders got in her borrowed shoes?

Her tent and the hard ground…or the couch and tomorrow's best man…

Each option had its advantages. Each had its draw-backs.

One thing was for certain. If she opted for the couch, that was where she would stay.

All night.

Seventeen

The rehearsal at Carriage Hill was brief and to the point, and no one freaked out—not even the bride's mother, which was saying something, because a year ago, Louise Frost would have turned ashen, started sweating and had to leave early. Having Samantha to focus on helped distract her. Louise had pulled Justin aside and told him how much she enjoyed meeting her, how different she was. "You've always wanted someone different, Justin."

He didn't get into it with her. He couldn't explain what was going on with Samantha to himself, much less to anyone else.

No regrets about kissing her, though. None. Stupid or not, there it was.

The rehearsal dinner was intimate, elegant and exactly what Jessica and her fair-haired, rangy, easygoing fiancé wanted ahead of the ceremony. They were happy, and that was what mattered to Justin—but his mind kept drifting to Samantha and whether she would be there when he returned to the sawmill.

As usual, Eric was the designated driver for the

evening. He edged over to Justin and Mark as they headed outside. "I can make multiple trips if need be. Wouldn't want anyone careening off the road on the dark drive home."

"We're meeting back at the Frost mill," Mark said. "Beer and stories by the campfire. Works for me. I'm not sleeping tonight, anyway."

"I'm fit to drive," Justin said.

His brother grinned at him. "Resisted sampling Scotch from Samantha Bennett's flask?"

"I should never have told you about that."

"I wonder if her grandfather had that flask in Antarctica."

"Feel free to ask her."

"I will," Eric said, oblivious to his younger brother's mood.

Eric collected the rest of his brothers and a few other guys while Justin took Mark—who wasn't fit to drive—in his truck. As they drove out to the sawmill, Justin decided to clear Samantha's presence at the wedding with his friend.

Mark shrugged. "Samantha Bennett? The treasure hunter you rescued?" He seemed vaguely aware of her. "Yeah, sure. No problem."

Justin grinned at him. "I could bring an orangutan tomorrow for all you'd notice or care at this point."

"Wait—she's an orangutan? I thought she was a treasure hunter."

"Forget it," Justin said. "You're too far gone. You're thinking about your bride-to-be and only your bride-to-be. As you should be."

"I'm getting married tomorrow, Justin."

"Yes, you are."

"To a Frost."

"To Jessica."

"Yeah. Jess."

Justin could hear the nervousness in his friend's voice, as if the reality of his imminent marriage was just hitting him. "It's going to be a great day tomorrow, Mark."

He nodded, staring out the window into the dark. "I used to think you'd end up with Olivia. Imagine that. If the two of us had married the Frost sisters. Liv and Dylan—they're good together. You, though, Justin. Hell." Mark shook his head as if he didn't get it. "You could have your pick of almost any single woman in Knights Bridge and probably a few of the married ones—"

"Tonight is your night, Mark. Beer and a campfire. Then a wedding in the morning."

Mark fell silent, for which Justin was grateful. When they arrived at Frost Millworks, Randy Frost had a campfire roaring out by the brook and beer in a cooler of ice. Samantha hadn't taken off into the woods with her tent. She was there, sitting on a blanket in front of the fire, with a smaller blanket from his couch around her shoulders. The firelight caught the gold in her eyes.

Randy patted her on the shoulder. "For those who haven't met her yet, this is Samantha Bennett, pirate expert and treasure hunter. She helped build the fire and load the beer into the cooler, and I invited her to stay for a while, at least until you guys get into a serious discussion about saving the world. Then she can call it a night." He grinned at the younger men gathering. "You all enjoy yourselves. Don't get yourselves arrested. I'll see you tomorrow at my daughter's wedding."

"Tomorrow will be great, Randy," Justin said. The rest of the guys chimed in with much the same as Randy headed up to his truck.

Brandon opened a beer. "Tell us about your pirates, Sam. I dressed up as a pirate for a masquerade ball in Boston a few weeks ago."

She started to get to her feet. "I should go—"

"No, no, stay," Brandon said, handing her his open beer bottle. "At least have a drink with us." He got another beer for himself and sat with her on her blanket. "What were real pirates like?"

Samantha sipped her beer. Justin had no doubt she could hold her own with the guys. "Depends on the pirate," she said. "Some were incredibly ruthless. Others weren't, although sometimes it was simply a question of practicality. For instance, taking over a ship and leaving the crew on an island, or giving them a vote, basically, on continuing as crew under the new command."

"Better than killing them but still wrong," Eric said. "Did a lot of them meet a bad end?"

She nodded. "Oh, yes."

"Shot?" Adam asked, grabbing a couple of beers, handing one to Justin, standing close to the hot fire and resisting the temptation to settle in next to Samantha.

"Hanging was the preferred method of execution," she said. "Some pirates also died at sea. 'Black Sam' Bellamy and most of his crew died in a major nor'easter off Cape Cod. The sunken remains of his ship, the *Whydah,* were discovered a few years ago.

They've yielded a lot of fascinating information about those aboard."

"And treasure?" Justin asked, keeping his voice as toneless as he could.

"Gold, yes," she said, no indication she thought he was goading her. "It can survive three centuries underwater, unlike valuable perishable cargo like cotton, cocoa, sugar, that sort of thing."

"Three centuries," Christopher said. "Long time."

Samantha drank more of the beer, then set it aside on the blanket. "Pirates were at their height in the Atlantic in the late seventeenth and early eighteenth century. The line between a legitimate privateer and an outright pirate was sometimes blurred. A ship captain could have a proper commission one day and be out of work the next."

"Who was the worst pirate?" Adam asked.

"Blackbeard is fairly notorious. He was an Englishman—his real name is Edward Teach. He was known, obviously, for his black beard. Some say he had forty wives."

"Ouch," Eric said.

"He had a fleet of pirate ships. Eventually a bounty was put on his head, and he was killed in a fierce battle off the coast of North Carolina. It's a grim ending." Samantha grimaced. "Let's just say he wasn't hanged."

"Go ahead and tell us," Brandon said, then added with a grin, "We can take it."

She stretched out her legs in front of her. "He was shot and stabbed multiple times, and the bounty hunter—a man named Maynard—cut off his head as proof he'd killed the infamous Blackbeard."

Mark gave a mock shudder. "Rough justice."

Adam, as well as Brandon, was now sitting cross-legged on Samantha's blanket. Justin stayed on his feet near the fire, watching her as she interacted with the guys. They weren't giving her a hard time. They were just hanging out, testing her a little, maybe, to see what she was like. They all knew how close she'd come to real trouble in the cider mill fire. That she'd trespassed, avoided telling anyone in town the whole story about herself and her reasons for being there—and that he was falling for her. Hard and fast. He could deny it, but his brothers would see right through him.

"Who's the pirate you think buried treasure out this way?" Eric asked.

Samantha faltered ever so slightly. "I never said—"

"Okay, okay," Eric said. "I get it. Top secret."

"I'm researching an American pirate named Benjamin Farraday." Samantha eased to her feet, leaving her beer bottle on the blanket. "I've only scratched the surface, but I'll spare you any more historical talk. Pirates fascinate me, obviously." She seemed momentarily uncertain what to say, then settled for a smile and a simple good-night. "See you all tomorrow."

Justin walked with her back to the sawmill. The night sky sparkled on the dark, still water of the millpond, and the brook flowed quietly over the dam. There was no wind, but the air was chilly, as cold a night as they'd had since last winter. "The temperature will bounce back tomorrow," he said. "I'm glad you decided not to camp out in your tent."

"I didn't say—"

"You didn't have to." He nodded back toward the fire. "The guys won't stay long. We're all in suits.

Can't be passing out drunk in a suit. Not that we would or ever have, mind you."

She smiled. "Paragons of virtue."

"We also have big brother Eric with his badge and reputation. He'd throw us all in jail, wedding or no wedding. We're just giving Mark a chance to calm down. Jess is staying with Dylan and Olivia tonight. They're making sure everything is set for tomorrow. Otherwise Dylan would be here."

"Is Maggie nervous, do you think?"

He noticed the moonlight catch her dark eyes and shook his head. "Maggie doesn't get nervous. She just said she'll poison any of us who show up tomorrow with a hangover. She wants everything to be perfect."

"I'm sure it will be."

"We have to be there by ten."

She licked her lips, just enough that it told him their kiss was on her mind. It was on his, too. It had been all evening. She glanced back at the sawmill, then again at him. "Justin—"

He opened the heavy front door. "Head on up. I'll be up soon. By the way, my feet hang off the couch but yours won't." His way of telling her he wouldn't be a problem tonight. He leaned in close to her. "Sleep tight."

As he returned to the campfire, he glanced back and saw that Samantha had gone upstairs to his apartment. He sat on her spot on the blanket with his beer. He noticed she didn't come back down with her backpack. The guys obviously noticed, too, but not one of them said a word. Eric did mutter, "Hell, Justin," under his breath, but that didn't necessarily have anything to do with Samantha Bennett.

After a few more stories, teasing and laughter, they
put out the fire, packed up the cooler and headed home.
Justin double-checked to make sure the fire was out,
and he scooped up a stray tie—Christopher's, he was
pretty sure. His youngest brother hated putting on a
suit.

When he went back upstairs, Samantha was sound
asleep on the couch. She had a quilt tucked up to her
chin. It was one his grandmother had made him as a
high-school graduation present—why, he didn't know,
but that was Gran. He doubted Samantha had anyone
in her family who made quilts.

She had one arm flung behind her. He could see
she was wearing navy flannel pajamas. They probably
weren't the deterrent for him that she hoped they were.

In fact, they didn't help at all. If anything they were
a particular temptation.

He ducked into his bedroom, imagining himself
peeling those flannel pj's off her, inch by inch.

Or just tearing them off her. That would work, too.

He got out of his expensive suit and left it in a heap
on the floor of his small closet. He climbed into bed.
Long day. Long week. Tomorrow would be good, with
Mark and Jess finally tying the knot. Having Samantha
there would be interesting. He didn't know if Olivia
and Maggie had been playing matchmaker, at least in
part. He wouldn't put it past them.

And just yesterday Maggie had been warning him
about his attraction to Samantha.

Justin stared at the ceiling and the shifting shadows
of the night. Only Eric knew about the gold coin, and
he probably hadn't thought about it in years—probably
didn't even realize Justin still had it. For all he knew,

it could be a copy, a worthless fake. He could think of a hundred innocuous reasons it could have been at the cider mill. Even that a real gold coin unrelated to pirate treasure could have been there.

Until Samantha Bennett and her mysterious Captain Benjamin Farraday.

He thought of stories he'd heard since he was a boy growing up out on Cider Brook, about the Hazeltons and other early settlers in the area. He'd figured most of the stories were "apocryphal," as Samantha had put it.

Now he wondered.

He rolled onto his side in his cold bed and swore under his breath. He was in a too-long stretch of celibacy with no particular end in sight, and here he was, alone in bed the night before his best friend's wedding, with a daring, impossible, crazily attractive woman asleep on his couch. But Samantha wasn't in Knights Bridge because of him—she was here because of the lost treasure of a pirate who'd been dead for three hundred years.

Eighteen

❧⟶⟶❧

The brigand Captain Farraday narrowed his black eyes. "You don't believe in romantic love, Bess?"

His words took her by surprise. Romantic love? What did a pirate know about such a thing? Of course, what did she know, the daughter of a loveless marriage—an arrangement— her mother called her relationship with Lord Fullerton.

Lady Elizabeth thrust her chin up at Captain Farraday. "If I do or I don't, I would never tell you."

He grinned at her. "You don't have to tell me. I have my answer."

As she sputtered in protest, he withdrew from the small, hot cabin.

Samantha smiled, remembering the passage as she made toast in Justin's galley kitchen ahead of the wedding festivities. She hadn't changed her mind with daylight. Maybe she should have. Maybe this one time, a Bennett getting cold feet would have been a good thing.

She found a small jar of peanut butter and smeared it thickly onto her toast. She'd made coffee, enough for two, but there was no sign of Justin yet. She'd gotten up early, folded her quilt, eyed her dress, debated sneaking out with her backpack—but here she was, still in her flannel pajamas, making herself at home.

When Justin ambled out of the bathroom, freshly showered and more or less dressed, she pretended not to notice that he didn't have his unbuttoned canvas shirt over a T-shirt this time, just his bare chest. He had on jeans and was barefoot, yawning as he shook off what she assumed were the aftereffects of his night out with the guys.

She pointed to the coffee press. "It's still hot if you'd like some coffee."

"Thanks." His gaze swept over her, but she was confident she didn't present a great temptation in her flannel pajamas. He smiled. "Hi there, Samantha."

She felt heat rush to her face. It was as if he were deliberately reminding her of the intimacy of their situation and their kiss yesterday. It was too much, his sexy smile, the glimpses of his bare chest, the two of them having toast and coffee in the close confines of the kitchen.

She made some vague excuse about needing to get dressed and bolted with the last of her toast. When she slipped into the bathroom with her backpack and wedding clothes, she saw in the mirror that she'd missed a critical button on her pajama top. *Surely* Justin hadn't noticed.

The bathroom was as outdated as the kitchen, but

everything worked and a small window looked out on the woods and fields past Frost Millworks. The morning sun seemed to hit every brightly colored leaf. As she took a quick shower and got dressed, she saw no evidence of another woman but didn't spend time looking. She was frustrated that she'd even thought of such a thing. It was that kiss and sleeping on the couch with Justin in the next room, so close—so dangerously close. She didn't trust their attraction to each other. She chalked it up to impulsiveness and the last vestiges of the fire.

Biology. Just a question of biology.

She did what she could with her limited supply of cosmetics. Needing a bit of lipstick for an unexpected dinner was different from getting herself ready for a wedding as the guest of the best man. Listening to the conversation last night, watching Justin, she'd realized that he had no enemies in Knights Bridge. He was a guy's guy—strong, competent, reliable, straightforward, if occasionally to the point of rudeness.

Then again, there hadn't been any women at the campfire. Maybe the female population of Knights Bridge was where she would find he had his share of enemies.

Samantha joined him in the living room. He had changed out of his jeans and was at ease and totally stunning in his best man's tuxedo. He wasn't a man who got worked up about every little thing—like having a fired treasure hunter thrust upon him for the day. She realized that she was drawn to him in part because of his self-confidence and self-control. He knew who he was and what he wanted.

It wasn't all broad shoulders and hard muscles, although there was that, too.

He pointed at her. "Some little hook thing isn't fastened on your dress."

"I have no idea what little hook thing—"

"Right here."

He took her by the shoulders and turned her so that her back was to him. She could feel his rough hands on her skin as he fastened a tiny hook and eye at the top of the back zipper of her dress.

When he finished, he gave his handiwork a little pat and stood back. "All set."

She turned to him. "Thank you."

"Easier to unfasten those things than fasten them."

Egad. She forced herself not to flush. "Right. I agree. I'm sure I'll manage to unfasten it." She almost choked. Had she *said* that? She rushed on before he could notice how uncomfortable she was. "I guess we're ready, then. Are you nervous at all about serving as best man?"

He grinned at her. "Not even a little."

She believed him. "Once you've fought a fire or two hundred, it probably takes a lot to get you worked up. Nervous, I mean." She coughed, covering for her awkwardness. Normally she wasn't someone who tripped over her words—or who worried that much if she did. "I'm not the nervous type, either, but I can still pack up my stuff and hit the road, finish my hike along Cider Brook."

"Your call. You won't know many people at the wedding, and the circumstances are unusual."

"If you think I should back out—"

"Didn't say that."

He hadn't, she realized. "It would be rude not to go at this point, and I want to go. Thank you. It's a great day for your friends."

"Mark says he thinks of it as Jess's day. He wants to make it the wedding she's always dreamed of."

"That's sweet. He seems like a great guy."

"Yeah." Justin shrugged. "He's Mark." He nodded to the door. "You go first. Might want to take extra care in those shoes."

Samantha did as he suggested, her shoes slipping slightly in the heels as she edged down the steep stairs. She glanced back at him, walking smoothly behind her, no hint he was uncomfortable in his tux. She almost slipped but righted herself as she came to the outside door.

A few minutes later, she was next to Justin in his truck, about to attend a Knights Bridge wedding—and the first-ever wedding at the charming Farm at Carriage Hill.

The wedding ceremony was short and perfect, taking place among gathered guests on the side lawn in the shade of an old maple tree, its leaves just beginning to turn a vibrant red-orange. Samantha could hardly take her eyes off the best man. As the ceremony ended, she had a moment of pure fantasy, picturing herself at her own garden wedding, with the man of her dreams.

Then Justin's gaze leveled on her, and he gave her a knowing grin. Blood rushed to her cheeks as if he could read her mind—which she was beginning to think he actually could. She bolted for the back garden. He would have to pose for pictures with the wedding party. That would buy her time to get her bearings.

Dylan eased in next to her with Buster on a leash. She smiled at them. "It was a beautiful wedding. Thank you for having me here."

"Glad you said yes." He nodded to a cluster of mostly spent light maroon coneflowers. "Coneflowers are also known as echinacea, did you know?"

"I did, actually. Just don't ask me to identify all the different kinds of mint."

"Olivia wrote to me on a Carriage Hill note card she designed. It was the first time I'd heard of her or Knights Bridge. I thought the chives were clover."

Samantha laughed, relaxing slightly. "Totally understandable, I would think." She glanced back toward the side lawn, where Justin was laughing with Mark and Jess, who looked stunning in her simple white wedding gown. Justin looked so at ease, so drop-dead handsome. She loved her borrowed dress, but she'd noticed another moth hole. She put that thought aside and smiled at Dylan. "Soon it'll be your turn for a Carriage Hill wedding."

"It won't be outdoors, that's for sure." He didn't show any hint of trepidation or second thoughts. "Mark and Jess are going out to California for their honeymoon. Noah and Phoebe are meeting them for dinner in San Diego."

"Phoebe is Maggie's librarian sister who discovered dresses sewn decades ago by a woman from Knights Bridge who went to Hollywood and became an Oscar-winning costume designer." Samantha took an exaggerated breath. "Did I get that right?"

Dylan smiled. "Exactly right. She and Noah are returning to Knights Bridge soon, but she's resigned as librarian. They'd have flown out here special for the wedding, but Mark and Jess talked them out of it. They want Noah and Phoebe to have this time."

"Will they make their home here in town?"

"Here and about seven other places, knowing Noah."

Samantha didn't know if Dylan was serious. "Your father liked Noah so much. He wanted him to find someone." She immediately regretted her words. "But you know that."

"My father and I didn't see as much of each other as we'd have liked." He paused as Buster flopped down at his feet. He reached down and patted the big dog. "We thought there was plenty of time, but there wasn't."

Dylan's simple statement conveyed a depth of emotion and loss that reminded Samantha that Duncan hadn't been just a spirited treasure hunter and adventurer to him but a father, if an elusive father. "I'm sorry—"

"You didn't say anything wrong, Samantha. I'm glad the weeks you worked with him were good ones for both of you. He only let you go because he hadn't asked enough questions about your background. I checked the records. You didn't lie to him."

"Deliberate omissions can be as damaging as lies."

"And you deliberately omitted a few things?"

"Just that I'd followed him out here. I honestly didn't think to tell him about my family."

"But it complicated things when he found out," Dylan said.

She nodded. "I wanted so much to work with him. Coming out here that one day in March was innocent enough—at least to me—but I knew it wouldn't look good. So I didn't mention it."

"You hadn't counted on Justin," Dylan said.

"I had not." She plucked a spent coneflower blossom and cupped it in her palm. "It's hard to believe the flowers are almost all gone." She tossed the blossom over the stone wall toward the adjoining field and added, half to herself, "I won't be staying long."

"Justin won't be able to get away for a while."

"That's fine. I can scoot off on my own."

"In those shoes?"

She made a face. "I almost forgot I don't have a car, and I left my backpack at Justin's apartment." She caught herself, but too late. "He offered me his couch last night. It was cold—"

"I'm not keeping up on sleeping arrangements," Dylan said with a small smile.

She wished she'd started walking to Maine to meet Caleb and Isaac, or to Amherst to call upon her grandfather's ghost to knock some sense into her. Clear her mind of the insidious, irresistible charms of Justin Sloan and his friends and little Knights Bridge.

She bent down, flicked a bit of mulch off the toe of her shoe and stood up again. "They're great shoes, but they aren't suited to trekking."

"So you're still at Justin's mercy," Dylan said with an enigmatic smile.

Time to change the subject. "Buster did great today, too. What a nice dog."

"He has his moments. Olivia's been a good influence on him. I don't know that I have, and Maggie's boys—those two love to get him excited." Dylan looked out toward Carriage Hill, then shifted back to Samantha. "I talked to Loretta Wrentham. Do you know who she is?"

"Your attorney." Samantha started to say more, then decided to leave it at that. It wasn't up to her to bring up Duncan's short-lived romantic relationship with his son's California lawyer. If Dylan knew, he knew. If he didn't—she wasn't telling him. "What did she have to say?"

"That my father told her you had nerve. He meant it as a compliment."

"Was that before or after he decided to fire me?"

"After."

After. Samantha felt a wave of regret and grief and fought back an urge to leap over the stone wall and run—get away from Dylan, Justin, the wedding. She could run through the fields of wildflowers, hike up Carriage Hill and look out at the valley where her pirate might have ventured three hundred years ago. Remind herself what she'd come to Knights Bridge to do.

"Your father was a remarkable man," she said quietly.

"He wasn't perfect."

"Who is? I liked him a lot, Dylan. Everyone on his team did."

"Did he remind you of your grandfather?"

"What? My grandfather—" Samantha stood straight, his question catching her by surprise—a reminder that this was a man who'd navigated launching a successful high-tech entertainment company and taking it public. She got her bearings, then responded. "In some ways, yes, your father did remind me of my grandfather."

"They died within a year of each other."

"Grandpa was much older. In his nineties. And he knew the end was near. Your father—"

"He didn't see the end coming. Just as well, maybe."

"He said you have good instincts about people and that was what Noah needed, why you two worked so well together."

Dylan smiled, his intensity easing. "Also helps that I can fight and Noah can't."

"I could take that as a warning, you know."

"You could."

He ran his fingers over some kind of mint that had the far corner of the raised bed to itself, bringing out the distinctive scent. "Loretta's known Noah and me for years, but she didn't meet my father until shortly before his death. It was around the same time you started working for him."

"Before Portugal but after Knights Bridge."

"That's right."

Samantha understood that he was indicating to her that he knew about Loretta Wrentham's affair with his father. It hadn't been a secret among his staff in Portugal, but Duncan hadn't broadcast it, either. He'd just clearly been very taken with her.

"Your father loved his work, but it was often more tedious than most people realize," she said carefully. "A lot of dead ends, false leads, digging into dry facts that might mean something and might not. I don't think he expected to fall in love with Knights Bridge."

"Loretta was here for the first time a few weeks ago." Dylan gave a small laugh. "She thinks I'm having a winter wedding just to torture her, but she'll be here. She'll just have to buy herself some boots and mittens."

"She sounds like a character. But she's worried about me being here, isn't she?"

"It's okay if she is. That's her job."

"Yep." Justin stepped over a raised bed onto their mulched path. "We can handle you. Can't we, Dylan?"

Dylan laughed. "I have a feeling you can handle Samantha all by yourself. And vice versa." He got Buster to his feet. "I'll see if Olivia and Maggie need my help. Maggie said to leave everything to her, but Olivia won't be able to resist. Pictures done, I take it?"

"The ones I had to be in are done. They're doing a few more with Jess and Mark. Mark's getting sick of smiling, but he'll get through it." Justin turned to Samantha, his tie, she noticed, already loosened. "Why don't I introduce you to some folks?"

She wasn't at all sure she answered before he swept her off to the terrace, where several elderly women had gathered at the table. "Ladies," Justin said, "this is Samantha Bennett, the pirate hunter I told you about. Sam, meet Grace Webster, Audrey Frost and Evelyn Sloan. Grace is Dylan's grandmother and a retired teacher. Audrey is Jess and Olivia's grandmother and a retired bookkeeper at the school. Evelyn is my grandmother and never worked a day in her life." He grinned at her. "Right, Gran?"

She seemed to be the youngest of the three women, if not by much, and looked at Samantha, a spark of amusement in her aged eyes. "I ran the nursery school that expelled Justin at four. He was incorrigible. He still is."

Samantha had no idea if Evelyn was telling the truth but she laughed. Justin pulled out a chair for her, and she sat. He remained on his feet, loosening his tie even more. As they nibbled on hors d'oeuvres in the early-autumn shade, the elderly women chatted with an ease and familiarity born of having known each other for decades. They all knew about the fire at the cider mill and Justin's heroics, which he waved off when they mentioned them.

Grace helped herself to a stuffed mushroom. "I understand that you knew Duncan McCaffrey. He was quite a character, wasn't he? He was my son, you know."

"I didn't know that when I worked with him, but I can see him in you." Samantha hesitated, then added, "I only knew him for a short time."

Grace, in her early nineties but alert, was clearly on top of her game. "I know you two had a falling-out." Her eyes softened. "Tell me about him."

Samantha glanced at Justin, but he wasn't coming to her rescue this time. He touched her shoulder and lowered his mouth to her ear. "They're a curious lot. Have fun. I'll get you a drink and get you out of here before they decide to fingerprint you."

He disappeared through the mudroom into the kitchen. Samantha smiled at the trio of women. "Duncan was an adventurer at heart, but he was serious about his work and his reputation. He liked to dig into a mystery that intrigued him, whether it was a painting missing for centuries or pillaged Portuguese gold."

"And you?" Grace asked, her gray eyes—so like her son's—narrowed on Samantha.

She kept her tone even. "I'm serious about my work, too."

"And your reputation?"

She nodded. "Yes."

Evelyn Sloan leaned forward and snatched a cracker with cheese from the tray in the middle of the table.

Nothing about her reminded Samantha of Justin, except perhaps her frankness. "Were you looking for treasure at Justin's cider mill?"

"I was getting out of the storm," she said, careful, diplomatic.

"What would you have done if Justin hadn't pulled you out of the fire?"

Samantha decided not to get into her assessment of the danger she'd been in, since the three women would no doubt agree with whatever the firefighters and police officer on the scene had told them. She grabbed a small square of cheese. "It doesn't matter now. I'm very grateful for Justin's help."

"I would be, too," Audrey Frost said half under her breath.

Samantha held back a laugh. "Because he arrived when he did, he was able to get the fire department out there in time to save the mill."

"It wouldn't have been a great loss if you ask me," his grandmother said.

Grace settled back in her chair. "You and your family have some experience getting yourself out of tight quarters, don't you, Samantha?"

Fortunately, Justin returned with a tray of iced tea. Samantha seized the moment. She took a glass of tea—complete with mint sprigs and a slice of lemon—and got to her feet, mumbling niceties and retreating as fast as she could without being rude. She had no particular destination in mind, just away from the scrutiny of the three older women and, especially, her own discomfort.

Her fourth day in Knights Bridge, and the locals had her thoroughly discombobulated.

And they knew it. *Especially* Justin.

She didn't realize he was behind her until she arrived at the lawn behind the older section of the center-chimney house, where tables were set up for the wedding lunch. Her throat tightened at the white cloths, silver, clear vases of hydrangeas, tinted burgundy with the arrival of autumn, and small, prettily bundled favors.

Justin looked at ease, but he would be comfortable here. These were people he had known his entire life. She was the outsider—the stranger.

Samantha spun around at him, almost spilling her iced tea. "Loretta Wrentham and Dylan don't think I had anything to do with Duncan's death, do they?"

"Whoa. I was thinking you were about to comment on lunch."

She should have. She wanted to have a normal conversation about the wedding, the lunch, the gorgeous day. But it wasn't possible. She was the treasure hunter Duncan McCaffrey had fired. The stranger with the weird family. The woman who'd be dead but for one of their own.

Better not to pretend she could fit in.

She tried not to sound defensive as she continued. "It never occurred to me that Duncan was having heart troubles. I never saw any signs of a problem. I wouldn't. I'm not a doctor. When he fired me, he wasn't screaming or upset—he'd let people go before. He'd been a businessman. It wasn't anything new. He wasn't happy about it, but there was no acrimony." She knew she was talking too fast—talking more to herself than to the man next to her. "I'm sorry. I should leave."

"Not before lunch." Justin caught a sprig of mint as

it was about to fall off the edge of her iced tea glass. He tossed it into the grass. He was calm, as if nothing about her rush of emotion got to him. He gave her one of his sexy winks. "It'd look like I said something asinine and ran you off. You don't want that, do you? Leaving me to explain myself."

Samantha sighed. "You're not worried about explaining yourself."

"Would you buy a little worried?"

"No."

He grinned. "See why I keep wanting to kiss you?"

"It's weddings," she said. "They addle people's brains."

"Maybe it's you." He placed a hand on her waist, as if she were his real guest for the day instead of one more or less foisted upon him. "All that talk of pirates."

She let herself sink into his hand, imagined it skimming over her hips. *Not good.* She stood straight, drank some of her tea. "I think you're just keeping an eye on me in case I lead you to buried treasure."

He flicked a fly away from her shoulder. "What if it's the other way around and you're the one keeping an eye on me?"

"Why would I think you could lead me to buried treasure?"

"The cider mill has something to do with your Captain Farraday and his missing treasure, doesn't it?"

"As I told you, tales of buried pirate treasure are mostly discredited."

"What about treasure aboard sunken pirate ships?"

"That's different," she admitted. "But it's complicated, and not a subject for a wedding reception—"

"It's okay, Sam. Relax. Throttle back for a bit and

enjoy the day." His deep blue eyes held hers, unreadable, but he smiled. "Lunch smells good, doesn't it?"

She hadn't noticed, but now she did, appreciating the mix of scents emanating from inside the house. Butter, apples, cinnamon, warm bread. "It does smell good, yes, definitely."

She wanted to let herself be distracted, to forget her reasons for being in Knights Bridge and the suspicion—the understandable suspicion—she was under by the people around her.

She returned his smile. "I think it's time for champagne, don't you?"

He drew her a little closer to him. "Or maybe some of that Scotch in your grandfather's flask," he said, then winked and headed back to his best man's duties.

It was a few moments before she got her breath back.

Samantha stayed for lunch but left before the cake was cut. Everything was perfect. The food, the company, the setting, the weather. Justin. Watching him with his friends and family, she saw there was more to the taciturn man who'd rescued her than she'd realized.

The best thing she could do for him—and for herself—was to accept that she didn't belong here and go about her business. "I have to go," she whispered to him as she rose from their table. "Thank you. It's been a wonderful day."

He didn't stop her. He had more best man duties, and maybe he wouldn't have, anyway. She slipped around the side of the house to the cars and trucks parked out front for the wedding, hoping to hitch a ride with a departing guest.

But no one was leaving, not yet.

"Well, damn. What now?"

No choice. None. She had to get herself back to Justin's sawmill apartment, fetch her backpack and figure out where to sleep tonight. *Not* on his couch.

Not in his bed, either.

Weddings, she thought. They absolutely did addle people's brains.

She sucked in a breath, called on the intrepid spirit of her grandfather and headed up Carriage Hill Road in her vintage dress and borrowed shoes.

Nineteen

Samantha had just passed Grace Webster's former property when Christopher Sloan pulled over in his truck. "Justin said you were stubborn. Climb in. I'm missing the dancing but I'm on duty in an hour. Where you off to?"

"To retrieve my backpack."

"It's still at Justin's place?"

She didn't want to get into the details and responded with a nod. "Did he send you after me?"

"Told me to look out for you." Christopher gave her what she was beginning to recognize as a Sloan smile. "Wouldn't want you getting blisters. Did you panic back there?"

"Panic?"

"It's not unusual to be jumpy at a gathering a few days after getting caught in a fire, even if you're normally not the type to have panic attacks." The grin again. "Must be a reason for you to run off in high heels."

"Two-inch heels aren't that bad. Anyway, I didn't panic."

"Right." As if now he knew what had gotten into her. "You have the key to Justin's place?"

She shook her head. "I didn't think of it being locked."

"Given your skills with his padlock, you could probably manage, but I know where he keeps his spare. Where are you going after you pick up your backpack?"

"The cider mill," she said without hesitation.

"I'll take you out there."

And he did, first showing her the extra key tucked by a gutter, then waiting for her while she changed her clothes and grabbed her backpack. She was half-way out the door when she went back and scrawled a note to Justin on a small pad on the kitchen counter.

Sorry to run but thank you for everything.
Yours truly,
Samantha

She frowned. *Yours truly?* It sounded stiff, but hugs and kisses was too familiar.

What was she doing?

She left the note on the counter and ran back downstairs. Christopher Sloan was drumming his fingers on the steering wheel, obviously impatient. "Thanks for waiting," she said, climbing in. "I know you must be in a rush. I can walk—"

"It's okay. We'll make it."

Samantha didn't change her mind as he drove her out to Cider Brook. He parked on the dirt road, not taking the time to venture down the driveway and back out. "I appreciate this so much, Christopher."

He shrugged. "Not a problem. You have a phone. Call one of us if you run into trouble."

He sounded as if he at least half expected she *would* run into trouble, but she jumped out of his truck with her backpack and headed down the rough driveway to the clearing and the nineteenth-century cider mill. Abandoned, partially burned and boarded up, it little resembled its earlier incarnation in the photographs at the Swift River Country Store and even less the cider mill in the painting in her grandfather's closet—so much so that she wondered if adrenaline and wishful thinking had made her see a similarity where none existed. It could have been another Cider Brook. One in New Hampshire or Vermont, maybe, or a creation of the painter's imagination.

But she didn't think so. She believed the painting was of *this* cider mill.

She saw the door wasn't padlocked and went inside. When she smelled the burned wood, her heart raced and her palms felt clammy. She ran back out and steadied herself as she sat on her boulder above the brook and watched the water tumble over the small dam.

She hadn't expected to flee the wedding.

Flee was the only word for it, as un-Bennett-like as it had been of her.

And it wasn't only the wedding that she'd fled. It was Justin and her attraction to him. She was getting in too deep with a man for whom she was, at best, a momentary distraction. Her history with Duncan McCaffrey and her search for answers about Benjamin Farraday had caused suspicion and distrust, a wariness toward her that she could well understand.

She glanced at the mill behind her. She couldn't go

back in time and change the choices she'd made once Caleb and Isaac had dropped her off. She couldn't find a different place to get out of the storm. She couldn't explain herself right from the start. She couldn't take away her own questions, suspicions, worries.

She could hear her grandfather and knew what he would tell her now. *"Don't be so hard on yourself, Samantha. You got out of that fire alive. Be grateful and move on."*

She sighed. It wasn't always so easy to forgive yourself, be grateful and move on.

Letting Justin kiss her—kissing him back—hadn't helped her sense of equilibrium.

"Gad. Why did you kiss him back?"

Too much reading about rogue pirates, she told herself, avoiding any deeper reasons, the ones that had to do with her heart. Ultimately, she knew, that was why she'd left the wedding. Fleeing had been an act of self-protection.

She pushed aside her thoughts and settled on a reasonably level, grassy section between the mill and the brook to pitch her new tent. It was a bit more complicated than she'd anticipated, but she managed, finishing up just as dark clouds moved in from the west. This time she did a thorough check of the weather on her phone. There was no threat of severe storms. A chance of a passing shower later and colder temperatures overnight. Nothing worrisome—nothing that would drive her from her tent back to Justin's couch.

She rolled up her jeans to just below her knees, pulled off her shoes and socks and stepped onto the narrow dam, inhaling sharply at just how cold the brook was. She stood still, watching the clear water flow from the millpond over her bare feet on the dam and then down the spillway. What an amazing spot. If only she'd waited until today to venture to Cider Brook. She would have arrived at the clearing now, with the owner at a wedding, instead of in the middle of a dangerous thunderstorm.

She heard a vehicle stop out on the dirt road, then a door shut. In another moment she was aware of Justin behind her on the driveway. "Thank you for not startling me," she said without looking back at him. "I don't want to lose my balance. I'd get very wet."

"Or you'd hit your head on a rock and get a concussion."

"I'd make sure I fell into the deeper water in the pond and not on the rocks." She steadied herself in the constant flow of water over the stone-and-earth dam. "The water is even colder than I expected."

"It warms up for five minutes on the Fourth of July."

His voice was close now. He had to be on the bank of the brook, but Samantha still didn't look back. "Don't make me laugh."

"I won't, but if you fall, you're on your own. I'm not jumping into that cold water to rescue you."

"The millpond probably isn't over my head. I'm more likely to get hypothermia and freeze to death than I am to drown."

"You won't freeze or drown," he said. "You'll just get wet and cold."

"The optimist."

She turned carefully, mindful of any slippery mud, sodden leaves or rocks hidden under the cold water atop the dam. Justin stood at the end of the dam, out of his wedding tuxedo now and back in jeans, a T-shirt and a canvas shirt. Whether in his usual clothes or in an expensive suit, he looked comfortable with himself and his world.

And fit and handsome. Always fit and handsome.

"Or are you just a pragmatist?" she asked him. "Neither a pessimist nor an optimist but someone who takes life as it is?"

"Doesn't matter. We all have to take life as it is."

"You don't believe we create our own destinies?"

He grinned at her. "I think you're creating your own destiny right now. You have cold feet and a cold night ahead of you in a tent."

Not, she saw, the time to make serious conversation, but, in a way, she had her answer. She made her way back along the dam. Justin put out a hand, and she took it as she jumped onto the bank.

"Thanks," she said, letting go of his hand. "Do you want to dip your feet into the water?"

"Why would I want to do that?"

"It's refreshing." She stood up on a flat rock, still warm from the sun. "Although my feet are so cold right now they hurt."

"That's quite an invitation, Sam."

She wondered if a hundred years ago Zeke and Henrietta had dipped their feet into Cider Brook. How romantic it must have been out here for a young couple, with the cider mill in full operation. But Samantha warned herself not to get carried away speculating about the unknown couple. She didn't even know if they *were* a couple. They could have been brother and sister, or mere acquaintances—and couple, siblings or acquaintances, the odds they had anything to do with Benjamin Farraday were slim at best.

"I think I can feel my toes again." She gave Justin a light smile. "I guess it's a good thing you weren't a bear coming through the woods. Now, that would have startled me. I can't say for sure I would have been able to control my fall and end up in the pond if you'd been a bear."

He shook his head at her. "It never occurred to you I was a bear."

"You said you have black bears out here. How was the rest of the wedding?"

"There was dancing after you left. I had to dance with my grandmother."

"I doubt you suffered for dance partners, and you would have danced with your grandmother whether or not I'd stayed." Samantha sat on her rock and pulled on a wool sock over her partially dry left foot. Her toes were numb, but she didn't regret her dip in the cold water. "What about your brothers? Did your grandmother dance with them?"

"Couldn't hold her back." He scooped up a sock that had ended up down toward the brook and handed it to her. "Gran grilled me about you."

"Oh, dear. What did you tell her?"

"Nothing she didn't already know."

"I'm a subject of town gossip. I guess it makes sense, given the fire, if nothing else." She put on her second sock, aware of Justin's eyes on her as she reached for her trail shoe. "Did your grandmother really expel you from nursery school?"

"Nah. That was just Gran and me joking around, but I wouldn't have put it past her. She didn't play favorites with my brothers and me just because we were her grandkids. We had to toe the line. I had my share of time-outs."

"What about high school?"

"Suspended once. Never expelled."

Samantha eased her foot into her trail shoe, relieved she hadn't gotten blisters from her borrowed shoes. "Why were you suspended?"

"A fight. No regrets." Justin nodded to her. "Your fingers look cold. Need help tying your shoes?"

"Nope. I can manage. Thanks." It was just too intimate to think about, Justin Sloan tying her shoes, although he did have a point about her fingers. They were cold from putting her sock and shoe on her cold foot. She had to tie more slowly than usual. "Who was the fight with that got you suspended? Were you settling a score with a bully?"

"Nothing so noble. Just fighting with today's groom."

Samantha sat up straight. "*Mark?* Did he hold his own with you?"

Justin smiled as he picked up a stick and tossed it into the brook. "He did not. That was the point of the fight, as I recall. He told me he could hold his own in a fight with me, and he had to prove it. He was wrong. He couldn't. He could be an arrogant SOB."

"And this morning you were the best man at his wedding. What about Brandon and Maggie? Did they get a chance to dance?"

"He grabbed her out of the kitchen for a quick spin."

Samantha put on her other shoe, her fingers warmer as she tied the laces. It would be a while before her feet warmed up. "I gather they were separated for a time."

"Longer than they should have been by their own

accounts. Maggie's two younger sisters are still annoyed with him."

"The wounds between a couple often spread to those around them." She stood, noticing the dark clouds had moved overhead, the gray light deepening the blue in Justin's eyes. She pictured him dancing and suddenly wished she had stayed longer. "I gather Maggie isn't still mad at Brandon, and he's not still mad at her."

Justin shook his head. "Haven't asked. Won't."

"But you'd be able to tell, wouldn't you?"

"Doesn't matter. I stay out of my brothers' romantic lives."

"Do they stay out of yours?"

His gaze settled on her, then he grinned. "Not a chance. Meddling bastards." He nodded to her tent. "Determined to stay out here, aren't you?"

"If you don't object, since it's your land."

"Now she cares," he said with a wink.

Samantha ignored his remark. "Staying out here feels like unfinished business for me, somehow. I suppose it's because of the fire, but I feel safe now." She smiled. "Bears or no bears."

"Suit yourself. I have no objection." He stood back, his expression hard to read. Deliberately so, it seemed. "Going to do a little treasure hunting while you're camping?"

"I suspect if a pirate had hidden treasure out here, someone would have found it by now." She kept her tone steady, if a little cool given his scrutiny. "It feels remote to me, but I keep in mind that much of this land was once cleared for farming, a cider mill operated successfully here for decades, and you, your brothers and who-knows-who-else partied out here. That's a lot of people for buried treasure to have gone unnoticed for three hundred years."

"Who would treasure found here belong to?"

"Eighteenth-century treasure? It would belong to you. It's your property."

"You could sneak off with it and say you found it in a spot where you could legally keep it."

"I couldn't do that, Justin, and I wouldn't. It's not how I operate."

He didn't look as if he regretted his comment in the slightest. "So, what's this pirate to you, Sam?" he asked, picking up another stray stick. "Why Benjamin Farraday?"

"His fate is a puzzle—a mystery I'm interested in solving. It's what I do."

Justin flung the stick across the brook. It hit a tree, then disappeared into the browning ferns. "Did you think Duncan would solve the mystery of your Captain Farraday first, before you could?"

Samantha forced herself to take a breath before she responded. "That he'd beat me to it, you mean? I hadn't reached that conclusion. I just wanted to know why he was in Knights Bridge." And that was *before* she'd discovered *The Mill at Cider Brook* and *The Adventures of Captain Farraday and Lady Elizabeth.* "When I realized Duncan's presence had nothing to do with Benjamin Farraday, I didn't say anything about having come here myself. It never occurred to me he would find out and think I'd been spying on him."

"But you had been spying on him," Justin said, blunt.

"It wasn't spying-spying. I never had plans to steal secrets from him or anything like that."

"What if he had been out here because of Farraday?"

"He wasn't, but I'd have asked to work with him on whatever project he had in mind."

Justin looked unconvinced as he moved closer to her tent, which hadn't collapsed or sunk since she'd pitched it—she must have gotten it right. He glanced back at her. "Mad at me for telling him about you?"

"As if you care if I am."

He grinned. "I care."

She rolled her eyes. "I think I like you better taciturn."

He leaned in close to her. "I think you like me best kissing you."

"Maybe that, too." Her head was spinning now. "Anyway, there was no reason for you not to tell Duncan about me, so, no, I'm not mad at you or anyone else—except myself."

Justin put a hand on the top of her tent, as if to test if it would collapse. "You went to work for him for legitimate reasons?"

"Totally legitimate."

"Nothing to do with Farraday?"

"I didn't say that. I wanted to learn from Duncan—and I did—but I also envisioned getting him interested in Farraday and perhaps helping to sort out what happened to him, the rumors that he'd fled west, the fate of his last ship."

"Somehow it figures that both you and Duncan McCaffrey ended up in Knights Bridge. A couple of treasure hunters here for different reasons." Justin turned back to her, the shadows bringing out the sharp lines of his face. There was no humor in his eyes now. "Meant to be, you think?"

"Maybe."

He stepped closer and traced her lips with his fingertips, then kissed her softly, just long enough to leave her with no uncertainty whatsoever of what he wanted. More, she thought. Much more.

"Go ahead and camp out here tonight, Sam." He tapped her chin and grinned, the humor back as fast as it had disappeared. "If you get cold, you know where to find me. You can always head up to my folks' place. By the way, they've invited you to a post-wedding brunch up at the house tomorrow."

"A brunch—"

"Loads of people will be there. Not as many as at the wedding, but plenty. Rain or shine, there'll be volleyball. It'll be good. Gran and my mother think you're cute."

"Cute?"

"It's the eyes. Your eyes are cute as hell, Sam."

She couldn't get a decent breath. "Right. Didn't I say weddings addle people's brains?"

He laughed as he started up the driveway, his boots crunching on the gravel. "Everyone's going to think you're camping out tonight because things got too hot between us last night at my place."

"How does 'everyone' know I stayed at your place last night?"

"I'll leave that one to your vivid imagination. In the meantime, one bit of advice." He turned, walking backward as he pointed at her makeshift campsite. "Zip up your tent."

She frowned. "I'm getting the new-tent smells out of it."

"Suit yourself, but I'd rather put up with the new-tent smells than bugs and critters crawling into my sleeping bag." He turned around, waving back to her. "'Night, Samantha Bennett. Sweet dreams."

She waited until he was out of sight before she dived into her tent, scoured every inch for any bugs and critters, and then zipped it up tight.

Dinner wasn't an issue. Samantha had eaten plenty of Maggie O'Dunn Sloan's incredible food at the wedding. She had energy bars if she did get hungry, but she doubted she would.

The cold, miserable rain, however, *was* an issue.

It started twenty minutes after Justin left, while she was investigating the stonework around the mill's foundation. She ran to her tent, slipped inside and zipped it shut again as raindrops splattered on the slanted top.

No thunder, no lightning, no fierce wind.

All was well.

She took off her shoes and smoothed out her sleeping bag and slipped inside, stretched out in her stocking feet. She wouldn't bother with flannel pajamas tonight and instead would just sleep in her clothes, but it was still relatively early. She wondered what Justin was doing. Drinking beer and telling stories in front of another campfire? Watching football? Helping his folks prepare for tomorrow's brunch?

She didn't have to be alone, but it was good that she was. Smart.

The rain stopped, then started again, hissing in the

woods, pitter-pattering on the brook. Samantha listened, cozy in her tent, warm and dry in her sleeping bag. *Totally safe.* She thought she could smell the faint odor leftover from the fire. She hadn't been safe then. Her mind was catching up with what her body knew, the denial lifting that she somehow had been fine, within her limits, unexposed to serious danger.

She took out the copies of the pages she had found in her grandfather's house. They were getting beat up, but they were still legible, even in the gray, fading light. She pictured her grandfather in his later years, still feisty and formidable—but also aware he was dying.

"I want you to have grand adventures, Samantha. It doesn't have to be to Antarctica. It can be to the clothesline with a basket of laundry. It's all in how you look at your life and your choices, and what you make of them."

She hadn't known, exactly, what he'd meant and why he'd brought up hanging laundry, even as a metaphor. He had loved that his eldest grandchild was interested in pirates and pirate shipwrecks, not for any monetary treasure but for the history, the mysteries, the clues and the pure adventure.

He had encouraged her to take up digging into Benjamin Farraday and his exploits, but Samantha wished she had an explanation for why he hadn't mentioned the cider mill painting and the unfinished story of Lady Elizabeth and Captain Farraday in his Boston office closet. Had he forgotten about them? Had he planned to show them to her but hadn't had a chance before he died? Had they come into his possession at different times?

Her grandfather had kept terrible records, so Samantha wasn't surprised that she hadn't found a note describing where the painting and manuscript had come from, whether he'd bought them or they'd been gifts.

She snuggled deeper into her sleeping bag. She wondered what would have happened if she'd gone back to Justin's sawmill with him. Would she have stayed on his couch through the night?

Now, there was a distraction from her long-ago pirate.

Justin hadn't worked too hard to persuade her to go back with him. Maybe the wedding—being with his family and friends—had jerked him back to reality.

Or he could have his own ideas about pirate treasure out here on Cider Brook. It'd been gnawing at her since he'd thrust her journal at her Thursday night—this notion that he knew more than he was saying.

That he was hiding something from her.

Samantha listened to the rain and kept her eyes open as darkness overtook her tent. She put the pages of her mysterious story away and got as comfortable as she was going to get on the hard, cold ground. She touched her lips and shut her eyes, reliving Justin's kiss.

"You're a true blackguard, Captain Farraday."
"Aye, Lady Elizabeth, I am."

Twenty

~◆◆~

Loretta took a bumpy, interminable red-eye flight from San Diego to Boston and arrived way too early. It was the middle of the night at home. She wanted to collapse onto the floor in baggage claim but figured some overzealous security type would arrest her. She didn't even have a bag to claim. She'd rolled up a few things and stuffed them into a small carry-on. She didn't know how long she would be staying on the East Coast. Not long, she hoped. She didn't want to have to deal with laundry at Carriage Hill. She could just see herself asking for some Woolite so she could wash her undies.

She wheeled her bag to the rental car counter.

"How was your flight, ma'am?" the middle-aged guy behind the counter asked.

"Flight from hell, but I got here alive, so no complaints."

He got right to taking care of business and telling her where she could find her car. Even so, she almost got lost. The car was a heap. She must not have specified "no heaps" when she'd rented it online. She shoved her bag onto the floor in front of the passenger seat and got behind the wheel and did all the checks. Blinker, headlights, wipers, emergency brake. She didn't know if she was up to driving, but she was good to go and figured she would find out.

"If I crash into the side of a tunnel, it's your fault, Duncan McCaffrey."

She could almost hear his booming laugh as she started the car and inched her way out of the rental garage. She should have at least had coffee before venturing onto Boston roads. Weren't there books about the pure hell of driving in Boston?

She'd slept in fits and starts on the flight, but the intervals of sleep had all been bad to awful. She'd kept dreaming about Duncan. Not sexy dreams. Sexy dreams would have been fine. These had been guilt-ridden dreams. She'd awaken with tears in her eyes, her heart pounding, and she'd choke back a cry of distress—absolutely not like her at all—and look around her to see if anyone had noticed. Of course, no one had.

"She's Harry Bennett's granddaughter. She's Malcolm Bennett's daughter. She lied to you, Duncan. You can't trust her. You just can't."

"Right, right. I know."

"My advice is just to get rid of her. Don't ask a lot of questions."

"Where are you now, Loretta?"

"What?"

"I want to picture you. Where are you?"

"Pacing in my kitchen in a bathrobe I've had for fifteen years."

Loretta remembered how he'd laughed. He'd always gotten such a big kick out of her. He'd been so filled with life. She'd thought he had time—that they had time—and she'd wasted too much of those last weeks bugging him about Samantha Bennett. Duncan would have dealt with her in his own way, in his own good time. He hadn't needed a La Jolla lawyer to harangue him about all the potential negative consequences of his impulsive hiring of a young woman who had followed him to a small Massachusetts town and omitted a few pertinent facts about herself.

Was Julius right? Was Samantha in Knights Bridge now to redeem herself?

Did she blame herself for Duncan's death?

Loretta felt her throat tighten and pushed back the flood of questions, the memory of her unsettling dreams. She concentrated on getting through some maniacal Boston tunnel alive.

She needed coffee. A bathroom so she could wash her face and brush her teeth.

A decent breakfast wouldn't hurt, but her body was convinced it was four o'clock in the morning. Whoever had thought red-eyes were a good idea, anyway?

The tunnel dumped her out in the city, and she missed her turn. Or maybe she'd already missed it and just hadn't noticed. GPS wouldn't do her any good if she didn't turn it on. She *always* got lost in Boston. She hated the damn place, as attractive a city as it was. There were several different routes west, and she hadn't taken any of them.

When she found herself on the city streets, she decided getting lost was a sign to take a break before continuing on to Knights Bridge. She parked on a promising-looking street, fed a meter a fortune and wandered into a small restaurant crowded with business people. She'd dressed all in black for her interminable flight and fit right in.

She sat at a small booth with romanticized pictures of Paul Revere on the wall above her. "He's the 'one if by land, two if by sea' guy, right?" she asked her waiter, who looked like a bored college student.

"Who is?"

"Paul Revere."

The kid obviously drew a blank. No idea the guy on the wall was Paul Revere, or probably even who Paul Revere was. College or no college. Loretta gave up and ordered a three-egg omelet with cheddar cheese, spinach and tomatoes, whole-wheat toast, orange juice and coffee.

"Do you want butter?" the kid asked.

"Yes, I want butter, and I want cream for my coffee."

While she waited, she checked her phone and saw she had an unread text from Julius. He had Harry Bennett's address in Boston. Beacon Street.

The man was a ferret. She wouldn't want to try hiding anything from one Julius Hartley, Hollywood-Beverly Hills-Los Angeles private investigator.

She checked the map on her phone and saw Bennett's address wasn't far from her restaurant. She could pour some more money into her meter and walk over there after breakfast. Take a peek and then get back on the road. She examined her map further and realized it wouldn't be that difficult to get out to Storrow Drive from Harry Bennett's house. At least on the map.

And it would be a good idea to get a sense of Samantha Bennett's roots—to better understand what she was like, what her motives could be, what made her tick.

Loretta almost wished she'd brought Julius with her, since he was better at that sort of thing than she was, but she knew she'd needed to come out here alone. He knew it, too.

The kid brought her plate. "That's one massive breakfast," she said.

He made no comment and withdrew. Next to her, two men in dark suits were discussing the Red Sox. Behind her, two women in dark suits were also discussing the Red Sox. Loretta smiled, feeling better already. She poured cream into her coffee, spread butter on her toast and settled into her booth for a good, long, enjoyable meal and then a leisurely walk to Harry Bennett's Back Bay house.

Really, she was in no rush to get to Knights Bridge.

Twenty-One

Justin woke up early and decided to get to work. He ripped out part of a wall in his bedroom. He'd needed to get a look behind it, anyway, and there was nothing like wielding a crowbar to ease his frustrations. Normally he planned his work and didn't end up with wallboard dust all over everything, but not much about the past few days had been normal.

He left the mess, took a shower, pulled on clean clothes and headed out. Because he'd been best man yesterday, he was off the hook for bringing anything to brunch. He figured that meant he would be on cleanup duty. Fine with him. Best to have things to do, given his restless mood.

Last night's rain had passed quickly, no real threat to the otherwise perfect weekend weather. With the crisp air and the changing leaves, autumn felt more and more locked in, summer a memory. It had been a summer of nonstop work for him. That was good, but it could also explain why he'd latched on to Samantha the way he had. Maybe it had nothing to do with pirate talk and his gold coin, or even the tempting curves of her fit little body. Maybe he just needed a damn break.

He parked on the dirt road and walked down the driveway to the cider mill. He hadn't wanted to arrive too early and have Samantha think he had been up half the night picturing her alone in her tent. Even though it wasn't that far from the truth.

He found her sitting cross-legged on her sleeping bag inside her tent, the flaps open. She gave him an unapologetic look. "The bugs and critters can have their way with me. I don't care. I got claustrophobic." She sighed, smiling at him as she climbed out of the tent. "Harry Bennett's granddaughter. Claustrophobic. It's just wrong."

Justin stood between her and the sparkling brook, noting that her hair was sticking out in odd places, as if she hadn't had that great a night herself. She was dressed, at least. No distracting flannel pajamas. "Is this your first time getting claustrophobic?"

"And the last, I hope. I'm more accustomed to tight quarters on a ship than tents. I called it a night earlier than I had anticipated because of the rain. That didn't help. At least it was only a passing shower, and my tent held up okay."

"Did you get cold? You look cold right now."

"Only because I got out of my sleeping bag. The worst thing was the sense I was sleeping among ghosts out here. Do you ever think about all the people who lived here before you arrived on the scene?"

He shrugged. "Not really."

"It was good, though. Being out here on my own. Imagining what it would have been like if Benjamin Farraday did make it this far west. There wouldn't have been old stone walls and a cider mill, of course, but still…" She paused, swooping up her jacket at the front edge of her tent. "I heard an owl but no bears."

"Was staying out here necessary to your mission?"

She pulled on her jacket. "I wouldn't go that far."

"It kept you from temptation, anyway." He reached out a hand and untucked part of her jacket collar, his fingers skimming her cool skin as he smiled at her. "Better the cold ground, owls and thoughts of pirates than sleeping on my couch again."

She angled a look at him. "Are you always this cocky?"

"Only when I have reason to be."

He thought she might have blushed, but it could have been the chilly air, too. She buttoned her jacket and pushed her hands through her hair, which didn't help much with the errant curls. The curls worked somehow, going with her general air of high energy and purpose.

"About this brunch," she said. "You're sure it's okay? I haven't taken a shower. I have bath wipes. They're great in a pinch, but they're not the same as a hot shower."

More images he didn't need. He wondered if she knew it. "You'll fit right in. It was a late night with all the partying."

"I should take this tent down before we leave. It'll only take a minute."

"I'll give you a hand. Where will you be tonight?"

She shook her head. "No idea." She pulled her sleeping bag and backpack out of the tent and set them off to the side in the grass. "Being as self-confident as you are, why didn't you have a date for the wedding?"

"Didn't get around to it."

"I gather you don't have a woman in your life at the moment."

"I have lots of women in my life."

"I'm not talking about your mother or your sister or your married and engaged women friends." Samantha picked up one end of her sleeping bag and started to zip it. "Are you hard on women?"

Justin walked around her and started dismantling the tent. It was a good design, easy to put up and take down. "Maybe women are hard on me."

"Ha. I doubt it. Need a hand with the tent?"

"I've got it. Might want to roll up your sleeping bag, or at least fold it so we can toss it in the truck."

"I'll do that." But she narrowed her eyes, assessing him with a frankness—an openness—that damn near took his breath away. She said quietly, "I'm guessing you're one of those men who isn't that easy to get. You like the hunt. You're not so sure about what comes after that. Home, hearth, the rest of it. Am I right? Are you a heartbreaker, Justin?"

"I break hearts by the dozen." He had the tent collapsed at his feet and knelt to fold it up while she finished zipping up her sleeping bag. "What about you, Sam? Have you left behind a trail of broken hearts?"

She grinned. "Damn, I hope so."

Her flippant answer caught him by surprise and made him laugh. "I gather you've had your share of pirates and brigands in your life."

"More like your average SOBs."

"But no man in your life now?"

"Not since before I went to work for Duncan Mc-

Caffrey." She winced as she dropped her sleeping bag into a heap. "Now, why did I tell you that?"

"Because you wanted me to know." He got the tent into a neat square and stuffed it back in its handy case. "Samantha, I wouldn't have kissed you if I had a woman in my life."

She waved a hand. "It was adrenaline left over from the fire."

"It was because I wanted to kiss you. Still do." He winked at her. "Maybe after that hot shower."

"Justin—" She paused, those dark eyes again meeting his. "I let you kiss me, and I kissed you back, because I wanted to."

"I know." He grinned at her. "Come on. Let's go to the brunch. You can meet Fred the Duck and the rest of the gang."

On the short drive up to the farmhouse, Samantha talked about woodpeckers and crows and whether they stuck around for the cold weather, but Justin suspected she wasn't thinking about birds. She was thinking about what was going on with the two of them. Whatever it was, it was real, and it wasn't going away.

The sprawling farmhouse where he'd grown up stood on wide, open ground, with a large lawn that sloped down to the road. Behind the house were fields marked off by stone walls lined with maples, oaks and white pines, in sharp relief against the clear morning sky. The barn that housed the Sloan & Sons offices was shut up for the day. Today was for relaxing, getting together with family and friends after yesterday's more formal and structured wedding festivities.

Fred waddled across the top of driveway. Samantha nodded to him. "The dogs don't give him any trouble?"

Justin laughed. "They wouldn't dare."

He introduced her to Charlie, the chocolate Lab—or, more accurately, Charlie introduced himself, nuzzling Samantha, wagging his tail. Justin didn't know if she was a dog lover, but she patted Charlie and seemed to appreciate his infectious personality. Heather's dog, Beaver, a mix of German shepherd and black Lab, was another story. Rambunctious, as spoiled as his owner, in Justin's not-so-objective opinion. The big dog almost knocked Samantha over before running off with Charlie.

"Why Beaver?" she asked.

"Heather thought he looked like a beaver as a puppy."

"Ah. He reminds me of Buster."

"We think he's Buster's offspring from his days before Carriage Hill. Don't tell Olivia."

Samantha laughed, obviously relaxing. Justin led her through the back into the kitchen. All four of his brothers were there, trying to help, but their mother shooed them out, pointing toward the dining room. At fifty-eight, Cora Sloan was still a force of nature. "Out. All of you. Thank you but everything's done, and right now I don't need to trip over size-twelve feet." She paused, smiling at Samantha. "I'm so glad you could make it, Sam."

"If there's anything I can do—"

"You can relax and enjoy yourself."

"And get out of the kitchen," Justin added with a grin, leading Samantha into the dining room, where

Heather and Maggie were standing next to the table, already crowded with food.

His sister was in the middle of an involved explanation of how she had accidentally left the egg out of the pumpkin bread she'd baked for the brunch. "It's a little burned on the edges, too," she said, "but it tastes fine. I tried it myself."

"I'm sure it's great," Maggie said.

"It won't kill anyone." She spotted Samantha. "You made it! We met yesterday. I don't know if you remember me in the crowd. Heather Sloan."

"The only one of us who can't be trusted in the kitchen," Eric said, grinning as he helped himself to a slice of apple from a tray of cut fruit and cheese. Heather just rolled her eyes as the eldest Sloan nodded to Samantha. "How was camping?"

If she wondered how Eric knew she'd pitched her tent last night, she gave no indication. "Perfect," she said, leaving it at that.

Eric munched on his apple. "Coldest night of the year so far."

"I wondered if that might have been the case. I'm definitely looking forward to coffee."

She headed for the coffee urn set up on the hutch, next to a window that looked out across the front lawn down to the road and a field below, at the bottom of which, out of sight, was the small cabin where Justin had lived for a few years.

He watched Samantha as she filled a mug. Eric stood next to him with his own mug of coffee. "I guess a cold night in a tent is nothing compared to an expedition to Antarctica," Eric said. "Must be hard to stand out in the Bennett family."

"I don't think camping last night had anything to do with standing out as a Bennett," Justin said, more to himself than to his brother.

Eric grimaced. "Not going there."

"Good. You trying Heather's pumpkin bread?"

"Only on a dare. You?"

"The same."

Eric grabbed another hunk of apple as Brandon came in with the boys and wandered off, and Justin joined Samantha at the coffee urn. She had a small rectangle of the pumpkin bread. "It's not bad, really. Do you like being from a big family?"

"I don't know any different," Justin said, pouring himself coffee.

"I feel a little like a stranger in a strange land."

"Fred the Duck likes you."

"How could you tell?"

"He didn't attack you. It's a good sign." He decided to bypass the pumpkin bread and instead opted for a mini muffin. "It looks like one Adam made. He's the best cook in the family. Heather and I are the worst, but she's a lot worse than I am. It's a point of pride with her."

"The youngest of six *and* the only girl." Samantha laughed in amazement. "I can't imagine."

"She's damn lucky is how I look at it."

"Do your brothers run off men who might be interested in her?"

"You're assuming there are any." Justin winked. "Kidding."

"It was a rude question," she said simply.

"You can ask any question you want, Sam. I don't get offended easily." He held up his muffin, still warm from the oven. "What kind of muffin do you think this is?"

"I've no idea—"

"Here," he said, "have a bite."

He ended up popping the whole thing into her mouth since it was so small. He could feel her lips brush against his fingers, and he was pretty sure Eric gritted his teeth and Brandon grinned.

"Your brothers are watching," Samantha whispered, swallowing the muffin.

He shrugged. "Everyone's watching. Life in my family. What kind?"

"Apple-walnut. It's wonderful. You chose well."

"Good. I'll have one." He grabbed another muffin off the tray and tried it. "Not bad."

Brandon was helping his sons choose from the finger foods, warning them not to overdo it since there would be hot food soon. His mother-in-law, Elly O'Dunn, arrived with a huge, bubbling pan of scalloped potatoes. She set the pan on hot pads on the table. She'd been at the wedding yesterday, but Justin didn't know if Samantha had met her. He made a quick introduction.

Maggie stepped into the dining room. "Mom raises goats. Nigerian dwarf goats. They provide all the milk for our soap making."

Justin got out of there. He had no objection to Elly's goats, but he'd heard all she had to say about them— which was a lot, once she got started. As he headed into the hall, Samantha was asking Elly follow-up questions on the qualities that made goat's milk such a good option for soap. Damned if she didn't sound genuinely interested. There wasn't a chance Elly or her goats could have anything to do with Samantha's pirate. That meant she had no ulterior motive—no reason to feign interest—and either wanted to learn about goats or to indulge Elly's passion for them. Either way, Justin couldn't figure her out.

He went out to the front porch. Dylan and Olivia were there, sitting on the porch rail across from Grace Webster, who was wrapped up in a shawl on a wicker sofa, facing the view of the fields and woods. Dylan glanced at Justin as if he wanted to pull him aside about something, but Samantha joined them, fresh from her lesson on goats. She and Olivia launched into a further discussion of the virtues of goat's milk soap.

Dylan gave the two women an exaggerated grimace. "You're not going to start talking about the benefits of lavender, are you?"

"Not lavender," Olivia said. *"Litsea cubeba."*

"I don't even know what that is," Dylan said.

"It's a small tree native to Southeast Asia. Every part of the tree is used in herbal medicine, but its fruit is commonly used to make a lovely lemon-scented essential oil." Olivia smiled, obviously enjoying the topic—and her fiancé's teasing. "It's uplifting. Maggie and I are going to try making our own *litsea* oil."

Justin looked at Dylan. "I'm dying here."

His friend grinned, but Olivia patted Justin on the shoulder. "I'll spare you and stop now," she said happily. "I smell your mother's homemade oatmeal bread. I want a slice while it's still warm. Slathered with butter and honey." She shifted to Samantha. "I'll have to walk home to burn off the calories, but it'll be worth it."

Dylan hopped off the rail and addressed his grandmother. "Would you like me to bring you a plate, or do you want to come inside?"

"I'll come in soon. Thank you, Dylan." With an aged hand, Grace patted the cushion next to her on the wicker sofa. "Sit with me a minute, won't you, Samantha?"

Dylan frowned but said nothing as he and Olivia went inside. Samantha dutifully sat next to Grace. Justin noticed his grandmother coming up the porch steps. "Hey, Gran. Need a hand?"

"I can manage, thanks."

Evelyn Sloan's standard answer. She breezed past him and sat on a wicker chair at an angle from Grace and Samantha. Justin leaned against the porch rail. Grace tightened her shawl around her and made small talk about the weather. His grandmother got settled, declaring it was warm enough now that she didn't need her coat. She took if off and glanced at Justin with a smile that struck him as not-quite genuine if not outright suspicious.

The two older women were up to something that involved the younger one. He was positive, but Samantha, not attuned to the ways of Knights Bridge seniors, looked oblivious. Grace and his grandmother would have ferreted out by now that he was attracted to Samantha. Did they also know this energetic, brown-eyed, treasure-hunting Bennett was attracted to him?

Because she was. No question in his mind.

It wasn't arrogance or wishful thinking on his part, and it damn sure wasn't adrenaline. He wasn't introspective by nature, but he was aware that he didn't have a lot of patience with self-delusion. He wanted to see things as they were.

Grace sat back with a certain satisfaction. "We don't always know where the heart leads us. It's the grandest adventure of all."

Justin felt his eyebrows go up. Where had that come from? He hadn't been paying close attention to the conversation.

Samantha seemed to be enjoying herself. "The cardinal sin in my family is to be boring."

"The Sloans are anything but boring," Grace said.

Justin grinned at her. "Listen to you, Grace."

"It's true. Remember, I had your father *and* your grandfather in school."

"I can't believe you're old enough to have taught Gramps."

Grace waved a hand. "I'm old enough to have taught Moses."

His grandmother looked wistful. "It's hard to believe Ralph's been gone almost five years. He was a tough customer. You remind me of him, Justin. No beating around the bush with either of you."

"And both good men," Grace said.

Justin noticed his grandmother took a second to respond, but then she glanced at Samantha and said, "Damn good."

He grinned. "Blunt bastards, the two of us, but reliable."

"There's a place for bluntness, to be sure," Samantha said, "and you wouldn't want to be unreliable."

His grandmother looked out at the view. "It really feels like fall today, doesn't it? I love this time of year." She turned to Samantha. "I understand you're curious about the Hazeltons."

She nodded. "I am. Do you remember them?"

"As far as I know, there were no Hazeltons in Knights Bridge when I was born, and I'm eighty. Grace is older, but she didn't arrive in town until 1938. They were long gone by then."

"But there were stories," Grace said, leaning forward.

Justin watched his grandmother lift a quilt—one she'd made even before he was born—off the back of her chair. She spread it, still half folded, over her lap. "The man who used to own this place before we bought it insisted the Hazeltons told him a hermit was living out this way when Scots-Irish settlers first arrived in the area." She winked at Samantha. "That would have been *well* before Grace's and my time. Before the American Revolution, even."

"Probably about 1730, maybe a little earlier," Grace said. "It was after war and disease had devastated much of the local Native American population. No one knew how long this hermit had been out here, or who he was. He hunted, fished, kept to himself."

"What happened to him?" Samantha asked.

Grace sat back. "People left him alone, as was his wish, and he died an old man. Or so goes the story."

Justin noted Samantha's clear interest, but she seemed to make an effort not to get ahead of herself. "Does anyone know this hermit's name?"

"I don't," his grandmother said.

Grace shook her head. "I don't, either."

"How did the Hazeltons come to hear this story?" Samantha asked. "Do you have any idea?"

Justin stayed quiet, watching the three women from his position on the porch rail. His grandmother smoothed out the old quilt, her hands no longer those of the young woman who'd sewn it. "The man we bought this place from had only owned it for ten or fifteen years," she said. "The Hazeltons had been here for a long time. The story could have come down generation to generation."

Samantha seemed transfixed. "It's fascinating," she said.

Grace looked at her, her incisiveness reminding Justin of her grandson, Dylan. "We understand you're interested in a pirate who might have ventured out this way."

"I have no proof of such a thing—"

"Oh, we know that. We wondered if the story of this hermit somehow generated whatever lead brought you here."

"It's possible. The lead I have isn't much. Slim at best."

Grace smiled knowingly. "And you're not going to tell us what it is, are you?"

"The word *pirate* has a way of causing trouble. Do you know if there was a Hazelton named Zeke or Henrietta?"

The two older women frowned. "I wouldn't know," Grace said.

Justin saw that his grandmother was less committed. "I'm not sure. Let me think. Why do you ask?"

"There's a photograph at the country store of a couple identified only as Zeke and Henrietta. They're standing in front of Justin's cider mill in 1915."

Justin had never looked closely at the cider mill photos at the country store, but now he would.

Samantha got to her feet and stood at the porch rail. Charlie rolled on his back in the grass and Beaver streaked past him with a softball, followed closely by Heather and then Brandon, griping about how she needed to train her dog. Finally Samantha turned to the two elderly women. "Does the name Farraday mean anything to you?"

It didn't, but Justin was intrigued by how engaged the two older women were by Samantha. She placed a hand on the rail. He noticed its shape and found himself thinking things that his grandmother and Grace would have rapped his knuckles for imagining. Yet at one time, the two of them had been where he was now, falling for someone who had surprised the hell out of their families. Evelyn, the daughter of Amherst shopkeepers, had fallen for a hardworking Knights Bridge carpenter who had dreamed of owning a plot of land and starting his own business. Grace, a teenager about to lose the only home she'd ever known in a town being obliterated before her eyes, had fallen for a British flyer on the run.

"My grandfather put me on to Benjamin Farraday," Samantha was saying. "I'm not sure how Farraday came to his attention. He's not a well-known pirate. For a short time I thought Duncan McCaffrey might be interested in him. Now…I'm just looking for answers."

Grace nodded. "Do you suppose this hermit could have been Farraday and he hid his loot out here?"

"My theory has Farraday cooling his heels in the wilderness west of Boston until the heat was off, then using his treasure—or at least part of it—to fund a new ship, which then sank, with him, his crew and whatever cargo they'd stolen."

"Those poor men," Grace said. "I can't imagine

drowning at sea. But if the Hazeltons' hermit was this Captain Farraday, and he died here as an old man…"

Samantha sighed. "It could mean he never brought treasure out here, or ever funded a new ship that sank at sea with him and his crew on board."

"What kind of man was he?" Grace asked softly.

"I've picked up a few bits and pieces about him, but not nearly enough," Samantha said. "He was well-educated, handsome and an astute businessman, but also daring and a real rogue."

"Pirates," Evelyn said with a scoff. "A lawless lot."

Samantha kept silent. Grace watched her closely. "Did this pirate Farraday have a woman in his life?" she asked.

"Not that I know of." Samantha glanced at Justin, and he noticed spots of color on her cheeks before she turned sharply away, smiling at the two older women. "It's been great chatting with you both. Do you think there are any records of this hermit at the library or historical society?"

Justin moved closer to his grandmother as she started to her feet. She looked a little unsteady, and he wondered if the talk of the past had unsettled her more than she realized. She said, "I've never thought to look. Do you think you'll stay in town and check the records yourself?"

Samantha must have noticed his grandmother's fatigue. "I might," she said, then smiled. "But right now, my mind's on all the great smells emanating from the house."

Justin put out his hand, and his grandmother took it as she rose. "A word to the wise," she said, addressing Samantha. "You might think twice about anything

Heather's cooked. My granddaughter has a big heart and I love her to pieces, but cooking isn't her long suit."

Samantha laughed. "Heather and I will get along fine, then. I'm not a fussy eater, and I never did learn to cook." She turned to Grace and put out her arm. "Shall we?"

Grace beamed, rising as she took the younger woman's arm. Justin felt his grandmother squeeze his hand, and she whispered, "I like your Samantha," as the four of them went inside.

Samantha made herself at home over brunch. There was nothing shy about her, and Justin thought she enjoyed the food—ham, scalloped potatoes, baked beans, a frittata made with veggies from his folks' garden, an array of salads and desserts. She seemed more at ease than she had yesterday at the wedding and stayed close to him, then pitched in and helped him clear dishes and load the dishwasher.

With the food put away and the dishes done, the gathering moved outside for a few games of volleyball. Justin and his brothers got the older crowd settled into lawn chairs, with blankets and mugs of hot chocolate.

Heather took it upon herself to create the teams. "Justin, Dylan, Eric on one team. Brandon, Adam, Christopher on the other team. That'll even things up. Maggie? You playing?"

"Only if I have to," she said, already on a blanket spread out on the grass.

"I don't blame you," Heather said. "Olivia?"

"I'll be on Brandon's team."

Dylan grinned at her. "You're going to lose."

"It's volleyball, Dylan, not hockey," Olivia said cheerfully, "and we've been doing this since we were in kindergarten."

"Okay, great," Heather said. "I'll be on Olivia's team. Sam, you'll be on Justin's team?"

Samantha nodded. "Sure. I don't know how to play volleyball, though."

Heather grinned. "Excellent."

Justin slung an arm over Samantha's shoulders. "Ball comes at you, hit it over the net. All there is to it."

Heather put their mother on Justin's team and their uncle on her team. Their father never played. Randy and Louise Frost sat with Randy's mother, Audrey, in the shade.

"We need one more for your team, Justin," Heather said.

He noticed his young nephews were looking dejected and said, "I want Aidan and Tyler."

The boys perked up. "Against *Dad?*" Aidan asked, obviously thrilled with the idea.

"Uh-oh," Brandon said. "We're in trouble, Heather."

They played three matches and barely kept score. Samantha got the hang of the game in no time. It took all Justin had to resist watching her as she jumped, ran and pounded the ball. He concentrated instead on making sure Aidan and Tyler had a good time, got in a few hits and didn't get run over by the rest of their teammates. As fit as they all were, there was no question Dylan was the experienced professional athlete among them.

Rain and wind ended the afternoon. Justin was putting equipment away in a small shed behind the house when Olivia found him. "Samantha left all of a sudden. She's walking down to the cider mill."

"Now? Or do you mean she's planning to?"

"Now," Olivia said. "Justin. She needs to come to Carriage Hill and stay with us. It's crazy for her to stay out at the mill by herself. I don't care if she is some badass treasure hunter who got herself into a mess with Dylan's dad. Water over the dam."

He shut the shed door. Why had Samantha left without saying anything? "You traipse down there and invite her, then."

Olivia crossed her arms on her chest, the wind blowing the ends of her dark hair. "I just might. It's supposed to rain all night and into tomorrow, you know."

Dylan eased in next to his fiancée. "I know Samantha is a Bennett and I'm from Southern California and not used to freezing my ass off in a tent, but I wouldn't want to be camping out tonight if I had a decent alternative."

"All right." Justin felt slightly less irritated. Maybe one of his brothers had said something asinine to Samantha. Maybe *he* had. "I'll go talk to her. If she wants to camp, though, I'm not stopping her."

"It's your land," Olivia said.

"You want me to play that card?"

She backed off, and Dylan said, "I've been meaning to talk to you, Justin. Loretta arrived in Boston this morning. She was going to drive out this afternoon, but when I told her about the brunch, she checked into a hotel and said she'll head out here tomorrow. I think she was looking for an excuse to delay coming out here. She sounded preoccupied."

Justin could understand if she'd been digging into the world of Samantha Bennett. "Did she have anything to tell you?"

Dylan shook his head, and Olivia said, "Certainly nothing that would stop us from inviting Samantha to stay with us tonight."

The rain had picked up and fog had rolled in by the time Justin got in his truck and drove down to the mill. He pulled into the driveway, splashing in deep puddles. Samantha had her tent back up, if not as securely as last night. She didn't come out, which meant he had to get out in the rain and go to her.

He peered at her through the zipped-up screen. She was sitting on top of her sleeping bag with her red-covered journal and a pen. "If the rain starts coming in through the screen," she said, barely looking up at him, "I'll zip up the outer flaps. I'm nice and cozy in here."

"Olivia and Dylan have invited you to stay at Carriage Hill."

"That's nice of them."

She still didn't look up. Justin kept his tone even as he continued, "We'll all sleep better knowing you're not out here by yourself."

Finally she raised her dark eyes to him. "It didn't bother you last night."

"They didn't know, and it did bother me." Despite his borderline annoyance, he grinned at her. "I kept picturing you stretched out here in the cold."

"Trust me, reality wasn't as good as your imagination. Is there reverse bonding? The rescuer with the rescued?" She set aside her journal and pen. "Never mind. Don't answer. It's raining, you know. You don't have an umbrella and you're not wearing a raincoat. You're getting wet."

"Not the first time. Gather up your stuff. I'll drive you over there."

"Is that an order?"

"A strong suggestion. An order would just get your back up."

"Think I'd cut off my nose to spite my face?"

He felt the cold rain in his hair, down his neck. "Wasn't that what staying out here last night was about?"

"No," she said, her voice quiet now, a seriousness in her dark eyes that he hadn't expected. "Today was amazing, Justin. I have bruises from hitting that ball, but it was all such fun. I'm sorry I ran out without saying thank you. But it hit me..." She cleared her throat and seemed to blink back tears. "I don't belong, Justin. You must see that."

"What I saw was a woman having a good time."

"I did have a good time." She sighed. "You know your grandmother and Grace Webster maneuvered me into talking about their hermit, don't you?"

"Maneuvered us both. Think he could be your pirate?"

"I don't know enough even to guess."

"They'd get a kick out of that." He wanted to unzip her tent and climb in there with her. Maybe she wanted that, too. But she'd come here, alone, for a reason. "I'm heading back to the house to help out with a few things. I'll stop by on my way home. You can tell me what you want to do. Sit here in the rain or sit by a nice fire at Carriage Hill."

* * *

When he got back to the house, Dylan and Olivia had left to take Grace home. Brandon and Maggie were off feeding the chickens with the boys. Adam and Heather were down at the office with their father and uncle and the dogs. Christopher was on duty at the fire station.

Eric had the vacuum and broom. Justin grabbed a wet cloth.

"You left Samantha out at the mill?" his older brother asked.

"Her call."

"Are you getting serious about her, Justin, or are you just having fun while she's in town?"

He attacked the dining room table and didn't answer.

Eric sighed. "She's a go-getter and cute as hell, but she's trouble. I don't mean bad trouble necessarily. Good trouble, maybe. The sort that stirs up your life."

"You saying my life needs stirring up?"

"I'm saying if you're going to insist on getting involved with her, at least stay out of her treasure hunts."

Justin stood straight and looked at his cop brother. "Too late."

Eric groaned with sudden understanding. "Not that damn gold coin you found?"

"You remember that?"

"Of course. I was there."

"The cop mind even then," Justin said with a grin. "Who the hell knows, Eric? Maybe that coin is part of Benjamin Farraday's pirate treasure."

"And maybe you're losing your mind, or at least not

thinking with it." He held out the vacuum and broom. "Which do you prefer?"

Justin took the broom, but he was thinking about ramming his crowbar into another wall back at his sawmill apartment.

Twenty-Two

$\sim\!\!\infty\!\!\sim\!\!\infty\!\!\sim$

It was a call from her uncle that convinced Samantha to return to The Farm at Carriage Hill. He and Isaac were winding their way back to Boston, thoroughly enjoying themselves in part, her uncle admitted, because they avoided topics of serious disagreement, which were many.

"There's a flood watch up where you are," Caleb said. "What will you do if Cider Brook overflows into your tent?"

"I'm on high ground. It's the wind I'm worried about right now. I think it's about to blow down my tent."

"One word—*hypothermia.*"

"That would be bad." She noticed her tent roof drooping dangerously but said calmly to her uncle, "I played volleyball with the Sloans and their friends this afternoon."

"I haven't played volleyball since high school. It's a fun game." Caleb seemed to be somewhat uncertain about what to say. "You aren't what they're used to and you feel out of place. So? Does that mean you can't accept the offer of a warm bed?"

"Uncle Caleb…" She thought of Justin peering at her through the tent screen, and of how much she'd wanted to invite him in.

"These people are getting to you, Sam. I understand. But you can't drown, freeze and eat dried-up energy bars because you like them and don't want to inflict yourself on them."

"You make it sound like I'm exposing them to a disease."

"That's what *you're* making it sound like."

"I just don't want to get in too deep and hurt them— or myself."

She heard Isaac in the background. "It's this volunteer firefighter, isn't it?"

Caleb swore under his breath, and Samantha quickly changed the subject and told him about the hermit. "What do you think? Could he be my Captain Farraday?"

"It's not much to go on, but you're going to pick at this thread, aren't you? Good. It shows these people aren't so much under your skin that you're willing to tuck tail and run when there's still work to be done. You'll need a good night's sleep. Go to the damn inn."

And that was that. When Justin returned, Samantha had her tent down, it and her sleeping bag more or less rolled up and her backpack loaded. Rain was dripping off her poncho and hood, and she was shivering with the cold. "I'm going to get your truck wet," she said.

He eyed her. "Yes, you will."

He said little on the way to Carriage Hill. She suspected he meant to drop her off and leave without going inside, but Olivia was out with Buster during a lull in the rain and insisted he come in. "I've made soup," she said. "I figure we're all stuffed after this weekend. Come on, Justin. You know you have nothing but beer at home."

"We drank all the beer."

"Then, no arguing."

He looked at Samantha with a half smile. "Olivia used to tremble before me."

Olivia snorted and ran to the house with Buster as the rain picked up again. Samantha laughed and climbed out of the truck, not sure what Justin would do, but he turned off the engine and met her on the stone walk. The cold rain and wind didn't seem to have any effect on him.

Inside, the kitchen was toasty warm. Dylan had bowls stacked on the butcher-block island. Samantha followed a soaked Buster into the mudroom. He shook off, and she hung her dripping poncho on the hook next to his leash, then slipped off her wet socks and shoes. Her lower pant legs were also wet, but otherwise she had fared okay in the rain. Contrary to Uncle Caleb's insidious worries, she would *not* have suffered hypothermia if she had stayed out at the cider mill— although her tent might have caved in on her.

She returned to the kitchen. Justin was leaning back against the counter by the sink, talking with Dylan. She ducked into the living room, where Olivia was curled up with Buster on the floor in front of a roaring fire. "There have been so many changes in Knights Bridge since Dylan's father came here," she said, stroking the big dog's back. "I know you were only here for the day two years ago, but can you notice any difference?"

"The new construction up the road," Samantha said with a smile. She sat on the couch, welcoming the heat of the fire even as she wondered if she'd done the right thing in getting back into Justin's truck with him.

Olivia laughed. "That is hard to miss."

"I didn't get this far down the road. This place was for sale then, wasn't it?"

"Not quite, but the couple who owned it had moved out by then. They did a great job renovating—well, the Sloans did the work. They're sought after far and wide for their skill with antique properties. Justin especially."

Samantha had no doubt. "My grandfather's house in Boston could use their expertise. It has a number of original features, but the plumbing, wiring, heat and everything else needs overhauling."

"You're keeping the house in the family?" Olivia asked.

"My father and uncle are figuring that out. I'm working on sorting through my grandfather's archives in London and Boston—which is a lofty word for most of it. Turns out he was quite the pack rat."

"That's what you've been doing the past two years? Since Duncan fired you?"

Samantha nodded, aware now of Justin in the doorway, listening. She tried to ignore her reaction to having him close by, but she could tell from Olivia's expression that she noticed. "I've continued research into Benjamin Farraday," Samantha said. "It'll be time soon to move on to other things. I just don't know what yet."

Buster yawned, then flopped his head on Olivia's lap. "I lived and worked in Boston until this past March. I always wanted to come back home. I assumed it would be on my own terms, but it didn't work out that way."

"You weren't fired, were you?"

"Outmaneuvered by a friend I'd helped get back on her feet. The writing was on the wall at work, and I guess I couldn't stand the thought of her elbowing me aside. It wasn't a pretty situation. I'm loyal. I don't let go of friends easily, and it was difficult for me to feel the knife in my back even when it was in deep." Olivia stretched out her legs, wiggling her toes close to the fire. Buster was dead asleep now. "But I took the kick in the pants and did something positive with it."

"The Farm at Carriage Hill," Samantha said.

"It led me to Dylan. I thought he was his father. I didn't know a thing about either one of them. I just had a name and an address. I sent him quite the starchy note to come clean up his dump of a yard or let me do it." Olivia laughed at the memory. "I never thought he would take to Knights Bridge. A dose of Southern California and McCaffrey are having an effect around here."

"This is such a great place to work, study, think, just be." Samantha sank deeper into the couch cushions. "I'm always on the move."

Justin moved into the room. "I've got a fire call," he said without any detectable emotion. "I have to go."

And just like that, he was out the front door and gone.

Olivia shuddered, her face pale even in the glow of the fire. "I hope it's not a bad one. I never can tell.

It's easier to find out about a call *after* they're all back safely." She got up and grabbed a log from the wood box and put it on the fire, readjusting the screen with the ease that came with practice. She turned to Samantha, her color back as the flames flared behind her. "You and Justin…"

"I'm the shiny new outsider," Samantha said simply.

"Oh, I don't know about that. Justin knows who he is and what he wants. He always has. He's wired that way." Olivia studied Samantha a moment. "I'm guessing you're a woman who knows who she is and what she wants."

Samantha gave a short laugh. "That doesn't mean what I want is sane."

"I hear you," Olivia said, sitting back on the floor next to her sleeping dog.

"I violated Duncan's trust, Olivia. That's why I'm here."

She nodded with clear understanding. "It's tough, I know. I trusted the friend who betrayed me. It was an awful experience, but it led me here, to where I am right now—and I wouldn't want to be anywhere else. I wouldn't want to be back in Boston, trying to compete with Marilyn Bryson. Samantha, I didn't know Dylan's father, but everything I've learned about him tells me he was a man who'd been around the block a time or two and had a few knocks along the way himself. I bet he'd forgive you."

"My father could be tough on people," Dylan said as he came into the living room with an armload of cordwood. "He was loyal, and he expected loyalty in return. He knew he could be hasty in making decisions, and that made him second-guess himself with you."

"He had reason," Samantha said.

"Maybe so."

"The way I see it," Olivia said, "the mistake Duncan made wasn't in trusting you. It was in thinking he couldn't trust you after he discovered you'd been here and you hadn't told him your family background."

Dylan dumped the logs into the wood box. "We talked about getting into adventure travel together but never got anything off the ground," he said, grabbing a log that tumbled off the pile and setting it back with the others. "I thought we might after Noah and I took NAK public, but by then it was too late."

"Your father had so many ideas," Samantha said. "Adventure travel would be a natural add-on to his treasure-hunting projects. He loved what he was doing, and he worked hard at it. I learned so much from him in such a short time. When do you think you'll have this adventure travel business up and running?"

"Not sure yet." Dylan sat on the floor next to Olivia. "Brandon Sloan will be working with us. He's not giving up Sloan & Sons. They're supportive."

"The Sloans might squabble among themselves, but they're a tight-knit family." Olivia sat back on the floor next to Buster. "Hurt one, hurt them all."

Samantha smiled. "I don't think I'd want the Sloans on my case."

"I had a crush on Justin Sloan when I was thirteen," Olivia said as Dylan sat next to her. "Every girl did. We all knew he'd stay in town but he'd be hard to catch— not my favorite phrase but you know what I mean."

"He's been decent to me since he pulled me out of that fire." Samantha didn't want to go into more detail and changed the subject. "Do you know what kind of fire they're fighting now?"

Olivia shook her head, her tight look back. "One thing about being home again, I get to hear when my father goes out on a call. I'm not used to it anymore. He's in great shape, but it's time to hang up his fire-fighting gear. He knows it. Anyway, tell me about your family, Samantha. What are the Bennetts really like?"

She seemed to want the distraction. Samantha didn't blame her. She could see the firefighters descending on the cider mill on Wednesday, attacking the fire without hesitation—determined and confident, but not reckless. She knew she hadn't been reckless, either, in finding herself caught in the fire, but she nonetheless felt as if she had something to prove. As if she had to pay them back somehow, Justin in particular. Now they were off somewhere fighting another fire.

"Samantha?" Dylan asked, a note of concern in his voice.

"Sorry. I was thinking about the guys out fighting the fire and the other day...." The fire in the fireplace crackled, and she jumped, then stared at the flames. Maybe she needed a distraction, too. "My family's close, but we don't all live in the same town. Hurt one of us, and the rest will stand by you but also wonder what you did to screw up." She added lightly, "I'm only half kidding."

"It must be like having Indiana Jones for a grandfather," Olivia said. "You're sort of a female Indiana Jones yourself, aren't you?"

"Not even close," Samantha said with a laugh. "Although I don't like snakes, either. I hate even thinking about that snake scene in *Raiders of the Lost Ark*."

Dylan got up and went into the kitchen. Olivia stroked Buster's back as she and Samantha both watched the fire burn in the old fireplace. Dylan returned with glasses of wine, a merlot from Noah Kendrick's winery. He handed one to Samantha. "Go ahead and stretch out on the couch," he said, sitting on the rug in front of the fire with Olivia and Buster.

Samantha took his advice and pulled a wool throw over her as she sipped her wine, grateful for the company. If she'd stayed in her tent, she probably never would have known Justin was out on a fire call. She heard Buster give a contented sigh in his sleep and noticed Dylan brush his lips on the top of Olivia's head. She was glad she wasn't alone, but the awareness that she didn't belong here—that she was an outsider, a stranger with an agenda—that had hit her yesterday at the wedding and again today at the Sloan brunch crept back. But she was determined not to run off this time.

Dylan glanced at her, as if he knew—even understood—what she was feeling, but he said only, "There's more wine."

A few minutes later, Samantha noticed headlights outside. Olivia jumped to her feet, Dylan following. Buster barked but settled down quickly. In a moment, Justin and Olivia's father entered through the kitchen.

"A chimney fire," Randy Frost said. "We got to it in time."

Dylan and Olivia joined him in the kitchen. Samantha remained on the couch while Justin came into the living room and stood by the fire. "This time of year, people start burning wood again and forget if they've had the chimney cleaned recently. Easiest way is to have it done annually on the same date. First week in September, last Friday in October, whatever."

Samantha got out from under her throw and stood next to him in front of the fire. "I'm not sure I do anything on the same date each year."

"Birthday, Christmas, Fourth of July."

"Good point. Everyone's okay, though?"

He nodded. "Shaken up but fine. Randy wanted to stop by. We're only staying a minute. I'll drop him off on my way home."

She noticed the flames reflected in his eyes. "You look tired, Justin."

He leaned in close to her. "A hot bath will do wonders. I'll think of you."

He gave her hand a quick squeeze and was grinning as he left, grabbing Olivia's father and saying good-night to her and Dylan.

Samantha couldn't remember when she'd felt so conflicted, an unsettling mix of loneliness and longing. She called out good-night to her hosts and headed upstairs to her pretty room. She knew when she'd ventured to Knights Bridge that she should keep her distance, but she hadn't. Now she was falling for a man she could trust with her life but maybe not her heart.

After a hot bath of her own, Samantha sat cross-legged on her bed and called her father. "Do you ever think about the souls who went down with the ship?"

"I always do," he said, "but I have to put those feelings aside in order to do my work."

"I'd hate to drown or suffocate in a submarine."

"I'd hate to be hanged as a pirate. What's with the gloomy mood?"

She stretched out her legs, the rustle of the sheets the only sound in the quiet room. "Looking into Benjamin Farraday is leading me to stories and people no one around here has thought of in ages, if ever. I don't know if any of them have to do with Farraday. There's a photograph of a couple in 1915…." Samantha leaned back against the padded headboard. "I have a feeling they don't have a happy ending. I can't pinpoint why since I don't even know who they are. Zeke and Henrietta. They're standing in front of the cider mill."

Her father hesitated before responding. "This place is getting to you, isn't it, Samantha?"

"Do you ever think about your ancestors?"

He grunted. "A lot of old bats."

"I'm serious, Dad."

"So am I. You've never been out to the old homestead where your Grandpa Bennett grew up. You'd understand why the Antarctic didn't faze him. Talk about a hardscrabble life. The past is past. It's not destiny. The past might deal you a set of cards, but then it's your hand. You get to make choices."

"Do you know why Grandpa put me on to Farraday?" Samantha asked.

"No idea," her father said. "When we got together, we tended to talk about the family and how long he had before he had to start spending money on house repairs. He was frugal, which is a polite word for tight."

Samantha smiled into the phone. "You're trying to cheer me up, aren't you?"

"I want you to be happy, kid. That's all. I know your mother and I didn't give you an *Ozzie and Harriet* upbringing, but we did our best and love you." He blew out a breath. "It's okay if you don't want the kind of life we've chosen. Not that you're looking for my blessing—"

"Blessing for what?"

"For whatever's next with you. You won't be cleaning out your grandfather's closets forever. Anyway, I was about to call you. We're bringing the party to you."

"The party to me? What party, Dad?"

"The reunion. We found a cabin to rent on a lake in Knights Bridge. Your cousins are starting to carve their initials in the woodwork here. They need some fresh country air. We figured we would all come out there."

Samantha restrained herself from groaning. Her family here? In Knights Bridge? "Was this Uncle Caleb's idea?"

"He and I conferred after your last crazy call. Any conversation that includes you and the words *flood watch, hypothermia* and *volleyball* gets my attention. We had the place rented in no time on the internet."

"Mom and Aunt Martha are in on this?"

"They think Caleb and I are meddling."

"You *are* meddling."

"You and this firefighter…" Her father sighed, unrepentant. "Bennetts don't do anything by half measures, Samantha. Yeah. We're meddling."

"This cabin and lake—"

"Just above the old cider mill that caught fire with you inside. It's owned by the Sloans. You should have had a dumber father. Believe me, there are times I wished I'd had a dolt for a father, too. I remember when I was fifteen and thought I was in love with this buxom cheerleader. Old Harry set me straight."

"I'm not fifteen and I'm not seeing anyone."

He ignored her. "We'll be there in time for dinner tomorrow. Eloisa is already talking about us all sitting around playing board games. That might be worse than volleyball. We'll see."

Samantha bit back a laugh. "It'll serve you right if you're bored out of your mind, you know."

"I'm never bored when I'm with my gang. See you tomorrow."

After she hung up, Samantha got under the covers, listening to the rain. It was a heavy, steady rain that promised to end tomorrow, probably well before her family descended on Knights Bridge. She appreciated her warm, comfortable room and the chance to reread her notes in peace, but she couldn't help but wonder what would have happened if she'd gone back to Justin's cozy sawmill apartment with him, or if she'd unzipped her tent and invited him in out of the rain.

Lady Elizabeth sank into her bunk and fought back tears. She knew the truth now but hated to admit it, even to herself, alone in the dark. It had been love at first sight for her with Captain Farraday. She ached to have him with her. She knew in her heart that he would give up his pirate ways for her. He would bring her back home to England, back to her family. They would welcome him and see that he was pardoned.

A loud knock startled her. She didn't know whether to pretend it hadn't awakened her or answer it. She settled for a little of each. "I'm sleeping," she called groggily.

"You're not sleeping," Captain Farraday said. "You're wide-awake, daydreaming."

"About going home, yes."

"About me, Bess. About us."

The door opened, and there he was. And she knew she was lost.

Twenty-Three

Loretta walked back to Beacon Street after dinner at an upscale Newbury Street restaurant that served the most outrageously wonderful macaroni and cheese she'd ever had. She definitely had to burn it off before she tried to get some sleep. Total carb load. Had to be nerves and jet lag, although she couldn't explain why she was nervous.

It was drizzling on and off, with heavy rain moving in from the west. She didn't own an umbrella, much less have one with her, and she'd only brought a leather jacket, which would do okay in the current conditions. She would need to get back to her hotel before the rain picked up. The jacket was just barely warm enough for the cool temperature. She'd have to buy a damn parka for Dylan's Christmas wedding.

Two young girls were out on the stoop in front of the Bennett house, wearing wool sweaters and sitting on raincoats they had spread out on the wet stone steps. Loretta slowed her pace and tried to hear what they were saying without looking like some kind of pervert. The girls seemed to be in a deep discussion about the questionable sanity of their parents. Apparently their cousin Samantha was right there in the screw-loose department.

"She's great," the younger girl, who couldn't have been more than ten, said, "but why can't we have a normal cousin?"

Her older sister, maybe twelve, gave a long-suffering sigh. "Isaac says she's falling for the guy in Knights Bridge who rescued her from the fire. She won't admit it, but Isaac can tell."

"Oh, wow. Think we'll meet him when we go to Knights Bridge?"

"I hope so. Isaac says this guy *carried* Samantha out of the fire."

The younger girl gasped. "Really?"

"This cabin sounds good," the older girl said. "Uncle Malcolm says he'll play Scrabble with us if we promise not to short-sheet his and Aunt Francesca's bed."

The two girls giggled. Loretta managed to get out of earshot and out of their line of sight without tripping. She didn't breathe until she got to the corner of the next block.

Knights Bridge? Samantha Bennett's young cousins were joining her in Knights Bridge?

Loretta continued up a side street toward her hotel in Copley Place. Maybe the Bennetts had decided to head to Knights Bridge because it was an attractive town and a good base for seeing the area and getting out of the city. A bunch of innocent reasons were possible. It didn't have to be anything involving Duncan and Samantha's treasure hunts. As desperately as she wanted to know what was going on, Loretta had no intention of walking back to the Bennett house, knocking on the door and asking Malcolm Bennett what was up with the entire Bennett family traipsing off to a cabin in Knights Bridge.

A nasty breeze gusted, bringing with it an unpleasant spray of rain. She picked up her pace. She knew she'd been dragging her heels about going to Knights Bridge. She'd had Julius with her that first time a few weeks ago. Well, *with* her wasn't exactly accurate. He'd been escorting his client, Daphne Stewart. The point was, Loretta was well aware that she hadn't had to face Dylan, Noah and the population of Knights Bridge by herself. She hadn't had to face the consequences of the two men she cared most about in the world—cared for like sons—having fallen in love with women from this little town on the other side of the continent. What that meant for her. Her life. Her hopes and dreams.

Julius had been singularly unsympathetic. *"Knights Bridge isn't on Mars, Loretta. It's not even in a different country. It's a plane ride from La Jolla. That's it."*

It felt like Mars.

She called him when she reached her room, about three seconds before the skies opened up. She'd never seen such rain. She paced in front of her window that looked out toward the river, marveling at the lights, the rain, the people running through puddles. It was so different from home and her view of her pool, her garden, the Pacific.

Her throat tightened as she gripped the phone. "I'm a coward, Julius."

"Getting cold feet about driving to Knights Bridge?"

"Frozen feet. It's all I can do not to get on a plane back to California tonight."

"Do it, then. There's nothing to stop you."

She sighed, sinking onto the bed. "You're calling my bluff, aren't you?"

"I'm trying to help."

"I know you are. Thank you. My conscience tells me I have to do this."

"Your obsessive-compulsive nature is telling you, you mean. Your conscience is clear, Loretta. You didn't do anything to hurt Duncan, Dylan, Samantha Bennett or anyone else, and you've told Dylan all you know. Right?"

Loretta was silent as she paused in front of the window, staring down at a line of cars, their headlights glowing in the pouring rain.

Julius wasn't giving up. "Loretta? I'm right, yes?"

"Yes, Julius." She could hear the irritation and impatience in her voice and softened it. "I'm sorry. It's not you. I'm just— Yes, you're right. My conscience is clear."

It was his turn to hesitate. "You didn't hurt Duncan during his last days in this life. Your head knows that, but your heart doesn't. That's why you're out there. You need for your heart to know it, too. Damn. I'm sorry I didn't see that sooner."

She frowned at her phone. "What do they put in the water up where you live? Head versus heart. Where did that come from? I have no idea what you're talking about."

"I'm empathizing."

"Don't empathize. I appreciate your thoughts. I do."

"You just need me to listen," he said. "Okay, when you want to talk, I'll be here, and I'll listen."

"Thanks." It came out sullen and curt, but she didn't try to correct it. He would understand. That was the thing about him. He got her in a way no other man in her life ever had. "I'm erratic right now. I admit it. What have you been up to?"

He seized on the slight change in subject. "Daphne wants to go back to Knights Bridge and do something with the O'Dunn twins."

"Phoebe's twin sisters. Does she want you to go with her?"

"She'd like her own entourage if she could get one, but she'd never put it that way. She and the twins think a master class might be a good start."

Loretta sat on the edge of her bed, kicking off her shoes. "A master class in what? Costume design?"

"She says she could do one on a variety of topics."

"Are you thinking about going with her?"

"She's asked me to. I told her I don't like New England winters. The only snow I want to see is on a ski slope in Utah. I like Southern California winters. She says the trip probably won't happen until spring, anyway."

"Then she's serious?"

"So she says. Daphne tends to do whatever she puts her mind to. She says once she figures out what she wants, everything else becomes clear. Things start showing up in her life to make it possible. Maybe that's your problem. You don't know what you want."

"I don't think like that. I just get up in the morning and do what I have to do."

"Maybe it's time to try a different approach and

think about what you want, beyond checking things off your to-do list. What will make you happy, Loretta?"

"Getting off this phone call," she said with a grin.

He laughed. "Good night. Sleep well. Think of me."

He'd just made it impossible *not* to think of him.

By morning, Loretta had her route to Knights Bridge plugged into her GPS, her phone charged and a bottle of water for the road. She bundled up in the warmest sweater that fit under her leather jacket. It was cold but not as wet and dreary as last night. For sure she would have seasonal affective disorder if she lived out here.

As she got on the road, she felt less jet-lagged, less erratic. She'd been weepy after hanging up with Julius. Weepy. Her. She didn't get lost on her way to Storrow Drive. She kept her eyes glued to the signs pointing west and concentrated on her driving—didn't let her mind drift to Duncan and the past or Dylan and Noah and the future, didn't get distracted by the passing scenery.

The landscape opened up the farther west she drove. The changing leaves against the clearing sky were nothing short of breathtaking. She slowed, pulling into the right lane and allowing herself a moment to take in a freshwater marsh surrounded by trees with bright red leaves that reflected in the still water. She'd never been in the Northeast during "leaf peeping" season.

"Stunning," she said aloud.

She cheered up, more herself, more hopeful that this trip wouldn't be a disaster after all. When she started onto the winding road into Knights Bridge, the scenery became too incredible to ignore. She pulled over on a ridge overlooking what she assumed was Quabbin Reservoir in the valley below and got out of her car. She walked down a gravel path to a rock outcropping, hugging her jacket and sweater to her as she gazed at the quiet waters and the surrounding hills and islands, vibrant with autumn color.

A cold wind blew across the ridge. Loretta shuddered, wishing she'd bought that parka already. She realized there were no houses, no people, in the beautiful drowned valley and imagined what it must have been like standing in this spot a hundred years earlier, looking down at a picturesque New England village. Dana, Prescott, Enfield, Greenwich. She knew the names of the lost towns but not which one she would be looking at now.

Knights Bridge was a picturesque New England village. Would it be what it was now if Winsor Dam and Goodnough Dike hadn't been built? If the three branches of the Swift River had been left to wind through the valley, en route to the Chicopee River and eventually the Connecticut River and the Atlantic Ocean?

Dylan hadn't come here just to see about the property his father had left him and to clean up the yard for a frustrated neighbor—Olivia Frost, the woman he was now set to marry. He'd come to Knights Bridge to get closer to his deceased father. Perhaps that was why she was here now. To get closer to Duncan and what they had meant to each other for those weeks before his death.

And, finally, to let him rest in peace.

She hadn't been the one who had died in Portugal

a little over two years ago. He had, suddenly, and far too soon.

His death wasn't her fault.

She watched some kind of bird float high above the reservoir. A big bird. A bald eagle, maybe. She smiled even as she blinked back tears, weepy again. Last night, alone in her Boston hotel room, she'd acknowledged that part of her resented Samantha Bennett because she'd gotten to be with Duncan during his last weeks, if not his final days. What if the stress of dealing with Samantha had tipped the scales for Duncan and ultimately done him in?

"I should have left well enough alone," Loretta said aloud.

The eagle—it had to be an eagle—disappeared into the endless expanse of wilderness. She got back into her rented car and cranked up the heat as she continued into Knights Bridge village. She didn't linger. She turned onto the road off the town green that led out to Carriage Hill Road and Grace Webster's old place.

Despite Dylan's updates, when Loretta pulled into the driveway, she was surprised to see how much had been completed on the house and barn he and Olivia were building. She parked behind a Sloan & Sons van and got out. It wasn't as cold and windy here as out on the open ridge, but it wasn't balmy, either. Everything was still dripping from last night's rain. She just missed stepping in a puddle as she took in the activity. Men working with hammers, saws and drills. A young woman with her hands on her hips as she had it out with an older man. Her uncle Pete, from what Loretta could gather. Something about keeping proper records.

Uncle Pete said, "Got it, Heather," waved her off and went back to the house he was helping to build.

What a spot, Loretta thought, taking in the rolling fields and old stone walls. They'd left most of the established shade trees from old Grace's days on the property.

Dylan walked down from the construction trailer. Loretta managed to grin at him. "I should have brought a wool hat and mittens. Damn, it's cold."

"Not by Knights Bridge standards." He took her hand and kissed her on the cheek. "How are you, Loretta? It's good to see you."

"I've been worse. Good to see you, too. What are you doing, getting in the way of the carpenters?"

He smiled. "I try not to get underfoot too much. I just met with Justin Sloan, the contractor."

"Our volunteer firefighter who rescued Samantha Bennett. She's still in town, right?"

"She stayed with us again last night."

"Guess you're not worried about her stealing the china. Look, I don't have to stay with you and Olivia."

Dylan sidestepped the deep puddle that had almost claimed her. "You do if you want to be in Knights Bridge and don't want to pitch a tent. There's a bed-and-breakfast that's almost never open, and that's it."

"The idea is to drive through town and keep on going?"

"I don't know that many people drive through Knights Bridge. It's a small town on the edge of a protected reservoir. Off the beaten track."

"But beautiful and not as out of touch with the rest of the world as appearances might otherwise suggest."

Loretta sighed, not quite sure she believed the out-of-touch part. "Where is Samantha now?"

"Up the road at Justin's old cider mill that almost burned down."

"Why?"

"Something to do with pirates, I think."

Loretta was spared having to respond when a tall, achingly good-looking man emerged from the trailer and joined them. Justin Sloan. She remembered him from her first visit to Knights Bridge, although they'd exchanged maybe four words. Not a big talker, she'd thought then. But get caught in a fire, she'd want him to rescue her.

Dylan started to introduce them, but she stuck out her half-frozen hand. "Loretta Wrentham. Good to see you again, Justin."

"Welcome back," he said, then turned to Dylan. "I'm off. Catch you later."

Loretta waited as Justin headed to a dusty-gray truck and climbed in. In thirty seconds, he was rattling up the narrow road. "Not one for small talk, is he?"

"I think he's taken with Samantha," Dylan said.

"I can't imagine a weirder match."

"Except for you and Julius Hartley?"

Loretta frowned at him. "What do you know about Julius and me?"

"What do I need to know?"

"Nothing. It's none of your business."

Dylan grinned. "Were you outspoken as a kid, or did law school teach you?"

"Working with you all these years forced me to speak my mind. You can't beat around the bush with you. Your head's too damn thick. Hockey players."

"Fair point." He turned serious. "You and my father were a case of might-have-been, Loretta. Don't let that stop you from enjoying your life now."

"Think that's why I'm here?"

"It is, isn't it?"

"This treasure hunter—"

"We can handle Samantha and whatever she's up to."

"Maybe I can help. You have time to drive with me to this cider mill? I'd like to meet her."

He glanced at her rental, then back at her. "We'll take my car."

Loretta glanced out the window as Dylan navigated a curve on the winding road—what other kind was there in this town?—out to the cider mill. "All the roads look the same around here with the trees," she said, just observing, not meaning to be critical.

"You start to notice subtle differences."

"Like what?"

"The stream was on the left side of the road and now it's on the right."

She glanced sideways at him. "You're not trying to be funny, are you?"

He grinned. "Come on, Loretta. It's a great little town. You won't find one prettier. Admit Knights Bridge is growing on you."

"It is nice. I could see having a country place here. Not me. A lawyer in Boston or something." She looked out the window again, swore she saw a rabbit hopping into the woods. Maybe it had been a woodchuck. "Your father never planned to live here, but I wonder if he might have changed his mind had he lived. I'm glad he got to meet Grace."

"Yeah. Me, too."

"How's she doing? How was the wedding? Is Carriage Hill up to being a wedding venue?"

Dylan filled her in, his affection for Grace—his grandmother—and his gratitude at having this chance to be a part of her life obvious. If anything, his love for Olivia had deepened. Loretta had never seen him this settled, this at peace with himself. Yet, at the same time, he was also as driven as ever, focused on his adventure travel business, the entrepreneurship seminars he and Noah had been talking about. Focused on the future, Loretta thought. A future centered here, in Knights Bridge, even if San Diego remained a part of his life and became a part of Olivia's life.

They pulled in behind Justin's truck on the edge of a dirt road.

"I don't see the mill," Loretta said.

"We walk in from here," Dylan said. "There's a driveway, but it's barely passable."

"Oh, great. I'm glad I had the foresight not to wear high heels out here." Her pricey ankle boots weren't much better. "I can't imagine what an old cider mill has to do with pirate's treasure. By the way, the Bennetts are arriving in Knights Bridge today, apparently en masse. They're renting a cabin. Did you know?"

Dylan clearly hadn't known. "This could get interesting." He nodded to her door. "Go on. It's a short walk to the cider mill. Watch for puddles and slippery patches in the mud."

"What about you?"

"I have a conference call with Noah and a couple of bean counters in twenty minutes."

"And you're just going to leave me out here in the woods?"

He grinned at her. "As fun as I know that would be for you, Loretta, no. Justin can give you a ride back to Carriage Hill."

"I'll try not to piss him off, then," she said, hopping out of the truck and landing in the mud up past her toes. She stepped out of Dylan's way and was positive he was laughing out loud as he turned around and headed back toward Carriage Hill.

Twenty-Four

━━━⟨∘⟩⟨∘⟩⟨∘⟩━━━

With the rain ended, Samantha had walked to the cider mill from Carriage Hill, enjoying the brisk air. The rest of the week promised to be clear and sunny. It would be good weather in Boston, too. She'd left her backpack at Carriage Hill but didn't expect to stay there tonight. She snapped one last picture of the cider mill to compare to the old photographs at the Swift River Country Store and the painting in her grandfather's office. First Justin had arrived, saying little as he went past her into the mill. He seemed to be a man with a purpose, but that was always the case.

Last night, replaying every word, every gesture, of their days together, Samantha was convinced he knew something about the background of his mill that he wasn't letting on. Something to do with Zeke and Henrietta, maybe.

Five minutes after Justin arrived, Loretta Wrentham had picked her way through the puddles on the driveway and introduced herself. She was taken with the mill and its surroundings, more so, apparently, than she had ever anticipated. Samantha liked her immediately.

Loretta was standing on the stone step, peeking inside. "All this old, dry wood. A wonder this place didn't burn to the ground." She shuddered, glancing back at Samantha. "And you were half dead on the floor?"

Samantha held her phone tight in her hand. "I dropped low to avoid the smoke from the fire."

"Fires scare the hell out of me. What does a nineteenth-century cider mill have to do with your eighteenth-century pirate?"

"Probably nothing."

"*Probably.* A devil of a word, isn't it?" Loretta jumped down from the step. Although she wasn't dressed perfectly for the conditions, she managed in her slim pants, leather jacket, silky scarf and urban ankle boots, and she certainly wasn't intimidated. She brushed bits of rainwater and wood chips off her manicured hands. "Is your interest in the cider mill a late development, or was it on your radar when you came to Knights Bridge to check out what Duncan was up to?"

"I hid here in a storm. I never said I came here specifically about the mill or—"

"Samantha. I'm a lawyer. You don't have to tell me anything you don't want to tell me, so don't worry, okay?"

"Fair enough."

"Good." Loretta shivered. "It's chilly, isn't it? Refreshing, I guess. By the way, I checked out your grandfather's house in Boston last night and overheard two of your cousins. Eloisa and...I didn't get the other one's name. A girl. Maybe twelve."

"Ann," Samantha said, sliding her phone into her jacket pocket. "The oldest two are boys. Isaac and Keith."

"Four kids. Heavens. The girls indicated they're heading to Knights Bridge later today. Did I hear that right?"

Samantha nodded. "I'm still wrapping my head around that one."

Justin materialized in the mill door, then stepped out. "They're renting our cabin." He pulled the door shut behind him, snapping on the padlock. "We rent it out sometimes. It's on a pond down the field across from the house. One night."

Samantha hadn't mentioned her family's impending arrival to him, but he hadn't said anything, either. He didn't seem at all offended or put out. Just matter-of-fact. But, she was learning, she didn't always know what he was thinking. "I wasn't sure how long they planned to stay," she said. "One night sounds about right for my father. He gets stir-crazy easily. My cousins can play board games for hours on end." She smiled. "The very idea gives my father hives."

"A man after my own heart," Loretta said. "Your family is different, but you must do all right. Otherwise you wouldn't all be staying in a cabin together even for a night. It's not like you can just kick everyone out to the mall or a movie theater for the afternoon."

"The cabin's not a bad walk from here if you want to go on up there," Justin said, nodding toward the trail alongside Cider Brook. "When you get to the bridge, you'll come out on the other side of the road from our place. You'll see a gap in the stone wall. The cabin's down through the field. You can't miss it."

"Is this the cabin where you lived for a few years?" Samantha asked.

His eyes held hers a beat longer than was comfortable. "It is," he said finally, then turned to Loretta. "You look as if you and Samantha here have some talking to do. I have some things I need to do, but I have to stop back at the office in a little while. I'll come by the cabin when I'm done."

Loretta didn't look enthusiastic, but she said, "Okay, then. Sounds as if I'm in for a walk in the woods."

Justin started out to his truck. "I can take you back to Carriage Hill when I finish up, but there's usually someone at the house if you want to head back sooner."

She nodded. "Good to know. Thanks."

He turned to Samantha, his eyes distant. "I figure you'll want to wait at the cabin for your family."

"Makes sense."

She wished she knew what was on his mind, but he continued out the driveway without another word, dodging the ruts and pits as if he knew them by heart. When he was out of sight, Loretta gave a low whistle. "The tall, dark and taciturn type, huh?"

Samantha tried to keep her tone light. "You should have seen him when he thought I'd broken into the mill."

Loretta's eyebrows went up. "Did you?"

"Only to get out of the storm."

"Did you know he owned the mill?"

"No idea, nor did I know he was the one who told Duncan about me."

Loretta adjusted her expensive-looking scarf, black and white with splashes of golden yellow. "You must have stood out that day for him to remember you and describe you to Duncan."

"It was snowing. No one had been living in the house for a while. I guess Justin wasn't expecting to see anyone there and I stood out."

"Well, I never would have noticed you, if that's any consolation." Loretta tucked the ends of her scarf into her sweater, as if she didn't want them in her way on their hike. "Are you done here?"

"All set," Samantha said. "It's not that far up to the bridge."

"How 'up' is up?"

"Water does run downhill, but it's not a steep climb."

They started onto the trail, wet from last night's rain but not too muddy. Samantha remembered her mad dash in the heat and humidity just a few days ago, with the fierce storm bearing down on her.

Next to her, Loretta was quiet. Finally Samantha said, "You investigated me after Duncan told you I'd been out here."

She didn't hesitate before answering. "I looked into you. I'm not an investigator. Duncan didn't ask me to get involved. I just plowed in on my own. I thought I was doing him a favor, but I was just sticking my nose where it didn't belong. I didn't work for him. I should have minded my own business."

"It seems to me you were trying to be a good friend," Samantha said.

"Think so?"

"Yes, I do. I think Duncan did, too. We didn't discuss you, but he told me a friend had checked me out and found out I was—how did he put it? 'Not just any freaking Bennett.'"

Loretta smiled. "That's a pretty good imitation."

"Burned into my brain. He'd heard of my grandfather, my father, my mother, my uncle. Knew their work in part because of his work. He said he couldn't take the chance I was up to something."

"That's because that's what I told him."

Samantha shook her head. "It was his decision to let me go. He emphasized that." She stepped over an exposed tree root, feeling the mixed emotions of the woman next to her—and her own. "I don't blame anyone but myself for what happened."

They paused on a short, fairly steep section of the trail, a jumble of rocks forming a small waterfall Samantha hadn't noticed before. The brook was high after the heavy rain. Loretta stared down at the mini waterfall. "So soothing. I love the sound of water. I walk on the beach at home to relax, think. I don't do it often enough." She shoved her hands into her jacket pockets. "Duncan and I were fond of each other. Fat lot of good it did him. I hounded him about you and next thing, he was dead."

"His death was a shock."

"Yeah. I guess I'm not over it."

"I'm truly sorry," Samantha said. "I've never really talked about what happened, certainly not with anyone as close to him as you were."

Loretta pulled her gaze from the waterfall. "We weren't that close. We were hoping to get close. At least I was hoping. Maybe he was looking to dump me. That's the thing about a sudden loss. You can be left off balance, not sure what was real, what was just wishful thinking." She pulled her hands out of her pockets and picked up a freshly fallen maple leaf, still wet but in perfect condition. "Pretty, isn't it?" She tossed it into the waterfall. "I hope nothing I did hastened Duncan's death."

Samantha went a few more steps up the trail, but all she could see was Duncan McCaffrey as he'd watched her leave his temporary office in Portugal after he'd fired her. He'd looked regretful, sorry—but not torn, she thought. In his mind, he'd done what he'd had to do. She turned to Loretta, still by the waterfall. "None of us on Duncan's team saw anything that indicated he would have a fatal heart attack. If he noticed any symptoms or was in a doctor's care, he didn't tell us."

"That would be just like him."

Loretta walked up to her. She was obviously in good shape but hampered somewhat by her inappropriate footwear. "He didn't need me haranguing him to get rid of you," she said with a groan. "He knew what to do. You're not the first person he'd had to fire. But he liked you, and I think he'd have liked to have given you a second chance and probably would have if he'd lived. He might have if I'd stayed out of it."

"Oh, he was determined to fire me."

"Maybe. My thinking…" Loretta shrugged. "I was affected by some of the things I'd seen with Dylan and Noah. The opportunists. The snakes in the grass."

"You're protective of them, and you were protective of Duncan," Samantha said as they continued up the narrow trail. "You can't possibly blame yourself for Duncan's death, Loretta. What you told him about me and what he should do—it's okay."

"He hated that he hadn't guessed you hadn't told

him everything about yourself. He said he should have asked you if you were related to Harry Bennett. Would you have told him the truth if he had?"

"I'm sure I would have. I've never denied my family to anyone."

Loretta slowed, her scarf working its way out from her sweater. "Damn. I can feel the jet lag." She looked at Samantha. "You're saying firing you wasn't that big a deal to Duncan?"

"I'm saying it didn't kill him," she said without hesitation. "He had a heart attack and fell. I wasn't there, but everyone I know who was doesn't believe it was brought on by stress or anything but undetected heart disease."

"I'm sorry. I had no right to insinuate the situation with you had anything to do with his death. It wasn't your fault."

"Or yours," Samantha said softly.

"It's crazy, maybe, but I haven't been able to shake the guilt…." Loretta cleared her throat. "What might have been. You know?" She smiled, the lines around her eyes visible in the dappled shade. "Then again, maybe you don't know. You're still awfully young."

"I wish I'd told Duncan the truth about myself from the start." Samantha heard the emotion in her voice. "I hate that I let him down. That everyone on his team knows I let him down. And myself. I handled the situation badly, but I never saw what I did as a breach of trust."

"You wanted to impress him. He was like that, wasn't he? A larger-than-life guy. It's not easy letting go of a man who seems indestructible. I'll bet your grandfather was like that. He's mixed up with your reasons for being here, too, isn't he?"

"Maybe so." Samantha could see the bridge through birch trees, their leaves turning yellow against their white trunks, and picked up her pace. "I miss him, but he had a long, good life. Duncan was only in his early seventies."

"Still a young man by comparison." Loretta kept up with Samantha as they followed the path under the small bridge. "He'd pour cold brook water on both our heads for talking about him this way. He went out fast, doing what he loved, before he had to slow down or even knew he was sick."

"There's some consolation in that," Samantha said.

"You'd think I'd have known him better, given the years I've worked with Dylan, but it's not the case. Duncan and Dylan's mother were divorced when Dylan was young. Duncan was always there for Dylan but maybe not always in the ways a son wants or needs. He and I didn't get to know each other until right before he died."

"You're quite a bit younger than he was."

Loretta grinned. "Nice of you to notice. The age difference didn't matter. Not to me, anyway."

Samantha went first up the steep bank to the road, across from where she had ducked down to Cider Brook on Wednesday. She pictured a posse of Sloan brothers charging down the trail as boys. What a place to grow up.

"Absolutely stunning," Loretta said, squinting out at the field and the line of trees beyond it. "But should I watch for snakes?"

"Ticks."

"I've never even seen a tick."

They found the gap in the stone wall that Justin had mentioned and headed onto a path through the tall grass and wildflowers of a wide, sloping field. Samantha welcomed the open ground, and a cool breeze helped to clear her head.

"Duncan wasn't happy about the situation with you, but it's not why he died," Loretta said, as if to convince herself more than Samantha. "He didn't die because you didn't tell him you'd been to Knights Bridge and were a Bennett, and he didn't die because I pushed him to fire you."

"I'm sorry I contributed to any turmoil in his last days."

"So am I, but Duncan didn't mind turmoil. I won't say he lived for it, but he sure did embrace it when it was thrust upon him."

Samantha didn't argue. Loretta seemed calmer, although she was obviously by nature an intense woman. As they continued through the field, she brushed her fingertips over lacy white wildflowers that came almost to her knees. "Has this trip to Knights Bridge been worth it for you, Samantha?"

"Right now I have more questions than I had when I arrived."

"About pirates or about Sloans?" Loretta asked with a knowing grin.

Samantha laughed, appreciating the cool breeze. "Both, maybe. I came here with a three-hundred-year-old pirate mystery, and now I've added a hundred-year-old mystery about a young couple photographed at Justin's cider mill. There's something about them… I can't explain."

"Do you trust your instincts?"

"Some days more than others."

"Dylan has good instincts about people. They were honed during his years as a hockey player and then working with Noah. Duncan thought he did, too, but his instincts about projects and opportunities were better than they were about people."

"I doubt anyone has ever said a Bennett has good instincts about people."

Loretta slowed her pace as they made their way through the field. She glanced sideways at Samantha. "What's your mother like?"

"Wonderful. She's intelligent, sophisticated—"

"She'd never break into an abandoned cider mill?"

Samantha smiled. "She'd never be in the position that she'd need to."

"Would she want to have anything to do with pirate treasure?"

"She and my father are deep into their work on sunken World War II vessels. Shipwrecks of all kinds can yield new evidence about the past—solve mysteries, dispel myths, answer questions about historical events and technical issues."

"Duncan used to tell me that his work wasn't about profiting from lost treasure." Loretta paused, gazing out at the rolling hills. "But there's a personal aspect to your interest in Captain Farraday, isn't there, Samantha? Piecing together this pirate's life and death was your last quest with your grandfather."

Samantha nodded, choking back unexpected tears. "Sorry."

"No apology necessary." Loretta's voice was surprisingly gentle for such a hard-nosed woman. They

continued on the narrow path through the tall grass
and wildflowers. "My grandfather died when I was
in college, and I still tear up when I think about him.
Look, I don't mean to stir up your grief over your
grandfather. Whatever your interest in this pirate is—
whatever he does or doesn't have to do with Knights
Bridge and that old cider mill—I wish you luck finding answers."

"Thank you," Samantha said. "I sometimes wonder
if I should leave well enough alone."

"Not your nature." Loretta gave a small moan as the
path curved down a slope and they came to the cabin.
"It would be a log cabin. I wouldn't be surprised if the
Sloans cut the trees for the logs themselves."

"Count on it."

"What a spot, though."

It was, Samantha thought. The cabin was situated
on a relatively flat stretch of open ground above a
small pond, rippling in a cool breeze. On the bank
opposite the cabin were woods, dominated by sugar
maples with their changing bright autumn leaves.

Loretta touched her arm. "You go on. I'll head back
up to the Sloan place and get one of them to take me
back to Carriage Hill. Dylan can show me what a tick
looks like."

"I can walk with you."

"It's okay. I'm glad we had this chance to talk. And
don't worry. Anything we've talked about remains
between us. I can keep things to myself. I'm an attorney, remember?"

"Justin knows most of what I've told you."

"It's what you haven't said out loud that counts,
though, isn't it?" Loretta smiled, plucking a golden-

colored wildflower. "If I were you, I might just take my time solving this pirate mystery. And don't ask me why, because you know why. I've met Justin Sloan. I've seen you two together."

"Yes, well..." Samantha grimaced. "He's about to meet my family."

"The guy's a rock. He can handle your family. Good to meet you, Samantha. I see now why Duncan liked you."

"How long will you be staying in Knights Bridge?"

"Not long. Maybe not past tomorrow." Loretta nodded up toward the Sloan house. "I noticed dogs in the yard. Do they bite?"

"They're very friendly. There's a pet duck, too. His name's Fred."

"Of course. I should have known there'd be a pet duck named Fred."

Loretta started back through the field, swinging her wildflower. Samantha liked her even more after their long conversation and felt they had cleared the air about Duncan McCaffrey and his last days.

She mounted the sturdy steps onto the cabin porch. The Sloans had obviously prepared for guests. The porch was swept, a large clay pot of orange mums set out by the front door, chairs and tables dusted and wiped down. She sat on a dark-stained wooden rocking chair. Her family would be along soon. She wondered if Justin would steer clear of them. Did she *want* him to steer clear? Meeting the Bennett brothers, their wives and her cousins could snap a man back to his senses.

Which, of course, her father and uncle knew.

And that, she thought, was why they were on their way to Knights Bridge. It had nothing to do with fresh air or her rambunctious cousins. It had to do with Malcolm and Caleb Bennett's suspicions that their daughter and niece was getting in too deep with one Justin Sloan of little Knights Bridge, Massachusetts.

Twenty-Five

Justin dropped Loretta off at Carriage Hill but didn't get out of his truck. He tried not to look impatient as she glanced sideways at him, her hand on the door latch. "Did you and your brothers cut the logs for the cabin? Samantha and I were wondering."

"My grandfather and my father and uncle did."

"Ah. It looks like a nice place. Rugged." She pushed open her door. "Thanks for the ride."

"Sure."

"You don't talk much, do you?"

"Mind's elsewhere. Sorry."

"Thinking about pirates, I imagine," she said with a wry smile as she jumped out of the truck. "Good seeing you again."

He made sure she was on the stone walk into the kitchen ell before he pulled away. It wouldn't be good to run over Dylan's lawyer. Loretta had been winded when she'd arrived at the office, worried about the dogs, dubious about Fred and totally freaked out about ticks. Justin had figured there was no need to yap at her on the drive back to Carriage Hill. Let her pull herself together before joining Dylan and Olivia.

And his mind *was* elsewhere.

On Samantha and the twists and turns that had brought her to Knights Bridge.

To him.

He shook off that last thought as he drove back to town. He stopped at the fire department, located in a solid, new building at the far end of the common, but he didn't go in. He walked around back to the old fire hall. It had been renovated and reconfigured years ago—before he had started wielding a hammer—and was now used as a training facility and for a meeting space.

Hazelton Hall, the main room was called.

Christopher had mentioned it in passing last night on their way back after the chimney fire. Justin had never paid much attention. He had no idea why it was named after a Hazelton but assumed it had to do with money, a donation the family had made to help fund the building. He'd asked Randy Frost after they'd left Carriage Hill last night. Randy didn't know, either.

Then, in the early-morning shadows, Justin had remembered a plaque on the back wall of the main room, and an old story—a near-forgotten story that was part of the fabric of Knights Bridge, of fighting its fires.

The room was maybe twenty feet by fourteen feet. Not that big. Shiny, polished oak floors and tall windows, sunlight streaming in on the bright afternoon. Folding tables were shoved up against a side wall, under a large bulletin board covered with information on training sessions, safety reminders, town goings-on.

The plaque was by itself on a white-painted wall

between two windows. Dark, coppery lettering against a lighter copper background that explained in the simplest, starkest terms why this was Hazelton Hall.

HAZELTON HALL
DEDICATED TO THE MEMORY OF EZEKIEL HAZELTON
APRIL 12, 1885–OCTOBER 6, 1915
HE DIED SO THAT OTHERS MIGHT LIVE.

Justin looked around him at the empty room. He'd attended functions and training sessions here countless times for as far back as he could remember, and never once had he read the damn plaque on the wall.

He left the hall, walking past Christopher out front. Christopher didn't say a word. Justin knew he must look stiff, unapproachable, but he was shaken to his core. He bypassed his truck and walked down to the country store. No one said a word to him here, either. He headed straight back to the camping gear and the photographs on the wall next to the bulletin board.

His gaze zeroed in on the young couple in the middle photograph.

Zeke and Henrietta, 1915

From the look of the trees around the cider mill and the wagon of apples, the photograph must have been taken in the fall, shortly before Zeke Hazelton's death.

He and Henrietta looked happy.

What had happened to her?

But Justin knew.

He died so that others might live.

Thirty years old. Younger than Justin was now. His life before him, sacrificed in a terrible fire that few remembered now, a hundred years later.

Justin went out through the back of the store, needing air—a moment to throttle back the emotion and resurface in the Knights Bridge of today, with its small, modern fire department and trained volunteer and professional firefighters. The courage and sacrifice of men like Zeke Hazelton had led the way.

Had Samantha sensed the tragedy of his and Henrietta's story?

Had she *known?*

No.

She hadn't known. Didn't know now. She might have ways Justin didn't get, but one thing he knew about Samantha Bennett—she was damn lousy at being anything but open and straightforward. It was who she was. Sneaking around, lying and pretending, didn't come naturally to her.

Then again, he'd been wrong about women before.

The Bennetts hadn't arrived yet when Justin walked up onto the cabin porch. He knocked on the side of the screen door, the main door wide open despite the cool weather. "Come on in," Samantha called. "I'm just getting ready for the family onslaught."

He smiled as he joined her in the front room, with its stone fireplace and comfortable, oversize furnishings. "You can't wait."

"It's true. We haven't had a family reunion in ages. All of us together." She grabbed a quilt off the back of a chair. "It'll be good."

"You just expected it would be in Boston."

"That was the plan." She set the quilt back on the chair. "The quilts are fabulous. I've always wanted to curl up under a stack of quilts on a cold, rainy day."

"You won't get your chance in the next couple of days. It's going to be sunny."

"Cool, though. The quilts look handmade. Are they?"

"Gran and my aunts sewed them. They love to quilt together. Everyone gets quilts for presents. When we decided to turn this place into a getaway, they got busy and made a bunch of quilts for it. They'd like it that you appreciate their quilts." He pointed to a log-cabin quilt on the couch. "That's got pieces of one of my old shirts. I wasn't ready to part with it, but I left it on Gran's living room floor one day and it ended up in a quilt."

"Then I'll think of you if I end up under it." Her cheeks flamed, but she laughed. "I really need to think before I speak."

"It's a good habit but not as much fun."

She nodded toward the screen door. "Want to get some air?"

He followed her outside. She stood looking out at the pond, a half-dozen gray birches along the bank. "How long did you live here?"

"A few years. It needed work. I put in a new bathroom and kitchen, painted, dug out the septic tank. That sort of thing."

"All while working for Sloan & Sons?"

"That was the deal." He sat on the rail, his knee brushing against her hip as she stayed on her feet. "There used to be a house on the other side of the pond, down the hill through the trees. Part of its foundation is still there. It burned to the ground in 1915."

Samantha's eyes narrowed. "Who lived there?"

"Zeke and Henrietta Hazelton and their son."

"The couple in the photograph." Samantha inhaled, her eyes wide now. "Justin…"

"They moved out here after they were married." Justin kept any emotion out of his voice, but he could feel it working its way through him as he looked back out across the pond. "Zeke worked in the country store and he and Henrietta ran the cider mill during apple season. This field used to be an apple orchard. You can still see a few old apple trees along the stone wall."

"I noticed them when Loretta and I were walking." Samantha's voice was quiet. She placed a hand on a post and looked sideways at him. "Justin—what happened to Zeke and Henrietta? Their story doesn't have a happy ending, does it?"

"Zeke was down at the cider mill. It was a dry, clear October afternoon. Henrietta and their little boy were home. The house caught fire. A kitchen stove fire that got out of control. Zeke smelled the smoke and ran home, but by then, the house was fully engulfed in flames."

Samantha inhaled sharply next to him. "His wife and son were trapped inside?"

"They'd been in the pantry putting up food for the winter. The exact wrong place. But Zeke knew that was what Henrietta had planned for the afternoon and checked there first. He got them out safely."

"So their story *does* have a happy ending—"

"He was overcome with smoke and collapsed in the back door. Henrietta set the baby in their wagon and ran to get help, but it was too late. She was driven back by the fire. They say if not for her son, she would have run straight into the flames and died with Zeke."

"How awful," Samantha whispered, pale and still.

Justin held in his own emotion. The woods across the pond were aflame with fall color, as they would have been the day Zeke Hazelton died. "It's been a hundred years. Zeke didn't have the training or equipment we have today. It's likely smoke inhalation, not the flames, killed him. There was nothing Henrietta could have done."

"What happened to her and their son?"

"They left town. Zeke's parents ran the store until their deaths. They sold the mill." Justin eased off the porch rail and turned to Samantha. "I don't know what connection Zeke and Henrietta could have to your pirate."

"Nor do I, and it doesn't matter—"

"Doesn't it, Sam? You were caught in a bad storm and then a fire. You've trekked up and down the roads and trails out here." He moved in close to her, touched a knuckle to her cheek. "You've let yourself get caught up with me. How far will you go to get your answers?"

Tears shone in her eyes, but she wasn't looking at him now. She was staring out at the woods across the pond. "Did you know about Zeke and Henrietta when you bought the cider mill?"

"Not really. I'd heard things here but never made the connection to the mill."

She shifted her gaze to him, tears glistening on her cheeks now. "I don't know how someone goes on after such a thing. Being rescued by the man you love. Having him die before your eyes."

"I don't, either, but I hope Henrietta found a way." Justin slipped his arms around Samantha, held her close, smelling her hair as he kissed the top of her head. "I have to get back to work. This is a good spot, Samantha. Enjoy your family."

Justin stopped at Carriage Hill after work. His brother Brandon was in the kitchen with Maggie and the boys, who were at the table regaling Loretta Wrentham with tales of their O'Dunn grandmother and her goats. "We help her muck out the barn," Aidan said.

"Muck out the barn?" Loretta frowned at them. "You mean shovel manure?"

Tyler nodded eagerly. "Grandma makes us wear work gloves so we don't get poop and stuff on our hands."

"Oh, well. There you go. Sign me up."

Maggie stepped into the mudroom. "I can't wait to tell Gran that you *like* mucking out the barn."

It was clear Aidan and Tyler liked getting a reaction out of Loretta more than they liked the work itself. They moved on to horrifying her with tales of slugs they'd found in Olivia's gardens. "I can buy that goats are cute," Loretta, obviously playing along, said, "but do not try to tell me that slugs are cute."

Five-year-old Aidan made an exaggerated face. "Slugs are *nasty.*"

Maggie emerged from the mudroom with a large clear-glass container of some kind of whole-grain flour. "The Bennetts have arrived, did you know, Justin?" She set the container on the butcher-block island. "Samantha's parents, her aunt and uncle and four cousins. They all fit at the cabin?"

He shrugged. "One way or the other."

"They're used to a Boston mansion," Loretta said from the table. "It needs work, but it's still a Back

Bay mansion." She held up a hand at Justin. "Not that there's anything wrong with your cabin. It's adorable."

"Adorable." Brandon, standing at the sink, grinned. "I don't think anyone's ever called anything associated with us adorable."

Loretta rolled her eyes. "I'm not going there."

"Smart move," Maggie said, turning back to Justin. "Your mother called me. I'm bringing the Bennetts food. Simple fare. You would think world-famous explorers would want something exotic, but lasagna and salad for dinner, toast and cereal for breakfast and some fruit and sandwich fixings will do it. Grab an apron. You can help. See what's up."

Justin shook his head. "I'm not grabbing an apron, Maggie."

Brandon grinned again at Loretta. "See what I mean? We are *not* adorable."

"All in the eye of the beholder," she countered. "I'm sure a girl slug thinks a boy slug is pretty darned adorable."

Justin was fairly certain Loretta had said "darned" because of the boys. Brandon got them off to do homework, leaving Justin to help Maggie load her van. Somehow he ended up going with her out to the cabin. She pulled in behind an old Mercedes.

Every light in the place was on, and it was not quiet.

They got out, and Maggie elbowed in next to him as he opened up the back of the van. Justin sighed. "What is it, Maggie?"

"Nothing. Absolutely nothing. Grab that big box there, will you? You can handle it."

"Maggie—"

"Let's just go."

She marched with her box up to the porch. Justin followed with the big box. The cabin was warm, a fire roaring in the fireplace. Two women were wrapped in quilts in front of the fire. They had glasses of wine and seemed to be enjoying themselves as two men— the Bennett brothers, Justin thought—set the table in the adjoining dining room. A teenage boy was laying out napkins, explaining that if he got into Amherst College, his top pick, he would check out all the old haunts of his deceased grandfather and his grandfather's friends.

Justin took Maggie's lead and went into the kitchen with her. Samantha emerged from a back bedroom, obviously surprised to see him setting a box of food on the counter. She made introductions as her father, uncle, cousin Isaac and then three more cousins— Keith, Ann, Eloisa—crowded into the kitchen. Maggie kept bumping into him as they unloaded the boxes. She wasn't even subtle. Justin knew she was reminding him who he was and where he belonged, and it wasn't with the offspring of Harry Bennett, explorer and adventurer.

When Justin headed out to the van for the last box of groceries, Malcolm Bennett followed him. He had on shorts and a sweatshirt but didn't seem to notice the cold temperature. He grinned as he reached for a jug of milk. "Not quite ready to meet the Bennetts, are you, Justin?"

He noticed that Samantha had her father's dark eyes. "I'm helping my sister-in-law."

"We appreciate her stepping in at the last minute. This is a sudden trip, but we're glad to be here. Caleb's kids haven't had a chance to see much of the New England countryside. It'll be good for the younger ones to see where their brother's going to school. He doesn't want to jinx himself, but he'll get into Amherst."

"Sounds good," Justin said, his tone neutral. "Hope you all enjoy your stay. Let us know if there's anything you need."

"My father grew up on a farm not that far north of here. This place reminds me of it. Funny the wobbles and turns our lives can take." Malcolm swung the milk jug next to him as they started back up to the porch. "Thank you for saving Samantha in that fire. Collapsing means it was too close for comfort."

"She would argue that she collapsed."

Malcolm didn't seem surprised. "We Bennetts aren't always good at acknowledging our limits. We're not reckless. We plan as best we can, mitigate the dangers, account for the risks, but sometimes you just don't know. Then what are you going to do? Chicken out because you can't know everything?" He nodded to Justin. "You'd never fight another fire if that was your answer."

Malcolm's young nieces had ensconced themselves under quilts on the porch. They stared up at Justin. "You're a *firefighter?*"

Their uncle scowled. "You girls quit gaping. You can be firefighters, too, you know."

"I'm a volunteer firefighter," Justin said. "I'm also a carpenter."

"We thought you were a caterer."

Maggie swung out the door. "He should be so lucky."

Malcolm looked out toward the pond, dark under

the night sky. "Knights Bridge is a lovely town. Would you ever leave?"

"I left once for a few years," Maggie said. "Now I'm back, and I'm glad of it. I've never been happier."

She trotted back down to the van. Malcolm looked expectantly at Justin. "You?"

Justin shrugged. "I'm here," he said, as if that explained everything. And maybe it did, he thought as Samantha came out to the porch.

Her father grunted and went back inside.

Justin started down the steps. Samantha joined him. They passed Maggie, who mumbled something noncommittal as she ran back up to the cabin with a small bag, the last of her delivery.

"Thank you," Samantha said as she and Justin came to the van.

He grinned at her. "This was brave of me, don't you think?"

"Ann and Eloisa already have crushes on you. Anyway, I just called and invited Loretta, Dylan and Olivia up for dinner. I was about to call you to see if you'd like to join us—"

"No, Sam," he said, interrupting her. "Thanks, but I'll see you later." He brushed her cheek. "Be with your family." He winked at her as he shut the back of the van. "And if you guys get bored playing Scrabble, there's also Monopoly."

Samantha didn't seem to think he was that funny. He laughed as he got back into the van. Maggie returned and slid behind the wheel, glancing up at the cabin. "The Bennetts are great. I wanted not to like them. Is that wrong of me?"

"Yeah."

She sighed. "You weren't supposed to answer."

She started up the van and backed out, the dark, open field behind them. The driveway, in considerably better shape than the one to the cider mill, curved around one side of the pond, then down through the woods.

Maggie spoke again when they reached the road. "When Brandon and I were living in Boston, I never thought about Harry Bennett being there."

"Harry was an old man by the time you were in Boston."

"I guess, but still. It's cool, getting to meet his sons. They're adventurers, too." She held the steering wheel with both hands. "I hope they like the food."

"Your lasagna's the best, Maggie. They'll love it."

She looked hesitant. "I didn't make it."

"Olivia?"

"Not Olivia."

"Brandon? He's a good cook. Not as good as Adam, but he can do lasagna."

"Heather," Maggie blurted. "Heather made the lasagna."

Justin grinned. "Uh-oh."

"I take full responsibility. She was at Carriage Hill, and Olivia and I were trying our hand at essential oils and not having great luck with our new still. I had all the ingredients for several batches of lasagna using Olivia's tomatoes. Heather offered to pitch in while I finished up with Olivia." Maggie winced as she glanced at Justin. "I didn't think of it until just now. Think it'll be okay?"

"It'll be fine. Even Heather can put together a basic lasagna. Your reputation is secure, Maggie."

"Phew." She smiled at him. "Samantha blushed when she saw you, did you notice? Her mother's beautiful, as well as smart. Of course, so is Samantha. They're both only children, did you know?"

"Maggie."

"What?"

"Just drive."

Twenty-Six

⟿⟾

"So the stud with the groceries is the one who saved you from the fire *and* ratted you out to McCaffrey?" Caleb Bennett shook his head as he and Samantha set the big table in the kitchen. "You remind me a lot of Pop, Sam. You don't do anything by half measures."

She sighed, grabbing the stack of napkins Maggie had thoughtfully included in her delivery. "You're making assumptions, Uncle Caleb."

"Based on hard evidence. It's a good thing we're here. A dose of your family will jump-start your brain."

"I'm not discussing Justin Sloan—or anyone else in Knights Bridge—given your mood."

"What mood?"

"You've been driving for several days with your eighteen-year-old son. Isaac's great and you love to drive, but you have a lot on your mind." Samantha set the napkins on the table for people to take as needed. "You're worried about Isaac going to school on this side of the Atlantic."

Caleb got the salad off the counter and set it on the table. "I went to school on this side of the Atlantic."

"Your parents lived in Boston."

"They weren't there all the time. We live in a big world. See what I'm saying, Sam? This town's affecting you."

"Don't let Caleb fool you," her mother said, joining them in the kitchen. "He knows you have to figure out the situation here for yourself, and what's next for you. So does your father."

"There's more to be done at Grandpa's house in Boston," Samantha said. "My skills are replaceable."

"But you're not," her mother said.

"Thank you."

Her father came into the kitchen and snatched a slice of cucumber out of the salad. "You're as driven and impulsive as any Bennett." He headed to the stove and got the lasagna out of the oven. "All kidding aside, Samantha, this is your gig. We'll do anything we can to help you, and we'll try to stay out of the way of you and this Justin Sloan character."

"Do you think there's pirate treasure out here?" she asked quietly.

"Anything is possible." He set the lasagna onto pot holders on the table. "Lightning did strike the other day."

As she stood in the warm kitchen with her parents and uncle, Samantha realized the aftereffects of her scare had eased. "All's well that ends well, as Grandpa used to say. He left me with unanswered questions about his own interest in Benjamin Farraday. He never mentioned him to any of you?"

"Not a word," her uncle said.

Her parents agreed. Samantha started to bring up *The Mill at Cider Brook* or *The Adventures of Captain Farraday and Lady Elizabeth,* but Olivia, Dylan and Loretta arrived, bearing wine from Noah Kendrick's winery.

Any lingering misunderstanding or doubts about Samantha's history with Duncan McCaffrey and Loretta Wrentham's role in getting her fired dissipated over dinner. The conversation centered on Olivia and Dylan's upcoming wedding, plans for The Farm at Carriage Hill and life in San Diego and Knights Bridge. Olivia and Isaac talked about Amherst, and she gave him more a sense of what it was like today versus eighty years ago when Harry Bennett had been there.

No mention was made of pirates, or of last week's fire and Samantha's rescuer.

After their guests left, she dug out a Scrabble set, and she, Ann, Eloisa and her father played a game on the dining room table. Samantha found an old score card of a series of games between Justin and his brothers. He'd lost every one of them—except the last one, which he'd won by a hundred points. She could see him letting his younger brothers win, then nailing them, just to remind them he could do it.

She bunked with Ann and Eloisa under the eaves in an upstairs bedroom. The girls were drooling over Dylan McCaffrey and Justin Sloan.

"If that's what the guys are like here," Ann said, "we're moving to Knights Bridge."

In the morning, Samantha led her father and uncle down the trail along Cider Brook to the old mill while her mother, aunt and cousins stayed back at the cabin.

The Bennett brothers examined the fire damage and interrogated Samantha about her interest.

"You didn't just happen on this place," her father said.

"I did and I didn't." She nodded to them. "Did Grandpa ever mention a painting of a cider mill to you? And a handwritten draft of a story about Farraday and a British aristocrat?"

The two men frowned at her. Caleb shook his head. "No."

Samantha filled them in as they walked back to the cabin together. Her aunt and cousins had been out kayaking on the pond. Her mother was reading a book on the porch, wrapped up in one of the Sloan quilts. They all had lunch together. Then Samantha waved Caleb and his gang goodbye, as they left in the old Mercedes, and saw her parents off in their rented car. They were all heading up to the old Bennett farm, via a stop in Amherst so Isaac's younger siblings could see where their grandfather had gone to college—and where Isaac hoped he'd be going. Then they would meet Samantha in Boston.

With her family safely back on the road, she walked down Carriage Hill Road. It was much easier without a backpack. She'd left hers on the cabin porch. She would fetch it once she figured out where she would be tonight. She ran through her options as she came to Grace Webster's old place. She noticed Justin's truck in the driveway. No surprise, since he was the contractor, but she still felt her heartbeat quicken.

Loretta was by the trailer and waved to her. Samantha headed up the driveway. "It's freezing," Loretta said, shivering in her leather jacket. "Dylan says

I'm being dramatic, but I swear I woke up with icicles on my bed. Apparently Olivia doesn't like to turn on the heat this early in the season, never mind the temperature."

Justin ambled out of the trailer, grinning at her. "It's sixty degrees out, Loretta."

"Fifty-nine. I just checked, and it wasn't fifty-nine this morning."

"Do you ever back down?"

"Never. Even if I know I'm going to lose, I at least find a way to save face." She gave a satisfied sigh. "It's crazy that I came out here, but it's good, too. Cathartic. I didn't realize just how much I had repressed the past two years."

"How long will you be staying?" Samantha asked.

Loretta glanced at her wristwatch. "Another forty-five minutes. I have a flight this evening that I don't intend to miss. Need a ride to Boston?"

Samantha hesitated only a fraction of a second. "Yes—yes, that would be great. I just have to stop at the cabin for my backpack."

"We'll pick it up on the way. My car's still at Carriage Hill. Let me say goodbye to Olivia and Dylan and meet you back here."

"Perfect. Thank you."

Loretta seemed pleased as she turned to Justin. "I'll see you again at the wedding. I'll be sure to bring my parka then. This trip…" She paused, glancing at the construction. "It was necessary and necessarily short." She straightened, smiled. "Anyway, Dylan mentioned a path along the stone wall, instead of walking back down the road. Can you point me in the right direction?"

"I'll walk you over there," Justin said.

Samantha waited by the trailer, watching the workers. She could tell they were watching her, too. She didn't blame them. When Justin returned, she noticed his broad shoulders, the shape of his mouth, his jaw. It was crazy, this awareness of him. Just as well her family hadn't stuck around. "My family just left," she told him. "They love Knights Bridge. They're off to Amherst and Grandpa Bennett's old farm in southern New Hampshire. I'll see them all again before they return to England and Scotland."

"In Boston," he said.

She nodded. "I hadn't thought about when or how I'd get back, and then Loretta said—well, you heard her. I seized the moment."

"Did your family have any insights into your pirate?"

"No, but it doesn't matter—"

"Doesn't it, Sam? And when this mystery is solved? On to the next one?"

"I don't know what's next. I'm counting on serendipity to lead the way."

"Serendipity," Justin said, with just a twitch of his lips. "Right."

She met his eyes, almost a midnight-blue in the shade. "There's something in Boston that I want you to see."

"There is, is there?"

"Two things, actually. You don't have to go there. I can bring them here."

"Do you own a car?"

"No, but I can wait for Uncle Caleb to come back with Grandpa's old car. It might be a few days." She smiled brightly, with more confidence than she felt. "I'll plan the next visit better than this one."

"Boston isn't that far. I have some business there I've been putting off. Maybe I'll take a drive over there."

Samantha pictured him pulling up to her grandfather's Back Bay house in his dusty-gray truck, and smiled at the image. "That would be great. When could you get there?"

He leaned in close to her. "Before your family gets back from their wandering."

Twenty-Seven

Loretta did the driving into Boston, veering into the left lane and staying there for most of the trip. On their way out, Dylan had warned Samantha to make sure her seat belt was securely fastened. Good advice, she thought as Loretta careened down Storrow Drive into Boston. They'd talked about Knights Bridge, and Samantha had told her new friend about Benjamin Farraday and the tragic couple in the photographs in the country store.

She looked out her window as they passed the Boston University campus. "I hardly slept last night thinking about Zeke and Henrietta. I have a feeling their story got to Justin, too."

"These tall, dark, silent types can have hearts of gold, you know," Loretta said, but without her usual half-serious tone. "It's quite a story, Samantha. I can't imagine what I would do if the man I loved died saving my life."

"I can't, either."

Samantha felt the flashback to her close call with fire coming on this time. She let it wash over her—let herself feel Justin's strong arms coming around her as she'd gasped for air, tasted the smoke, felt it burning in her eyes, her throat. The moment passed, and she exhaled a long, slow breath before she continued.

"Okay?" Loretta asked her.

"Yes, thanks. I keep thinking I'm missing something that's right in front of me."

"Maybe getting away from Sloan testosterone will help."

Samantha smiled. "Maybe."

"I'll write down these names once I get to my gate. Farraday, Hazelton. Do we know Henrietta's maiden name?"

"Justin might. I don't."

"No worries. I know a guy who can find out anything about anyone." Loretta pointed at an exit off Storrow. "This is where we get off for your grandfather's house, isn't it?"

"Yes, but I don't mind getting you out to Logan. I can take the subway back into town."

Loretta already had her blinker on. "It's all right. I've got this down now. If I get lost after I drop you off, I'll dump this heap on the side of the road and flag a cab. Nobody will miss it. Isn't it the worst car rental ever?"

Samantha laughed. "It is pretty bad."

With no need of Samantha's guidance, Loretta pulled in front of Harry Bennett's Back Bay house without making, or even almost making, a wrong turn. She grinned as she parked crookedly. "Serendipity, but I'm not staying. I want to give myself plenty of time to get to the airport and turn in this car." She reached over and grabbed Samantha's hand, giving it a quick squeeze. "I'm glad I came out here and met you, Samantha. I have a feeling we'll be seeing each other again before too long. Knights Bridge is under your skin." She added in a conspiratorial half whisper, "More to the point, so is Justin Sloan."

"Things did kind of explode between us," Samantha said. "But he's coming to his senses."

"Yes, he is, and he's about to realize that having you in his life is worth the chaos."

"We haven't even known each other a week."

"All it takes sometimes. Duncan and I…" Loretta sighed, wistful, not as manic and sad as she had been yesterday. "Hours."

"And now you're going home to this guy who can find out anything about anyone—"

"Who is a total pain in my backside," Loretta said with a laugh. "I'll be back in touch if we find out anything. See you, Samantha."

"Safe travels."

After Loretta pulled away in her creaky rental, Samantha dragged her backpack to the front stoop of her grandfather's house. She hadn't managed to refold her tent as neatly as Justin had, but she didn't care. She wouldn't be using it again for a while.

She had her keys out when a movement down on the street caught her attention. She looked back and saw Justin standing on the street with an apple in one hand. He put one foot on the bottom step. He had on his usual canvas shirt, T-shirt, jeans and scuffed boots. "Hey, Sam. I thought you'd never get here."

"How did you beat us?"

"Loretta doesn't know the roads. I do. I passed you in Concord."

"Concord terrified her."

"She's all drama. Nothing terrifies her."

Samantha stuck her key in the door. "What about your business in Boston?"

"It'll keep. It's not why I'm here."

She pushed open the door and led him into the front entry. Her gaze landed on her grandfather's umbrella still in its stand in the corner, as if he were about to go out for a walk on the esplanade.

Justin grabbed her backpack and set it inside the door. "I have to be back in Knights Bridge tonight. I'm on call, and I have work in the morning."

"You've lost a lot of time already since I came to town." She pointed to the curving stairs. "My grandfather's office is on the second floor. That's where the things are that I want to show you."

"Lead the way."

"This place could use a good contractor," she said. "Carpenters who know old houses. You'll see."

As Samantha headed up the familiar stairs, she was aware of Justin behind her, watching her, taking in everything, as if he were gauging whether their worlds were so different—too different.

She came to the landing and pointed to the open door to her grandfather's office. "In there. I think I've spent more time in Grandpa's office during the past three years than he did in all the time he lived here."

"You love this place."

"Because it reminds me of him and the amazing life he led."

"He set quite a standard. Tough to live up to?"

She took in a breath. "I don't think he wanted us to see it that way. My father, Uncle Caleb, my cousins, me. I think he wanted us to find our own path in life and embrace whatever it is, wherever it takes us."

"Within reason," Justin said. "Bet he didn't want you to be bank robbers."

She laughed, not as tense and self-conscious about having him here, close to her, in this place she loved. She went first into the cluttered office. Justin stood back, taking in the massive old desk, the mix of glass-front and open shelves, the credenza, the filing cabinet, the heavy drapes and Persian rug.

Samantha walked over to the closet, the door still cracked open from when she'd been up here last Wednesday morning. "Grandpa used to say that the main reason he became an explorer was so he didn't have to sit in an office. I've worked here on and off since he died, more steadily since Duncan fired me. Grandpa managed to squirrel stuff away all over the house. I've got most everything sorted out in his London apartment. We'll be getting rid of it soon."

"Will you be putting this place on the market?" Justin asked.

"I don't know. It's not up to me."

She opened the closet door wide and stepped in, the cider mill painting and the original pages of *The Adventures of Captain Farraday and Lady Elizabeth* right where she'd left them. With a quick breath, she brought them out into the office. She set the small painting against the credenza that held her grandfather's Scotch decanters and handed the pages, in their worn envelope, to Justin.

"I didn't know about these when I went to Knights Bridge two years ago," she said. "If I had known, I might have handled things differently. But I knew about them this trip."

"That's my cider mill," Justin said softly, his gaze narrowed on the painting and its rich colors.

Samantha saw now that it could be no other cider mill but the one on Cider Brook in little Knights Bridge. Run-down, abandoned, no longer a vibrant red, it was without question the model for the romanticized one in the anonymous painting.

Justin turned to her. "Where did this come from?"

"I don't know. Grandpa didn't keep good records. Grandma did what she could, but she had her own work and died twenty-five years ago."

He opened the envelope and read the handwritten title page. He smiled at Samantha. "Your pirate rogue?"

"A highly fictionalized version of him. The story's just a rough draft. It was never finished. Captain Farraday rescues a British aristocrat after she's kidnapped by one of her wealthy father's enemies. They have numerous adventures on the high seas."

Justin laughed. "I'll bet they do." He set the pages on the desk and picked up one of the decanters. "Is this what you filled your flask with?"

"That's the Lagavulin, yes. There are still a few unopened whiskey bottles in the closet. Grandpa had a friend who sent him good Scotch at Christmas."

"A good friend to have." He nodded to the closet. "Mind if I have a look?"

Samantha shook her head. As Justin stepped into the closet, she sat on the edge of the desk, noticed the afternoon light was less direct in the office, a hint of the shorter days to come.

He emerged from the closet with an Ardbeg single malt, still in its distinctive box. "Another good Scotch. Ultra peaty."

"I'm not that up on Scotch. I just poured some into the flask in kindred spirit with Grandpa."

"Adam's the Scotch drinker in our family. I've learned a bit from him." Justin set the whiskey on the credenza next to the decanters. "I grabbed this one because there's a card with it."

Samantha jumped off the desk, and he handed her the small white card, tucked in a matching envelope. She opened it and read the neatly printed note. "'Warmest regards, Ben Magowan.'" She smiled, placing the card back in the envelope. "I should have known, but I haven't thought of Ben in forever."

"Who's Ben Magowan?"

"He was one of Grandpa's closest friends. They met at Amherst College and stayed in touch until Ben's death—it must be ten years ago now. He encouraged Grandpa's work and helped fund his Antarctic expedition. I met him several times. He was from Boston." Samantha pointed vaguely in the direction of Beacon Hill. "Louisburg Square."

"So he was well-off," Justin said, not making it a question.

"Well-off, and a man of many and varied interests."

"Scotch being one of them." He traced the Celtic *A* on the Ardbeg box. "Want to see what else we can find?"

"I'd like that," Samantha said.

They dug through the closet together, pulling out two more unopened bottles of expensive Scotch and several loose photographs that depicted Ben Magowan with her grandfather. Justin laid them side by side on the desk. In each shot, the slightly older, distinguished-looking Ben was always conservatively dressed, calm and smiling next to high-energy, often disheveled Harry Bennett.

Only one photograph was labeled. Justin found it. "Hell, Sam," he whispered, pointing at the inked cursive handwriting on the back of a photo of a young Ben and Harry grinning at the camera as they stood in front of a building at Amherst College.

Harry Bennett and Benjamin Hazelton Magowan

Samantha's shock was so complete that she couldn't speak. Justin stepped back from the desk where he'd set the photo. "I think we know what happened to Zeke and Henrietta's son."

"I had no idea." She touched her fingertips to the regal man standing with her grandfather on some mountaintop. "Ben was married. His wife's gone now, too. They never had children. I didn't spend much time with him, but I..." She looked up at Justin. "I don't think he did the painting of the cider mill or wrote the pirate story, but what if he gave them to Grandpa? For him to figure out what they meant. Or something."

Justin brushed an errant curl off her face. "Your grandfather encouraged your interest in pirates. He put you on to Farraday. Maybe he wanted answers, too, for his own reasons, and never got around to telling you the whole story."

"I wonder if he forgot the painting and the story were up here, or if he never really looked at them." Samantha realized she was shaking. "Justin...I didn't see this coming."

"Zeke and Henrietta named their son Benjamin."

Justin frowned at the bottles of Scotch, the array of old photos and the general mess that was her grand-father's office. "This is a start."

"The answers aren't here. They're in Knights Bridge."

"Then come back when you're ready."

"I'm ready now."

"You don't think that's your impulsive nature talk-ing?"

"I don't care if it is. Justin, I need to know what happened to Henrietta Hazelton. I need to know—"

"Everything," he said, finishing for her.

"Yes. Everything. If Ben Magowan gave my grand-father the painting and story, where did he get them? And why would he do that?"

"Lots of questions," Justin said.

Before she could respond, he swept her into his arms and kissed her, not a restrained peck on the fore-head, either—a lift-her-off-the-feet kiss that left her breathless, wanting more, when he set her back on the thick carpet.

He winked as he started for the door. "See you, Sam."

She listened to his footsteps on the stairs, heard the front door shut. Could she wait for her family to return to Boston, then drive back to Knights Bridge after they boarded their flights?

No.

She ran up to the third floor to her bedroom. She stuffed things into the overnight bag her mother had given her at ten, anticipating, she'd said, that her one and only daughter would need a proper bag, given who she had for parents. Samantha paid little attention to what she grabbed—just enough to get through a day or two at Carriage Hill, in her tent, on Justin's couch—it didn't matter.

Except it did matter. She wanted to be with Justin.

It wasn't a wheeled bag. She slung it over one shoulder and slipped back down to the second floor and into her grandfather's office, debating only a few seconds before she tucked the cider mill painting under one arm. She would be careful, but she wanted it with her in Knights Bridge.

She ran down the stairs and out the back door, barely remembering to lock it behind her. She took a shortcut through the alley and caught up with Justin before he reached Storrow Drive.

She pulled open the door with her free hand. "Your truck's easy to spot, and I know Boston streets," she said. "There's a difference between being impulsive and acting on what you know you want. I want to go back to Knights Bridge."

His deep blue eyes settled on her. "Get in before someone runs you over."

Once they cleared the city, Samantha called her father. "I know why you and Uncle Caleb came to Knights Bridge and why you went to Amherst."

He sighed. "Because of you, Sam."

"Because of Benjamin Hazelton Magowan. I remember him smoking cigars and drinking Scotch with Grandpa, but I never made the connection." Her heart was still racing with the realization. "I didn't know Hazelton was his middle name."

"Caleb and I started wondering. We didn't know the Hazelton part, either, or didn't remember if we did know. Isaac told us. He's fascinated with Pop's history at Amherst College, and Ben's name came up on the tour. I think there's a building or something named after him on campus. We wanted to be sure before we said anything."

"There are still so many unanswered questions," Samantha said.

"You'll find answers. That's why Pop put you on this thing. You don't give up. It's who you are, Samantha. Tenacious as a terrier." Her father added, "And we love you just as you are. All of us do."

"Even if I never find lost pirate treasure?"

"Oh, I don't know about that...." He laughed. "Would it be corny to say you're all the treasure your mother and I ever wanted?"

"Very corny."

"Yeah, but it's true. Where are you now?"

"Driving back from Boston."

"Caleb still has the Mercedes. You rented a car?"

She glanced over at Justin and smiled into the phone. "I'm with Justin Sloan."

"I guess that's no surprise at this point."

She laughed. "Talk to you soon, Dad. Say hi to the gang for me."

When she disconnected, Justin downshifted, almost at the turnoff for Knights Bridge. "Your family doesn't give you any peace, do they?"

"Not a minute."

"Then the Bennetts aren't that different from the Sloans after all."

Twenty-Eight

Justin set Samantha up on the couch again. He was being stubborn, or just plain stupid. But he was fast learning that it was first things first with her. She lived an open-throttle life. What he saw wasn't just courage and high energy, but also vulnerability. She trusted easily and needed people in her life who could help her see the rakes, scoundrels and jackasses coming.

The way he'd felt when he'd kissed her in her grandfather's crazy office…

He was all of the above, he thought. Rake, scoundrel, jackass.

If not for having to be back in Knights Bridge, he'd be in bed with her somewhere in that big Bennett house now—or on the office floor. The rug would have served nicely for the kind of lovemaking he'd had in mind.

She didn't seem that put out about the couch. Maybe she could see through him to what he was thinking, feeling, imagining.

Hell if he couldn't be her pirate rogue.

He grinned at her as she set her overnight bag on the

floor by the couch, but a call came in that shut off any conversation. A fire. A big one at a factory just west of town. A five-alarm blaze requiring the response of every available unit in the area.

"I have to run," Justin said, then winked at Samantha. "Be good."

An hour after Justin left, Samantha was up on her feet, pacing in the dark, quiet sawmill. Usually she wasn't one to pace. She would just decide what she wanted to do and do it. But what she wanted now was to have Justin's safe return—to have an idea of the danger he was in—and that, she knew, was out of her hands.

Then Maggie and Olivia arrived, alone, without either Brandon or Dylan. "It's a bad fire," Maggie said, entering the small apartment. "It's scary as hell."

"We thought my mother might be at her office," Olivia said, "but she's with my grandmother—Audrey. My father's mother. You met her the other day."

"Then we saw the light on up here," Maggie said. "We thought it might be Justin."

"He was on call," Samantha said.

Olivia nodded, pale.

Maggie crossed her arms over her chest, shuddering as she plopped down on the couch. "Brandon used to think about becoming a volunteer firefighter. I don't think his mother could take another first-responder in the family."

Olivia pointed at the cider mill painting, leaned up against the coffee table. "That's Cider Brook, isn't it? And Justin's mill?" She glanced back at Samantha. "Where did he get this?"

Samantha seized on the distraction. They all needed one. Her stomach twisted as she relived again, just for a few seconds, the cider mill fire. Justin hadn't waited. He'd taken action. He would be doing the same now, she realized. And tonight's fire wasn't an ordinary chimney fire or lightning strike. It was something different—or Maggie and Olivia wouldn't be here now.

"I found the painting in my grandfather's office," she said. "It's quite a story. We don't have the ending yet, but would you like to hear what we have so far?"

Olivia sank onto a chair, nodded tentatively, as if she understood she needed to keep her mind occupied but wasn't sure she could. Samantha started with her grandfather introducing her to the privateer-turned-pirate Benjamin Farraday and took Maggie and Olivia through to digging in his Back Bay office closet with Justin. She didn't mention their spine-melting kiss, but she had a feeling the two women could guess that part.

"Let's have a look at this painting," Olivia said, easing off her chair and kneeling in front of the small oil. "*The Mill at Cider Brook.* Simple but enticing." She drew the painting toward her and checked the back. "There's a paper backing. We could cut that off without damaging the painting."

"Think there'll be clues to the identity of the painter?" Maggie asked, obviously intrigued.

Olivia shrugged. "Maybe."

Samantha was already on her feet, rummaging in a kitchen drawer for a sharp knife. She found a paring knife that would do the trick and returned to the living room with it, sitting on the floor next to Olivia.

"It's your painting," Olivia said. "You do the honors."

"You're the artist. Tell me if I'm screwing up, okay?"

Carefully, working slowly, Samantha cut away the brown-paper backing around the edge of the frame, keeping as much of the paper as possible intact. Olivia peeled it away and set it on the coffee table.

"What's that say?" Maggie asked, pointing at a few lines of writing on the back of the canvas.

Samantha recognized the neat, feminine handwriting—it was the same distinctive writing of the author of *The Adventures of Captain Farraday and Lady Elizabeth.*

"It's an inscription," she said.

They all read the simple words at the same time:

To the girl I once was and to the man she loved with all her heart. Oh, what might have been on Cider Brook. I owe you my life, and our son's life, my beloved Zeke. HHM

Olivia covered her mouth. "Oh…oh, I'm going to cry."

Maggie was already crying. "That's the sweetest, saddest thing."

Samantha sniffled, crying, too, hot tears streaming down her cheeks. "Henrietta painted a scene from the life she and Zeke had dreamed of having together." She got out Grandpa Bennett's silver flask and she, Maggie and Olivia each took a quick sip of the Lagavulin. "Courtesy of Benjamin Magowan, Zeke and Henrietta's kind and extraordinary son."

She started to pass the flask for another round, but Brandon and Dylan arrived. Brandon, especially, was pale. "It's a nasty damn fire," he said, taking Maggie into his arms.

"What's happened?" she asked.

"Eric called. Damn, Maggie…"

"There are injuries," Dylan said, finishing for his friend. "We don't know who or how many—"

"How bad?" Olivia asked.

He shook his head. "We don't know."

They waited together in the sawmill apartment before Randy Frost finally called his daughter. She listened to him, ashen, then disconnected. "Christopher is hurt. He's in the emergency room. He's likely to be admitted, but he'll be okay. A beam fell on him. Three firefighters from other towns were also hurt. Their injuries are serious but not life-threatening." She finally breathed. "It's still chaotic. We'll know more soon."

"Your father?" Samantha asked.

"Good. Fine. It'll be a while before he gets freed up." Olivia reached for her jacket on the back of a chair. "I need to go be with my mother and grandmother."

Dylan was already on his way to the door.

Olivia hesitated. "I've got your cell number, Samantha. I'll call if I hear anything else. Justin…" She swallowed, obviously controlling her emotions. "He got Christopher out just in time. Dad says it was close. Too close."

Maggie looked at her husband. "We need to be with the boys."

"Go," Samantha said. "Please. I'll be all right here. Be with your families."

Brandon Sloan gave her a quick, brotherly hug. "Trust me, Sam. Justin will want you here when he gets back."

* * *

Samantha was awake when Justin returned at dawn, gray-faced, exhausted. He didn't say a word until he got a beer out of the refrigerator, opened it and sat next to her on the couch. He had a long drink, then turned to her. "How are you, Sam?"

"I've been into the Lagavulin."

He grinned, but there was little spark in his eyes. "Good for you."

"And how are you, Justin?"

"Hell of a night. Christopher will be all right. They wanted to keep him overnight, but he's up at the house. He's got plenty of people watching over him."

"It really was a close call, wasn't it?"

"Yeah. It was close." Justin drank more of his beer. "I almost died saving my baby brother's sorry ass."

"That's what we call gallows humor."

He winked at her. "That's what we call Sloan humor. 'Gallows' makes me think of dead pirates. No one died tonight."

"I'm glad of that."

"I know you are, Sam." He set his beer on the coffee table and touched a fingertip to her cheek. "We have unfinished business."

She thought she said his name. She might not have, not out loud, at least. As tired as he was, he still managed to sweep her up off the couch and carry her into his bedroom without any apparent effort.

"I was hoping you might be in your flannel pj's," he whispered as he laid her on his bed. "I've been dreaming about taking those damn things off you."

"In one fell swoop or inch by inch?"

"Both," he said, his mouth finding hers, his hands

raising her shirt, finding the warm skin at the small of her back. "When does it stop, Samantha? When do you quit trying to prove yourself and let yourself off the hook? Live your life."

"I am living my life right now."

He laughed softly, easing her pants over her hips. "Damn straight. I'm more about action than words." He coursed his palms along her bare skin. "Shall I demonstrate?"

Her answer was a small moan of pleasure, and he took advantage, deepening their kiss. She slipped her arms around his waist, under his canvas shirt, pulling at his T-shirt until she had it out of his jeans. She could feel the warmth of his skin, the hardness of the muscles in his back, his hips, his thighs.

He moved against her, as if they were already making love. Any fatigue seemed to lift off him, and he rolled onto his back, taking her with him. She ended up on top of him but saw right away it was only so that he could get her clothes off. Pants, shirt, bra. They were gone in a flash, cast off onto the rubble on the floor from his bashed-in wall. She didn't care where they ended up.

He held her still, straddling him, and gazed at her. Then he lowered her slowly to him, taking one nipple between his lips, then his teeth, until she felt the wet heat of his tongue. She tore at his clothes but with little effect, given the distractions of his mouth. She could feel his erection through his jeans, stark evidence of what lay ahead. She outlined it with her fingertips, felt him thrust hard against her hand even as she ended up on her back, flat against the cool sheets.

His mouth again, tongue and teeth working their

delicious torture down her stomach. He smoothed her underpants over her hips and down her legs, flinging them aside as his fingers slid between her legs. No words. Just the pure ecstasy of his touch. When she thought she would melt under him, he followed his fingers with the flick of his tongue.

She didn't know when he got his clothes off, or how, but she was quivering with want, aching, when she realized he was naked. She took him in her hand, guided him to her. "Justin...now...please..." But he was thrusting into her before she finished her last plea.

As if just to torture her some more, he went still, raising himself above her.

"Samantha," he said softly, lowering his mouth to hers. "Damn."

And as he kissed her, he moved inside her, eliminating any chance that she would be able to entertain a coherent thought anytime soon. She pulled him deeper into her, gave herself up to the heat roaring through her, the sensations—physical, emotional, all jumbled together. She clawed at him, cried out and then couldn't breathe, could only feel the letting go, the release...hers and his.

She collapsed against him, placing her head on his chest, and in a moment of stunning clarity—even if it was the last one of the night—she knew she was in love with this man. Hopelessly, miraculously and forever in love. Maybe it made no sense, but she didn't care. Not now, in the milky dawn light, with Justin Sloan's arms around her.

Twenty-Nine

In some respects, Samantha thought she could safely assume that making love would have resolved some of the tension and adrenaline left over from how she and Justin had met, but when she woke up alone in his bed, she knew nothing about him was simple or easy or ever would be.

She took a shower, got dressed and discovered his truck was gone.

Of course.

Even after two bouts of incredible lovemaking, she had energy to burn and went out into the cold, clear Knights Bridge morning and started walking to town.

Randy Frost picked her up in his truck. "Looking for breakfast?" he asked.

"Breakfast would be great," she said as she climbed into his old truck. "What's the word on Christopher Sloan?"

"A week recuperating and he'll be back on the job."

"That's a relief."

Randy nodded. "Yes, it is. A hell of a night. Don't

let Justin fool you. It was a near thing for him with this fire, too."

He dropped her off at Smith's and went on his way. The restaurant was crawling with Sloans and Knights Bridge firefighters. Justin got up from his booth with Eric, Brandon and Adam and headed to a small booth at the back, nodding to Samantha.

She slid into the booth across from him.

"Lively night," Justin said. "I woke up hungry. I see you did, too."

Dylan McCaffrey entered the restaurant and headed straight for their table. "I'm not staying," he said. "I just heard from Loretta, who heard from Julius Hartley, the L.A. private investigator she knows. I thought you'd like her report."

Samantha scooted over on her bench. "Have a seat."

Dylan sat next to her but shook his head when their waitress brought two mugs and asked him if he wanted coffee. When she withdrew, he said, "Henrietta Hazelton arrived in Boston in early 1916 as a very wealthy young widow with a small son, Benjamin. She married a widower, also wealthy, a banker fifteen years her senior named James Magowan. He adopted Ben. He and Henrietta had no other children. He died at eighty." Dylan paused, sitting back against the booth. "Henrietta loved to make up romantic adventures and eventually took up painting. She and Ben remained close until her death at eighty-five."

"Zeke Hazelton did all right, but he wasn't wealthy," Justin said.

Samantha drank some of her coffee, just to buy herself a moment to think. "My grandfather told me that Ben often said he didn't know the whole story about his mother. That she'd left out some parts of her past, and not everything added up. Grandpa didn't mention Knights Bridge, or the fire. Nothing like that."

Dylan nodded. "I'm not surprised. Henrietta kept the Hazelton name but that didn't mean she wanted to revisit what happened here." He rose, clearly as taken with Zeke and Henrietta as Olivia had been. "I know there's more to this story, but that's all Julius and Loretta have at the moment."

"Thank you," Samantha said. "And, please, thank them for me."

Dylan glanced at Justin, then shifted back to her. "I hope you'll be able to thank them yourself in person one day soon, but they were happy to help. It's a fascinating tale."

As Dylan left, Samantha looked across the table at Justin. "A lot going on this morning."

"All good."

"Randy Frost said it was a near thing for you last night."

"My brother's okay. The rest doesn't matter. What are you having for breakfast? Did you even have dinner last night?"

"If I order a huge breakfast, everyone here is going to know we…"

"They know, anyway, Sam," Justin said, amused. "It's what we call obvious."

"You're all a bunch of know-it-alls," she said, and, ignoring Justin's grin, ordered fresh-squeezed orange juice, whole-grain pancakes with real maple syrup and local bacon, cooked crisp.

Her orange juice arrived at the same time as a text from her uncle. We're at the family farm. Our sec-

ond cousin has done a great job with the place. Says
Ben and Pop visited several times over the years. Ben
always said his mother insisted she was descended
from pirates.

She texted him back. Farraday?

No names. Hell, Sam. Pirates.

She handed her phone to Justin and sat back, drinking her juice and remembering her talks with her
grandfather in his last days. "I'm positive that Grandpa
never mentioned the painting or the story," she said.
"I'd remember."

"His friend Ben could have dropped them off before he died but never told your grandfather what they
were all about." Justin shrugged but was clearly interested, despite last night's fire. "Ben might have been
torn about digging into his mother's past."

Samantha nodded. "I can see him being ambivalent.
Wanting to know her true story, but afraid he couldn't
take it—that it was sad beyond words."

Justin leaned forward. "My guess is your grandfather decided you were meant to be the one to figure
out Henrietta's story. You were relentless enough to
follow the leads wherever they took you."

Here, she thought. *To Knights Bridge.* "Grandpa
must have met Henrietta. Maybe my father and Uncle
Caleb did, too. Wouldn't it be ironic if Grandpa's first
expeditions were funded with pirate treasure?"

Justin winked at her. "Par for the course with your
family, if you ask me."

Her breakfast arrived—the pancakes and little
pitcher of syrup steaming, the bacon with a smoky,
maple smell. Samantha grabbed her fork, ready to dive
in, when the waitress returned with a little bowl of

plain yogurt and granola and set it in front of Justin. "Yogurt, Justin? Really? After last night—"

"I don't want too much in my stomach. I'm going back to bed after breakfast." He pointed his spoon at her. "You eat up, though."

"You're going back to bed?"

"Mmm. Long night. Didn't sleep much. I'll see Chris this afternoon after he's caught up on his sleep."

"I could eat a few bites of these pancakes and get the rest to go."

"We could share them for a late lunch."

Samantha raised her eyes to him. "You know every one of your brothers and firefighter friends is watching us right now, don't you?"

He grinned. "Get used to it."

A warmth spread through her, and she smiled at him. "I already am."

Thirty

"You do have your ways, Julius," Loretta said, sitting on a cushioned lounge chair beside her pool. No New England autumn foliage, but there was bougainvillea, her pots of miniature roses, her avocado tree, warm sunshine, and it was home. Julius had driven down from Hollywood and met her at the airport.

He was next to her on a matching chair. She knew she looked as if she'd done an emotional whirlwind trip to the East Coast, and he looked great. Rested, dressed in his damn country-club clothes. "Finding out the basics about Henrietta was a snap once I had names and dates. That's the hard part. Piecing together the rest of her story will be tough. Maybe impossible."

"The money, you mean."

"Either she robbed a bank or dug up pirate treasure."

He wasn't kidding, either. Loretta stared out at her glimmering pool. "There's something about that town, I swear. Grace Webster's secret love affair with the jewel thief—"

"Your Duncan's birth parents."

Her Duncan. She swallowed. "Then there's Daphne Stewart's story. Debbie Henderson. Abused, frightened, dreaming of a new life. And now we have Henrietta Hazelton, rebuilding her life after an unbearable tragedy."

Julius set his iced tea glass on the table next to him. "It's every town if we only stop long enough to find out."

"Do you think this Benjamin Farraday was Henrietta's ancestor?"

"It's what she believed. No question in my mind. Wherever her money came from, it helped her to shut the door on her life in Knights Bridge. She had to, in order to go on—to create a new life with her son."

"I can see Ben and Harry getting together as old men," Loretta said with a smile. "Smoking cigars, drinking Scotch, talking about Antarctica and skirting the rest. The father who died saving you and your mother. The mother who somehow slipped out of town with a fortune."

Julius gave a heavy sigh. "Life, huh?"

"Ben would have had a happy life if Zeke had lived and there'd been no money. The cider mill, the general store, the winding roads and the people." Loretta realized her eyes were misting. She sucked in a breath. "Damn jet lag. Messes with my emotional equilibrium."

"Your what? Never mind." Julius got to his feet and took her hand. "Loretta, I have something to say to you."

She rose, frowning. "You're not moving East, are you?"

He laughed, but his eyes were intense, serious. "I'm

not moving East, but I would if that's where you are. I'm crazy about you, Loretta."

"Or just crazy."

He swept both her hands into his and drew her toward him. "Marry me."

Her heart jumped. "Julius—"

"You'll like my daughters. They're Hollywood lawyers. One works for a studio, one for an agency. We get along great. No strife there. They want me to be happy, and I want them to be happy." He kissed her on the cheek and whispered into her ear, "Think about it, okay? I know marriage is a big step for you. Take your time. I'm not going anywhere."

Loretta stood back, gaping at this man she loved. How had it happened? How had her life changed so much in such a short time? She laughed suddenly, a little maniacally. Julius looked taken aback, but she grabbed his hand and held it tight. "I don't need to think. I don't need time. I've been thinking about this since the day I thought I might have to call the police on you." She smiled at him, her heart racing. "Yes. Yes, Julius Hartley, I'll marry you."

He had a ring. A beautiful diamond. "I'd have gone down on one knee, but I was afraid you might kick me into the pool." He smiled at her, slipping the ring on her finger. "We're going to have a good time, Loretta."

She eyed the ring on her finger, the diamond glittering in the sunlight, and she kissed him. "I feel like a kid. I love you to pieces, Julius. You know you'll have to go back to Knights Bridge for Dylan's wedding."

He rubbed the back of his neck. "Probably for Daphne, too."

Loretta looked around at her quiet, pretty backyard. "I'm open to change in my life, but this is home for me, Julius."

"I know, kid. I can do my job from down here." He slipped an arm around her. "I'm the luckiest man in the world."

"We're going to be a couple of fun old people."

"In thirty years. We have lots of time."

Thirty-One

Samantha saw her family off to Scotland and London. She would be seeing them again soon. They were all certain there was more to be unearthed about Harry Bennett and Benjamin Hazelton Magowan, who, it seemed, had included his best friend in his will. Only Harry had never done anything about it.

Isaac wanted to help Samantha with her research when he was at Amherst. His father was thinking about teaching there for a year, maybe longer. Her parents didn't plan to be in Scotland forever.

Her father pulled her aside at the airport, while his nephews and nieces unloaded the trunk of their grandfather's old Mercedes. "Are you staying in Boston?" he asked her.

She shook her head. "I'm going back to Knights Bridge."

"Will you be staying at the Sloan cabin again?"

She thought of Justin and smiled. "Maybe." Her father groaned, and she grinned at him. "What?"

"Nothing." He kissed her on the cheek. "You always did want a guy who could fix things."

She hugged everyone goodbye and headed off before airport security started to get antsy. She drove through the tunnel and pointed the big car west. No need to stop back at her grandfather's house. She was prepared for Knights Bridge this time. More or less, anyway. Backpack in the trunk, water bottle up front with her, her grandmother's recipe for apple pie.

No tent, though. If she needed a tent…well, then, she wouldn't be staying long at all.

In less than two hours, Samantha pulled into Carriage Hill. More leaves had turned, glowing orange, red and yellow in the afternoon sunlight. As she walked past the pots of yellow-and-white mums, she could hear laughter from the kitchen.

Maggie opened the door, still laughing. "Samantha! Welcome. Come on in. We're making applesauce."

The kitchen was warm with the smell of cooking apples, steam rising from two large pots on the stove. Empty canning jars were lined up on the butcher-block island. Olivia and Dylan were at the sink, paring knives in hand, colanders filled with apples on the counter next to them.

Justin was there, too, leaning in the mudroom doorway. His truck wasn't out front. He must have walked down from the construction site. Samantha noticed bits of sawdust on his clothes—the uniform black canvas shirt, dark T-shirt, jeans, scuffed boots. A few days away, she thought, and nothing had changed.

"I wanted to say hi," she said. "My family's on their flight. I figured I would stop out at the cider mill before—" She stopped there. She didn't know what to say. Before what? Before she went back to Boston?

But she didn't want to go back. She wanted to stay here.

Justin eased into the kitchen. "I'll go out there with you." He nodded to his friends. "It's a good year for apples. Let me know if you need more."

He walked out to the old Mercedes with her and got into the passenger seat. She smiled at him. "Good that I have a car this time, don't you think?"

"You probably don't want to take it onto the mill's driveway."

"You're right, I don't."

Samantha had no trouble navigating the back roads out to the cider mill. She parked under a large oak tree as gray squirrels chased each other along a branch. She got out of the car, shoving her hands into her jacket pockets at the unexpected cold.

Justin started down the driveway toward the cider mill. "You never thought your Captain Farraday would lead you here, did you, Sam?"

"In some ways, he seems as elusive as ever."

They walked down to the clearing. A dozen bright-colored leaves floated in the millpond, and clear, coppery water flowed over the dam. The acrid fire smells had dissipated, the exterior of the little nineteenth-century mill showing no visible signs of damage. Samantha could see it now as Henrietta had seen it, painted a vibrant red, churning apples into cider, a part of the fabric of the community of Knights Bridge and of her life with Zeke.

"Come on," Justin said. "There's something I want to show you."

They went inside. He'd pulled the dirty, cracked plastic off the windows. The sun streamed in, and she saw that he'd cleaned up from the fire. He wouldn't be one to waste time.

A gold coin was on the worn sill of a front window, leaning against the glass.

"What's this?" she asked.

He picked it up. "You tell me."

"It looks like an eighteenth-century Spanish coin, but that doesn't mean it is. Where did you get it?"

"I found it one night when the guys and I were out here horsing around. I kept it. Figured I'd do something with it one of these days." He took her hand, opened her fingers and placed the coin in her palm. "I did some digging out here and checked town records. The mill's built on an old cellar hole. It's likely to belong to one of the earliest houses in the area."

"The hermit your grandmother told me about."

"Your pirate."

Samantha rubbed her thumb along the markings in the coin. "Why didn't you tell me?"

He shrugged. "I wasn't sure what you were up to."

"You knew all along my interest in Cider Brook had to do with pirates."

"Let's just say I doubted Duncan McCaffrey's pirate expert had come here to follow Cider Brook into Quabbin. I figured you'd left out a few things." He nodded at the coin in her hand. "Can you tell if the coin is part of Farraday's lost treasure?

"Maybe. The Hazeltons built the mill. Did Henrietta's family own the land before them?"

"Just the few acres around the mill. Her father sold them to the Hazeltons in 1872. His name was Smith, by the way. Benjamin Smith." Justin was silent a moment before he continued, "There's a story that after

Zeke died, Henrietta would take little Ben out here and spend hours and hours on their own. People were worried she would take her own life. Then she and her son quietly left town."

"She found Benjamin Farraday's lost treasure, or at least some of it—what he hadn't sold to support himself or for bribes to secure his freedom."

Justin looked out toward the brook. "If the hermit was your pirate, he could have decided he liked his simple life here."

"He was wanted by the crown by then."

"Unloading a lot of ill-gotten gold and whatnot would only draw unwanted attention to himself. Better to keep the bulk of his treasure buried than to risk a hanging."

"Then Benjamin Farraday never went back to Boston and bought a new ship," Samantha said. "That was a ruse on his part to throw off authorities and to keep anyone from looking for him out here."

Justin settled his gaze on her. "There's no pirate shipwreck for you to find, then."

She sighed. "That's the way it goes. There are a lot of false leads and dead ends in treasure hunting."

"What now?" he asked. "Think there's more treasure out here?"

"I doubt it. My guess is Henrietta found whatever there was to find, and I'm glad of that."

"What are you going to do with no treasure to hunt?"

"You've seen my grandfather's office. There's so much yet to go through there, and that doesn't count all the other places he has stuff squirreled away—and now we have whatever Ben Magowan left him, too.

Who knows where that will lead?" Samantha stepped into the threshold of the mill door and looked out at the brook tumbling toward the reservoir. "I've been thinking a nice, quiet cabin in a pretty New England town with a cute guy up the road would be a good spot to cart stuff and go through it."

"A cute guy, huh?"

"That would be your brother Christopher." Samantha turned back to Justin and smiled. "You would be—how did Loretta describe you? Tall, dark and taciturn."

"Not cute, though. Good. I was worried for a second." He tapped her hand with one finger. "And the coin?"

"It belongs here, don't you think?"

"Sam…"

She placed it in his hand, curled his fingers around it. "You know what to do with it, Justin. I think you always have. That's why it's not in a vault."

He surprised her with a kiss. "We'll have to create our own treasures. I'm in love with you, Sam. I fell in love with you when I felt my padlock in your jacket pocket. I want to get to know you better, but it's not going to change how I feel." He brushed his fingers through her hair, down to her lips. "That's forever."

"Forever." She kissed his fingertips. "I like that word. I think I've been in love with you since you plopped me out by Cider Brook and told me to stay put."

"You weren't intimidated."

"Never."

He grinned and hooked an arm around her middle, lifting her as he headed outside. He set her down by the millpond. Then, without a word, without so much as a glance at her, he flung Henrietta's gold coin into the millpond. It hit a yellow leaf, then sank into the water. In no time at all, it would disappear in the muck at the bottom of the pond.

"To Henrietta and Zeke," Samantha whispered.

She and Justin stared at the water as the ripples from the coin faded and another bright leaf dropped from a nearby tree.

They heard a commotion up on the trail along the brook. Heather Sloan and her nephews arrived in a panicked search for Beaver, the big Sloan dog that looked so much like Olivia and Dylan's Buster.

Justin turned from the pond and looked at Samantha. "Beaver's not a long-lost pirate, but want to help find him?"

She took his hand and smiled. "Let's go."

"Ah, Bess. I'd do anything for you. I'd die for you."

"I know you would die for me, as I would for you," Lady Elizabeth whispered in the dark of their bunk. "May it never come to that, my love."

Captain Farraday held her close. "I'll get you home and I'll keep you safe."

"I know you will. You're not such a rogue after all, are you, Captain Farraday?" She touched his scarred cheek with her fingertips and smiled. "You're my hero. You always will be, no matter what happens to us."

* * * * *